at the heart of it

USA TODAY BESTSELLING AUTHOR

AWNA FENSKE

PRAISE FOR TAWNA FENSKE

LET IT BREATHE

"This charming romp from Fenske evokes the best of romantic comedy, with its witty characters and wacky but realistic situations."

—*Publishers Weekly*, Starred Review

ABOUT THAT FLING

"Fenske's take on what happens when a one-night stand goes horribly, painfully awry is hilariously heartwarming and overflowing with genuine emotion . . . There's something wonderfully relaxing about being immersed in a story filled with over-the-top characters in undeniably relatable situations. Heartache and humor go hand in hand in this laugh-out-loud story with an ending that requires a few tissues."

—*Publishers Weekly*, Starred Review

THE FIX UP

"Extremely charming and undeniably sexy . . . I loved every minute."

—Rachel Van Dyken, *New York Times* and *USA Today* bestselling author

"Sexy banter in the boardroom, romantic movies with a sexy alpha geek, and humor that will leave a smile on your face until the very last page."

—Kelly Elliott, *New York Times* and *USA Today* bestselling author

*Nominated for Contemporary Romance of the Year, 2011
Reviewers' Choice Awards, RT Book Reviews*

"Fenske's wildly inventive plot and wonderfully quirky characters provide the perfect literary antidote to any romance reader's summer reading doldrums."

—*Chicago Tribune*

"A zany caper . . . Fenske's off-the-wall plotting is reminiscent of a tame Carl Hiaasen on Cupid juice."

—*Booklist*

"This delightfully witty debut will have readers laughing out loud."

—*RT Book Reviews*, 4½ Stars

"[An] uproarious romantic caper. Great fun from an inventive new writer; highly recommended."

—*Library Journal*, Starred Review

"This book was the equivalent of eating whipped cream—sure, it was light and airy, but it is also surprisingly rich."

—*Smart Bitches Trashy Books*

BELIEVE IT OR NOT

"Fenske hits all the right humor notes without teetering into the pit of slapstick in her lighthearted book of strippers, psychics, free spirits, and an accountant."

—*RT Book Reviews*

"Snappy, endearing dialogue and often hilarious situations unite the couple, and Fenske proves to be a romance author worthy of a loyal following."

—*Booklist*, Starred Review

"Fenske's sophomore effort is another riotous trip down funny-bone lane, with a detour to slightly askew goings on and a quick U-ey to out-of-this-world romance. Readers will be enchanted by this bewitching fable from a wickedly wise author."

—*Library Journal*

"Sexually charged dialogue and steamy make-out scenes will keep readers turning the pages."

—*Publishers Weekly*

FRISKY BUSINESS

"Up-and-coming romance author Fenske sets up impeccable internal and external conflict and sizzling sexual tension for a poignant love story between two engaging characters, then infuses it with witty dialogue and lively humor. An appealing blend of lighthearted fun and emotional tenderness."

—*Kirkus Reviews*

"Fenske's fluffy, frothy novel is a confection made of colorful characters, compromising situations, and cute dogs. This one's for readers who prefer a tickled funny bone rather than a tale of woe."

—*RT Book Reviews*

"Loaded with outrageous euphemisms for the sex act between any type of couple and repeated near-intimate misses, Fenske's latest is a clever tour de force on finding love despite being your own worst emotional enemy. Sweet and slightly oddball, this title belongs in most romance collections."

—*Library Journal*

"*Frisky Business* has all the ingredients of a sparkling romantic comedy—wickedly clever humor, a quirky cast of characters, and, most of all, the crazy sexy chemistry between the leads."

—Lauren Blakely, *New York Times* and *USA Today* bestselling author

at the
heart
of it

ALSO BY
TAWNA FENSKE

Stand-Alone Romantic Comedies

This Time Around

Now That It's You

Let It Breathe

About That Fling

Eat, Play, Lust (Novella)

Frisky Business

Believe It or Not

Making Waves

The Front and Center Series

Marine for Hire

Fiancée for Hire

Best Man for Hire

Protector for Hire

The First Impressions Series

The Fix Up

The Hang Up

The Hook Up

The List Series

The List

Schultz Sisters Mysteries

Getting Dumped

The Great Panty Caper (Novella)

at the heart of it

TAWNA FENSKE

Montlake
Romance

Text copyright © 2017 Tawna Fenske
All rights reserved.

Published by Montlake Romance, Seattle

www.apub.com

Amazon, the Amazon logo, and Montlake Romance are trademarks of Amazon.com, Inc., or its affiliates.

ISBN-13: 9781542047302
ISBN-10: 1542047307

Cover design by PEPE nymi

Printed in the United States of America

To my brother, Aaron "Russ" Fenske.
For years of tasteless jokes and tasty crepes.
For screening out my bad boyfriends and befriending the good ones.
But mostly, for giving me a reason to write about loving brothers
and all their delightful, obnoxious, endearing quirks.

CHAPTER ONE

Kate Geary stepped onto the sunny back patio of the B&B and scanned the breakfast tables. Each held a bouquet of daisies and a noisy array of her fellow guests. As she smoothed the skirt of her ankle-length black sundress, Kate breathed in the scent of maple syrup and assessed her options.

Four octogenarians discussing the merits of hip-replacement surgery as they devoured plates of German apple pancakes.

Two fortysomethings bickering about the aesthetic distance and dramatic unity in the Shakespeare production they'd seen the night before.

One thirtysomething guy sitting alone, munching an impressive heap of bacon while reading a children's picture book with a pig on the cover.

Kate headed for Swine Guy, figuring he was most likely to let her eat breakfast in peace. He looked up from his book as Kate approached, hitting her with the full force of the most striking eyes she'd ever seen. The color, somewhere on the palette between green and amber, reminded her of tree moss or spearmint. They were framed by a pair of black-rimmed glasses and gazed back at her in a way that suggested their owner wasn't thrilled by Kate's intrusion.

Kate touched the back of a chair, as much to keep herself steady as a request for permission to plant her butt in it. "Is this seat taken?"

Swine Guy looked at her for a few beats, then picked up another piece of bacon. "Nope. Feel free."

"Thanks."

She pulled out the chair and sat down, then spread a blue-and-green checkered napkin over her lap. A server walked past en route to the next table, and Kate heard her stomach growl. She glanced at Swine Guy, wondering if he'd noticed. His eyes were glued to his book again, but maybe he was being polite.

"I love German apple pancakes," she said, then wanted to kick herself. Hadn't she sat here precisely to avoid conversation? But here she was, blathering like an idiot. "And the bacon smells incredible. I thought nothing could top yesterday's crêpes suzette, but everything looks amazing."

Swine Guy glanced up, then followed her gaze to where the octogenarians were debating cemented versus uncemented hip-joint replacements as they passed around a white platter loaded with thick slices of ham. He nodded and bit into his bacon, chewing for such a long time that Kate thought he might not respond at all.

"I'm not much of a sweets-for-breakfast fan, so I asked for a bunch of extra bacon," he said. "I'd offer you a piece, but that seems creepy."

"Offering bacon to strangers, you mean?"

"Right. Or offering any food to strangers, really." He gave her a one-shouldered shrug and the faintest hint of a smile.

Kate stuck out her hand, and Swine Guy wiped his fingers on a napkin before grasping hers in a firm handshake. His palm was big and warm and enveloped hers almost completely.

"Kate Geary," she said.

The moss-green eyes flickered with mild interest as he let go of her hand. "Jonah Porter."

Kate grinned. "Now we're not strangers. May I have a piece of bacon?"

He laughed and shoved the plate toward her. "Nicely played. For the record, I wasn't hoarding it. I just figured you'd want your own."

"I do, but I'm starving. I'll share mine when it comes." Kate chose the smallest piece of bacon and bit into it. "Oh my God. You weren't kidding."

"I never kid about bacon." Swine Guy—er, Jonah—picked up another piece and chewed quietly as he set down his book atop a pile of others.

"Would you like coffee, ma'am?"

Kate turned to see one of the servers holding a silver urn. Kate nodded and flipped over the bright-green mug beside her place mat.

"Thank you." She watched as the server filled her mug, then set the plate in front of her with a flourish, presenting her with her very own German apple pancake and four crisp slices of bacon.

"This looks fabulous," Kate said as she got to work doctoring up her breakfast. A little syrup, some powdered sugar, a squeeze of lemon . . .

Jonah picked up another piece of bacon, and Kate let her gaze drift to his left hand. No ring. *Single?* It looked that way, but she'd learned not to judge too quickly.

"Jumping to conclusions is a lousy form of exercise!"

It was a quote from one of Kate's favorite books, and she smiled to herself as she thought of it.

She forked up a bite of pancake and glanced at Jonah again. He'd set the pig book on top of a larger pile of children's books, which seemed interesting. Was he the father of a young child, or a guy with unambitious reading habits?

Jonah caught her staring and nodded. "I own a bookstore," he said, resting his hand on the stack of books. "Customers have been trying to talk me into expanding the children's section, so I'm checking out some new releases."

"Ah." Kate smiled and chewed a bite of pancake, oddly charmed by his profession. There was something cultured and intelligent about a guy who owned a bookstore. The fact that he was here in artsy little Ashland said something, too. This time of year, nearly everyone in town was here for the city's renowned theater productions at the Oregon Shakespeare Festival.

"Before you assume, try asking." There went Kate's brain again, reciting words from Dr. Vivienne Brandt's most famous tome on relationships and positive communication. *"You learn much more asking questions than you do by painting the walls inside your own mind."*

Kate picked up her coffee and took a sip. "Which plays are you seeing?"

"Oh, I'm not here for a play," Jonah said. "I just came for the bacon."

She must've looked startled, because he laughed and shook his head. "Sorry, I'm kidding. I saw *Julius Caesar* last night, and I'm seeing *Off the Rails* tomorrow night. I was hoping to see the matinee of *Shakespeare in Love* today, but it's sold out. How about you?"

"Oh, I wanted to see *Shakespeare in Love*, but I couldn't get tickets either," Kate said. "I saw *Hannah and the Dread Gazebo* instead, which was amazing. How did you like *Off the Rails?*"

"It was terrific. Sort of a *Blazing Saddles* meets Shakespeare kinda thing."

"Isn't it OSF's first play by a Native American writer?"

He nodded and gave a small smile. "Yeah. It's sort of a comedic musical about Indian boarding schools. Cedric Lamar gave an amazing performance. Really powerful." He picked up his coffee mug. "Are you seeing anything else?"

For a breathless instant, she thought he'd asked if she was seeing anyone, and she started to blurt out her availability. Luckily, her brain worked quicker than her mouth did. "I'll probably go lurk around the

4

theater this afternoon to see if anyone's selling any last-minute tickets," she said. "I have to leave early tomorrow morning."

"Sounds like you're quite the theater buff."

Kate shrugged and took another bite of pancake. The lemon she'd squeezed over it lent the perfect zingy contrast to the warm maple syrup. "I guess so. I actually studied acting in college, but wised up by the time I hit grad school and learned to be on the other side of the camera instead."

"You're a filmmaker or something?"

"Close. I work for a production company in LA, but I got my start making documentaries."

"Is that what you're doing now?"

Kate shook her head, not sure why she hesitated a little before answering. "I'm actually in unscripted television."

"Unscripted television?" He gave her a curious look. "Is that a fancy way of saying reality TV?"

"Bingo." Kate took a bite of bacon. "Don't judge."

"I'm not." He smiled and shook his head. "I don't watch much TV myself, but my sister is crazy about *The Bachelor* and *Survivor* and a bunch of other shows like that."

His expression shifted to a sort of fond admiration, though there was something else, too. A flicker of melancholy, maybe, though Kate was probably reading it wrong. She wanted to press for details about the sister's favorite shows, but decided this wasn't the time for market research.

"Where's your bookstore?" she asked instead.

"Seattle," he said. "One of the few indie bookstores that's still thriving in the age of the e-book."

"What's your secret? Free bacon with every book?"

He laughed and picked up another slice. "I put in a full-service bar and started bringing in live music a few times a week. There's also a room where guests can interact with adoptable cats. My sister runs an animal shelter, so it's been a great way to socialize them and help them find new homes."

"That's a great idea."

"Thanks. *Travel + Leisure* featured it in a piece about America's best bookstores."

"Nice!" Kate wrapped her hands around her coffee mug. "Maybe I'll check it out when I'm there next month for work."

Jonah studied her a moment, looking thoughtful. "Why did you say that earlier about acting? About wising up and moving to the other side of the camera?"

Kate's fingers tightened around the mug as her gut pinged with surprise at which detail he'd latched onto. Normally, everyone pumped her for details on filmmaking or television, eager to hear if she knew famous people or if they'd seen anything she'd worked on.

But that's not what Jonah wanted to know. He was curious about the path not chosen. She took a sip of coffee and considered how much to share. "It didn't seem practical," she said. "Building a career in acting takes so much time and luck."

"You miss it, though? Acting, I mean?"

Kate shrugged. "Sometimes. But it's just not a good career choice for someone who wants stability, a family—things like that."

As her brain caught up to the words tumbling out of her, she fought the urge to wince again.

Jesus, Kate. Why don't you stand on the table and announce you're a thirty-four-year-old single woman whose most exciting risk in the last decade was returning a library book two days late?

But if Jonah thought any of that, his face didn't show it. He opened his mouth to say something just as two older ladies stepped onto the patio with matching cotton-ball perms and colorful cardigans Kate recognized from the window display in one of the expensive, artsy shops on Main Street.

"Honestly," the taller woman was saying. "Far be it from me to criticize a passionate performance, but do they not realize how thin the walls are in this place? I could hear every creak of the bedsprings."

Jonah gave a soft snort while Kate stifled a giggle behind her napkin as the pair drew closer to the table.

"Their headboard must be right up against our bathroom wall," the other woman was saying. "Maybe we can speak with the manager about leaving a note or something. I don't want to embarrass them, but maybe they just don't realize how noisy they are."

"All that banging. And the moaning and the groaning—"

The two were mere steps away, and Kate realized the only two vacant seats were at her table. She started to scoot right to make the newcomers welcome when a hand brushed hers.

She looked up to see Jonah with a straight face and an unreadable glint in his eyes. "You said you missed acting," he murmured. "Want to take a shot at it?"

Kate stared at him for a second, mystified by what he might be suggesting.

Which seemed like the perfect reason to agree.

◆ ◆ ◆

The fact that Kate nodded in agreement before Jonah had told her a damn thing about what he had in mind said a lot about her personality.

She was naturally trusting. Curious. She either took risks or wanted to look like someone who did.

A decade of serving as a counterintelligence expert in the US Marines had left him trained to interrogate subjects, and analyze visual and auditory clues. Military training aside, he had a knack for reading people.

Not that the skill had kept him from making some pretty stupid choices in relationships, but it was still a handy ability to have.

Kate was looking at him with a curious expression, somewhere between intrigue and anxiousness. Hell, he wasn't normally the kind of guy to suggest a spontaneous game of make-believe, but bringing up his sister had reminded him of the game they'd played as kids. Still played, actually.

"You pretend you're a Turkish oil wrestler with a head injury, and I'm your translator," Jossy would whisper as they walked into a grocery store together, giggling as she got into character.

Not that Kate was anything like his sister. And he definitely wasn't feeling brotherly toward her. There was something about Kate that filled him with an odd mix of boldness and giddy energy. It was a far cry from how he'd felt in his marriage, content to let his wife be the creative free spirit while Jonah remained the fuzzy background noise.

The old ladies drew closer. As they seated themselves at the table, Jonah covered Kate's hand with his. The women were still chattering about the noisily amorous couple in the room next door, and Jonah cleared his throat.

"Ma'am." Both women looked up, and Jonah flashed an apologetic smile. "I couldn't help overhearing your conversation. About the couple staying next door to your room?"

The two women blinked, frozen in the act of placing their napkins on their laps. The shorter one in the blue sweater spoke first. "Yes?" They exchanged a glance, then looked back at Jonah.

"Right," he said. "I just wanted to apologize for that." He smiled at Kate, his best attempt at nervous fondness. While he'd never studied acting the way she had, he knew damn well what a chagrined lover might act like. He watched as Kate's brown eyes widened, but she gave nothing away.

Across the table, the shorter woman tilted her head to one side. "I beg your pardon?"

"My wife and I are on our honeymoon." Jonah slung his arm around the back of Kate's chair, relieved when Kate leaned into him. But not quite as relieved when she kicked him under the table.

He wasn't sure if it was a reprimand or an agreement to play along, but he had his answer soon enough.

"Of course, we're very sorry." Kate's voice quivered a little, and Jonah wondered if it was nerves or part of the act. Either way, it fit the situation. She brushed a shock of straight, dark hair from her eyes and smiled at him. "My husband gets a little carried away by passion sometimes. I tried shoving a sock in his mouth, but you know how it is."

Jonah stifled a laugh as the two women stared. They didn't look embarrassed or angry, which was a good sign. This was Oregon, after all, and a liberal artsy town at that. People probably had sex on street corners and called it performance art.

"Well." The taller woman glanced at the shorter one, and the pair seemed to come to some sort of unspoken agreement. She looked back at Jonah and offered a cautious smile. "Congratulations to both of you. Where are you from?"

"Eugene," Kate offered, and Jonah wondered if that was true or part of her character. "My husband owns a store that sells novelty socks, and I'm a painter."

"A sock store?" Both women eyed Jonah with confusion before glancing back at Kate. "What do you paint, dear? Watercolors or oils or—"

"Houses," Jonah interrupted, earning himself another shin kick. His arm was still around the back of her chair, and she felt damn good there. Warm and soft and her hair smelled like vanilla. "And commercial buildings. Especially skyscrapers," he added. "You should see her up there on that crane with a paint sprayer in her hand and a hard hat on her head."

"Isn't that something!" The shorter woman extended her hand as the server bustled over and began pouring coffee. "I'm Carol, by the way, and this is Marilee."

"Pleasure to meet you," Kate said.

They all shook hands while the server arranged a large tray of bacon and ham at the center of the table and set a German apple pancake in front of each of the new arrivals. Jonah watched as Kate took another bite of hers, and he tried not to fixate on the lovely bow of her mouth. Her features were unique. Not beautiful, but striking. She had sharp cheekbones and chin-length hair that might've looked black without the glint of late-August sunlight lending it slashes of mahogany.

She met his eye then, catching him in the act of staring, but not seeming to mind all that much.

"So," she said, turning her attention back to Carol and Marilee. "What plays are you seeing?"

"We saw *The Merry Wives of Windsor* last night and plan to see *UniSon* tomorrow at one thirty," Carol said. "How about you two?"

"*Off the Rails* was terrific," Kate replied, glancing at Jonah. "There's this really captivating story line about Indian boarding schools in the American West. Cedric Lamar gave an amazing performance."

"I saw that earlier in the season!" Carol said. "What did you think of Barret O'Brien's performance?"

Jonah expected to see a flicker of panic in Kate's eyes, maybe an uncertainty over whether the actor in question was male or female. He readied himself to answer. But her expression didn't waver a bit, and her reply was cool and even.

"I thought Barret's performance was surprisingly understated, but still delightfully irreverent," Kate said. "How about you?"

"I agree." Carol's gaze swung to Jonah, and he held off biting into the slice of bacon he'd just lifted. He could sense another question coming. "So tell me about your wedding. Where was it?"

Marilee's face lit up. "I want to hear about the flowers and the music."

"We just adore weddings!"

A tiny snap of anger zinged through Jonah's chest, and it took him a few beats to remember this wasn't a real question. Not about his real marriage, anyway. The one that hadn't ended well.

Luckily, Kate was quicker on her feet than he was.

"It was beautiful," she gushed. "We had it out at Brasada Ranch resort in Central Oregon. Do you know it?"

Carol tilted her head to one side. "That's in the desert part of the state, right?"

"It's the high desert, yes," Kate replied. "But there are so many trees and glorious mountain views. We got married right at sunset on the big grassy lawn with these little wild rabbits hopping around everywhere and tall vases of gladiolas in all different colors. You could hear coyotes yipping and smell the sagebrush on the breeze. It was magical."

Jonah looked at her, struck by the image she'd just painted. Was this something she'd envisioned for herself, or just an act? Something she'd experienced at some point?

She turned to look at him, and he couldn't help feeling moved by their imaginary ceremony. "She walked down the aisle to Pachelbel's Canon, and the recessional was the throne room song from *Star Wars*."

Kate laughed, which was the opposite of what his ex-wife had done when he'd suggested it for their wedding.

"You know I love your whimsy, darling," she'd said, placing her hand on his arm the way she used to. "But maybe we could find something with more meaning for the two of us together?"

"It was awesome," Kate said, jarring Jonah back to the present. "And afterward, we served cupcakes instead of regular cake."

"Great combinations," Jonah added. "Flavors like salted caramel and rhubarb pineapple and grilled peach with lavender."

"And the dance," Kate continued, sounding a little breathless now. "Our first dance was 'Happy' by Pharrell Williams. Everyone was jumping all over the place, especially little kids. I've never seen so much joy in one place."

"Lovely!" Marilee clasped her hands on the table and glanced at Carol with a wistful look in her eye. "Weddings are so much fun!"

Carol gave a coy smile and dabbed the corner of her mouth with a napkin as she leaned in close across the table. "Don't tell anyone, but sometimes we like to crash them."

Kate laughed, and Jonah glanced over, surprised to see such delight in her eyes. They were brown, but not a dull brown. More like the color of copper or toffee.

"I don't like the word *crash*," Marilee was saying. "*Attend without an invitation* sounds nicer."

"It does," Kate agreed, placing her left hand over Jonah's right one, which was resting next to his plate of bacon. She looked down at their pile of fingers and palms, then frowned and pulled her hand back.

But she wasn't fast enough for Carol, whose gaze skimmed over Kate's bare ring finger. "They're being soldered," Jonah said. "Her rings. She really wanted to wear them for the honeymoon, but there was a mix-up at the goldsmith and they didn't have them done in time."

Kate shot him a grateful look, and Jonah smiled, glad the women didn't seem concerned by his own lack of a wedding band. Even when he'd been married, he'd never worn one. Not really his style, and his ex had never minded.

Stop thinking about your ex-wife, asshole.

"This is such a lovely place to honeymoon," Carol said, smiling at the two of them. "You're seeing *Shakespeare in Love*, aren't you?"

"Unfortunately, we couldn't get tickets," Kate admitted. "It's okay, though. We'll make plenty of romance of our own."

She smiled up at Jonah, and he felt his heart leap up and lodge itself in his throat.

"Don't worry, ladies," he assured their tablemates. "We promise to keep it down from now on."

"I know!" Carol looked at Marilee with an excited gleam in her eye. "We were going to skip *Shakespeare in Love* today anyway so we could go wine tasting. What if we made the tickets a wedding gift?"

Kate's eyes went wide. "Oh no. We couldn't possibly."

"I insist," Marilee said. "We were planning to gift them to someone at the box office anyway as our good deed for the day."

"They're front row," Carol added. "Very nice seats."

Jonah shook his head, not willing to let the charade go this far. "Really, you shouldn't—"

"No, we insist!" Marilee fished into the little pocketbook she'd brought with her, pulling out a pair of tickets. "We want you to have them."

Kate's gaze dropped to the tickets, and Jonah knew how much she wanted them. "We'll pay you for them," he offered. "Those aren't cheap."

"Absolutely not," Marilee said. "I got them free anyway for being a longtime donor. We were just planning to give them away."

"And you two look nice," Carol added.

"Very nice."

Jonah watched Kate's throat move as she swallowed. She looked up at him and gave a cautious smile. "What do you think, sweetie?"

He smiled back, his chest tightening with excitement for more than the play. "I think it's a date."

CHAPTER TWO

They dropped the marriage act before they got to the theater, which was fine by Kate. But they didn't drop the "date" act, which was also fine by her, especially once the play had ended.

"Here, try this." Jonah held out a spring roll filled with shrimp and fresh cilantro, and for an instant, Kate wasn't sure whether to take it from him or bite it out of his hand.

She decided to err on the side of caution.

"Thanks." She plucked it from his fingers and took the politest bite she could manage. "Mmm, you're right. The peanut sauce is delicious."

They'd both been hungry after the show, and found their way to a quaint little Thai restaurant near the theater. It seemed platonic enough, except that they'd been seated at a candlelit table on the patio beside Lithia Creek, with a canopy of twinkle lights strung through the trees overhead.

"I love this place," Jonah said as Kate forked up a spicy bite of eggplant from her green curry. "Especially that little mouse over there that keeps darting onto the patio for crumbs, and then running back when the waiter comes out."

Kate glanced behind her at the bushes to see the tiny pink feet scurrying away. "How do you know I'm not afraid of mice?"

Jonah grinned and poured the last dregs of wine into each of their glasses. "Because I saw you slip him a noodle when you thought no one was looking."

Kate laughed and lifted her glass, enjoying the crispness of the rosé, the coolness of the evening, the warmth of Jonah's company. "Guilty as charged," she admitted. "You're a very observant guy."

"I try." Jonah took a slow sip of wine, then set his glass down and looked at her. "So you just came to Ashland by yourself?"

She felt herself bristling, then relaxed. He was here alone, too, so there was clearly no judgment in the question.

"Yep." She trailed her fork through the green curry, looking for another bite of chicken. "I used to come here all the time with Anton— that's my ex. I guess I started thinking of it as 'our place.'"

"So you're here to reminisce?"

"God no." She didn't realize she'd jerked back until her cardigan slipped off one shoulder. Tugging it back up, she shook her head at Jonah. "It's the opposite, really. I'm here to reclaim it."

"Reclaim it?"

She shrugged and scraped a pile of rice to the middle of her plate, not wanting to miss a bite of it. "There's this book I really love about getting on with life after a bad breakup—" She stopped, reconsidering how far she wanted to go down that path as she shoveled sauce-soaked rice onto her fork. "Anyway, it talks about reclaiming memories and places after a split. I used to come here with my parents as a teenager, so it's really more *my place* than ours. Anton's and mine, I mean. I realized I was being silly letting it stay haunted by ghosts of relationships past."

"Ghosts of relationships past," he repeated, giving her an odd look. "That's an interesting turn of phrase."

"I can't actually take credit for it," she said. "It's from that relationship guide I mentioned."

Something flickered in Jonah's face, but it was gone in an instant. Maybe he wasn't used to women admitting they read self-help books, but Kate refused to feel embarrassed. If anything, it was a point of pride, a reminder that she was willing to improve and grow and embrace change. Anyone who'd judge her for it was not the sort of guy whose opinion she valued.

"Breakups are tough," he said. "Sounds like you've done a good job moving on."

"I like to think so." She studied him for a moment. "You're not married, are you? Sorry to be blunt, but the last three guys I've gone out with turned out to be married. Not that this is a date, but—"

"Divorced." The answer was firm and decisive, but he didn't volunteer anything else. Kate lifted her wineglass.

"Well, here's to having the self-assurance to vacation solo," she said. "Feeling confident dining alone or seeing a movie by yourself or whatever."

"Cheers to that," he agreed, clinking his glass against hers. "Some of my happiest moments have been totally solo. No offense, of course."

Kate grinned. "None taken. Enjoying the pleasure of your own company is one of the greatest skills to master."

She replayed her own words in her brain and wondered if they sounded entirely too masturbatory. Jonah didn't react, so she was probably overthinking things.

She watched him drain the last of his wine and tried not to be disappointed their plates were empty. Despite her assertions about the importance of flying solo, she'd enjoyed his company. A lot, actually. True, there was no point starting something with a guy who lived in another state. Or a guy from anywhere, *really*—

"Wait, no, you don't have to do that." She made a grab for the credit card he'd handed the passing waitress, but she missed and ended up grabbing the woman's hip instead. "Sorry about that," Kate said as she fished into her purse for her wallet. "Please, let me—"

"It's fine, Kate." Jonah grinned at her and caught her hand in his. He didn't let go right away. "I'm not paying so you'll put out."

The waitress giggled and hurried away, and Kate felt herself blushing all the way to the tips of her hair. She sat back in her chair with a grimace. "Sorry. I'm a little out of practice at this. But, you shouldn't have to foot the whole bill for this."

"I think I can manage."

She must have looked dubious, which was pretty lousy of her. It wasn't like she had any idea how much a bookstore owner made.

Seeming to read her thoughts, Jonah grinned. "I have other sources of income," he said, pausing long enough to scrawl his signature on the bill the waitress handed him. Reading upside down, Kate could see he'd left a generous tip. "The bookstore isn't my only revenue stream."

"Oh. That's—that's good."

She waited to see if he'd volunteer more, but he seemed to be done discussing his finances. She thought about what else she wanted to know about him. How long had his marriage lasted? Did he have any kids? Any tattoos or pets or—

"Don't be afraid to ask blunt questions at the start of a relationship!" Kate's brain quoted matter-of-factly from one of Dr. Brandt's older books. *"Someone who'd judge you for being inquisitive and straightforward isn't worth getting to know, and walking on eggshells only makes your toes cramp!"*

It felt weird to hear the words echoing in her head now, considering this wasn't a relationship and she'd probably never see Jonah again.

They both stood and Kate tugged her cardigan tighter around her shoulders. The fall evening had turned chilly, and she shivered as she started up the stairs leading from the courtyard to the street. She was conscious of Jonah right behind her, and wondered if she had panty lines showing through the thin jersey fabric of her dress. The hemline came all the way to her ankles, and part of her wished she'd worn something knee-length or maybe gone commando.

"Something's making you smile," Jonah remarked as they reached the street and fell into step together.

Kate couldn't tell if it was a question or a statement, but she blurted an answer anyway. "Underwear."

He laughed as they headed back toward the B&B. "I guess that's something to smile about. Did you know nine percent of American men have underwear that's at least ten years old?"

"That's—wow." She looked up at him. "So you might be wearing underwear purchased around the first time you legally bought beer?"

He grinned as his elbow bumped hers. "Was that a roundabout way of asking how old I am, or a roundabout way of assessing my hygiene?"

"Neither, really. Just an observation." Kate shrugged as she side-stepped a crack in the sidewalk. "I don't usually hold back if I have a question or something I want to say."

"That's a good trait to have. Straightforwardness, I mean. I'm thirty-six, by the way. And I bought all new underwear after my divorce."

Kate laughed. "That's an interesting post-divorce ritual."

"Not a ritual so much as reestablishing my identity," he said. "She liked boxers, but I'm more of a boxer-brief guy."

"Reclaiming your sense of self with underwear. I like it." Kate hesitated, not sure if she should press for more. But hell, he'd been the one to bring up the ex. "You've been divorced awhile?"

He shrugged. "A year or so."

"Was it ugly?"

Jonah kicked a pinecone out of their way. "Nah, it was pretty amicable. Well, as amicable as divorce can be when one person gets fed up and pulls the plug while the other is sitting there like a dumbass wondering what the hell just happened."

"Which were you?"

"The dumbass." He gave a funny little laugh. "Probably part of the impetus for the divorce."

Kate smiled to herself and tugged her cardigan tighter around her waist. "I don't think dumbasses generally use words like *impetus* and *amicable*."

He turned and looked at her, a flash of surprise in his expression. "Good point."

A breeze kicked up, sending a pile of dry leaves skittering across the road. Kate didn't realize she'd shivered until Jonah began shrugging off his jacket. "Here. We've got two blocks to go. I don't want you freezing to death."

"I don't want *you* to freeze either."

"I've got a long-sleeved shirt under a sweater," he insisted as he settled the chocolate-colored suede around her shoulders. "I'm good."

She started to protest again, but the jacket felt warm and smelled like cloves and cedar dust. It was five sizes too big, but she snuggled into it and tucked her hands up inside the sleeves.

"Thanks," she said as they started walking again. "You're very chivalrous."

Jonah laughed. "My sister would say overprotective, and meddling, but I'll take it."

Kate smiled and breathed in the scent of crushed leaves and the warm leather of the jacket, letting the soft suede collar brush her cheek. She wondered if this qualified as a date. If it did, it was one of the nicest ones she'd had in months.

She was almost disappointed when they reached the B&B. He held the little white gate open for her, and Kate filed through, shuffling slowly up the steps. She hesitated at the top, pivoting on the wide front porch to face him.

"This has been a really fun day," she said. "Thanks."

"My pleasure. I enjoyed getting to know you."

He lifted his hand, and she thought he might reach for her. Pull her in for a good-night kiss or a romantic cheek graze. She thought she might want him to.

Instead, he curled his fingers around the chain holding a white, painted porch swing under the eaves. He glanced at the front door, but made no move to go inside.

"Did you get one of the rooms on the ground floor, or on the second floor?" he asked.

Kate hesitated. He must have noticed, because he held up a hand and shook his head. "Wait, don't answer that. I didn't mean to sound like a creepy stalker. I was just making conversation."

"No, it's okay. I'm on the second floor."

"Ground floor," he said. "Right off the library."

"Mm, I hear that room's nice," she said. "It's got that antique, claw-foot tub, right?"

Oh shit. Did that sound like a request for an invitation? She hadn't meant it to.

But Jonah just smiled and nodded. "It does. I haven't used it, but you're welcome to check it out if you want."

Kate bit her lip. She was so out of practice. On one hand, she didn't want to end the evening. On the other hand, she didn't know what else to do. Invite him to her room? Suggest a nightcap? Was that even something people did, or were nightcaps only a thing in old movies?

She took a deep breath. "Look, I don't do one-night stands."

"What?" Jonah barked out a laugh. He was still gripping the chain of the porch swing, and the whole thing began to shake as he convulsed with laughter. He was laughing so hard he had to sit down in the swing, and Kate seated herself on the edge of the swing beside him, feeling silly.

"Sorry," he said as he took off his glasses and wiped his eyes. "I didn't see that one coming." When he finally looked at her, he cocked his head to the side. "Was there a 'but' coming next? *I don't normally have one-night stands, but with you—*"

"No." She shook her head, wishing she could restart this conversation. "That's not what I was getting at. I just wanted to be clear; I'm not having sex with you. I also don't do long-distance relationships."

"I see," he said, still sounding amused. "And there's nothing in between those two?"

Kate's cheeks were burning, and she folded her hands in her lap. In her quest to be a forthright communicator, had she turned herself into a social moron?

But Jonah pushed his feet against the wood slats of the porch and sent the swing into a gentle sway. They glided back and forth a few times, rocking in a gentle rhythm that gradually began to soothe Kate's tattered nerves. "I wasn't planning to seduce you," he said. "Not that I'd object if *you* wanted to seduce *me*. You're very hot. And smart. And funny. Did I mention hot?"

He grinned, and Kate's insides liquefied. Maybe she'd been too quick to dismiss the idea of a one-night stand.

No, of course she wouldn't do that. It wasn't her style. Still—

"You're hot, too," she acknowledged as she leaned back against the swing and kicked her feet. "This is nice. Just swinging. It's such a pleasant night."

"That it is." He kicked off the porch again, giving them a little more momentum. "Swinging soothes the soul."

"Can we sit here and talk for a while?" she suggested.

"I'd like that." He smiled. "And maybe you'd let me hold your hand?"

Kate grinned and slid her hand onto his knee. He wrapped his fingers around hers, forming a comfortable web of digits. "I'd like that," she said. "I'd like that a lot."

Jonah leaned a little closer, and Kate gave a little sigh of pleasure. "And maybe eventually," he murmured, "you'd let me kiss you good night?"

Kate looked up at him, admiring the soft creases in his forehead, the fringe of dark lashes, the sparkle of streetlights in those amber-green eyes.

"Why wait for eventually?" she murmured back.

Then she leaned up and kissed him.

♦ ♦ ♦

Four weeks later, Kate was still thinking about that kiss.

Well, she thought about other things, too. Like the fact that she was on the brink of one of the biggest breaks in her career.

"So the rest of the network guys liked the pitch?"

Kate nodded. "They loved it." She glanced over at her assistant producer in the passenger seat. Amy's wild blond curls fluttered in the current from the rental car's air vents, and her manicured fingers drummed the stack of books in her lap. The sight of those books sent a pulse of happiness through Kate's body.

She knew every one of them by heart.

There was *But Not Broken*, Vivienne Brandt's debut memoir about finding love after an abusive relationship.

On the Other Hand was the follow-up, a sort of relationship self-help guide for couples.

The newest title, *Making It Work*, had only been out a few weeks and featured Vivienne Brandt's advice for real-life couples experiencing challenges in their relationships.

"I still can't believe you convinced Vivienne Brandt to do a reality show," Amy said, jarring Kate back to the present.

"I'm still kind of stunned myself," Kate admitted. "Don't forget we're avoiding the term *reality show*. At least when we're talking to Dr. Vivienne."

"I know, I know," Amy said. "It's 'unscripted television.'" The implied air quotes said plenty about Amy's opinion of the nitpicky word choice, but Kate didn't care.

"We can call it whatever we want when we're alone," Kate said. "But it's important to Vivienne that we keep things sounding sophisticated and educational."

"Hey, whatever keeps the good doc happy."

Kate steered the car off I-5 with a flutter of anticipation. She couldn't believe she was here in Seattle. The whole thing had happened so quickly. Well, quickly in TV terms.

And somehow, she'd made it all happen. First, she'd convinced Vivienne Brandt—her freakin' *idol*—to do a television show. And then she'd convinced the studio to back it. And yesterday morning, she'd gotten a tentative okay from the Empire TV network. The sizzle reel she and Amy had put together was one of the best they'd ever done, and the whole thing was almost in the bag.

Almost.

As though reading her thoughts, Amy cleared her throat. "So you think the network is going to pick it up?"

"They want to," Kate said. "We just have to get Dr. Vivienne to agree to their changes."

"She *has* to," Amy said with all the determination of someone still relatively new to the television industry. "Besides, the network's title is better anyway. *Relationship Reboot with Dr. Viv* has such a cool ring to it."

"I agree," Kate said. "It's not the title I'm worried about. It's the *other* change that might be an issue."

"Right." Amy shuffled the books in her lap, bringing *On the Other Hand* to the top. The cover featured the interlaced fingers of husband and wife, wedding rings on casual display. It was one of Kate's favorites, both the cover and the book itself. She used to keep it on her nightstand and read sections aloud to Anton. Chapters about communication techniques and relationship-building exercises and—

"Do you think she's going to go for it?" Amy asked.

Kate glanced at her. "Having her husband involved?"

Amy nodded. "I mean, I loved how they wound up together at the end of *But Not Broken*," she said. "And his sidebars in *On the Other Hand* were terrific. So lighthearted and genuine. Maybe even better than *her* parts."

Kate cringed. "Please, please don't say that in front of her."

"Obviously," Amy said with an eye roll Kate didn't see, but could hear in her tone. "It's true, though, right? I mean, why else would the network be so adamant about adding him?"

"Dr. Vivienne is the one with the PhD in psychology," she reminded Amy. "He just wrote the sidebars. Besides, we didn't pitch this show as a two-person act. This was just supposed to be Dr. Vivienne's show."

"But you think she'll do it?"

"I don't know. She was pretty guarded when I told her about it on the phone yesterday. I'm guessing she has some concerns."

"So that's why she wants to meet with us alone before we sit down with the network team?"

"Yep." At least Kate hoped so. She had an uncomfortable feeling in the pit of her stomach.

Amy continued chattering as Kate took a sharp right. "I've been reading old reviews of *On the Other Hand*," Amy said. "Female readers really connected with the whole Average-Joe thing. I think it'll add a lot to the show."

"But her new book doesn't have that at all," Kate pointed out as she continued down the narrow street lined with gated properties and towering stucco houses. And trees. So many trees. Must be a Seattle thing.

"I'm only a couple chapters into that one," Amy said.

"*Making It Work* is just Dr. Vivienne's perspectives on a whole bunch of different relationships in jeopardy, and it's been on the *New York Times* bestseller list for weeks."

"Her career is definitely hot right now," Amy said. "Putting her on television is a fabulous idea."

"It is great timing," Kate agreed as she pulled up to the gate and punched in the code Dr. Vivienne had given her. Her stomach did a triple backflip of anticipation. She'd met Dr. Vivienne before, of course, but never at her home. Never like this. Here she was, Kate Geary, driving alongside the hydrangea bushes of the woman who'd written the books that got Kate through the toughest times in her life.

She took a deep breath and eased into the circular driveway.

"Nice place," Amy said as she eyed the massive house. "The self-help gig must pay pretty well."

"She's done other things," Kate said. "Speaking engagements and workshops."

Amy looked at the house again. "We're not all going to hold hands and talk about our feelings, are we?"

"I highly doubt it," Kate assured her as she parked the car, then checked her lipstick in the rearview mirror. "She's really down-to-earth. I'm sure you'll love her."

Kate stepped out of the car and smoothed down the front of her gray pencil skirt. She wore a conservative navy blouse and low heels, her all-business look. She grabbed her leather briefcase from the backseat and started toward the front door with Amy right behind her. "How's my hair?" Amy asked.

Kate pivoted on the doorstep and paused to adjust the bobby pin holding Amy's wild blond curls back from her face. "Perfect."

"Here, you've got a smudge of eyeliner right here." Amy dabbed the corner of Kate's cheekbone with a damp thumb.

"Did you just spit on me?"

"Yes, but I did it with the utmost respect." Amy grinned. "You're all good."

Kate reached up and rang the doorbell, braced to be greeted by a stiffly attired butler or maybe Dr. Viv's personal assistant.

But when the door flew open, it was the woman herself who greeted them. Vivienne Brandt's trademark long, dark hair was swept back in a low ponytail, and she wore only the faintest hint of makeup on her flawless porcelain skin. The thin gold bangles on her right wrist chimed when she lifted her hand. She looked elegant in loose linen slacks and a simple black T-shirt, and as she shifted to acknowledge Amy with a smile, Kate couldn't help envying the delicate arches of her bare feet.

"Kate! It's so good to see you again!"

Vivienne clasped Kate's hand in hers, replacing Kate's intended handshake with a friendlier grasp that left Kate wondering how long she should stand here holding hands with a relative stranger.

"Hello, Vivienne," Kate said, turning just enough to free her hand. "I'd like you to meet our assistant producer, Amy Bartholomew."

"Ma'am," Amy said. "I absolutely love your books."

"Such a pleasure to meet you," Dr. Vivienne said as she gave Amy the same hand-holding treatment. "Please, call me Viv. And come on in! I've got water and herbal tea and some light refreshments in the parlor."

"Light refreshments in the parlor," Kate recited in her mind as she followed Dr. Viv down a well-lit corridor lined with cool Italian marble and Asian artifacts. There was something lovely and lilting about the phrase, and it gave Kate a fresh boost of confidence about how well Dr. Viv would do on camera.

"This is a beautiful space," Kate remarked, taking in the tall, floor-to-ceiling windows, the clean lines, the modern sparseness of the décor.

"Thanks." Viv halted in the center of the room—the parlor, Kate presumed—and swept her arms in a wide arc. "You can see now why I wanted the team to consider filming here in my home. It's sleek, but intimate. Cozy, but professional. I think it sets the perfect tone."

"Very modern," Amy murmured, nodding as she paused to scribble something on her ever-present notepad.

Kate glanced at her watch. "We have two hours until the network guys show. You said you wanted to go over their proposal?"

"Right." For the first time since they'd arrived, Viv's perfect smile seemed to falter just a little. Still rooted in the center of the parlor, she shifted from one bare foot to the other, then gestured to a buttery-looking leather sofa in a soft gray. "Please, have a seat. Help yourselves to the cucumber water, fresh fruit, nuts—whatever you like."

Viv's new uneasiness made the hair prickle on the back of Kate's neck, but she seated herself on the edge of the sofa and grabbed a small handful of raw almonds. She slipped one in her mouth as Amy filled three glasses from a pitcher brimming with slices of cucumber and lemon and slid a coaster under each one. They waited for Viv to sit, but she remained standing.

"So," Viv said, clasping her hands together. "I was a little surprised by the title change, but I'm fine with it. *Relationship Reboot with Dr. Viv* is casual and catchy, and I'm sure it will resonate better with viewers."

"Excellent." Amy plucked a handful of grapes off the platter. "I'll get the paperwork rolling on that end."

Viv nodded, and Kate watched her fiddle with the gold bangles, then take a deep breath.

"All right, I'll just come out and say this." Viv cleared her throat. "I wanted to tell you this in person, rather than on the phone or in an e-mail. And I wanted you to see the space first, so you can see how perfect this would be."

Kate felt Amy stiffen beside her. "The space is lovely," Amy said. "I'm sure the network will consider it."

Kate kept her attention on Viv. "What do you need to tell us?"

Vivienne took another deep breath, then gave a nervous little laugh. "Goodness, look at me. I've written all these books encouraging forthright communication and blunt honesty, and I can't seem to spit out the words."

"It's okay," Kate said, struck by how human Viv seemed. How down-to-earth. She'd idolized Vivienne Brandt for years, and there was something sweet about seeing her so uncertain. "Take your time."

Kate glanced at Amy, who looked jumpy on the sofa beside her. She turned back to Viv, who was still working to compose herself.

"All right." Viv took a few more breaths, then arranged her expression into one of lovely serenity.

That'll look great on camera, Kate thought, even as the back of her neck continued to prickle.

"The network's request—the one about having my husband be part of the show?" Viv began.

Kate felt herself nodding as Amy bumped her knee with the side of her notebook.

"They liked the idea of breakout sessions," Amy said. "You do most of the counseling, but then bring your husband in for a round of 'Straight Talk with Average Joe.' They think it'll resonate with male viewers in particular."

"Right, well—that's going to be a problem." Vivienne unclasped her fingers and reached up to fiddle with the bangles again. "I need to just lay this out there. Joe and I went through a very difficult time in our marriage between the completion of the manuscript for *On the Other Hand* and the release of the actual book."

"A difficult time?" Kate frowned, picturing plates hurled at the wall in anger or heated arguments about which way the toilet paper should roll.

"Nothing violent or overly contentious," Viv amended softly. "Just a—a slow dying of love."

"Oh," Amy murmured as Kate's heart began to race.

"By the time the book was released, we weren't even living together anymore," Viv said.

"But—but—" Kate dropped the almond that had been en route to her mouth. She thought about grabbing for it, but that was the least of her concerns right now. "I don't understand. You did that whole publicity tour together. Book signings and magazine interviews and—"

"We scrapped all the television appearances, and stuck with things that minimized public appearances together." Vivienne sighed. "I know what you're thinking. I know this goes against everything I've written about authenticity and being true to yourself, but our publicist thought it would be best if we pretended everything was fine just to get through the PR obligations together. We were still technically married at that point, and we figured we could go our separate ways once the limelight was off us."

Kate blinked. "So you're divorced?"

Viv nodded and looked down at her hands. "It was final long before *Making It Work* came out. Almost eighteen months now. Things had died down after all the hoopla for *On the Other Hand*, and the paper-work went through quietly. We were still friendly enough to handle all that ourselves, so there was no need to involve lawyers or make a big deal about it. We just—cut ties and moved on."

Amy shook her head, her expression nearly as dumbstruck as Kate felt. "So that's why he's not mentioned in your new book," Amy said, earning herself a slow nod from Vivienne. "That's why *Making It Work* is all about case studies and other people's marriages with no personal anecdotes of your own."

"But you thanked him," Kate said. "In the acknowledgments for *Making It Work*—you wrote, 'And thank you to Joe: For everything.'"

Okay, in light of what she'd just heard, it wasn't the most romantic thing one spouse had ever written to another in the acknowledgments. Still—

"The split was friendly," Viv said. "And I am thankful for Joe's part in my life, even if we're no longer together as a married couple."

Kate nodded. There was a humming in her ears, and she could see this whole plan going up in smoke. She licked her lips.

"This is going to be a problem for the network," she said. "I'm sorry, but I have to be honest with you here. I know when we first approached you and talked about a stand-alone show that just featured you, everyone was on board. But the network is only interested if Joe is part of the plan. I'm almost certain that's the only way they'll bite. If we'd known this sooner—"

She stopped, not wanting to play the blame game. Not wanting to finish by saying *then* would have been the time to mention the divorce.

But Viv had spent enough time as a counselor to know damn well what Kate was thinking. "I hear you," she said. "It would have been easier to scrap the show and go with something else if I'd let you know the situation sooner. But I wanted to give you the chance to consider an alternative."

"An alternative?"

Viv nodded. "I feel confident I can still convince Joe to be part of the program."

"With his ex-wife?" Amy's tone was incredulous, but Kate couldn't blame her. She was thinking the same thing.

"As I said, the split was amicable," Viv said. "We're still adults who are capable of working together in a professional capacity. We already proved that during the publicity blitz for *On the Other Hand*, didn't we?"

"True," Kate acknowledged, still reeling a little from the shock. "So Joe—he's on board with this plan?"

"And what would this even look like?" Amy asked. "Would you pretend you're still married, or do the show as exes, or—"

"These are all excellent questions, and I'd love it if we could all sit down and discuss them together." Vivienne glanced at her watch. "He should be here any minute."

Amy frowned. "He's on his way here now? Average Joe?"

"The one and only." Viv offered a smile that seemed a little forced, and Kate felt a knot in the pit of her belly.

"And he's willing to go along with this?" she asked.

"I'm sure as soon as we explain the whole concept to him, he'll see this is a positive move for us bo—"

"Wait." Kate blinked. "You mean you haven't *told* him about this?"

"I thought it would be best if you were here to answer questions." Viv glanced toward the front window and smiled. "Ah, here he is now. Excuse me one second."

Vivienne scrambled up and strode from the parlor on enviably long legs. Kate gaped after her, too stunned to form words.

"This is nuts!" Amy stage-whispered. "Why would she wait until now to bring it up?"

"Well, we did just find out yesterday that the network wanted Average Joe in the program," Kate whispered back. "It's not like she had a lot of time to plan."

"Still, she could have called him or told him in person before we flew all the way out here."

"It's a technique," Kate said as a male voice murmured a polite-sounding greeting in the foyer. "She talks about it in chapter six in *Making It Work*. This idea of getting everyone together in one place to have the difficult conversations so everyone's hearing the same story and there are no games of telephone or miscommunications or—"

"Everyone's in here, darling." Vivienne's voice echoed from the hall-way, and Kate snapped her attention to the parlor doorway. "I'll explain in just a second why I've asked you to join me today."

"Jesus, Viv," muttered a male voice. "Always with the drama. Can't we just have a conversation like normal fucking pe—"

The words died in his throat as the man froze in the doorway. His eyes locked with Kate's, and she heard herself give a startled gasp. She started to stand up, but bumped her water glass with her knee and sent it toppling onto Amy's lap and the tidy glass table in front of them.

Amy gasped, too, so at least Kate wasn't the only one who sounded like a hyperventilating hyena. Tearing her eyes from the doorway, Kate yanked off her cardigan and threw it over the blossoming puddle of cucumber water before it reached the edge of the table.

Then she turned and met those amber-green eyes again.

"Jonah?"

CHAPTER THREE

Jonah had several questions buzzing around in his brain and wasn't sure which one to ask first.

He decided not to choose. "Why the hell am I here?" He leveled the first question at his ex-wife before turning to face the whip-smart woman with the sleek mahogany hair and the lips he hadn't stopped thinking about for a month. "And why are *you* here?"

Kate flinched, and Jonah felt like an asshole. Okay, so that came out a little gruffer than he meant it to. The question—or maybe the bluntness of it?—seemed to catch Kate off guard. She opened her mouth, but no sound came out, leaving Jonah staring at those perfect, soft lips for a little too long.

Way too long. Jesus.

He swung his gaze back to Vivienne. "What's going on here?"

"You two know each other?" Vivienne looked genuinely perplexed, which wasn't like her. That killed his initial theory that this was some sort of weird matchmaker scheme, which was totally something Viv would do. Helping her ex-husband find love again would make a great bestselling self-help book.

"I—we—" Kate was still fumbling for words, and Jonah couldn't help remembering how cool and composed she'd been for their newly-wed playacting in Ashland. That meant she was really rattled.

He looked back at Viv again, trying to make sense of things. His ex-wife gave a stiff smile and swept an arm out over the parlor. "Please, Jonah—have a seat."

Christ. She only used his full name when she wanted something. After the publishing house had slapped him with that ridiculous "Average Joe" moniker during edits for *On the Other Hand,* Viv had taken to calling him Joe all the time.

At least until she needed something from him.

"I'm sure we can get this all sorted out," Viv was saying as she poured him a glass of cucumber water. "Can I get you something else? A beer, maybe?"

She was really laying it on thick. Beer? Really? At ten in the morning, when she used to flip him shit for drinking the stuff at all?

She'd tried for years to make him a passionate wine connoisseur instead, signing them up for a couples' pinot noir tasting class and booking a romantic vineyard getaway when all he'd wanted was a goddamn pale ale and a quiet afternoon with a good book.

And now here he was getting worked up over the beer issue again when he still had no idea why Kate was sitting in Viv's living room.

Jonah shook his head and took the water glass. "Water's fine, thanks."

He surveyed the array of seating options in the parlor and selected a leather club chair the color of squash puree. It looked new, something she'd acquired in the months since their divorce, along with this house. He'd been here only once before to pick up a cookbook that had belonged to his mother. They'd been cordial enough then, but something told him this was a different sort of meeting.

He set the glass on the sleek glass coffee table, deliberately avoiding the coaster just to watch Viv blanch. Then he sat back with his hands on his knees and looked from one face to the next—Viv, Kate, and a curly-haired blonde who seemed so flustered she'd forgotten to introduce herself.

"So what's going on here?"

The words came with an echo, and Jonah realized he and Viv had spoken them at the same time. He stared at her for a moment, resisting the urge to call "Jinx!" the way they might have in the early years of their marriage.

Viv looked away first and focused on Kate. "I'm confused. You told me yesterday that you'd never met Joe. You were even joking about how you couldn't find photos of him online."

"Jonah," he muttered, not that anyone was listening.

The blonde gave a vigorous nod and stared at him like he'd emerged from a spaceship. "It's true about the photos. The only things we found when we Googled you were a couple pics from college and this one where you had a big lumberjack beard."

Jonah frowned, wondering why the hell any of these people would be Googling him. "The military required me to keep a low profile for a number of years," he said.

"And then he refused to have photos in the books," Viv said in a tone that suggested she was still irritated about it.

"Oh," the blonde said as realization seemed to dawn. "We were also Googling *Joe* Porter, not Jonah."

Kate seemed to find her tongue at last. "Vivienne. This is—wow, such a coincidence." She looked at Jonah then as though expecting him to correct her, but he apparently knew even less than she did.

She licked her lips—a nervous gesture that sent his libido reeling— and flicked her gaze back to Viv's. "So, uh—Jonah and I met four weeks ago in Ashland. We stayed at the same bed-and-breakfast and ended up going to the same play that afternoon and—"

"Oh dear." Vivienne raised a hand to her lips, eyes wide with amazement. Someone who didn't know her well might mistake the look for dismay, but Jonah knew better. Viv lived for serendipitous shit like this.

She looked at Jonah. "You two slept together?"

"No!"

This time it was Kate whose words came out in an echo of his, and Jonah looked at her again. She was shaking her head like the thought of sleeping with him was only slightly less repugnant than the thought of bathing in a pit of raw sewage. He tried not to take offense.

"Definitely not," Kate said. "We saw a play together and had dinner together and—"

"Pretended to be married," Jonah supplied.

Hell, might as well put it all out there.

"That's not as scandalous as it sounds," Kate said with exaggerated patience. "There were these two old ladies talking about the people next door having really loud sex, and Jonah and I—" She stopped there, probably realizing that any additional detail would make things sound more meaningful than they were. Kate cleared her throat. "Anyway, we saw a play together and had dinner afterward, but we didn't even exchange phone numbers."

Jonah watched her speaking, intrigued that she didn't mention the kiss. And that's all it had been. Just a kiss, or more accurately, several long, drawn out, passionate kisses. Making out, if you wanted to call it that. The sort of kissing-for-the-sake-of-kissing that most people forget exists sometime between, "Are you taking the SAT prep course?" and, "I now pronounce you man and wife." Kissing as the endgame, rather than foreplay.

God, he'd loved that.

But if Kate wasn't going to say anything about it, he wouldn't either. He still didn't know what the hell was going on here, but he sensed he was better off not volunteering too much. He turned back to Viv, who was studying them both with that clinical, analytical look she always got when she was trying to burrow into a client's brain and wiggle her fingers around in the dark, slippery layers.

But she didn't press for more information, so it seemed like a good idea to get on with whatever the hell had prompted her to invite him here.

"So," he said to Viv. "Want to tell me what this is all about?"

Vivienne folded her hands in her lap and nodded. "Of course. In a nutshell, the Empire Television Network would like me to star in a new unscripted television program called *Relationship Reboot with Dr. Viv*. They'll follow one couple each episode from the point where they first appear in my office for counseling to the point where they leave with a decision to save the marriage or mindfully disentangle themselves from the union."

Mindfully disentangling themselves from the union was exactly what he and Viv had done, or at least what she'd suggested when she'd brought up the idea of divorce in the first place. The words still grated on him, and brought out his inner chest-thumping caveman the way it always did around her.

Maybe that's what she wanted. Why he was sitting here right now.

"Let me take a guess," he said, pulling off his glasses so he could polish them on the hem of his T-shirt. "You want me to be part of this show."

He regretted the words the instant they left his mouth. He'd look like a dick if he'd guessed wrong.

But he wasn't wrong. He could see from the way Viv pursed her lips, and the way Kate shifted uncomfortably on the sofa and looked down at the floor.

Viv cleared her throat. "Based on the success of our co-authored book, and the fact that—"

"No."

All three women frowned, but it was Viv who spoke first. "Jonah—"

There she went again, using his full name. To this day, he regretted that stupid Average Joe moniker. Playing the Neanderthal to his ethereal, educated wife had seemed like a good idea at the time. But now . . .

"We were able to function beautifully together during the publicity push for *On the Other Hand*, despite our separation," Viv continued in her soothing-therapist voice. "Very maturely."

Jonah put his glasses back on and folded his arms over his chest. "Not that maturely."

"Having you as part of the show would lend an authenticity to it," Viv said. "A relatability element."

Kate cleared her throat. "For what it's worth, the focus groups we've tested the concept with so far found a male element to be vital for a show like this. Your contributions to *On the Other Hand* were some of the most compelling, heartfelt sections in the whole book. They literally changed my life."

She was selling it pretty hard, though there was an earnestness in her voice that almost sounded real. But hell, she knew how to act. He'd seen that firsthand.

He looked away, needing to keep his focus on the subject at hand instead of the lushness of Kate's thighs crossing and uncrossing under that snug little skirt. Jonah tugged at his collar and turned his attention back to Viv. "You swore when we finished that publicity tour that we'd be all done. No more."

"I know that," she said. "It was a promise I meant at the time, but things change."

"No shit."

God, he sounded like a bitter ex-husband. He wasn't really. The divorce had been friendly enough, and they'd parted on decent terms. What was it about sitting here with her that made him turn into a goddamn cretin?

"Jonah," Viv tried again. "Just hear us out."

"I don't think so. Have you forgotten the fact that I hate TV appearances? Remember how many we did during the push for *On the Other Hand?*"

"Zero." Viv pressed her lips together. "We did zero. You also wouldn't pose for a book jacket photo. Not even the hands on the cover are ours."

A flash of hurt shot through Viv's eyes, but she looked away before he could even think about apologizing.

"Exactly," Jonah said, trying to soften his voice but not succeeding. "I hate having my picture taken. So what makes you think I'd agree to do a fucking TV show?"

Viv sighed. "We've been apart for almost two years, Jonah. I've certainly changed in that time. I was hoping maybe you had, too."

She was baiting him, he knew. Trying to gain the upper hand in the game of who's-the-most-mature-and-enlightened-party-in-this-divorce.

It was a game he'd never won, never *tried* to win.

He glanced at Kate and the woman sitting next to her, though it was Kate who held his attention. Kate, whose copper-colored eyes made him think that even though he damn sure wasn't doing any television show, sitting here in her company for a few more minutes wouldn't be the worst thing in the world.

She held his gaze a few more beats, then folded her hands in her lap. "Would you like to at least hear the proposal?"

Jonah hesitated. Recalled how willingly she'd gone along with his harebrained acting scheme in Ashland. Recalled the feel of her lips brushing his, the softness of her hip as he'd skimmed his hand up her body as they kissed.

Not the most helpful memories, under the circumstances. Jonah sighed.

"Not really," he said. "I'm sorry to waste your time."

The blonde winced as Jonah started to stand, but Kate's expression didn't falter. To his left Jonah heard Viv's voice again.

"Jonah, please give this a chance," she pleaded. "The network executives will be here in less than two hours."

He frowned. "And that's my problem?"

Viv folded her hands in her lap. "I thought you'd be open to hearing about this," she said. "Keeping an open mind."

"Huh," Jonah said. "I guess you thought wrong."

◆　◆　◆

The afternoon light was waning and so was Kate's energy by the time she caught up with Jonah walking a red-and-brown fox-sized dog along the waterfront pathway in Alki Park.

At least, she assumed it was Jonah. She'd never seen him with his shirt off, so she hung back a good twenty paces behind to make sure it was really him.

Okay, maybe she was checking him out. Good Lord, the man was chiseled. He had muscles in his back that Kate hadn't known existed, and a tattoo of a sword on one shoulder blade. The contrast of that tattoo against his tanned flesh and against Kate's own memories of the cultured bookstore owner she'd met a month ago made her palms clammy and her pulse drum in her head.

How had she not noticed before how ripped he was?

Kate wasn't the only one noticing.

"Oooh, can I pet your dog?" A buxom brunette approached from Jonah's left and didn't wait for an answer. Just stooped down to pet the cinnamon-colored mutt wearing an orange vest that read *Adopt Me!*

Jonah stopped walking and shifted the leash to his other hand, preventing his canine charge from clotheslining his new admirer. "That's Buster," Jonah said, reaching up to adjust his glasses. "He's up for adoption at Clearwater Animal Shelter."

Kate moved closer and watched the brunette make an extra effort to provide a glimpse down the front of her top. "I just love little doggies," she said. "You want to come home with me?"

Her gaze lifted to Jonah when she said it, and Kate watched his face to see if he'd taken it as an invitation. He still hadn't noticed Kate, and studying him now gave her a voyeuristic thrill.

But Jonah seemed unaffected by both the cleavage and the flirtation, which only seemed to pique the brunette's interest. Her eyes widened as he fished into the pocket of his navy athletic shorts and pulled out a card.

"Here's the info for Clearwater Animal Shelter," he said. "They're just three blocks that way, and they have a lot of other great animals up for adoption."

"You work there?" The brunette straightened up, glancing once at Kate as though assessing the competition. Finding it lacking, she returned her gaze to Jonah.

That's when he seemed to notice her. Jonah turned to look her direction, holding her gaze as Kate took a few steps closer. He didn't smile, but she could have sworn she saw a warmth that hadn't been there two seconds before.

"I'm a volunteer," Jonah said, sliding his gaze back to the brunette. "Will you excuse me? I need to make sure Buster gets his exercise."

"Absolutely." The brunette gave a chipper little wave, then turned on her heel and flounced away.

Jonah didn't watch her go. Instead, he turned his gaze back to Kate and watched as she covered the few steps that still separated them. Something about the way his eyes swept her body made Kate feel as topless as he was.

He was first to speak. "Either Viv told you where to find me, or the level of coincidence here has just gone from 'crazy' to 'I need a restraining order.'"

Kate shook her head and offered a nervous smile. "Nope, it's still just crazy." She wiped her palms down her gray pencil skirt and wished she'd stopped at the hotel to change. She felt stiff and overdressed standing in heels and a navy silk cowl-neck top beside a shirtless man with pecs she really should stop ogling. There was a faint dusting of hair on his chest and Kate wondered if it would feel as soft as it looked.

She cleared her throat. "Viv told me you'd be here," she continued. "I felt bad about the contentious turn things took back at her place."

"It wasn't your fault," he said. "I apologize. Sometimes I can be a little hotheaded when I'm caught off guard."

Kate nodded, remembering one of the chapters in *On the Other Hand* where Viv and Jonah bantered about each other's most unfavorable traits. *Temper* and *forgetfulness* had topped Jonah's list.

Bossiness and *self-righteousness* had topped Viv's.

"It's okay, I understand," Kate said.

"No, it's not okay. I'm sorry. I don't always react well to surprises."

"Understandable," Kate said. "Those were two pretty big ones."

"Thanks!"

Kate turned with a start as a busty blonde jogged past with a wave for Jonah. With a grimace, Kate ordered herself to keep her voice down. She turned her attention back to Jonah, who seemed oblivious to the awkward exchange.

"Mind if I walk with you for a bit?" Kate asked him.

Jonah shrugged. "Suit yourself. It's a free country." He turned on his heel and started walking again. Kate fell into step beside him, hustling to keep up with those impossibly long legs.

"It is a free country," she repeated, glancing up to watch his expression. "Interesting choice of words. One might say your military service played a role in the whole 'free country' thing. You might have mentioned that when we first met."

"Why?" He looked at her. "It was a long time ago, and not what I'm doing for a living now."

"It might have given me a clue who you were," she said, though the odds seemed slim she would have put the pieces together even then. "Anyway, I was hoping we could talk alone for a minute."

Jonah raised an eyebrow at her. "Yes. I seem to recall the conversation flowed a little more smoothly when my ex-wife wasn't there."

The comment sent a flush of heat through her face and throat, which was dumb. He was talking about conversation in general, not where the conversation had led that evening on the porch swing.

"Right. There's that." Kate took a deep breath as she hurried to keep up with him. "Look, I had no idea who you were when we met in Ashland."

"The comic relief guy from a shitty relationship guide?" His tone was dry, and Kate felt an unexpected surge of defensiveness.

"You know, that book has changed a lot of people's lives," she snapped. "The advice about communication and honesty and—"

"Hi, can I pet your doggie?"

Kate turned to see a woman with a blue-blond pixie cut approaching from the right. Jonah stopped so fast that Kate nearly ran into him. She put a hand out to catch herself, grazing a shoulder blade that felt like flesh-covered steel.

"Sure," Jonah said to the blonde, fishing another business card out of his pocket. "Buster is a terrier-heeler mix, and he's available for adoption at the Clearwater Animal Shelter."

"So sweet!" The blonde glanced at the card, then knelt down and stroked the dog's ears, earning herself a lick on the cheek. She smiled up at Jonah, and Kate caught a smolder of suggestion in the woman's eyes. "I've been thinking of getting a dog. Which days are you there if I wanted to come by and check out what you have?"

"My schedule varies, but the shelter is open nine to five on weekdays and ten to four on weekends."

"What a sweet, sweet puppy." The woman accepted a few more sloppy kisses while the dog wagged and wriggled and seemed genuinely thrilled at the attention.

"So I'll see you around," she said to Jonah as she stood, beaming as she stole a quick glance at the broad expanse of his chest. She ignored Kate completely, probably assuming based on their mismatched attire that she was his boss or sister or parole officer. Kate straightened her skirt and watched her sashay away.

When the blonde was out of earshot, Kate looked up at Jonah. "This must happen to you a lot?"

He grunted and gave a curt nod. "That's the idea."

"The idea?"

He stooped down to adjust the dog's *Adopt Me!* vest, then gave the little guy a quick booty scratch before straightening up.

Since Jonah didn't reply, Kate was forced to guess. "You're whoring yourself out for dog adoptions?"

"Pretty much." He started walking again, putting an end to that line of questioning.

"So why didn't you mention it when we met?"

"That I'm a shirtless dog walker?" He shrugged. "Didn't seem relevant."

Kate rolled her eyes. "That's not what I meant and you know it. You're smarter than you're pretending to be right now. For the life of me, I can't figure out what the hell that's about."

She thought she saw him flinch, but he kept walking, not missing a stride. He said nothing for a long time. She'd just decided it was pointless to keep pressing for information when his voice came out in a low rumble.

"You're asking why I didn't mention I'm the co-author of a bestselling relationship guide?" he said. "You figure that's the sort of thing that might have come up during several hours of conversation, followed by an hour of heavy petting?"

"There was no heavy petting!" she argued, earning herself a startled look from the middle-aged joggers running past. She glared and lowered her voice. "You might have had your hand under my jacket—"

"*My* jacket—"

"But you certainly didn't grope me or even—" She stopped and frowned up at him. "Wait. Are you trying to distract me?"

Jonah sighed. "It was working until you decided to get technical. I may have learned a technique or two from four years married to America's leading authority on communication strategies."

"Unfortunately for you, I've read all those books."

"That is unfortunate."

He walked a little faster, and Kate had to pick up her pace to keep up.

"I'm just saying," she continued, struggling not to sound too breathless. "That night in Ashland—we talked about literature and careers and even my breakup," she said. "Hell, I even quoted from *But Not Broken* during dinner."

"You did," he acknowledged. "Though I didn't write anything for that book."

"But you were *in* it," Kate argued. "You were part of her happily-ever-after at the end."

Jonah grunted but said nothing, and it occurred to Kate she was arguing the wrong point entirely. "Jonah, come on. Why didn't you say anything?"

He raked his fingers through his hair, but didn't look at her. He kept walking, but his pace slowed just a little.

"All right, fine. Look, I wasn't thrilled with the way I was portrayed in the book."

"*But Not Broken?*"

"No, *On the Other Hand.*"

"The way you were portrayed?" She frowned. "Didn't you write it?"

"I wrote the *sidebars*. The comic relief. And yeah, the words were mine—mostly—but not the spin. The whole Average Joe thing—that wasn't me at all."

"How do you mean?"

Jonah shrugged and caught her hand. For a second she thought he was trying to hold it, but she realized he was guiding her around a puddle of spilled milkshake, saving her expensive Prada heels. He let go the instant they were past it, and Kate hated the small flutter of disappointment in her belly.

"I did counterintelligence work in the Marines," Jonah said slowly. "I was trained in elicitation techniques—ways of evoking trust and comfort in a subject to procure information."

"You mean like interrogating spies?"

"Something like that. There's more to it than that, but the bottom line is that I've studied communication techniques from some pretty unique angles. The book was supposed to reflect that. To give my insights from that perspective."

"It did mention you were a Marine," she said. "Right inside the dust jacket, it said you were a military veteran."

"It didn't say what I *did* in the military," he pointed out. "Just that I was a Marine. And a football fan. And an avid fisherman. And a 'handy guy' who stomps around the house in a tool belt, fixing shit." He cleared his throat and glanced over at her. "For the record, I don't own a tool belt. And I haven't been fishing since I was eight."

Kate frowned. "What do you mean?"

"I'm saying the publisher decided I was more marketable as an everyman. A regular fella. Not as a cerebral guy, but a blue-collar one. The all-American, Average Joe."

"You couldn't be both?"

She watched his Adam's apple bob as he swallowed, but he didn't look at her. "Not according to the publisher."

"And you went along with it," she said. "You pretended to be someone you weren't."

He shrugged. "I was star-struck and love-struck and blinded by newlywed bliss," he muttered. "The publisher said the book would sell better that way, and they were right."

Kate kept walking, trying to digest the new information. "So you're saying you're not really the guy in the book. The guy who wrote, 'A relationship is like a fart: if you have to work real hard and strain and force things, it's probably shit.'"

Jonah laughed. "Actually, I liked that one. And it's true."

"Then what's the problem?"

He sighed, but didn't say anything. Kate was getting used to these long stretches of silence. In a way, it was nice knowing he cared enough to take the time to formulate a response instead of blurting out the first words that came to mind.

They kept walking, passing a pair of twentysomething women on a park bench who cooed and leaned down to pet Buster. Jonah doled out the business cards and ran through his spiel about adoptable pets at Clearwater Animal Shelter. Kate watched him, mystified by these dual versions of the same guy.

And by his abs. God Almighty, the man should never wear a shirt.

They started walking again, and Kate waited, wondering if he'd pick up the conversation where they'd left it. When he finally spoke, his voice sounded defeated. "Look, I just can't go back there."

"To that persona, you mean?"

"The persona, the role—the relationship with Viv."

She felt a dull ache in her belly and a sharp pang in her chest. Physical manifestations of feelings she couldn't quite name. Sympathy for him, maybe, and something a little like jealousy. That was dumb. It's not like she had any claim on Jonah, or any reason to resent his ex-wife's claim on him.

"Sit with the feelings!" Viv called in her brain, an echo from chapter five in *But Not Broken*. *"You don't need to analyze or categorize or judge them. Just feel them."*

Kate took a deep breath and ordered herself to keep an impassive expression. "You still love Viv?"

"God, no! Not like that, anyway. Don't get me wrong, we're still friendly. And I don't hate her either, if that's your next question."

"Then what's the problem?"

"I've moved on. She's moved on. It's better that way for both of us."

"I see."

She was trying to see, anyway. Part of her wished he'd tell her more, that he'd explain the arc of his love affair with Viv and how they'd reached this point.

But part of her—a tiny, jealous part—didn't want details. Didn't want to imagine the two of them together laughing, touching, exchanging loving glances across a crowded room.

She was still thinking about it when Jonah spoke again. "What do you remember about the way Viv described me in *But Not Broken?*"

His voice was so soft and the question so random that Kate thought she'd heard wrong at first. "Um—well." She thought back to chapter twelve, the point in the book where Viv had healed her broken heart was getting to know the man who would become her husband. "She liked that you were rough around the edges," Kate recalled. "That you were so different from the abusive asshole she'd been with before—that Ivy League professor?" She took a deep breath of salt-tinged air, feeling more than a little awkward. "She loved that your size and your strength made her feel safe instead of scared."

"Right," Jonah said, glancing over at her. *"Here was a man who'd served his country with dignity and honor,"* he recited, startling Kate with the sound of Viv's words spoken in the low rumble of the man they'd been written to describe. *"A man who didn't need cocktail parties or college lectures to validate his self-worth. A man who could sit for hours with my feet tucked under his thigh on the sofa, comfortably enjoying silence without needing to fill it with the sound of his own voice."*

Tears pricked unexpectedly at the edges of Kate's eyelids. She blinked hard, wanting to stay professional. "That's beautiful," she said. "I always thought so."

"It's bullshit."

She turned and gave him a sharp look. "What?"

"I mean she fell in love with an idealized version of me," he said. "The opposite of her, the opposite of the guy she'd been with. But that wasn't the whole me. It was a caricature."

Kate opened her mouth to protest. To defend Viv's intentions or meaning. But Jonah got his words out first.

"Look, I'm not saying she was the only one who screwed up," he said. "I did the same damn thing. We both had this idea that our differences complemented each other. We liked the *idea* of each other, but not the day-to-day drudgery of it."

"I can see that, I guess." Kate thought about her last relationship. How she'd started out fascinated by Anton's passion for expensive Scotch and glamorous parties, but in the end, those were the things she'd grown to resent.

"The only thing opposites really attract is misery," Jonah said softly. "And I just can't go back to that."

"Oh."

Well, hell. She couldn't really argue with that. If the guy didn't want to work with his ex, who was she to tell him he ought to? She couldn't blame him. The thought of having to work with Anton made her stomach knot up in a big, sour ball.

Still, the circumstances were a little different. Jonah might not know how different. She owed it to him to spell it out.

"Look, Jonah. There's something else you should know."

"What's that?"

"After you left Viv's place, we had a meeting with some executives from the Empire network. She, uh—let them know you're uncertain about being part of the show."

"Uncertain?" He frowned down at her. "What part of *fuck no* sounded uncertain to you?"

"I'm just relaying what she said," Kate replied evenly. "But I was also going to share what the executives told me after we left the meeting."

"Which is?"

"They want you. Obviously. And they're willing to pay handsomely to get you."

"I'm not hard up for money," he said. "Between the royalties from *On the Other Hand* and profits at the bookstore, I'm doing just fine."

"I'm sure you are," she said. "But the kind of money we're talking about—it's more than 'just fine.'"

He didn't say anything to that, but she heard an invitation in the pause. Kate reached a hand into her purse and slid out a large stack of paper. She stopped walking, hoping he'd do the same. He got three steps ahead, then turned.

"We worked up a series bible and budget before we approached you," she said. "This afternoon, the network asked us to sit down and hammer out a new set of numbers. A budget that accounts for the possibility of you joining the lineup."

Jonah glanced at the sheaf of papers in her hand. "I assume that's what you have there?"

Kate nodded. She hesitated a moment, knowing this was a risky move. But the execs had told her to do what it took to get Average Joe on board. That's what she was doing.

"These documents are confidential," she said. "I'm not allowed to distribute them at all. In fact, I was specifically asked not to show Viv at this stage in the game."

Jonah frowned and shoved his glasses up his nose. "But you're offering to show me?"

She hesitated, then nodded. "I think you should have all the information before you make up your mind."

Flipping the folder open, she let her gaze drift to the page on top of the stack. The word *confidential* was stamped in red ink across the top, and under that, the words *Proposed talent budget for* Relationship Reboot with Dr. Viv.

She flipped to the page with his name at the top, then turned the folder around so he could see it. Then she looked up to watch his face. The amber-green eyes drifted slowly down the page, back and forth, taking in the information, the columns of numbers she'd seen for the first time only an hour ago.

"Holy shit." Jonah glanced up and locked eyes with her. "That's per year, or—"

"That's per *episode*," she told him, flipping the folder closed. "If the pilot takes off, the network intends to order fourteen episodes in the first season."

He stared at her. "But that's insane. That's more than ten times what I've made with *On the Other Hand*."

"I know. That's why I wanted you to see what they're proposing. This isn't some third-tier programming on a no-name network. This is prime time, Jonah. The big leagues."

His hand drifted to the center of his chest and he scratched absently at the edge of one pectoral muscle. Kate ordered herself not to look. Not to let her gaze drop even an inch. Not even for a peek.

"How much do you get?"

Kate swallowed. "What do you mean?"

"Are you being fairly compensated for this as well?"

She nodded. "Fair enough."

"What else is in it for you?"

She hesitated. "A chance to do something meaningful. These books—Dr. Viv's whole outlook on things—they changed my life. Changed my outlook on relationships and the way I interact with the world."

He quirked an eyebrow at her. "That's a lot of meaning to ascribe to a bunch of paperbacks you bought for five ninety-nine on Amazon."

"I bought them in hardback," Kate shot back, pretty sure he was trying to distract her again. "Besides, this show would be a big feather in my cap career-wise. A chance to work with my favorite author. *Authors.*"

He smiled. "That was never really my book. You know that."

"Your part in it was important. Just because you're not the one with *PhD* behind your name doesn't mean your contributions didn't touch people."

Jonah cleared his throat. "Speaking of touching people, why didn't you tell her?"

She thought about pretending she didn't know what he was talking about. But asking "Who?" or "What?" would just be a forestalling mechanism or a game, and she was too old for that.

"I didn't tell Viv about the kiss because it seemed irrelevant."

"Beeeep!" he shouted, making the dog's ears prick to attention. "Incorrect answer. Try again."

She sighed. "Is this one of your spy-catching techniques from the Marines?"

"Yeah. We're trained to say *beep* when they lie to us," he deadpanned. "Come on. The kiss was *not* irrelevant."

"Okay, you're right," she said. "Maybe it's because it seemed entirely *too* relevant."

"How so?"

"If Vivienne Brandt is considering inviting her ex-husband into her television program—into her home, for crying out loud—it'll complicate things if she knows the producer and her ex played tonsil hockey once upon a time."

He nodded. "Now there's an honest answer. A good one, too."

"So you agree. We probably shouldn't mention one innocent little kiss?"

Jonah snorted. "I was there, babe. That was no innocent kiss. And there wasn't just one."

Kate shivered, but ordered herself to keep her composure. "Fine. But now that you've seen the numbers, is your interest piqued even a little?"

He looked away, his gaze drifting out over Puget Sound. "A little."

Okay, so that was a start. Kate slid her hand into her bag and pulled out a business card. Since he wasn't looking at her, she pressed the card into his palm and watched as his gaze swiveled back to hers.

"All my contact information is here—my cell, my e-mail, everything," she said. "And in case you want to talk privately, I'm staying at the Westin in Bellevue. Room 906."

Now why had she said that? It wasn't on the card, and she hadn't planned to just blurt it out. Jonah stared at her for a few beats, then looked down at the card.

"If I say no, are they going to pull the plug on the show?"

Kate looked at him, not sure how to answer. "Are you asking because you want to help her out, or because you like knowing you can kill your ex-wife's TV show?"

He shoved the card in his pocket and met her eyes. "The fact that those are the two possibilities that occur to you means I'm probably not going to get a straight answer."

"I don't know," she said, ordering herself to hold his gaze. "I don't know what'll happen to the show if you won't do it. That's the truth."

He stared at her for a long time. So long Kate couldn't help letting her gaze stray from his, drifting quickly down his bare chest and then back up to those amber-green eyes that seemed to be staring straight into her soul.

"I'll be in touch," he said.

Then he turned and walked away, the little fox dog trotting along beside him.

CHAPTER FOUR

Jonah walked through the doors of the Clearwater Animal Shelter and handed Buster's leash to the redhead wearing a mischievous smile and a nametag that said "Josslyn."

"I gave out six business cards and fielded nine requests to pet the dog," he reported as he moved past his sister behind the counter.

Jossy grinned and shoved a shock of curly red hair behind one ear. "How many requests to pet you?"

Jonah grunted. "Two."

He rummaged under the counter for his T-shirt, feeling oddly self-conscious. It's not like he wasn't used to walking bare chested around Alki Park, but it always left him feeling like an aging frat boy. Fall was on the way, and with it the colder weather. He felt relieved. It meant he could graduate to a skin-tight thermal shirt for the winter.

"Here," Jossy said, shoving the T-shirt into his hand. "You left it in the back room again. I swear you'd lose your balls if they weren't stapled on."

"And if I didn't have women checking them for me every time they try to stick their phone numbers down the front of my shorts?" Jonah took the T-shirt and began hunting for the neck hole while Jossy made cooing noises at the little terrier.

"You're exaggerating again," Jossy said. "That only happened once."

"Twice."

"And didn't you say she was drunk?"

"You're implying that's the only way I'd get groped?" Jonah finished tugging down his shirt and looked at his sister.

"Yes, because you're a disgusting boy."

"If I'm that repulsive, why do you keep making me work as your shirtless dog walker?"

"Because apparently, a lot of women are charmed by your repulsiveness." Jossy looked up at him, pausing in the middle of scratching Buster's ear. "Seriously, Jonah, I owe you."

Her expression was still teasing, but there was a glint of adoration now. Hero worship. Jonah's heart twisted. He wasn't worthy of her admiration. He was the one who owed her. Owed her everything and then some, which is why he spent as much time as he did "whoring himself out," as Kate had so eloquently put it.

"I was running the stats this morning before my meeting with the accountant," Josslyn said as she led Buster to a red silicone water dish and gave him a long drink. "Ever since you started your shirtless dog-walking campaign, adoptions are up almost thirty percent. Unsurprisingly, they're nearly all women."

Jonah dug out a bottle of lukewarm iced tea from where he'd left it under the counter and pried the top off. He took a long drink before wiping his mouth with the back of his hand. "Don't hate me because I'm beautiful."

"Don't worry. There are plenty of other reasons to hate you."

"You know you love me."

"Only because Mom says I have to," she said. "Also, that's disgusting. Warm iced tea?"

"If there's no ice in it, can't we just call it tea?"

"Not if you're drinking it from a bottle. There are rules for these things."

"Remind me to read those never."

Jossy rolled her eyes and Jonah felt a soft squeeze of fondness for his sister. He'd been feeling it for thirty-three years, since the day his parents brought the tiny pink bundle home from the hospital. His father had knelt before him in dress blues just a few weeks later, moments before shipping out to some country Jonah couldn't pronounce yet.

"You're in charge," said the hulking Marine to his three-year-old son. "It's your job to take care of your baby sister. Understand?"

Jonah had nodded, resisting the urge to stick his thumb in his mouth or hide behind his mother's legs. He had a job to do, and he took it seriously.

He kept taking it seriously through high school, when he was a senior and Jossy a sophomore with flame-red hair and a bubbly personality that made her a magnet for attention.

But it was her talent on a bike that made her a contender for the US cycling team at only fifteen. With their father gone—killed in the line of duty—Jonah knew it was up to him to keep watch over her. To make sure Jossy was safe and protected and happy and healthy.

And a damn shitty job you did with that, he reminded himself.

"Thanks again for watching the front counter earlier."

Jossy's words startled Jonah back to the present. He took another gulp of tea to rinse away his dark thoughts.

"How did things go with the accountant?" he asked.

Jossy shrugged and glanced away. He watched her carefully, noticing the shift in her demeanor, the way she wasn't meeting his eyes. "It was fine," she said. "The nonprofit world kind of sucks right now, but I'm making it work."

She moved across the lobby, her limp more pronounced than it had been earlier in the week. Jonah was primed to notice. Had spent more than a decade noticing.

He opened his mouth to ask if the prosthetic was bothering her again, but stopped himself. There was no point. She'd just tell him everything was fine and change the subject.

He watched her open the latch on the largest kennel in the lobby and usher Buster inside. Three spotted puppies scampered over and jumped on the terrier, and the four dogs collapsed into a roly-poly heap of play snarls and dog slobber.

Jossy closed the gate and wiped her palms down the front of her jeans. "Any chance I could persuade you to watch the front counter for an hour next week?"

"I think so," Jonah said. "I have to check my schedule. How come?"

"The accountant asked to meet again," she said. "Apparently there's some stuff we should to deal with on the financial front."

"You need money?"

"I'm good!" she said with cheer that almost sounded real. "Well, aside from needing help watching the counter for an hour. And the service of your disgusting, shirtless body once a week like always."

Jonah watched her for a few more beats, trying to get a read on what was bothering her. Money was always tight, and he helped out whenever she let him. Running a nonprofit, no-kill animal shelter wasn't a ticket to fame and fortune, but his kid sister had always been able to make ends meet. Was she struggling more than he realized?

She sure as hell wasn't going to tell him, so Jonah gave up watching her and stepped over to the kennel closest to the counter. He peered inside and found himself staring at the oddest feline features he'd ever seen. The cat had a white face with a lone black polka dot on its left cheek. Its eyes were framed by black slashes of fur that looked like eyebrows arched in disdain.

The cat wore a look of permanent judgment, though Jonah couldn't tell if it was displeased by its surroundings, its life, or Jonah himself.

"When did this guy come in?" he asked Jossy.

"About an hour ago," she said. "And it's a *her*, not a him."

"That explains the look of perpetual disdain."

"Be nice!" She smacked him on the shoulder. "I think she's striking."

"I think she's plotting to rip my eyelids off."

"Want her? She's really sweet."

"Eh." Jonah turned away and started tidying the counter, turning all the pens in the holder so they faced the same direction.

"Never mind. I forget you have commitment issues."

"I do not have commitment issues," he muttered. "I'm holding out for the right pet."

"That's right," Jossy teased. "One who *speaks* to you."

"You make it sound like I'm waiting for a dog to serenade me Disney-style," Jonah muttered. "I'm just waiting for the right fit. The one I look at and instantly think, 'Here's what your life is missing.'"

"I've got news for you, bro," Jossy said. "The pet-sized hole in your life could be filled by any one of a hundred animals. You're just being picky because you spent so long with your control-freak wife saying you shouldn't get a pet."

"It would have been tough to travel," Jonah muttered, not sure why he was defending Viv.

"You have a sister who doubles as a pet sitter," Jossy pointed out, shaking her head. "You know, if any of these animals could speak for real, they'd tell you to pull your head out of your ass."

"That's exactly what I need," he muttered. "A pet who passes judgment."

He let his gaze slide back to the cat, whose disapproving eyebrows seemed to lift a fraction of an inch. Something began to buzz like a malfunctioning refrigerator, and it took him a moment to realize the cat was purring.

Jonah turned as Jossy bumped into him en route to the file cabinet. He saw her grimace as she bent down to shove a manila folder inside. The cabinet was gray and battered, a castoff she'd gotten for free when a warehouse had closed down a few weeks before she'd opened this place.

Jonah had hauled it in for her, along with all the other furniture and cages. He'd given her the seed money from his portion of the advance for *On the Other Hand*, insisting she take it as his personal contribution to animal welfare.

He watched Jossy try to hide a wince as she stood up. This time, Jonah couldn't help himself. "Your leg bothering you again?"

"It's fine."

"You know, they've made a lot of new advancements in prosthetics. If you want, I could check into—"

"I'm *fine*, Jonah. Seriously."

Her amber eyes flashed as she stared him down, not blinking at all. Jonah sighed. "Just be gentle with yourself, okay?"

"Yeah, yeah."

She moved past him, skirting a bucket half-full of muddy-looking water. He looked up to see the rainwater ring on the ceiling had grown larger over the last week. He'd already patched it half a dozen times, so it was probably time for a new roof. Maybe there was a way to convince her to let him pay for it.

"You've got your own business to worry about," Jossy always insisted, which was true. Still he wanted to help her. *Needed* to help.

"So tell me about your day," she said, and Jonah stopped staring at the ceiling. "You whipped in here and grabbed Buster before I had a chance to talk to you."

"Not much to report," he said, leaning back against the counter. "I got a new shipment of cookbooks at the store, spent some time doing inventory, told my ex-wife to go fuck herself—"

"Wait, what?" Jossy laughed and shook her head. "That's right, I totally forgot she wanted you to go over there today. What did Snobby McBitcherson want?"

Jonah felt a stab of guilt for starting this round of bad-mouthing his ex. Jossy had never liked Viv, not even when she and Jonah had been married. They'd always been cordial to each other, but there was an undercurrent of unpleasantness between them. Jossy found Viv's attempts at empathy to be patronizing, and Viv found Jossy repressed and out of touch with her own grief.

Still, Jonah felt bad feeding the animosity. "I didn't literally tell her to go fuck herself," he admitted. "But I did impolitely decline to be part of some stupid reality TV show she's doing."

"Reality TV?" Jossy rolled her eyes. "Please tell me it's *Survivor*, and she'll have to eat cow brains and pee in the woods. Or no!" Jossy smacked her hand on the counter. "It's *The Bachelor*, and she's going to have to dress slutty and degrade herself to get the attention of some schmuck who uses grammar like, 'Viv and mine's relationship is very much good.'"

"A nice thought, but no."

"So what is it then? *Cake Wars? Deadliest Catch?* What?"

"Actually, it's a brand-new show. She'd be the star. Couples would come on and she'd try to fix their relationship problems and wrap everything up in a neat little bow at the end of the thirty-minute segment."

Jossy frowned. "So what does she want you to do?"

Jonah shrugged. "Show up and throw out one-liners and straight talk, I assume. Stuff like, 'Dude, you've gotta go down on her first if you want regular BJs. And keep the hedge trimmed. No woman wants to feel like she's licking the dog.'"

Jossy made a gagging sound. "So you're going to do the Average Joe shtick again?"

"No. Did you miss the part where I said I told her I wasn't interested?"

"I heard it. I just know Viv has a way of talking you into things."

Jonah felt a stab of annoyance. At Jossy, at Viv, at himself—he wasn't quite sure. He stuck a finger through the bars of the eyebrow cat's cage to scratch under her chin, and was rewarded by a gravelly purr that brought his blood pressure back to normal.

"Trust me," Jonah said. "If I were going to change my mind, it wouldn't be because of anything Viv said."

His brain flashed on a memory of Kate huffing along beside him, asking real questions instead of firing crap at him about how great the show was going to be or baiting him with reasons he owed it to people to do it. Had Viv told her to try the money angle?

Unlikely. True, Viv knew about Jossy's special needs and about the animal shelter, of course. But she had no way of knowing how badly the money might be needed. Not small amounts either. Not the few thousand dollars here and there that Jonah persuaded Jossy to take as donations to the shelter. The amounts Kate had shown him on those forms, those were different. Not keep-things-afloat amounts. They were life-changing amounts.

While Jonah might like his life just fine, he'd give almost anything to improve his sister's.

"What are you looking at, dork?" Jossy asked.

He'd been staring at her, but there was no way he'd admit that. "What's the story with this cat, anyway?" he asked.

"Owner surrender."

"What the hell for?"

Jossy shrugged and slipped a finger through the bars to scratch at the base of cat's fluffy black tail. The cat boosted her butt in the air and purred harder. "They tried to give some bullshit reason about her being 'not the right fit' for the family, but that's code for 'I liked the idea of having a cat more than I like actually having a cat and now I don't want to scoop the litter box.'"

"Poor girl." Empathy tugged at Jonah's gut, and he thought back to his conversation with Kate.

We liked the idea of each other, but not the day-to-day drudgery of it.

Beside him, Jossy sighed. "It's okay. We'll find her the right home."

The cat opened her eyes and looked at Jonah. Her eyebrows lifted, shifting her expression from mild disdain to "What the fuck is wrong with you?"

A damn fine question.

"That reminds me, Beth called," Jossy said.

"Why is my store manager calling you now instead of me?"

"Because I'm nicer," she said. "And I'm the one who keeps your cat café full of adoptable felines, moron."

"Can you repeat the part about you being nicer?"

"She said they adopted out two more cats yesterday," Jossy continued, ignoring him. "So I need to send you with a couple more. You want this one?"

"This one?" Jonah looked at the eyebrow cat. The cat twitched her nose, lifting the beauty mark on her upper lip.

"Her vaccines are up-to-date, and I'd just as soon get her into a social situation instead of having her stuck here in a cage."

Jonah looked back at the cat and something shifted in the center of his chest. A cat-shaped hole, maybe. He grunted.

"Sure. Go ahead and stuff her in a box."

◆ ◆ ◆

"What do you think about this giraffe sculpture?"

Kate turned to see Amy standing under an enormous bronze monstrosity. The assistant producer gestured like a game show hostess, sweeping her arms wide and tossing her blond curls with dramatic flair.

Kate laughed and checked the price tag.

"Not bad," she said. "Bonus points for the giraffe reference."

"Hey, that was one of my favorite chapters in *On the Other Hand.*" Amy patted the giraffe's rump. "I love the part about emulating the land mammal with the largest heart."

"The quiz was my favorite," Kate admitted. "Where you sit down with your partner and figure out which animal best represents your communication needs?"

"And then you spell out your 'animal needs.'" Amy grinned and made claws with her fingers. *"Rawr."*

Kate smiled and pretended to study the pedestal at the base of the giraffe. Very sturdy, which was more than she could say for the basis of her relationship with Anton. It was stupid to still find herself thinking about him, but she blamed the giraffe. She remembered reading that chapter aloud to Anton in bed one lazy Sunday morning while he sipped coffee and did the crossword puzzle in the morning paper.

"C'mon," she'd urged, snuggling up next to him with the book in her lap. "Just answer the question."

"Are you serious?" He'd leveled her with a look like she'd asked him to strip naked and run through the neighbor's sprinkler. "You want me to pretend to be a jackal?"

"That's not what I'm saying at all," Kate had said. "I just want to understand which animal you think best represents you and figure out which one represents me and talk about how we relate to each other when—"

"How about we just build the beast with two backs and call it good?" Anton had flashed her a salacious grin and set the paper down.

And Kate—who'd been looking for some form of connection with him anyway—had tugged her sleep shirt over her head and did her best to convince herself it was romantic.

"Kate?"

She turned to see Amy snapping a photo of the giraffe. "Would you mind standing next to it to give it a sense of scale? That way we can give the props team an idea of how big it is."

"And Viv," Kate pointed out. "If this thing's going in her house, she'll probably want to have some say in it."

"True. Though the contract does specify the team will have first say over décor choices and props."

Kate sidled up to the giraffe and refrained from commenting. The likelihood of the show happening at all still seemed precarious, so there was no point reminding Amy that they needed to choose their battles when it came to details like giraffe sculptures and mood lighting.

"There," Amy said as she clicked off a photo. "Should we go look at area rugs next, or did you want to scope out things for the boudoir scene we talked about for the pilot?"

"I think—" She stopped midsentence as her phone began to buzz. She slipped it out of her purse and felt her arms start to tingle as Jonah's name popped up on the screen. She'd programmed it in after Viv had given her the number, wanting to be prepared in case he did call. "Sorry, I need to take this," she said, stepping away from the giraffe as she tapped the phone screen to answer.

"Hello, this is Kate Geary," she said in her best professional voice.

"Kate Geary," he repeated, his voice smooth and warm the way it had sounded over dinner in Ashland that night. It was so different from how he'd sounded at Viv's house earlier that day or when she'd chased him down the boardwalk during his shirtless dog-walking exercise. "This is Jonah Porter."

"Hello, Jonah."

"Tell me something, Kate Geary," he said.

"What would you like to know, Jonah Porter?"

Kate wasn't sure if the name or the flirtatious note in her voice made Amy look up. The assistant producer lifted one eyebrow and turned to look at a copper shelf on the wall.

Jonah laughed on the other end of the line and Kate had another flash of memory to their night in Ashland. The way he'd laughed with his whole body, nearly knocking himself off the front porch of the B&B when she'd declared herself unavailable for a one-night stand.

"Do you have my number programmed into your phone already or do you always answer the phone that stiffly?" he asked.

She tried to think of a reason to be coy or pretend she didn't know what he was talking about, but she couldn't see a point to it.

"Did your military super-spy-catching skills tell you that, or are you hiding behind a giant giraffe watching me?"

He laughed again. "I'm afraid to ask where you are that you're lurking near a giant giraffe."

"I'm at a consignment shop at the moment. To what do I owe the pleasure of your call?"

He didn't answer right away, and Kate glanced at Amy to see if she was following along. She was studying a mirror in the shape of a vagina, but Kate was pretty sure she was listening.

"I'm not saying yes," he said. "To the TV thing, I mean."

"Okay."

"I need to put that out there up front. But I'm rescinding my 'fuck no' and replacing it with an 'I'd like to hear a little more about it.' Is that still an option?"

Kate nodded, which was ridiculous. He couldn't see her. But she was almost afraid to speak, not wanting to scare him away.

"Yes," she said. "I'd be happy to tell you anything. What would you like to know?"

"Not on the phone," he said, sending another ripple of excitement through her.

Kate gripped the phone a little tighter. "What did you have in mind?"

"I'd prefer to meet in person."

She glanced toward Amy again, this time catching sight of her own face in the vagina mirror. Holy hell, that wasn't the look of someone having a business call. That was something else entirely. She forced her features into a neutral expression and hoped Amy hadn't noticed.

Kate straightened up and looked away from the mirror. "I'm sure that could be arranged," she said. "My assistant producer and I would be happy to meet with you to go over—"

"No," he said. "Just you. Sorry, I'm sure she's a lovely woman. But I want to keep this casual. And I want fewer people involved."

"Any reason?"

She expected him not to answer, or to make up some bullshit story. His answer surprised her. "When I got railroaded into doing the Average Joe thing for the book, it was in a big committee meeting. Everyone started throwing out numbers and statistics and research and Viv was pleading and—I guess I just caved."

"I appreciate your candor. I can't promise I won't throw out statistics and research, but I can promise I won't plead."

Jonah laughed. "That's unfortunate."

"If you make a crack about wanting to see me on my knees, I'm hanging up right now."

He burst out laughing, and she could picture his exact expression in her mind. The image made her smile again.

"No blow-job jokes, no one-night stands, no long-distance relationships," he said. "I know what's on your no-fly list now. What do you like to eat? Besides Thai food?"

"I'm not picky," she said. "Let's go someplace quiet so we can talk."

"Oh, I already have the place picked out. Just wondering what sort of takeout food to order."

"Where are we going?"

"You're coming to my bookstore. How's eight tomorrow evening?"

"I can do that," she said. "I'm eager to see where you work."

"I'll text you the address. See you then."

Kate clicked off and slid the phone into her purse, careful to wipe any trace of smile off her face. She looked up to see Amy studying her.

"Aren't you at least going to pretend you weren't eavesdropping?" Kate asked.

Amy shook her head and grinned. "Do you want me to?"

"Not really."

"Do you want a tiny bit of advice?"

"Not really." Kate smiled and shook her head. "I'm kidding, it's fine. Lay it on me."

Amy bit her lip. "Be careful with Jonah."

"What do you mean?"

"I mean I saw the way you looked at each other at Viv's place. It was probably shock, I get it."

"Shock is an understatement," Kate said. "I swear I had no idea—"

"I know," Amy said. "That was pretty obvious. So was the fact that there's some pretty intense chemistry between you."

"No way," Kate said. "I mean, yeah, the guy is hot. And yeah, I'll admit the first time we met in Ashland, I was sort of attracted to him."

"And now?"

Kate shook her head. "Please. He's the ex-husband of my freakin' idol."

"Hero worship doesn't preclude you from wanting to knock boots with her ex-husband."

"It's not like that. This program has the potential to skyrocket our careers to the next level. The show has the power to change a lot of lives. Any passion you're picking up on is all about that."

"That sounded really good." Amy smiled. "Almost like you believed it."

Kate rolled her eyes. "What's that supposed to mean?"

"Hey, your secret's safe with me. I don't care if you really did sleep with him or—"

"I didn't," Kate interrupted. "I swear."

"Okay," Amy said. "I believe you. But I also believe something else might've happened. Just be careful, okay? We don't want anything to get in the way of the show."

"Nothing's more important to me than the show," Kate said. "Cross my heart and hope to die, I'll be careful."

Amy grinned and grabbed her arm. "Good. Now let's go look at dining room tables sturdy enough to fuck on," she said. "I'm thinking ahead to episode five."

Kate laughed and let Amy tow her across the store, ordering herself to push Jonah out of her brain.

CHAPTER FIVE

Kate appeared on the doorstep of Cornucopia Books precisely at eight just as a woman with a nose ring and a bright-pink pixie cut was flipping the door sign from *Open* to *Closed.*

Kate's surprise must have registered, because the woman smiled and pushed the door open. "Are you Kate?"

"That's me."

"Come on in. I'm Beth. The boss man's in the Cat Café. He's elbow deep in some project in the kitchen, so he asked me to let you in."

"Oh. Thank you." Kate ran her hands down the front of her navy striped T-shirt dress and wondered if she should have dressed down more. Maybe skipped the blazer or gone for casual-casual instead of business-casual.

"Come on," Beth said. "It's right this way."

The young woman led her across rustic wood floors through a spacious lobby filled with racks of postcards and reading glasses and bright mugs printed with phrases like *Never judge a book by its movie,* and *My book smells better than your tablet.*

They continued past a barista station with a gleaming espresso machine and tap handles boasting the names of breweries Kate had never heard of. Then again, she wasn't a beer drinker, though it was clear from the chalkboard menu listing a dozen kinds of beer that it was a popular choice here.

At a red door marked *Cat Café* Beth halted and turned to Kate. "You can wash up at that sink right there and go on in. He's either in the kitchen or in the lounge area already."

"Thank you." Kate pushed up the sleeves of her jacket and turned on the taps, wondering if she looked like someone who might have cat diseases.

"It's because I'm letting you into the food-prep area," Beth said, reading Kate's mind. "The boss is really strict about OSHA stuff. Things you wouldn't even think about. Like anyone who's had litterbox duty that day isn't allowed in the kitchen during the same shift."

"Oh. That does seem like a smart policy."

"Yeah." Beth smiled. "You have a cat?"

"No. I like cats, though. I guess I just travel too much for work."

"We get a lot of folks like that here." Beth whipped a rag out of her back pocket and started dusting a waist-high steel sculpture of a cat. "Can't have a cat of their own, so they come here to get their feline fix. It's good for the animals, too. Helps them get comfortable around people so they're more adoptable."

"That's a great idea."

Beth smiled. "The boss man's full of 'em."

The pride in the young woman's voice was evident, and Kate lathered her hands and stole a glance at her. Beth straightened a black-and-white cat photo on the wall as Kate pumped a little more soap from the dispenser shaped like a cat.

"Have you worked here long?" Kate asked.

"Since the day he opened. It's a great place. Indie bookstores are dying off by the dozen, but this place is doing okay. Jonah's a smart businessman."

"So I'd gathered," Kate said, remembering what he'd said in Alki Park. How he'd chosen to cast aside his cerebral self to fill the Average

Joe persona. How much would it suck to think you could only be one or the other? A military counterintelligence expert and bookstore owner, or a straight-talking, blue-collar handyman known for writing hilariously brash sidebars in a self-help book?

One or the other, but not both.

Then again, hadn't Kate faced the same conundrum? More than once, really. *An art-minded actress or a family-focused female with a stable career. A documentary filmmaker or a money-making reality TV producer.*

What a dumb choice to have to make. To have to decide at all.

"I should get back to closing out the till," Beth said. "Could you let him know the restrooms are clean and we're getting low on cold brew?"

"Clean restrooms, almost out of cold brew," Kate repeated. "Got it."

"Thanks! Have a good night."

Beth turned and vanished back through the lobby, making Kate grateful for a few moments alone to compose her thoughts as she dried her hands on a paper towel. She dropped it into a black metal wastebasket engraved with silhouettes of cats whose tails were intertwined. Then she took a deep breath and pushed open the door marked *Cat Café*.

She heard the singing before she saw him. The voice was coming from the other side of a huge stainless-steel oven, and sounded vaguely like Jonah. The tune sounded like Meghan Trainor's "All About That Bass," but the lyrics were something else entirely.

"I love to stuff my face, stuff my face, more kibble—"

"Jonah?"

The singing stopped, and Jonah poked his head around the oven. Kate expected him to look embarrassed about being caught in an off-key serenade, but he just grinned at her.

"Hey," he said. "Thanks for coming."

Kate smiled back and stepped around the oven to join him at the bright-red enameled counter. He was stirring something in an industrial-sized stainless steel pot, and steam billowed around him like marshmallow fluff.

"Beth said to tell you the restrooms are clean and you're almost out of cold brew," Kate reported. She watched as Jonah continued stirring the pot. "Don't let me stop the concert. By all means, keep singing."

He laughed and flipped off the gas burner. "I hadn't gotten very far with the lyrics yet," he said. "This one's in honor of Porky."

"Porky?"

"Yeah, he's one of the cats we've had here the longest. Everyone thinks since he's a little overweight, he's not as desperate for a home as the other guys. The vet suggested we switch up his diet to see if there's a food allergy going on, so that's what I'm working on."

"You're cooking him a meal?"

"Sort of. It's just some chicken. Trying to work in a little lean protein to balance out his regular food."

"And a song to go along with it."

Jonah grinned and stirred the pot again. "I hadn't made it past the first couple lines."

"I love to stuff my face, stuff my face, more kibble?" Kate only meant to speak the words, but found herself singing the last few in her best Meghan Trainor voice. She laughed and continued on, leaning against the counter as Jonah wiped his hands on a dish towel.

"My mama, she told me to always eat all your foooood," Kate sang. "If you don't lick your bowl clean, the humans will think you're rude."

Jonah laughed and tossed the dish towel on the counter. "You know I might be a thick kitty, but I got lots of heart."

"So just feed me some chicken, and don't mind it makes me fart."

Jonah cracked up, shaking his head as he tossed the dish towel onto the counter. "I can't believe you just said that," he said. "That was awesome."

"Thanks," Kate said, irrationally proud of the compliment. "Maybe if this TV production thing doesn't work out, I can become a professional cat composer."

"It's good to have goals. Come on. You hungry?"

"A little bit," she said. "That smells really good."

"It does, but that's not our dinner. That's for Porky, remember?"

"Porky's got it pretty good."

"Not yet, but he will. As soon as we find him a home. Come on, I'll show you the Cat Café. We've been trying to get some of these guys used to being in a room with people eating and not jumping up on the table, so this is good practice."

He reached into a compartment above the oven and pulled out a pizza box.

"Would you mind grabbing those plates?" He nodded at a pair of paper plates rimmed with pictures of cartoon cats, and Kate scooped them up and followed after him.

"Careful," he said as he held the door for her. "There are a couple escape artists in here and one new girl who's not too sure about things yet."

"I know the feeling," Kate said. "Which one's new?"

"Judgey-eyebrow cat over there." He pointed to a fluffy black-and-white tuxedo kitty on the windowsill. The cat lifted her impressively arched brows and studied Kate with a look of intense scorn.

Kate laughed. "I see what you mean."

The cat had the most unusual markings she'd ever seen. Her body was black fluff with white socks, and her face was white, too. She had a little black spot on one side of her face and eyebrows that gave her a permanently skeptical expression. The brows lifted a bit as Kate approached.

"If you could caption her right now, she'd be saying, 'Lady, I don't think so,'" Kate said as she stroked a hand down the cat's back. The cat allowed it, but her expression suggested serious doubt about Kate's petting skills.

Jonah grinned and pulled the door shut behind him. "She's been looking at everyone like that today. I heard a guy this morning say, 'If

I wanted someone judging my every move, I'd get a wife. At least then I wouldn't have to clean a litter box.'"

"Very nice." Kate set a plate on each side of a bright-blue table and pulled out a chair as Jonah set the pizza box in the center of the table. She moved a chrome napkin dispenser out of the way and sat down. A fluffy orange tabby hopped into the center of the table, then jumped down as Jonah made a *psst* sound.

"Sorry, but it's how they learn," he said. "We want them to have manners when they go to their new homes. That way there's less chance of them getting returned to the shelter."

"Sort of like cat finishing school."

"Exactly."

He opened the pizza box, and Kate breathed in the heavenly aroma of pepperoni and sausage. A little gray cat with white feet stretched up to bat at the box top but didn't make any moves to jump for it.

"I'm impressed by your commitment to animal welfare," she said as Jonah handed her a bottle of iced tea that didn't feel particularly iced. "Have you always been such an advocate?"

"Nah." He sat down across from her and twisted the top off his own bottle, taking a swig before he continued. "I don't even like cats that much."

She blinked at him. "Then why—" She stopped, remembering their conversation in Ashland. "That's right, you said your sister runs a pet rescue center?"

"Yep." He set down his drink and grabbed a piece of pizza out of the box. "She owns Clearwater Animal Shelter. She also owns me, come to think of it." He grinned and took a bite of pizza, but there was something in his eyes that Kate couldn't read. It was somewhere between pride and sadness, which seemed so incongruous that she knew she wasn't reading him right at all.

Kate slid a slice of pizza onto her own plate and wondered if it would be weird to ask for a fork. Probably. She needed to just go with the flow. If she wanted any hope of persuading Jonah to do the show, she needed to come off as friendly and unassuming.

Requiring flatware to eat pizza wasn't very unassuming.

"I have to admit I don't know a whole lot about reality television," Jonah said. "What's your job in all this, exactly?"

"For this show, I'm the executive producer," Kate said. "But I've also asked to be on-site as a field producer."

"Is that unusual?"

"Sort of. The executive producer is the one with the big-picture vision for the show, and the field producer is on the ground helping to capture footage and steer the day-to-day filming. In this case, I wanted to do both."

"That sounds like a lot of work."

"It is, but it's important work." She smiled, feeling a little awkward as she spread a few paper napkins over her lap. "This show is kind of my baby."

"I caught that." Jonah helped himself to another slice of pizza.

"So," Kate said, taking a small bite before she continued, "you're open to hearing about the TV show."

"Yes. May I first tell you what I'm *not* open to?"

"This isn't sounding like a good start for openness."

He shrugged and took a big bite of pizza, chewing and swallowing before he spoke again. "I just don't want to waste anyone's time here, so I need to put this out on the table."

"By all means."

Jonah cleared his throat. "I'm not willing to fake it," he said. "I'm not going to make up handyman projects or talk about NASCAR or scratch my junk on TV or anything else they think will help me look more like an average, blue-collar guy."

"Okay." Kate nodded and made a mental note to put *No junk scratching* in an e-mail to the network execs. "Would you be okay with continuing to offer the sort of blunt, no-filter commentary you gave in *On the Other Hand*? That's the part of Average Joe that everyone fell in love with."

"Maybe," he said. "I'm not willing to play dumb. And I don't want to be made to *look* dumb."

"Understandable." She took another bite of pizza as she waited for him to continue. "What else?" she prompted. "What are your other conditions?"

"I'm willing to collaborate and be friendly with Viv because we *are* friendly," he said. "More or less."

"I got that from the kind and tender way you told her to fuck off."

Jonah offered a small, chagrined smile. "Sometimes exes bring out the worst in us."

"Can't argue with that."

Jonah leaned back in his chair and took a swig of tea from the bottle. A cat the size of a small automobile took it as an invitation to jump up onto his lap.

"Get down, Porky," Jonah said as he eased the enormous beast onto the floor. "Your dinner is cooling."

The big gray cat growled and sauntered away. Jonah turned his attention back to Kate. "I suppose Viv would say you can't blame someone else for making you act a certain way," he said. "That people control their own words and actions."

"You don't agree?"

He shrugged. "You can't blame others for your actions, but you also can't help how you feel. And sometimes certain people bring out the worst kind of feelings in you. It's up to you whether to act on them, but feeling like shit never brought out anyone's best personality traits."

"I suppose that's true." Kate took a sip of tea. "So is that it for your conditions?"

"No, that was my preface to the biggest one."

"Which is?" Kate braced herself, hoping it wasn't a demand she couldn't meet. Hoping the network would agree to it, whatever the hell it was.

"I won't pretend Viv and I are still married," he said. "I don't know if that idea has been tossed around or if the TV people are jonesing for the happily married vibe they got from us in *On the Other Hand*, but I can tell you right now I won't do that. I won't pretend we're in love or that there's some kind of undercurrent of unrequited emotion between us. There's not, and I refuse to fake it."

Kate nodded as relief sluiced through her. She told herself it was relief that his condition was fairly minor. The network would agree to it, she felt pretty certain.

But she knew there was more to her feelings of relief. That deep down, she was cheered by the vehemence in Jonah's denial of feelings for Viv.

"I hear what you're saying." Kate dabbed her mouth with her napkin, even though she'd taken only a couple of tiny bites of pizza. "It's true that networks love arced stories when it comes to reality tel—to unscripted TV." She paused there, wondering if he cared one way or the other whether they called it reality television or something else. "I can't make any promises, but I can definitely make it clear to the team that you're not willing to fake a relationship that isn't there. Under the circumstances, I feel confident they'll be fine with that."

"Good." Jonah chewed thoughtfully for a while. Kate watched as his gaze drifted to the windowsill where judgey-eyebrow cat sat watching them with disdain. A lean little tiger-striped cat tried to jump up onto the sill beside her, but eyebrow cat stuck out one paw and whacked the kitten on the forehead.

Jonah laughed. "Denied."

"You know, her eyebrows aren't her only striking feature," Kate said. "That little spot on her cheek makes her look a little like Marilyn Monroe."

"Marilyn." Jonah looked at the cat. "That's a good name for her."

"She doesn't have a name?"

"She just came in. Owner surrender. When that happens, we usually come up with a new name for the cat in case they have negative associations with the old name."

"That makes sense." Kate wiped her hands on a napkin and reached for her own bottle of tea. She took a slow sip and wondered why the hell he'd served it warm. "So your conditions sound reasonable. Is there anything you'd like to know from me about the show? About what the network has in mind?"

She expected him to ask something obvious. The format, the timeline, the way his name might appear in the credits.

She didn't expect the question he really asked.

"Why are you doing this?"

"Me?"

"Yes, you. Why are you so fired up about the TV show, first of all? And why do you give a shit whether I'm part of it?"

Kate thought about how to answer. She picked up her pizza and took a small bite, surprised to find it still warm. She chewed carefully as she considered how much to tell Jonah about her reasons for wanting to make this show.

Bravery, openness, transparency, honesty, Viv coached in her head. *The acronym is BOTH, and it's your key to connection with another human. Your ticket to understanding and being understood.*

Kate cleared her throat. "My father used to hit my mother," she said.

Jonah blinked. "Jesus."

"It was a long time ago. He died in a car accident when I was fifteen, so my mom has been safe ever since." Kate fought the urge to look down at the table, wanting Jonah to see why this mattered to her. To understand the importance of this TV show beyond a paycheck. "I was really angry about it for a long time. All the way into my late twenties, actually. I was angry at my mother for putting up with it, and angry with my father for doing it in the first place. Angry with myself for not doing something about it."

"But you were just a kid."

"I know. I understand that now. And I understand the dynamics of abusive relationships. I also understand how to move past all that. How to break the cycle. I owe that to Vivienne Brandt and the words she wrote in her first book about escaping an abusive relationship. I read that book when I was twenty-eight, and it was like someone shining a flashlight into my brain."

She watched his face for a reaction, wondering if he heard the reverence in her voice. Wondering if it bugged him to hear his ex-wife referred to as some kind of life-altering shaman.

But she *was* that to Kate, and she needed Jonah to understand.

Jonah nodded, all traces of the flippant bravado erased from his face. "That book helped a lot of people," he said. "*But Not Broken* was Viv's best work."

"I disagree."

Jonah frowned. "What?"

"I think the next book was. The one you wrote together. *On the Other Hand* was more than just a memoir or a trendy self-help guide. It made the issues relatable. It wasn't just a woman on a pedestal giving her advice on communication strategies. It was two people—two very different people—giving their perspectives on communication and relationships and all the messy stuff that comes along with human connection. Jonah, that book changed lives. You were a part of that."

Jonah stared at her for a long time. When he spoke, his voice was softer. "That wasn't me. That was Viv."

"It wasn't just Viv." She shook her head, needing him to believe this. "Your contributions may have been smaller, lighthearted pieces of the equation, but they were equally vital. They're what got people buzzing about the book. They're what made men pay attention and actually *read* instead of rolling their eyes when their wives brought home a silly relationship guide."

Kate's voice had gotten louder, and she watched Marilyn, the judgey-eyebrow cat, shift positions. The cat's brows lifted a fraction of an inch, and Kate imagined her remarking, "You're laying it on pretty thick, lady."

She was, but she didn't care. She needed Jonah to hear this. Needed him to understand. He still hadn't said anything, and she wondered what he was thinking. Were her words having an impact at all?

"Thank you," he said softly.

"For what?"

"For what you just said. About the book mattering. About my parts of it. I know I've been acting like sort of an asshole about the whole book thing, but it means a lot to hear you say that. That it mattered."

Tears pricked the back of her eyelids, but she fought them off. "It did matter. It still does."

She looked down at the table, struggling to get her bearings. She couldn't afford to get too emotional over this. It was business, and she needed to stay professional. She thought about picking up her pizza and taking another bite, but she wasn't sure she could get it past the lump in her throat.

The rumble of Jonah's voice made her look up again.

"Who was he?"

◆　◆　◆

Kate blinked, her expression so startled Jonah knew he'd hit a nerve.

"Who—what do you mean?" she asked.

"The guy who broke your heart. Who was he?"

He watched her take a few steadying breaths, watched her glance up and to the left. A neurolinguistic indicator, sometimes an indication that the subject was accessing a part of the brain that forms fabrications.

Or maybe she was looking at judgey-eyebrow cat again.

"His name was Anton." Kate's words were soft, and Jonah could tell she was speaking the truth. "I mentioned him over dinner in Ashland."

"Did he hit you?"

Kate shook her head, but she blinked when she did it. Something was off here. "No," she said.

"But?"

He watched her swallow, and he kept his gaze on hers, channeling all his energy into using the subtle elicitation skills he'd honed in his counterintelligence training for the Marines.

"Abuse takes more forms than fists," Kate said. "I'm quoting Viv again, I know. But I'm trying to tell you how much those books meant to me. How much I learned about what a healthy relationship looks like. *But Not Broken* may have taught me to recognize signs of an unhealthy relationship, but it wasn't until *On the Other Hand* that I understood what a healthy one looked like. That I shouldn't settle for anything else."

Something tightened in Jonah's chest. A pang of guilt, or maybe regret. He remembered the first meeting he and Viv had with the editor contracted to work with them for *On the Other Hand.*

"You two have such an amazing relationship," the editor had gushed, folding her hands on a polished ebony desk as she beamed at Jonah and Viv sitting across from her. "You have an important gift you can give people here. The gift of seeing what a healthy relationship should look like."

Viv had smiled and twined her fingers through Jonah's, and Jonah had squeezed back as the lump formed thick in his throat. By then they were already sleeping in separate bedrooms, already talking quietly about "taking some time apart."

Deep down, he'd known then that they were past the point of no return. He hadn't wanted to believe it, but it had sat there between them like an angry cat. Even if Viv had been the one to pull the plug, he'd known where things were headed.

"We'd love nothing more than to set a positive example," Viv had told the editor while pressing the tip of her toe against his instep. "To help other people."

Even then, Jonah knew she'd meant it. That was Viv for you. Maybe her words weren't always genuine, but her desire to be of service never wavered. Her urge to help others, even at her own expense sometimes. It was the thing he'd always admired most about her.

Jonah shook himself back to the present. Back to the woman sitting across from him with wide toffee eyes and a calico cat on her lap. She'd barely touched her pizza, and he wondered if he should have cleared his choices with her before ordering.

But now wasn't the time to be fretting about pepperoni. He reached across the table and touched her hand.

"Hey," he said, keeping his voice low. "Thank you for sharing that with me."

She nodded, then gave a small smile. "Yeah."

He thought about sharing his own story then. Telling her everything about Jossy and that horrible day eighteen years ago. He looked down at his plate, trying to form the words.

"Owl."

Jonah looked up at Kate. "What did you say?"

"I didn't say anything."

"It sounded like you said *owl*."

"I heard it, too, but it wasn't me." She glanced toward the window. "I think it came from over there."

But there was no one there. Just the weird-looking black-and-white cat with the judgey eyebrows and the Marilyn Monroe beauty mark. Jonah looked back at Kate.

"Weird."

"Very."

"So this TV show. Would we be filming at Viv's house?"

"She suggested it, and the network seems to like the idea. Some of it comes down to licensing and insurance. That's Amy's department, so she's looking into—"

"*Ooowl!*"

The voice was more forceful this time, and it was definitely coming from the window. Judgey-eyebrow cat seemed to lift one brow, or maybe it was Jonah's imagination. If a cat could speak, would it really choose to say *owl?* Her expression looked more like, *"You people are fucking idiots."*

He was probably reading too much into this.

"I really think it's the cat," he said. "Judgey-eyebrow cat."

"You have to stop calling her that," Kate said. "She's not judgey. Just misunderstood."

Jonah laughed. "Funny. I think I said that to my sister the first time she met Viv."

"That's nice," Kate said. "That you stuck up for her. Viv, I mean."

"Sure," he said, wishing he hadn't said that. He needed to watch his mouth, especially around a woman who made a living in reality television. It was juvenile to be hanging up their dirty laundry so long after the divorce.

He looked at the cat again, wondering what the hell her deal was. She had a sweet face, regardless. The cat stared back at him, then opened her mouth.

"*Owl!*"

Jonah shook his head. "Apparently she has something important to say about Strigiformes."

"Strigiformes?"

"It's the order owls belong to," he said. "In the animal kingdom. It includes a couple hundred species of solitary, nocturnal birds of prey known for an upright stance, a broad head, binocular vision, binaural hearing, sharp talons, and feathers adapted for silent flight."

"Wow." Kate did her own eyebrow raise, though it wasn't nearly as impressive as the cat's. "You really are kind of a geek."

Jonah grinned. For some reason it sounded like the best compliment anyone had paid him in a long time. "Thanks."

"Have you always been such a nerd?"

"Pretty much."

Kate laughed and took a bite of pizza. She seemed ravenous all of a sudden, and he watched her wolf down the rest of the slice in just a couple of bites. Then she wiped her hands on her napkin and stood up.

"Look, I know it's important to you to get out of the shadow of the Average Joe thing." She carried her plate to the trash can and dropped it in, then smoothed down the front of her dress. "To have the opportunity to be known more for your brains than your favorite sports team."

Jonah started to nod, then stopped. That wasn't it exactly. "It's not as much that I care how other people see me. It's more about how I see myself."

"How do you mean?"

"I know I'm a smart guy," he said. "Intellectually, I know that. But I haven't always *felt* smart."

"How do you mean?"

"I grew up with dyslexia," he said. "I'm still dyslexic, of course, but I've learned ways to manage it."

"Wow," Kate said. "And you co-wrote a bestselling book and own a bookstore?"

Jonah nodded and watched Kate's face. He waited for the barrage of questions. The gentle probing he'd always get from Viv about how he felt about his disability or what motivated him to overcome it.

Instead, she smiled. "That's impressive. I worked on a documentary about dyslexia a long time ago. The people we interviewed talked about being made to feel stupid or lazy." She smiled, and Jonah's heart twisted. "I think it's pretty obvious to anyone who spends more than five minutes with you that you're neither of those things."

Jonah swallowed hard and wondered if she knew she was saying exactly what he needed to hear. He wasn't sure why he'd volunteered that information in the first place, considering he didn't know Kate all that well.

But there was something empowering about being the one to share it. About telling the story on his own terms, in his own way.

Or maybe it was just Kate. There was something about her that made him want to open up his chest and his brain and the whole big mess of himself and let her have a look at whatever might be in there.

"Right," he said, feeling a little sheepish. "Opening a bookstore had been my goal for a long time. I didn't have the balls to do it until things started winding down in my marriage."

"It's pretty admirable," she said. "Talk about confronting your fears."

Jonah smiled. "Yeah. Anyway, besides the dyslexia, I'm forgetful as hell. It's partly an ADD thing, partly just me being—well, *me*."

The way she looked at him with eyes flooded by admiration made Jonah's chest ache.

"That's the *you* people fell in love with in the books, Jonah," she said. "The guy who's self-aware and eager to fight his own demons."

"Thanks," he said, his heart snagging a little on the word *love*.

Kate looked at him for a while, leaning back against the counter. Then she nodded. "I hear where you're coming from," she said. "For what it's worth, if you agree to do the show, I'll do my best to make sure you're portrayed in the best light."

He stood up, feeling dumb for sitting on his ass while she was on her feet. She was probably itching to go. Waiting for him to ask more questions about the TV show or to give her an answer or something. She hadn't come here to make idle chit-chat.

He stepped into the space next to her and rested a hand on the counter, making a gray-and-white cat growl from the center of a round pet bed he'd set there. "Thank you for coming here tonight," he said.

"For sharing everything you've shared this evening. You've given me a lot to think about."

Kate looked at him, her gaze holding steady. "Do you have any more questions about the show?"

He shook his head, captivated by her eyes. Had he noticed before how many colors they held? Copper, cinnamon, something that almost looked like amber.

"Are you—leaning one way or another?" Kate asked. "About the show?"

"I think so." Jonah didn't say anything else. He knew what he wanted to do. What he *needed* to do. He'd take a night or two to think about it, maybe look at some contracts or something. But the money alone was enough to consider it. And even without the money, getting to work with Kate—

No. Don't think that way. You already know what a mess it is to do this sort of work with a woman you're sleeping with.

That was the wrong thought to have. The idea of sleeping with Kate, touching her and holding her and sliding into her—

Jesus Christ, knock it off.

Kate's gaze was still locked with his, and Jonah wondered if she'd blinked at all in the last few seconds. She was standing close enough for him to feel her breath against his skin. For him to reach out and slide an arm around her waist if he wanted to, which he did want, but he couldn't, and he really ought to stop thinking about—

Suddenly, she was kissing him. Or he was kissing her. No, she was definitely kissing him, but he was kissing back, and they were all tangled up with fingers and tongues and breath and little sighs of pleasure that Jonah wasn't sure were coming from him or her or one of the cats.

He slid his hand up into the curve of her waist and she leaned into him like she craved his touch as much as he craved this—all of this. He heard a soft purr behind him, or maybe it was coming from Kate. She was soft all over and tasted like something spicy and warm.

"Jonah," she murmured as he broke the kiss to place a trail of kisses down her throat and across one collarbone. Her hands cupped his ass and he could feel her nails digging in. Is this what it would be like to have her? So much dizziness and passion and forbidden heat?

Forbidden.

The word stuck in his brain. Jonah froze. He drew back slowly, his body screaming at him to keep going while his brain screamed at him to knock it the hell off.

He looked Kate in the eye and swallowed. "We can't do this. Not if we're going to be working together."

Kate blinked. "We're going to be working together?"

"I—"

"Did you just say yes?"

He hadn't meant to. Or hell, maybe he had. He was a little mind whacked with Kate still pressed up against him like this. Jonah took a breath.

"Yeah," he said. "I guess I did."

Kate broke into a grin. She gave a delighted little bounce and let go of his ass to place her hands on his shoulders.

"Oh my God, Jonah! I'm so excited."

"Yeah," he muttered, already slipping back into Average Joe mode as he thought about his raging erection. "You and me both."

Lucky for him, Kate seemed to miss the crude joke. Or maybe she was too polite to say anything, which was probably just as well. He'd meant what he said. There was no place for screwing around if they were going to be working together, along with his ex-wife.

Like magic, Jonah's hard-on went down.

But Kate was still bouncing like a giddy kid, so he had to feel at least a trace of her enthusiasm.

"This is going to be great," she said. "You'll see. I promise to do my best to portray you as a multifaceted guy with dignity and wisdom."

"Owl."

Jonah tore his eyes off Kate to see Marilyn eyeing him from the windowsill with a look of silent distaste.

Well, not so silent. *"Owl,"* the cat insisted, standing up and stretching. She hopped down off the sill and padded over to him. She sat down at his feet and looked up at him for a moment, then butted her head against his shin.

"I think she likes you," Kate said.

"Yeah, I could tell from the head-butting." Of course, he knew enough about cat psychology to recognize it was probably true. Cats bumped heads against anyone or anything they saw as their own. As a member of their tribe or a possession to be claimed.

Something warm spread through Jonah's chest as he looked down at that weird little whiskered face and those judgmental brows.

"Marilyn," he said, testing it out. He liked the way it sounded.

Apparently, so did the cat. A low rumble sounded in her chest, and she rubbed her face on the leg of his jeans as she continued to purr.

"Do you ever end up adopting the cats you have here?" Kate asked.

"I never have. Yet." He thought about what his sister had said the other day about Viv being the reason behind his pet-free life. Did Jossy have a point?

"I think this cat is trying to tell you something," Kate said.

Jonah studied Marilyn, mostly because he couldn't bear to look at Kate with her flushed cheeks and kiss-stung lips.

"Marilyn," he said again. "Would you like to come home with me?"

The cat narrowed her eyes, unimpressed by the offer. Then she head-butted him again, the queen of mixed messages.

"Typical woman," he muttered, tearing his eyes off the cat to meet Kate's gaze again. "Not you; the cat. Though I guess if I'm doing the Average Joe thing again, here's where I call you a cock-tease and suggest you get your sweet ass home unless you want me to grab it again."

Her eyes widened. She licked her lips, and he got the sense she didn't find his piggish behavior nearly as offensive as he did.

"Is it wrong to admit I kinda want that?" she asked.

"Go on," he said. "You should get out of here."

"I suppose so."

She seemed to hesitate, and he watched her open her mouth like she wanted to say something else. Instead, she closed it.

"And we probably shouldn't do that again," he said.

"The kissing?"

"Yeah. Not a good idea, under the circumstances."

"Okay." Kate pressed her lips together. "Thank you, Jonah."

"For the pizza you hardly touched?"

"For saying yes to the show. I promise you won't regret it."

He looked at her, fighting the urge to tell her that a small part of him already regretted it. That he'd been fueled by regret for most of his adult life.

"Don't mention it," he said, then bent down to pick up his cat.

CHAPTER SIX

With her heels clicking on the black maple floor, Kate strode across the front of the hotel conference room, handing out printed packets. She kept her eyes averted from Jonah's, remembering Amy's words about the chemistry between them.

It wasn't true, obviously.

Even so, she couldn't afford for it to *look* obvious to any of the studio reps and network execs who'd shown up for today's pre-production meeting.

"What's this?" Jonah asked as Kate handed him his packet, and she fought the urge to strangle him. Clearly he didn't share her intent to avoid direct conversation between them.

Kate let her gaze skim the room, skipping eye contact with Jonah in favor of directing her response to the dozen other people in the room. "These packets contain basic information about the pilot episode," she said. "Shot lists, intro and outro materials, that sort of thing."

"Are the patients in there, too?" On the opposite side of the conference table, Viv accepted her packet from Amy and began flipping through it. Her dark hair was held back by a polished ebony clip, and her flowy peasant blouse made her look effortlessly chic. "I'd like to get started learning about who we'll be helping."

"Profiles of the proposed subjects are at the back of the packet," Kate said. She ran a hand down the front of her slim black skirt and wished she'd taken a few extra minutes that morning to wear contacts instead of her glasses.

Then she cursed herself for giving a damn what she looked like. This was a business meeting, not a dating show.

"We've identified five couples with strong potential to be featured in the pilot episode," Kate continued as she scooted past Amy to make her way to the other end of the table. "You'll see all the details spelled out there about the struggles they're facing and what we think is going to resonate best with our viewers."

"These are real couples," Amy pointed out to Viv as she performed an expert sideways dodge to avoid the grabby hands of some dickhead network producer. Kate made a mental note to keep an eye on the guy. "We pre-screened them all with an eye on what we think will play well with our audiences," Amy continued. "First and foremost was relatability. A sense of genuineness. These are real people, not actors."

"Well, some of them are actors," Kate amended. "This is show biz, after all, and a lot of these folks are coming from LA. Everyone's an actor."

"True enough," Amy acknowledged. "Which does help with the vetting process as far as making sure everyone's comfortable being on camera."

"But we plan to do most of the filming in Seattle, of course," Kate said with a quick smile at Viv. "That keeps us out of hot water as far as where Dr. Brandt is licensed to practice, plus we'll catch audience interest with the fresh setting."

"Thank God," muttered a network exec to Kate's right. "If I have to watch one more reality TV show set in LA or New York City, I'm going to stab my eyeballs with a fork."

Kate glanced at Viv, hoping she hadn't heard the reality-TV remark. Viv had already flipped to the section of the packet with the profiles of the couples they'd pre-screened for the pilot episode. She was reading with a serene, thoughtful expression, and Kate breathed a sigh of relief.

It was a good sign. One of 684 reasons she'd always loved Vivienne Brandt was that her desire to help people was genuine. That shone through in her books, and Kate felt certain it would come through on camera, too.

She glanced away from Viv and let her gaze drift around the room. *Don't look at Jonah,* Kate willed herself. *Don't think about how hot he looks in that red shirt. Or how hot he looked the other day with no shirt. Or how his lips feel when he brushes them across your—*

"Jeez, you guys aren't messing around." Jonah whistled low under his breath, and Kate felt her gaze swivel his direction without her consent.

"What do you mean?" she asked.

"This first couple—Sam and Elena?"

"Those are their real names," Amy interjected. "They've already signed confidentiality agreements."

"I hope they signed a prenuptial agreement, too," Jonah said. "They don't have kids, but they have two mortgages on a four-thousand-square-foot home, and she hasn't held a job the entire twelve years they've been married?"

"It says here she's been in school," Vivienne pointed out as she slid a fingertip down her own page. "Working on her PhD in philosophy."

"To do *what?*" Jonah asked, flipping through the pages like he might have missed something.

"It doesn't say," Viv said. "But is that even the point? She's working to expand her mind, to broaden her horizons, to—"

"Avoid reality?" Jonah turned to the next page, and Kate watched him nudge his glasses back up his nose. "How did these people have the wherewithal to plan a ninety-thousand-dollar destination wedding with three hundred guests, but not to have a simple conversation about their expectations for careers and money?"

"Judgment, Jonah," Viv murmured in a sing-song tone that told Kate this was a familiar refrain. "We're here to help them, not scold them."

"They need more help than we could give them in a thirty-minute reality show," Jonah muttered.

"Unscripted television," Viv corrected. "And we're just giving them the tools they need to find their way."

Jonah snorted. "Judging from what I'm seeing here, these two couldn't find their asses with a map and a flashlight."

"Perfect!"

All eyes swiveled to the head of the table, where Empire TV's executive director clapped his hands together and looked pleased. "This is excellent," Chase Whitfield added. "I love the dynamic already!"

"I agree," murmured Luke Sheehan, one of the high-level execs from the studio. Kate had already forgotten his job title, though it clearly involved agreeing with everything the Empire TV team had to say.

"They're very fiery together," added another Empire TV exec, almost as though Viv and Jonah were two actors in another room instead of two ex-spouses sitting right here in this one.

"This is some solid-gold shit right here." Chase Whitfield whacked the packet with the back of his hand, and Kate tried to tamp down the irritation she'd always felt around him. He was one of the biggest names in the business, and they were lucky he'd taken an interest in the show.

That didn't mean she had to like him.

"You know," Chase continued, "it's actually so much better having them divorced."

"Amen to that," Jonah muttered as he continued to the next section in his packet and adjusted his glasses again.

"There's something we can agree on." Viv crossed her legs, exposing one bare knee as her red silk skirt rode up. Kate wondered if Jonah noticed. At what point did you stop being affected by the bared body parts of someone you'd once loved?

"You see this quote on page two-sixteen from the husband?" Viv continued. "The one where he says, 'the feelings just aren't there anymore.'"

Jonah glanced at the page and grunted before looking up at Viv. "So he's boning someone else."

"That's typically what it means," she mused. Then she frowned and looked at Kate. "Wait, is he allowed to say *boning*?"

Kate folded her hands in front of her and glanced quickly at Chase. "It's ultimately up to the network, but there's usually more leeway with cable television," she said. "A few appropriately timed curse words are usually acceptable."

"Define appropriately timed." Jonah looked at Kate. "If someone is being a fucking dumbass and I tell him so—"

"In a spirit of love and compassion," Viv interjected.

"Sure," Jonah agreed. "If I tell him in a spirit of love and compassion that he's being a fucking dumbass, is that appropriate?"

Across the table, Amy was trying—and failing—to keep a straight face. "I suppose it depends on the circumstances."

Jonah raised one eyebrow. "How about if he's being a fucking dumbass?"

"I suppose that *would* be appropriate circumstances," Amy agreed.

"I think we're getting off track here," Viv said. "How about we take a look at the second couple?"

There was a rustling of pages, and Kate flipped forward in her own packet. She stole a quick glance at Jonah and wondered what he felt like being here now. Did working with an ex feel awkward, or was he able to see Viv as just another body in the room?

There were no cameras rolling, which had been Viv's idea. She wanted to ease him in slowly, despite the Empire TV team's desire to start test shooting right away. From what Kate could see, Jonah would look fantastic in front of a camera. Whether he'd enjoy it was another matter.

"Did you find out if we can get Pete Waller as the lead cameraman?" Chase asked.

"If we're able to start filming right away, he's available," Amy said.

"We've had a terrific working relationship with him in the past," Kate said. "He's very talented."

"And he's got that whole teddy-bear vibe about him," Amy added. "That'll help put all the couples at ease."

"He knows how to get the dirt, too." Chase grinned, and Kate tried not to cringe.

"He's a professional," she said mildly, glancing at Viv and Jonah to make sure neither looked alarmed.

They were both engrossed in their packets. Kate turned the page and skimmed the bio on the second couple. Roger and Abby, married for eight years with two young kids under the age of five. Roger complained Abby was never in the mood for sex, and Abby complained that Roger didn't help around the house.

"The oldest story in the book," Jonah murmured, taking the words right out of Kate's mouth.

"So sad," Viv said, tapping the page with one manicured fingernail. "Sounds like they had a terrific sex life right up until their son was born."

Jonah flipped to the next page. "If by *terrific* you mean they both enjoyed dressing up in animal costumes and humping each other in public places, you're right on the money."

Viv glanced at Chase. "Is *humping* better than *boning*? Because I think either would be better than *fucking*, but I want to make sure we're all on the same page here."

"All depends on who's doing it, babe," Jonah muttered.

Kate's face heated up, and she was grateful both Viv and Jonah had their eyes glued to the words on the paper as Chase muttered something about fine-tuning language preferences at a later time.

"There's nothing wrong with the animal costumes," Viv pointed out. "Furries are becoming more mainstream every day, and it's impor-tant for these two to have a shared passionate interest—one we should help them to rekindle."

Jonah looked up and locked eyes with Kate, and a lightning bolt hit her straight in the libido. "Did you guys go out of your way to pick freaks and drama queens?"

"Judgment, Jonah," Viv sang again, but Jonah ignored her.

Kate cleared her throat. "Certainly the couples we've identified have characteristics and interests that maximize their entertainment value."

"Fair enough," Jonah said before looking back at Viv. "So what would you recommend for our friends Roger and Abby?"

A flush crept into Viv's cheeks, and Kate wanted to kiss Jonah for deferring to her. For knowing the right tone to set in casting Viv as the expert. She crossed her fingers that formula would keep working.

"Well," Viv said, "I think they could benefit from some alone time. Regular date nights, any opportunity where someone could take the kids for the night. Do they have family nearby?"

Amy nodded. "The wife's parents are both in town and available for sitter duty. We already looked into that possibility, anticipating you might suggest a romantic getaway."

Someone from the product-placement team piped up from across the table. "Brasada Ranch resort in Central Oregon offered to put them up in one of their luxury suites for the weekend. Romantic dinners, sunset horseback riding, the whole nine yards."

"That place is amazing," Kate said, making an effort to avoid Jonah's eyes. Did he remember that as the site of their imaginary wedding?

"I hear it's very romantic," he said. Kate felt his gaze on her, but she refused to look. Her face was burning enough as it was. "Mountain views and little bunny rabbits hopping all around."

Amy caught Kate's eye and frowned.

"You okay?" she mouthed.

Kate nodded and picked up a glass of water from the conference room table. She downed it in two gulps, earning herself a baffled look from the props-department girl to whom the glass belonged.

"Sorry," Kate whispered. "I'll get you another."

"A romantic getaway does sound nice," Viv continued, thankfully unaware that Kate was considering a leap out the window. "A change of scenery could certainly help a couple in crisis, and we could do some on-location filming."

"I agree," Amy said. "As an alternate destination, there's a vineyard we could send them to with—"

"Or we could order them not to touch each other."

All eyes swung to Jonah. Amy frowned. "What?"

"No touching." He set his packet on the table and crossed his ankle over one knee. "At all. Hands off completely. Tell them it's to preserve the sanctity of the counseling process or some shit like that."

Amy frowned. "Do we really want to tell a married couple they're not allowed to have sex?"

"He's right, actually." Vivienne folded her hands on the table and glanced at her ex. "In a case like this, what you'd hope to have happen is that the couple will be titillated by the hands-off rule."

Amy's eyes widened. "You want them to fail?"

"Not fail, exactly," Viv said. "The goal is to create a sense of unity from their mutual rebellion."

"The goal is to get everyone laid," Jonah added. "Orgasms do wonders for unity, especially if they're supposed to be off-limits."

Across the table, Chase banged a hand on the back of the empty chair next to him. "Fucking brilliant," he said. "Reverse psychology at its finest."

"I agree," Luke said, and Kate wondered if she should start recording the number of times he uttered the phrase. Was that three or four?

Amy scribbled furiously on her notepad while Kate began mentally sketching out how much of this they could show on television. Obviously they couldn't follow the couple to bed with cameras, but they'd be miked up outside the bedroom. She'd have to make sure the cameraman captured any suggestive banter beforehand, any discussion of plans for an illicit tryst. And if the conversation didn't flow the way they needed it to, they could always make it work in editing. Maybe an interview segment with one spouse, and then a cutaway shot with a little frankenbiting, piecing the clips together to make it look like one solid—

"What about this couple here?" Jonah said. "The third couple on the list. Suzie and Ken. This one sounds pretty toxic. Name calling, finger-pointing, blaming—"

"At least they're communicating," Viv pointed out. "It's the couples who've shut down completely that are harder to help. The ones who aren't even trying to make themselves understood."

"There's a big difference between listening to understand and listening to reply," Jonah shot back. "Trying to make yourself heard isn't the same as making an effort to hear someone else."

Viv tapped her pen on the table and looked at Chase. "I'd suggest an immediate communication workshop. They could benefit from learning NVC."

"Nonviolent Communication," Kate supplied, thrilled to see the master at work. "That's a great idea."

"Learning compassionate communication tools is essential here," Viv continued. "Also establishing some basic rules, like making a habit of never going to bed angry."

"I disagree," Jonah said. "For some couples that's pointless. Trying to resolve everything before hitting the sack just makes people irritable and sleep deprived the next day. It's better to get a good night's sleep and talk once you're rested."

"Easy for you to say, Mr. I Never Have Any Problem Falling Asleep," Viv countered. "Some people can't fall asleep when they're upset or stressed or—"

"So what do you want them to do, stay up all night screaming at each other?" Jonah interrupted. "Look, it's simple science. Did you read the study last month that talked about the importance of sleep in replenishing the adenosine triphosphate molecule that serves as energy currency for the body? When the ATP molecules are depleted, the body can't—"

"Whoa, whoa, whoa—" Chase interjected. "Let's save the science speak for Dr. Viv. Jonah, you're doing great when you stick with things about boning and orgasms. All the things viewers want to hear from Average Joe."

Kate bit her lip. She watched Jonah's eyes flash. Saw him clutch his pen in one fist and look down at the page. She took a deep breath, wondering if she was about to see his famous temper flare.

But Jonah said nothing.

Kate clapped her hands together. "Look, why don't we take a break for a little bit?" she suggested. "It's clear tensions are running high here, and there are going to be some kinks to work out before we reach a point where we're ready to start filming."

Jonah looked up, then set the paper down on the table and pulled off his glasses. He dragged his hands down his face and sighed. "I think it's clear this isn't working," he said. "All we're going to do is argue. No one wants to see a couple of exes squabbling."

"Actually, you're wrong there," Chase said. "This was brilliant. Absolutely perfect."

"I agree," Luke said. "Viewers love these kinds of fiery interactions."

Kate resisted the urge to roll her eyes, wondering if the man had ever had an original thought. But at least he was right.

"It's exactly what they want to see," Amy agreed, glancing at Kate before looking away quickly. "The arguing, the shouting—this is all great for ratings."

Jonah gave her a skeptical look. "Are you serious? People want to watch us fight on a show about trying to save doomed relationships?"

"Judgment, Jonah," Viv said. "They're not doomed. They're coming to us for help. To determine if things *can* be saved."

Jonah dragged his hands down his face again, and Kate had a sudden urge to wrap her arms around him.

"God help them," he muttered, and picked up his packet again.

◆　◆　◆

Jonah tossed his keys on the dining room table and headed straight for the fridge. He was pretty sure he had a beer in there, maybe even two left over from the six-pack he'd grabbed a few weeks ago.

Right now he wanted nothing more than to crack a cold one and sit down on the couch with a bag of chips and a good book.

You should probably skip the book, his brain chided. *Might as well turn on ESPN and get back into character as Average Joe.*

He sighed and rounded the corner into the kitchen, then stopped in his tracks.

A ball of fluff blocked his path, her white feline face and silvery whiskers a startling contrast against the explosion of black fur that made up the rest of her body. She was lying in front of the fridge, white paws stretched sphinxlike in front of her.

The cat opened her eyes and took him in. *"Owl,"* said Marilyn.

Her eyebrows lifted in silent reproach, and Jonah felt like a kid caught egging the neighbor's house.

"What?" he said. "I was just going to get a beer."

The cat stared at him with huge gold eyes, the beauty mark making her look like a judgmental prom queen. She twitched her tail and sighed as though his presence was a grave inconvenience.

Jonah crossed his arms. "What, you're my mother now? I just want a beer."

"Owl." The cat stayed fixed in front of the fridge.

"Look, I'm not going to let you start dictating my beverage choices," he pointed out, ignoring the fact that he was arguing with a cat. "I happen to like beer. I don't care if wine seems more sophisticated. I know for a fact there are a couple of pumpkin ales left in the fridge, and maybe even an IPA—" Jonah sighed and dragged his hands down his face. "Why am I having this conversation?"

Marilyn sniffed and yawned, then twitched her tail again. It would be easy enough to nudge her out of the way of the fridge, but for some reason Jonah didn't have the heart. He heaved another sigh, then turned and grabbed a lukewarm bottle of iced tea from the pack he'd left sitting on the counter God knows when. He popped the top and took a swig, then yanked open a cupboard door and pulled out a bag of chips.

"You win, cat," he muttered as he headed for the living room. "You've obviously pegged me as a guy who's used to being overruled by a pushy female."

"Owl."

Jonah stalked toward the sofa, his steps accompanied by the tiny tinkle of a bell. Either fairies were stalking him, or Marilyn was on the move, jingling the collar he'd managed to wrestle onto her the night before. He glanced over his shoulder to see her trotting along behind him, disapproval radiating from her like laser beams.

She'd decided he needed to be monitored.

"This okay?" Jonah asked as he dropped the chip bag onto the coffee table.

The cat said nothing, but jumped up onto the arm of the sofa and stared at him. Jonah sat down and grabbed a paperback off the coffee table. He'd dog-eared the page where he'd left off—a habit that used to bug the crap out of Viv—and flipped to the middle of chapter seven. Grabbing a handful of chips, he began to read.

"Owl." The cat head-butted him—*hard*—then jumped onto the coffee table and gave a half-hearted sniff at the potato chip bag. Deeming it unsuitable, she hopped to the opposite arm of the couch, the one closest to Jonah. She curled into the shape of a comma and began to purr against his ribs.

Jonah looked at her, then shook his head. "You're a strange one, cat."

He went back to reading, settling against the couch with the book in one hand. Somehow, his free hand found its way to the cat's slender body, and he began stroking the silky fur. She purred louder and tilted her rump to give him a better angle.

The book had held his interest all week, but for some reason it wasn't cutting it. He'd read the same paragraph three times and still had no idea what it was about. He would have liked to blame the cat for the distraction, but that wasn't it. He couldn't even blame Viv, really, though she was part of it.

He did blame himself, though. For falling back into old patterns in that damn pre-production meeting. For letting his ex get under his skin. For arguing just for the sake of argument, instead of because he gave a shit.

For not being able to keep his mind off Kate and what she might've been wearing under that slim black skirt and her silky blouse the color of caramel. Did she wear sleek satin underthings, or basic white cotton? Black lace thong or conservative bikini panties in nude?

Focus, dipshit, he ordered himself.

He'd just flipped the page in his book when the doorbell rang.

"Owl."

"Yeah, thanks. I got it." Jonah heaved himself off the sofa. He expected to see the UPS woman with some package he'd ordered on Amazon and forgotten about, same way he did every week.

What he didn't expect was Kate. She was standing there on his front porch like he'd conjured her with his thoughts. No longer wearing the skirt and silky blouse, she'd changed into jeans and a blue sweater that looked unbearably soft. Cashmere, maybe, and Jonah realized that if he opened the door instead of standing here staring like an idiot, he might find out for himself.

Kate met his eyes through the floor-to-ceiling side panel window next to the door. She lifted a hand in greeting, but there was something timid in her expression. An uncertainty he hadn't seen before in her face.

He opened the door, half-nervous about why she'd come, half-thrilled-to-fucking-pieces she was here.

"Hey," he said. "Everything okay?"

Kate started to nod, then stopped mid-gesture and shook her head. Her odd coppery eyes glinted under the porch light, and he watched her chest rise and fall as she took a deep breath.

"We need to talk."

CHAPTER SEVEN

Kate saw Jonah hesitate as she stood there on his doorstep, feeling the glare of his porch light beating down on her like a spotlight. She took a deep breath, wondering if she should have come here at all. If she should have kept texting or maybe sent an e-mail.

Then he stepped aside and waved her into his home, and Kate released the breath she hadn't realized she'd been holding.

"Come on in," he said. "I was just helping the cat get settled."

Kate looked at Marilyn, who was standing on the back of a tan leather sofa with her eyebrows arched in silent judgment.

"Hey, kitty," she said, stepping over to stroke the cat's ears. "I'm glad he decided to keep you."

"Me, too," Jonah said, and Kate thought she caught a note of embarrassment in his voice.

"You're her hero."

"Please," he muttered. "I'm her butler."

"Same thing to a cat."

Jonah shoved his hands in his pockets and looked at her, probably wondering what the hell she was doing in his living room. "I'd offer you a beer, but the cat doesn't seem to approve."

"Your cat disapproves of beer?"

"Apparently the cat I acquired to break free from my ex-wife's pet ban is now enforcing my ex's beer ban," he said. "Don't think the irony is lost on me."

Kate laughed, relieved he was still joking with her. That he wasn't as pissed as she knew he had a right to be. "That's okay," Kate said. "I'm not really a beer fan anyway."

"Not a beer fan?" Jonah shook his head in dismay. "What's wrong with you?"

Kate grinned and scratched the cat under the chin. "Just because I happen to think Budweiser tastes like a skunk that's been run over?"

Jonah made a face. "It *does* taste like that. Budweiser? Are you serious?"

"That's the only beer I know of."

"Do you live in a cave? Haven't you had *real* beer? Not Budweiser or Coors some other mass-produced, yellow, fizzy mess. I'm talking craft beer."

"Isn't all beer pretty much the same?"

Jonah shook his head a little sadly, and Kate wondered if this whole conversation was his way of distracting her from what she'd really come to discuss. Wasn't it male habit to shut down any conversation that began with a woman saying, "We need to talk"?

"Don't stereotype!" Viv urged in her brain. *"Making generalizations about the person with whom you're in a relationship is a one-way ticket to conflict."*

But since she wasn't in a relationship with Jonah, and since she was standing here in his living room hearing echoes of his ex-wife's voice in her head, maybe the whole point was moot.

Kate stroked her hand down the cat's back again, soothed by the soft rumble emanating from Marilyn's fluffy body. "Look, I'm sorry about just showing up like this," she said. "I tried texting and calling, but there was no answer, and I really wanted to talk with you privately."

"I shut off my phone," Jonah said. "I wasn't in the mood to debrief with Viv about how today went."

"You think she'd want to debrief?" Kate lifted an eyebrow. "Seems a little presumptuous. I'm guessing she'd be as eager as you were to put today behind her."

Jonah didn't answer. Instead, he picked up his phone off the counter and switched it on. As soon as it powered up, he held it out to her. Kate looked down at the screen, which was lit up with the opening lines of three different text messages.

Jonah, I'm concerned with how . . .
We really need to . . .
I think we should have a conversation about . . .

Jonah drew the phone back. "Just a hunch, but I think she wants to talk about how today went."

Kate swallowed and nodded. "Probably a good guess."

She thought about asking why he didn't just have the conversation and get it over with, but the exhaustion on his face made her think twice about that. Could she really blame the guy for not wanting to follow up a day spent with his ex-wife with an evening spent talking to her on the phone?

"Jonah, I want to apologize," Kate began. "I didn't expect today's session to be quite so—"

"You know, you really should try a *good* beer," he said, "before you write off the whole beverage based on exposure to an inferior product."

"I, uh—"

"Hang on," he said. "I have a really good pumpkin ale from Elysian Brewing. They're based in Seattle."

Kate started to protest, but it was clear this was something that mattered to Jonah. Maybe it had something to do with the beer ban he'd mentioned, and a need to force his way out from under Viv's thumb.

Or maybe her earlier suspicion was right and he just wanted to distract her. Either way, he had a point. She probably hadn't given beer a fair shake.

"Sure," she said. "If you think the cat will allow it."

Marilyn looked up. *"Owl."*

Her expression was one of silent judgment, but she stayed rooted on the back of the sofa.

"You distract the feline police," he said. "I'll make a break for it."

He turned and hustled toward the kitchen, and it took Kate a few seconds to realize she was staring at his ass. He wore jeans that looked worn and soft as flannel, and a blue T-shirt that said *Semper Fi* across the back.

The cat gave a low growl and Kate looked down to see the animal regarding her with a knowing eyebrow lift.

"Sorry," Kate whispered. "I didn't mean to look."

"Owl."

"Oh, come on. Like you haven't admired the view?"

"Are you talking to the cat?" Jonah called from the kitchen.

"We're just discussing the finer points of filmmaking."

"That seems fitting. Maybe she's a reincarnated movie critic."

Kate glanced at the cat, whose expression did suggest an abundance of freely spoken opinion.

"You can't judge a girl by her looks," Kate said.

"It's not just her looks," Jonah called. "It's the attitude. I'm telling you, it's like living with a perpetually disgruntled boss who's critiquing my job performance."

"Maybe you need to step up your game."

"Maybe so." He sauntered back into the living room, carrying two pint glasses filled to the brim with a pumpkin-colored liquid. He handed one to Kate and nodded toward the couch. "Come on. If you're going to make me talk about how today went, let's at least sit down someplace comfortable."

Kate followed him around the sofa, a little surprised by his willingness to return to the subject he clearly didn't want to discuss. But maybe the beer made the difference. She had to admit, holding the pint glass in her hand made her feel casual and relaxed.

Jonah seated himself on the sofa, and Kate hesitated. It would probably be more professional for her to sit on the loveseat, but would that seem weird? Jonah patted the seat beside him.

"You planning to sit, or are you going to stand there lecture style and tell me all the things I did wrong today?"

"You?" Kate dropped onto the sofa, the distance thing forgotten for now. "You didn't do anything wrong. What are you talking about?"

He shrugged and took a sip of his orangey-looking beer. The flicker from the fireplace reflected on his glasses and brought out the amber in his eyes. Kate felt herself getting dizzy and started to blame the beer before remembering she hadn't tasted it yet.

"I know today was awkward, but trust me, that it wasn't your fault," Kate said.

"I'm not sure everyone shares your opinion."

Kate shook her head and rested her glass on the knee of her jeans. "If anything, it's my fault. Clearly the whole situation was more contentious than I expected it to be. That's why I came here. I wanted to apologize for that."

"It was exactly as contentious as *I* expected it to be," Jonah said. "No need to apologize."

He didn't seem angry or bitter about that, but still. Kate felt bad. "Obviously we knew it was going to be awkward to have two ex-spouses working together, but I don't think I realized what a toll it might take on you."

"On me in particular, or are you having this conversation with Viv as well?"

Kate gripped her glass tighter. It hadn't occurred to her to have this conversation with Viv. Only with Jonah. She tried not to read too much into that.

"I'm concerned about both of you," Kate said, deliberately avoiding the question.

"But more about me."

She wasn't sure if it was a question or a statement, but clearly he wasn't going to let the subject lie. "Viv has been on board with this TV program from the start—the planning, the pre-production, the discussions of what it would and wouldn't feel like. You sort of got thrust into it at the last minute."

Jonah grinned. "Here's where Average Joe would make an inane comment about last-minute thrusting being a great way to save a relationship."

"Right." Kate felt a sharp stab of guilt. "I guess that's what I mean. I worry that I pushed you into something you didn't have time to think through. That maybe you agreed to this without considering the challenges of being pushed back into the Average Joe persona when you've been trying to break out of that."

Jonah shifted his glass from one hand to the other, but didn't take a sip. He studied her with an intensity that made her want to look away, but she didn't.

"You're not responsible for my decision, Kate."

She bit her lip. "I can be pretty persuasive."

A ghost of a smile tilted up one corner of his mouth. "I don't doubt that."

"I just—look, I've been thinking about the other night in your bookstore. About what happened."

"What happened?"

His smile was full-on, and she could tell he was teasing her. But if she'd learned nothing else from all these damn self-help books, it was the importance of saying what was on her mind. Not skirting the difficult conversations.

"I kissed you," she said.

"And I kissed back."

"Right. But what if I only kissed you because I was trying to manipulate you into doing the show?"

He looked amused by that notion, which Kate probably should have taken as an insult. She waited for him to respond, but instead he lifted his glass and took a slow sip of his beer. She watched his throat move as he swallowed, and for some reason her mouth began to water. Glancing down at her own beer, she wondered if she should try it. Instead, she set it on the coffee table.

Jonah lowered his glass next to hers and looked at her, eyes glinting with amusement. "You think I was so dazzled by your skillful use of tongue that I signed on the dotted line before my hard-on had gone down?"

"Jesus." His words took her breath away. It was probably the shock value, not the thought of Jonah aroused. Not the thrill of thinking it might have been her who aroused him.

"You're good, don't get me wrong," Jonah said, reading her thoughts. "But I have a little more self-control than that. The best thing I took away from my divorce is the ability to decide for myself what I want."

He lifted the beer in a mock toast, then took a sip. Kate glanced at Marilyn, who was still parked on the back of the sofa. The cat's expression was one of disapproval, but the fact that she was here in the first place underscored Jonah's words. The man could make his own decisions, so maybe Kate hadn't pressured him into the show.

She looked back at Jonah, letting her gaze drop to his mouth. She shivered as her brain filled with memories of what it felt like to kiss him. What it felt like to have his hands in her hair, his body molded against hers. With a shaky breath, she lifted her gaze to meet his. "It doesn't bother you to think I might have been trying to manipulate you?"

"By kissing me?"

She nodded. "Kissing you and rubbing myself against you and—"
The words made her dizzy, so she decided to stop there.

"*Were* you trying to manipulate me?" He sounded more charmed
than annoyed.

She hesitated, then glanced down at the beer. "I don't think so, but
I can't say for sure. How self-aware is anyone, really, about why they do
certain things?"

"Anyone ever tell you that you overthink things?"

"All. The. Time." She meant for her tone to convey the gravity of
the situation, but caught herself starting to smile. Okay, so this was a
little absurd. She took a breath and met his eyes again. "I just don't want
you to blame me. If things go wrong, I mean."

"Kate."

"Yes?"

"I solemnly swear not to blame you—or your delectable lips—
when things go wrong."

Her breath caught on *delectable*.

Her brain caught on his choice of *when* over *if*.

The rest of her body was humming like she'd swallowed a shot of
whiskey. She glanced at the beer glass on the coffee table and wondered
if she'd absorbed some through her fingertips.

"Okay," she said, though she couldn't recall if she was agreeing to
something or acknowledging what he'd said. What had he said again?
The living room felt hot, and she wasn't sure if it was the fireplace or
another heat source.

"Tell you what," Jonah said. "How about we balance things out?"

Kate swung her gaze back to his. "How do you mean?"

"Well, since you seem so concerned about your own culpability and
your intentions in kissing me, it only seems fair that I should kiss you
now." He smiled. "Just to set things right."

Heat flooded her face. She tried to swallow but discovered she couldn't. "I—I'm not sure that's a good idea."

She *knew* it wasn't a good idea. So why was she leaning closer?

She had every intention of standing up then. Putting some distance between her body and Jonah's, maybe even leaving. It was late, and she'd said what she'd come to say. She really should go.

But somehow she found herself leaning in, pressing her palms to his chest, breathing in the woodsy scent of him as she tilted her head back and pressed her lips to—

"Nope." Jonah drew back, and Kate started to yank her hands off his chest. But Jonah was quick, catching her wrists to pin her palms in place.

"Not like that." He grinned. "What part of '*I* should kiss *you*' didn't make sense?"

Kate swallowed. "The part where we both agreed we shouldn't kiss at all."

"Right, that part." Jonah smiled again. "And that's totally legit. Right after this kiss."

Then his lips were on hers. Any thought of leaving vanished the instant his hand slid around her waist to settle in the small of her back. He pulled her against him, kissing hard and deep as Kate responded in kind.

She knew in theory it shouldn't matter who kissed first when both parties were willing, but Jonah was right. There was something different about this. Maybe it was the way he angled his mouth against hers, the way he tasted like pumpkin spice.

Maybe it was his hand in her hair, the way he pulled her so tight against him that her body ached to slide onto his lap.

Maybe it was the thrill of knowing they shouldn't be doing this.

Or maybe it was something else entirely, the knowledge that they seemed incapable of keeping their hands off each other no matter how often they agreed it would be best.

Jonah broke the kiss first, but he didn't let go of her. With his fingers still in her hair, he held her gaze with his. "Okay then."

Kate took a shaky breath. "So we're done with that."

Jonah nodded. "I think we proved our point."

"Which was?" Kate's voice was high and tight, and she barely recognized it as her own.

"I forget." Jonah let go of her then and reached for his beer. He picked it up and took a drink, then looked at her.

"So we got that out of our systems then."

Kate stared at him, her body still buzzing where he'd touched her. She looked at her own glass, then picked it up. It was still cold, and had a soft froth of white across the top. She took a big gulp, then sputtered.

"Easy there, cowgirl!" Jonah grabbed the glass out of her hand while Kate coughed and gasped.

When her eyes stopped watering, she looked at him. "That was—not good."

"You're supposed to sip craft beer," he said. "Not gulp like it's water. Try again."

He put the glass back in her hand, and Kate thought about resisting. But she tasted hints of graham cracker and nutmeg and allspice, and wasn't sure if that was the beer or the kiss. Either way, she wanted more.

She wrapped her fingers around the glass and lifted it to her mouth. This time, she took a moment to breathe it in.

"It smells really good," she admitted. "Like pie and cream soda."

"Olfactory senses are really important when it comes to tasting beer," he said. "Well, tasting anything, really, but we're talking about beer here."

Kate sniffed again. It really was nice. "I don't think I've ever sniffed any drink that wasn't wine."

"Then you've been missing out. There's a lot of sensory response that takes place in the zone where smell and taste meet."

Kate laughed and sniffed again. "Wow. And to think I assumed you just chugged it at a tailgate party."

"Perish the thought."

She tilted the glass and took a tentative sip. Not bad. Not bad at all. She swallowed and sipped again.

"Take your time," Jonah said. "Experiment with different ways of moving it over your tongue and swallowing."

Kate grinned. "I can't believe you're instructing me like I've never consumed liquid before."

"Not this kind of liquid," he said. "Different parts of the tongue taste different things—salty, sweet, sour, bitter, umami. You could spend hours experiencing the flavors in totally different ways."

Kate took one more sip and set the glass down. She'd barely made a dent in the contents of it, but she felt an odd sense of accomplishment. "That wasn't bad at all. It was actually kind of nice."

Jonah smiled at her. "That's what I like about you." He said it like he was just realizing something important.

"What do you mean?"

"On the surface you seem like someone who'd be set in her ways," he said. "Who wouldn't want to try new things. But you're actually one of the most experimental people I've met."

There was a warmth in Kate's belly that might have been the beer, but she didn't think so. "That might be one of the nicest things anyone's ever said to me."

It was true. So much better than if he'd told her she had beautiful eyes or nice hair. What was it about being seen by someone—really seen—that felt like such a gift?

She picked up her glass again and took another swallow. Something about it reminded her of when her father used to pick her up from school and take her out for a butterscotch malt. The faint nuttiness, the cool sweetness on the back of her tongue.

She closed her eyes and took another sip, breathing in notes of creamy caramel and maybe cinnamon buns. Balancing the glass on her knee, she swallowed and felt the bubbles tickle her throat on the way down.

Her eyes were still closed when his lips brushed hers again.

This time, the kiss was soft. She didn't open her eyes. Just slid her free hand into his hair and kissed him back, savoring the taste of cloves and cinnamon and something forbidden.

When she opened her eyes, his amber-green ones were locked with hers. He hadn't drawn back yet, but there was a finality in his expression.

"I had to do that," he murmured. "Just one last time."

"I'm glad."

"But that's really it," he said. "We have to stop now."

Kate nodded and took another sip of beer. "Okay," she said, and lifted her glass again.

◆　◆　◆

Jonah half expected Kate to leave right after the second kiss. He wouldn't blame her. What the hell was he thinking, planting one on her like that when they'd already agreed that was a horrible idea?

Maybe she was sticking around for the beer.

That seemed unlikely, since she wasn't exactly chugging it. But she did sip it slowly as she answered all of his questions about the television show. The ones he hadn't thought to ask before.

"It's called an airable pilot," Kate explained, shifting a little on the sofa. "All the color correction and sound mixing will be up to broadcast standards. That way, if the network says go, we're ready to roll."

"So they'd put it on the air just like that?"

"More or less. Amy's making sure all our ducks are in a row as far as releases and legal clearances. We've got a good head start already on the paperwork side of things."

"So what happens after they air it?"

"We cross our fingers for a series order from the network." Kate shifted again, bumping his knee with hers. Jonah didn't think it was on purpose, but part of him wished it was. "We're hoping for fourteen episodes to start."

"Fourteen?" He stroked a hand down Marilyn's back, glancing over to see the cat looked as surprised as he felt. "I can't believe you have that many victims lined up."

"Victims?"

"Contestants—subjects—what are we calling the people whose relationships we're supposed to fix?"

"Oh—I'm not sure yet. Viv wants to call them *patients*, but the network guys think that's too clinical."

"It sounds like we're treating them for venereal disease."

Kate laughed. "Exactly. I think for now it's safe to say *couples*. And yes, casting has about four dozen of them pre-screened and ready to go in case we do get picked up."

Jonah leaned back against the sofa and took another sip of beer. His glass was almost empty, but he didn't want to leave this spot, this conversation, to get up and grab a refill.

"What do you think the odds are?" he asked.

"That the network will pick us up?"

Jonah nodded, and Kate tipped her head to the side, considering. "Above average," she said. "Obviously we don't even have a pilot yet, but I can see it in my head."

"And how is it?"

She grinned. "Very good. Excellent. I have a pretty nice track record."

"I'm glad."

Jonah glanced down at his glass, not sure he was telling her the truth. Did he want the show to get picked up? He thought so, but his reasons for it had nothing to do with helping troubled couples. They were selfish reasons. Or maybe *selfish* wasn't the right word. He was doing it for Jossy, but wasn't that still selfish?

Or maybe he was trying to make up for the selfishness in the first place. That seemed like a better story.

"Can I ask you something?" Kate said.

Jonah looked up. "Fire away."

"Why did you say yes? If it wasn't my kissing skills, I mean?"

She gave him a small smile, but there was something serious in her eyes. Something that told him she knew there was more to his story than he'd let on so far.

Jonah hesitated. "I want to help my sister."

"Ah. That makes sense." Understanding flashed in her eyes. "The one with the animal shelter?"

"Exactly."

"That's noble of you."

He thought about dispelling that idea. Just opening his mouth and letting the whole story come spilling out. But he bit back the words and gave a small shrug. "Not really. It's family. You help each other out when you're family."

"Your father was killed in the line of duty?"

He must have looked alarmed, because Kate reached out and touched his arm. "I'm sorry, I didn't mean to get too personal. Viv mentioned it in that first book. I wondered if maybe that had something to do with why you're protective of your sister."

Jonah nodded and studied her face. There was nothing there to suggest she knew the rest of the story. Even so, he wondered. Maybe Viv had said something.

But no. Kate's expression wasn't calculating. It wasn't pitying. It was sincere. That much he could tell.

She lifted her glass and drained the last few drops of pale-orange liquid. Then she rested the glass on her knee. "Just be careful, Jonah. You don't want to sell your soul to be someone else's savior."

Something in those words was familiar. He thumbed fast through the Rolodex in his brain, trying to place them.

"Viv wrote that," Kate said, reading his mind. "It's a line from *But Not Broken*. I think it was in chapter twelve or thirteen, right after she leaves the abusive relationship."

"Right, of course." His gut churned. "I remember now."

Kate looked down at her glass. "I should probably go."

She stood up before he could say anything else, and Jonah wondered what she'd seen in his face just then. Had something tipped her off that her words had touched a nerve? Or had he kept his expression as impassive as he'd hoped to?

He didn't have time to ask. She'd already carried her glass to the kitchen. He could hear her rinsing it out in the sink. Then she walked back into the living room and stood behind the sofa, stroking a hand down Marilyn's back.

"I'm really happy to be working with you, Jonah," she said. "Even if we got sort of a weird start."

"I'm happy to be working with you, too." That was true, even if he wasn't entirely sure how he felt about the show itself.

"I think this series is going to touch a lot of people."

He nodded, ignoring the voices in his head that told him the only thing he really wanted at the moment was to touch her. That wasn't going to happen. Her body language was making that perfectly clear, even if they hadn't already agreed there would be no more kissing.

Jonah set his empty glass down and stood up. "I'm glad you came by. I definitely feel better about the show. About what happens next."

Kate began walking toward the door, and Jonah fell into step beside her while something inside him screamed at her not to go. At the threshold of the door, she turned and looked at him.

"You think you'll feel ready to start shooting in a couple days?"

"Ready as I'll ever be."

"Good. Well, then." She took a deep breath, and Jonah waited for her to say something else. To tell him she felt the same way he did, even though he had no idea how either of them would put that into words.

"Good night, Jonah."

"Good night."

There was an air of finality in the word. An echo of goodbye, even though they'd be working together. Even though they'd be seeing each other every day for the rest of the foreseeable future.

But they wouldn't be kissing again. They'd both made that clear.

"See you Wednesday at ten," she said. "At Viv's place."

"Viv's place," he repeated as a tight ball formed in his chest.

CHAPTER EIGHT

When Jonah pulled into Viv's driveway for the first day of filming, he was right on time. It went against his inner caveman's desire to piss her off by showing up late, which must mean he was maturing. That he was meeting his goal of being his own man instead of basing his actions around Viv's expectations.

The fact that you're even thinking like this means you've got a long way to go.

Jonah sighed as he made his way up the walk. He didn't know why being around her made him feel like a surly teenager. She'd been nothing but cordial. Well, cordial with a side of nagging bossiness, judging from the eight billion text messages she'd sent over the past few days.

"Hello, Jonah," his ex-wife said as she greeted him at the door wearing black leggings and some sort of flowy white shirt. Her feet were bare, of course, and her smile was guarded but genuine. That was something. She'd also called him Jonah instead of Joe, which he appreciated.

"Hey, there." He stepped over the threshold as she waved him inside and then shut the door behind him. "Sorry I didn't get back to you. I needed a little time to decompress."

There. That was good. An apology. And he meant it, too, even if it wasn't the whole story.

He couldn't see her face as she led the way to the parlor, but her voice seemed calm and casual. "Don't mention it," she said. "We have a little time to get on the same page before the shooting begins this afternoon."

"Is the crew here yet?"

"The camera guys are doing something in my study—setting up lights and checking the sound. I forget what they called it."

"And what about—" He started to say her name but stopped himself, not wanting to sound too eager. "What about the studio people?"

Viv turned in the doorway of the parlor and gave him a thoughtful look. Jonah ordered himself not to blink, not to let his eyes show even the faintest flicker of interest.

"Kate and Amy will be here in about thirty minutes," Viv said. "They had some last-minute emergency meeting with the casting department. Something about a disagreement with the network people over which patients we should select for the pilot."

He couldn't help noticing she'd used the word *patients*, despite Kate's mention that the network had already nixed the word. He also noticed a pang of disappointment in his chest at the news Kate wasn't already here.

It has nothing to do with wanting to see Kate, he assured himself. *Just the annoyance of having to make conversation alone with Viv for half an hour.*

He looked away from Viv and surveyed the room, admiring the black-and-white color scheme with splashes of color here and there. An orange chair, a cobalt vase, a grass-green throw rug at the threshold of the door that led to the other end of the hall.

"I like what you've done with this place," he said. "It looks like you."

"Thank you."

Viv beamed, and Jonah wondered if she'd taken it as a commentary on her physical appearance. The space was beautiful, of course, though that's not how he'd meant it. It was also tidy, expensive, and set up to be the perfect TV backdrop.

But there was no point in saying any of that, so Jonah shoved his hands in his pockets and waited.

"Can I get you something to drink? Herbal tea or some lemon water?"

"Any chance you have a pot of coffee?"

"I gave up coffee almost a year ago," she said with a breezy wave of one hand. "Too many toxins."

"Toxins are delicious."

"Right." Viv frowned. "I suppose I can check to see if there's some stashed in the pantry somewhere."

"That's okay. I'm good." He'd had plenty of coffee already—he just wanted something to do with his hands.

He went back to surveying the room. Probably ought to sit down and get comfortable. He started to move toward the chair he'd sat in the last time he'd been here, then stopped. Would she read something into the notion that he had a favorite chair at her place? He moved toward the sofa instead. Halfway to sitting, he wondered if he should have picked the loveseat instead. Would Viv notice that he'd opted to plant his butt where Kate had sat before?

Way to overthink things, Jonah. You're turning into Kate.

He grunted and sat down on the sofa, annoyed with himself. This was why he hated spending time with Viv. Every move was up for analysis. He could pass gas and spend the next two hours knowing she was interpreting it as a subconscious rejection of social norms and Viv's own hospitality. Or maybe a reflection on his upbringing or dietary choices.

The possibilities were endless.

Viv folded herself into the club chair he'd chosen last time, and poured two glasses of water. Jonah reached out and grabbed two coasters, setting one in front of each of them. Good, this was good. They were getting along nicely.

Viv set a glass of water in front of him, then took a sip from her own. She studied him over the rim, and Jonah fought the urge to look away.

"I'm actually glad we have a few minutes alone, Jonah."

"Oh?"

"Right." Viv set her glass down. "I know things were a little tense at the meeting, but I want you to know how grateful I am that you chose to do the show. You didn't have to, of course."

He shrugged. "It's fine." He started to add some offhanded quip about the money being good, but stopped himself. Hadn't Kate said the budget numbers were confidential? He wondered what Viv's agreement was with the network. The numbers he'd seen had only reflected his own salary. How much more were they paying Viv? She was the big draw, while he was the last-minute addition.

He hoped she was being paid well. Okay, most of him hoped so. This was her gig, after all. He was just the comic relief. Then again, he did have experience. He didn't have the psychology degree, but he hoped he'd have a chance to add more than dick jokes to the lineup for the show.

Viv cleared her throat. "I know you're a little camera shy—"

"I'm not camera shy," he interrupted. "Just not a fan of that kind of permanency. Something that lives on forever on the Internet or TV reruns."

"That's right." Viv pressed her lips together and gave a serene little smile. "Commitment was never really your forte."

Something flared in his chest. "Seriously? You're the one who wanted the divorce."

"Honestly, Jonah. If I hadn't proposed to you—"

"Like a modern, empowered woman taking charge of her own life," he snapped. "You wrote a whole chapter about it in your book."

Viv pressed her lips together. "You can't look me in the eye and tell me you *wanted* to get married."

"I can look you in the eye and tell you I didn't *want* to get divorced," he shot back. "That was your idea, babe."

"Based on the amount of emotional neglect and—"

"Wait a minute." Jonah shook his head as a realization dawned. "Are you baiting me?"

Viv blinked. "What do you mean?" Her expression was one of calculated innocence, but Jonah knew better. He'd seen that look before.

"You're trying to rile me up," he said.

"I don't know what you're talking about." She glanced down at her water glass, spinning it around in her hand.

"Pissing me off on purpose so I'll be ready for the camera," he said. "The emotional equivalent of a fluffer on a porn set."

She laughed and did her breezy hand wave again, dismissing the accusation and apparently, the whole conversation. God, she was good. She had her Average Joe sound bite and the cameras weren't even rolling yet.

"Anyway, I do hope you'll be able to act natural once the cameras are rolling," she said. "Some people aren't comfortable around them."

Jonah only half heard her, still stuck on what she'd said about commitment and how he hadn't wanted to get married. Was that true?

"I adopted a cat," he blurted, then felt like an idiot.

Viv stopped laughing and looked intrigued. "Really?"

"Yeah. Her name's Marilyn. Marilyn of the Judgmental Eyebrows."

"That sounds—interesting."

"She came from Jossy's rescue center."

Viv's expression softened into one Jossy once dubbed "serene healer," which was always said with a snide tone. She'd never said it to Viv's face, and Jonah had always felt a little bad using the phrase himself.

"How *is* Josslyn doing?" Viv asked as she touched a hand to her chest.

"She's fine. Sends her regards."

Not entirely true, unless "regards" could be expressed with a middle finger. But sharing that would be unhelpful, so Jonah picked up his glass of water and took a sip.

His brain flashed back to a conversation with his sister not long after he and Viv had gotten married.

"I don't like how she treats people," Jossy had complained when he'd demanded to know why his sister had turned down every dinner invitation for the last six months.

"She's a therapist," Jonah had tried to point out, feeling defensive of his new wife. "She treats people with kindness and compassion, and yeah—sometimes a little tough love."

"You forgot the condescension," Jossy had muttered. "Which is odd, since she reserves an extra dose of it for you."

Jonah set his water glass down harder than he meant to, annoyed by the memory. Maybe his sister had had a point. Was that any reason to feel irritated now? He was clear of Viv, divorced and free as a bird, removed from the scene of his own discontent.

Okay, so not entirely. How would Jossy feel if she knew the reason he'd agreed to do this stupid TV show? That his whole plan was to help *her*, his baby sister, the one he should have helped a long time ago?

She'd be mad as hell.

"I have to say, I'm a little surprised you agreed so quickly," Viv said, jarring Jonah back to the conversation. "Though I suppose Kate's a pretty talented persuader."

She watched his face and waited, and Jonah recognized the question in her eyes. He sure as fuck wasn't going to answer it.

"She said you told her I'd be at Alki Park the other day," he said, not bothering to mention the other two times he'd seen Kate alone. "That you sent her there to talk to me."

"I wouldn't say I sent her there, exactly." Viv sipped her own water. "I did suggest to her that you might be more open to persuasion from someone besides me." She smiled and leaned forward just a little. "I also might have suggested she undo a button or two on her blouse."

Jonah gripped his water glass tighter. "She wasn't wearing a blouse with buttons."

"Oh, so you noticed?"

Jonah wanted to hurl his glass at the wall, but he settled for draining the contents and refilling it. Viv's, too, since he was a goddamn gentleman. He sat back on the sofa and wondered how much longer he had to make conversation.

"Did I tell you how Kate persuaded me to do the show?" Viv asked.

"Did it involve undoing buttons? Because I've gotta say, I think girl-on-girl stuff would resonate well with cable TV viewers."

Viv ignored him and slid her silky ponytail from one shoulder to the other, then tucked her bare feet up onto the chair.

"She wrote me the most amazing fan letter," Viv said. "Truly, I've never seen anything like it."

Jonah thought of the passion in Kate's eyes when she'd told him about the concept for the show. About the heartfelt explanations she'd given over pizza at the Cat Café. "I can see that," he said.

"She didn't come right out with her request at first," Viv said. "But she explained her job and asked if she could fly me out to LA for an all-expenses-paid trip. Said she had something she wanted to talk to me about. And get this—the hotel where she set me up was the same one I talked about in *But Not Broken*. The scene where I flew out and met with the shaman who—"

"Right, I remember."

"Of course you do. Anyway, the whole trip was like that. Kate picking up on little details—my favorite wine, a significant quotation, having hydrangeas on the table at dinner because she knows I love them—all the little things that showed she was a serious student of my work and not just a fan."

Viv had the good grace to blush at that, and Jonah wondered if she'd been working on sounding less pretentious. She might have her faults, but Viv was pretty good at identifying her own weaknesses and looking for ways to improve.

He took another sip of water and wondered if he was supposed to add to this conversation or just let Viv talk.

"Anyway," she continued, "when it came time for her to do the real pitch, Kate pulled out all the stops. Every persuasive technique she used, every communication strategy—it was straight out of my books. It's like she was not only making her case for why I should do the show, but why I should pick *her* to produce it."

"That must have been flattering."

"Yes. Well. That's Kate for you. Knows exactly what buttons to push to make things happen. I admire her tremendously for that."

Jonah nodded, searching his ex-wife's face for a bigger sign of that admiration. It was there, of course. But so was something else. Something Jonah couldn't quite put a finger on.

"Oh!" Viv clapped her hands together and stood up. "I almost forgot—I bought some of those sourdough scones you used to love so much. The ones we used to eat with the honey butter? They're staying warm in the oven right now. Let me go grab those."

She bustled out before Jonah could argue that he wasn't in the mood for scones. That he wasn't entirely sure what had just happened in that conversation, but he knew he probably shouldn't let his guard down. Not with Viv, not with anyone, really.

He glanced at his watch and wondered how much longer he had to wait before Kate would arrive. She'd texted this morning when he was in the shower, and Jonah had read the message while standing naked on the bathmat dripping water onto the screen.

Don't stress about what to wear today, she'd written, even though Jonah had been doing no such thing. Jeans and a T-shirt are fine. Or long-sleeved flannel. Or solid. Just no busy prints.

Jonah had smiled to himself and typed a response before winding a towel around his waist. You mean I'm not required to be shirtless like I am when I walk dogs?

There had been a long pause, and Jonah wondered if he'd crossed a line. When her response popped up, he'd laughed out loud.

LOL! Camera crew has been discussing what you'd look like shirtless and whether you'd do it for TV. They didn't believe me when I said I witnessed it firsthand. Kinda wish I'd nabbed a photo of you at the park.

He'd hesitated, not wanting to read too much into that. But hell, it wasn't like he didn't parade around shirtless all the time. He'd aimed his phone camera at the mirror, careful not to shoot anything but his torso. Fired off a couple of shots, then glanced at the screen, making sure he hadn't gone too low or captured his messy bathroom counter.

Then he'd pulled up his text exchange with Kate, attached an image, and hit "Send" before he had a chance to change his mind.

Holy shit!!! Kate had texted back less than two seconds later. You just made my morning.

Before Jonah could respond, she followed up with another message.

I meant that in a purely professional way. OMG. The camera crew will be delighted. That's assuming it's okay to share?

Share away, he'd written back, feeling a weird mixture of pride, embarrassment, and longing.

"Here we go!" Viv swept back into the room and presented the scones with a dramatic flourish. She set down a small stack of plates in varying hues of yellow and robin's-egg blue, along with a small white bowl of honey butter with a tiny spoon in it.

"Thanks," Jonah mumbled as he helped himself to a scone. He felt awkward and out of sorts. Part of him wanted to be guarded about any show of kindness from his ex-wife. Hadn't that always come with a price before?

But part of him—the part he really wanted to embrace—felt like a jerk for not giving her the benefit of the doubt. They'd be working together, after all. Maybe he should make more of an effort to mend fences.

He slathered butter on his scone and tried to come up with a suitable olive branch. "Thanks for being gracious about this," he said. "I don't mean the scones." He cleared his throat and looked at her, noticing she wore a guarded expression. "I know it wasn't your idea to have me as part of the show. I know deep down, it probably pisses you off that the network insisted on dragging me into this."

There was a flicker of something in her eyes. He watched in that split second she wavered between denying any angst and acknowledging that yeah, she was mad as fuck.

She settled for a tight nod. "Thank you." She lifted her water glass. "Here's to making the best of things, even when they don't work out the way we expected."

"Cheers to that," Jonah agreed.

It was probably the last time they'd be agreeing on much for a while. If the network got what they wanted, Viv and Jonah would be at each other's throats for the foreseeable future. It's how they seemed to want this show to go.

Across the table, Viv picked up a scone and began the delicate process of slathering it with honey butter. "Anything you want to discuss before all the network people start showing up?" she asked. "I don't imagine we'll have much time after this for private conversation."

She probably meant the show. About casting or protocol or what sort of boundaries they wanted to set.

But what came out of his mouth had nothing to do with the show. "Why did you give up?"

Viv's mouth opened and closed, then opened again. It was clear she hadn't expected the question. Hell, Jonah was surprised by it himself.

"On our marriage, you mean?"

Jonah he gave a tight nod, then took a bite of his scone. He chewed for a long time, trying to formulate his next words a little better than he'd formed the question. "I'm not asking because I'm bitter or pissed off or because I'm sitting over here pining for you like some sort of love-sick fuck," he said. "I think it's pretty clear we're both over each other."

"Certainly."

Was that sarcasm in her voice? Jonah refused to take the bait, so Viv took a deep breath and set down her scone.

"We had a great four years together," she said. "Five, if you count the year before we married. Truly, I thought we'd stay together forever. Eventually, though—"

"You lost feelings for me?"

There was a hard edge to the question, and Jonah hoped she heard it the right way. Not as an accusation, but as a shared joke.

"In our case, it wasn't code for *I'm boning someone else*, as you so eloquently put it." Viv looked down at her scone. "I hope you know that."

"I do."

She looked up at him, and the earnestness in her expression made his chest feel tight. "I'm not fucking with you," he said. "I believe you when you say there wasn't anyone else."

"Thank you."

"But can you tell me what it was?"

She was quiet a long time, and Jonah wondered why he'd never had the balls to press for answers before. Sure, they'd talked about it. When she'd asked for the divorce, she'd buried him in piles of psych-sounding words about the evolution of feelings and the inherent challenges of cohabitation.

But he'd never flat-out asked *why*.

"I guess when you get married for such a fragile reason, there's always a risk."

"When you get married for sex?"

The corner of her mouth tipped up just a little, but she didn't smile. "Love," she said. "I did love you, of course. But we humans have so little control over who we fall in love with in the first place. That also makes us powerless against falling *out* of love." She bit her lip. "Obviously you can work at it. That's what I teach people, of course."

"Of course," he murmured, though he couldn't help noticing she'd framed it as an afterthought.

"But there's only so much you can force. The human heart is a fickle thing. It stands to reason that a love-based marriage is just as fickle."

He started to argue. To insist there were plenty of strategies for staying in love. Plenty of books said how to do it—hell, Viv's own books went on about it endlessly.

But the truth was, he didn't disagree. Not completely, anyway.

Which was a pretty damn good reason he planned to avoid the whole love-and-marriage mess in the future.

Jonah picked up his scone and took a bite. It was probably time to end this line of conversation. Hell, he probably shouldn't have brought it up in the first place. It was just that he'd never gotten answers before.

Maybe this show was his ticket to closure and forgiveness.

"So are we good now?" Viv asked.

Her voice was oddly small, and Jonah felt a stab of guilt followed by a flicker of anger, which just pissed him off. At what point did exes stop having the power to jerk your emotions around like a paddleball?

"We're good," he said, and took another bite of scone.

They didn't say anything for several minutes, both feigning intense interest in their pastries. When Viv's voice broke the silence, Jonah nearly jumped off the couch.

"Here they are!"

She bounded out of her chair like it was on fire, dusting nonexistent scone crumbs off her shirt.

Jonah glanced toward the front window and watched a nondescript sedan pull into Viv's circular driveway. He looked at Kate behind the wheel, her dark hair slicked back from her face and held tight at the nape of her neck with a silver clasp. Her fingers were long and graceful on the steering wheel, and he remembered what they'd felt like tunneling through his hair.

His heart did a stupid little shiver in the center of his chest, and he hoped to God Viv wasn't looking at him. He turned away, annoyed with himself, and took a fierce bite of scone.

◆　◆　◆

Kate walked into the makeshift hair-and-makeup studio and glanced at the clock on the wall. They had fifteen minutes before the crew would start to get cranky, and Elena still had half of her head covered with hot rollers.

Ginger, the hair and makeup artist, glanced at Kate and gave a nervous smile. "Sorry. I know we're running behind, but we had a little flatiron mishap. Don't ask."

"I won't," Kate assured her, though she did sort of wonder. "You're not making her look dramatically different from yesterday, are you?"

"Relax. She'll still look like the same person from the B-roll footage. Just a little glammed up for the in-studio shots, that's all."

Lead cameraman Pete Waller lumbered into the room, looking like a kindly grizzly bear in a khaki vest. "Ladies." He set a cardboard drink holder on the dressing table and nodded to Kate. "Hot chocolate," he said. "Figured I'd grab some for you before the lugheads on my crew started filling their thermoses."

"You're a lifesaver." Kate picked up a paper cup and peeled back the lid to blow inside. "Oh my God, I love you. There's whipped cream and cinnamon."

Pete nodded, then turned to look at Elena in the mirror. Scratching his beard, he studied her with a thoughtful expression. "When you and your husband go out to the sunroom to talk about how the day went, we're gonna have cameras stashed all over," he said. "Just act natural and have a normal conversation. But don't say anything you wouldn't want on TV."

Elena nodded and gave him a nervous smile. "Thank you."

Pete grunted and walked out of the room. Kate took a sip of cocoa, grateful they'd landed him for this show. He'd worked on some of the most scandalous reality TV programs in the business, but there were lines he wouldn't cross. Filming people without their knowledge was one of them, not even when participants had signed ridiculously broad agreements like the ones required for this show.

"Kate! There you are!"

She turned to see Amy hustling into the room, her blond curls a bit more disheveled than normal. "Craft services wants to know if they can set up lunch in the kitchen or if we need to shoot in there."

"That's fine, we're not doing the cooking sequence until late afternoon or maybe tomorrow." She glanced at her watch again as her nerves jittered in time with the second hand. "Are Viv and Jonah ready to go?"

"Jonah's been sitting in the parlor reading for at least an hour," she said. "I think Viv's meditating or something."

"She'd better not mess up her hair," Ginger muttered as she unfurled a hot roller from Elena's head and finger-combed the fresh waves.

"Okay." Kate took a deep breath, tamping down the butterflies that threatened to surge up her throat. "Did the sound guys fix whatever was wrong with that boom mike?"

"No, but they had a spare. Oh! And we got Sam to cry in his side interview, so that's golden."

Kate stole a nervous glance at Sam's wife. Elena seemed unperturbed as Ginger unfastened another roller from her hair. She caught Kate's eye in the mirror and nodded. "Don't worry. I can cry on command, too."

"Right." Kate took another breath. "It's important to just be yourself, okay? Let the emotions flow, even if they're not pretty. Authenticity is key here."

"The mascara's bulletproof," Ginger added helpfully. "Just try not to rub your eyes too much."

Gripping her cocoa in one hand, Kate edged toward the door. "Will you excuse us a moment?"

She pushed her way into the hall and Amy followed, pulling the door closed behind her. Kate reached down and switched off her two-way radio, then waited for Amy to do the same.

"How does he seem?" Kate whispered.

Amy shrugged. "He's good. Got a little bristly when the props girl suggested he put down the Ann Patchett novel and read *Sports Illustrated* instead, but overall I think he's fine."

Kate felt a flush of relief, both that Jonah seemed fine and that Amy hadn't forced her to spell out who "he" was. Then again, maybe that wasn't a good thing. Was it that transparent Jonah was on her mind?

"How's Viv?" Kate asked.

"Good. Centered, according to her. She was studying a bunch of notecards when I saw her last. I reemphasized the importance of making sure this sounds unscripted."

"She's good at that," Kate said. "Remember her last appearance on *Oprah*?"

"She was adorable."

"Exactly. Just remind her to bring more of that."

Kate glanced at her watch again and tried not to feel nervous. Today would be their first time shooting with all four players—Viv, Jonah, and the couple they were tasked with helping.

"How's his cat?"

Kate looked up to see Amy giving her a tiny smirk. It wasn't a judgmental one, so at least there was that.

But Kate couldn't afford to have her going doing that path. She shrugged and gave her best look of nonchalance. "Beats me. I haven't seen Jonah outside work since I went over and talked to him right after the pre-production meeting."

Technically, that was true. But that didn't mean they hadn't texted each other regularly. Sometimes it was all business, sometimes it was flirty, but it definitely toed the line between professional contact and something more.

Last night had been more of the same.

I e-mailed you a new draft of the contract, Kate had texted around 10:00 p.m. as the tub was filling in her hotel bathroom. Have your attorney look at it if you like, but we need signatures by Friday. Also, there's been a venue change for next Wednesday's shoot. I'll forward the info.

She'd finished pouring bubble bath into the tub before climbing in, resting her phone on the edge with a silent prayer of thanks for the invention of the waterproof phone case. She hadn't expected Jonah to text back, but felt a tiny shiver of pleasure at the new message chime a few seconds later.

Got it. Thx.

Was it wrong to feel disappointed by the brevity? Yes, of course. This was business. They were business colleagues, and they couldn't afford to be chatty or too friendly.

Even so, excitement fluttered in her belly when the phone buzzed again.

Tell me the truth: Do you ever stop working?

Kate smiled to herself, then texted back.

I'm not working now. I'm actually relaxing.

There was a brief pause, then a bubble to indicate he was texting back. An image popped up on screen, and Kate clicked to see what it was.

Marilyn, the judgey-eyebrow cat, does not believe you.

Kate laughed at the cutesy meme of his cat, her feline features arranged in a look of perfect skepticism. She stared at the photo a few more seconds, then typed a response.

I promise I am. Look.

She hit the icon for her camera, then aimed it at the beer bottle perched on the edge of the tub. She turned it a little to the side, angling the camera so she could get the words *Jamaican Me Pumpkin* and *10 Barrel Brewing* in the photo, along with a froth of bubbles visible on the edge of the tub.

The second she hit "Send," she wondered if she should have done it. Would it seem too flirtatious? Had she meant it to be?

Of course not, she reassured herself. *You're just making a friendly connection with a cast member. It's perfectly innocent.*

Which she knew wasn't true. Knew she'd deliberately slipped one bare leg up through the suds, lending a backdrop of naked flesh to her bathtub beer pic.

But the beer was in the foreground. Maybe that's all he'd notice.

That looks amazing, Jonah texted back, and Kate had smiled to herself. See? They could do this. Chat about beer like good friends.

Two seconds later, he'd texted again.

The beer looks good, too.

Okay, so he was flirting. She should have put a stop to it. But instead, she'd just lain there in the tub, feeling warm and languorous while soap suds fizzed around her.

"What are you smiling about?"

Amy's question jolted Kate back to the hallway, where they waited for Elena to emerge from hair and makeup. Kate clawed her way through the recesses of her brain for something that wouldn't give away her illicit memories.

"This hot chocolate," she said, lifting the paper cup Pete had given her. "It's—uh—really good."

"It must be good if it's giving you that I-just-had-a-dirty-thought look."

"There's whipped cream."

"Okay."

Amy tucked a blond curl behind her hair and gave Kate a knowing look, but she didn't say anything else. Not for a moment, anyway. Then her eyes darted to something just over Kate's shoulder, and her expression shifted to a smirk.

"Hey, Jonah!" Amy called, and Kate's heart started to gallop.

She kept her eyes on Amy, reminding herself not to react, not to smile or flush or hold eye contact for too long. Turning slowly, she took in the faint stubble on his chin, the wind-tousled look of his hair, the weathered-looking chambray shirt with the sleeves rolled up to his elbows. Jesus, the man had beautiful forearms. Kate licked her lips and commanded herself not to stare.

"Amy." His voice was a low rumble. "Kate."

Kate swallowed, glad he'd used that order for their names. She wiped her palms on her skirt, not sure why she felt queasy.

"Good morning," she said. "Looks like wardrobe got you all squared away."

"Wardrobe?" Jonah looked down at himself. "These are my clothes."

"Oh. Well, you certainly look the part."

He quirked an eyebrow at her. "I look the part of myself?"

"Um—"

"You look authentic," Amy declared, and Kate said a silent prayer of thanks.

Jonah looked from Kate to Amy, then back to Kate again. "So how'd you like that beer last night?" he asked.

All the blood drained from Kate's face. She could feel Amy's eyes on her, and she looked over to see the assistant producer's brows rise.

"I texted him a photo of a pumpkin beer I found at that little shop around the corner from the hotel," Kate said. "I thought he might like it."

Amy's eyebrows strove valiantly for her hairline. "I didn't know you even liked beer."

"I'm learning," she said, ordering herself not to make a big deal out of this. She turned back to Jonah, focusing all her energy on looking professional, but courteous. "The beer was kind of intense," she said. "I couldn't drink very much of it, but I liked what I tried."

"It's an imperial, isn't it?"

"I don't know what that means."

"They're usually really big, bold beers," Jonah said. "Much higher alcohol content, too. Sometimes up to twelve or thirteen ABV."

"No wonder I felt a little loopy," she said, hoping that explained why she'd been bold enough to send that photo. Maybe he'd buy that.

"If I remember right, 10 Barrel has another pumpkin beer that's a little less intense," he said. "I sampled it a few years ago when Viv and I were down there doing the Bend Ale Trail."

The thought of Jonah and Vivienne on a romantic autumn retreat in Bend, Oregon, was enough to splash cold water on Kate's libido.

This is why we're here, dammit. The two people who were married to each other, who wrote a bestselling relationship guide together and traveled and made love and—

"God, I'd almost forgotten about that trip," Jonah muttered, almost to himself. "Viv hated it. We were out there for some film festival, but I talked her into the beer tour for a couple hours. You would have thought I'd asked her to drink from the toilet."

Kate rearranged the mental picture she'd formed moments before, hating herself for liking this version better. The version where Viv was stuck-up and surly and closed off to new experiences.

"That's too bad," she said carefully, gripping the paper mug a little tighter. "We should probably get down to the parlor. The crew's going to start getting restless if at least a couple of us aren't down there."

"Should we nudge Elena again?" Amy asked.

Kate glanced at her watch. "Let's give them a couple more minutes. Ginger gets touchy if we try to rush her."

She turned and led the way down the hall, then into the well-lit parlor. The room was packed with camera equipment and lights, but the film crew had all dispersed. Only Viv sat there looking serene and centered, in a chic red kimono top and black silk slacks. She looked up as the three of them entered and smiled broadly.

"Hello, everyone," she said. "Are you all as excited as I am to get started?"

"So excited," Jonah muttered under his breath.

Kate resisted the urge to laugh, especially when she saw twin frown lines appear between Viv's brows. Having them both a little edgy was fine, but Kate hoped they wouldn't get too riled up before the cameras started rolling.

Skirting around Jonah, Kate moved into the center of the room and glanced at the antique clock on the wall. She set the cup of cocoa on a coaster and turned back to face the group. "Vivienne, Jonah—we've probably got another ten minutes until Elena is out of hair and makeup.

Why don't you two warm up by doing one of the communication exercises you talked about in *On the Other Hand*?"

"Oh, that's a great idea!" Amy beamed. "How about the Five Things exercise? That seems like the perfect way to get the two of you on the same page."

Jonah looked at Kate as though she'd just suggested they take off their clothes and paint their bodies with ketchup and mustard. Vivienne, on the other hand, looked delighted.

"That *is* an excellent idea. How about something like five things we admire about each other or five ways we've been inspired by one another?"

Jonah's expression grew pinched, and Kate wondered if she should have kept her mouth shut. Then again, it was important to have them ready for filming. To make sure the two stars of the show were on the same page, more or less.

"Maybe something a little more neutral," Jonah suggested. "Five favorite uses for duct tape?"

Viv smiled, though it looked a little strained. "That's a perfect example of the first one I was going to share," she said. "I admire the fact that Joe is already getting into character as the charmingly surly ex-husband with the dry sense of humor. That's such a critical part of this process, and I admire him for committing to the role."

Kate caught the subtlety of the backhanded compliment, and she wondered if Jonah had, too. Did poring over every word Vivienne Brandt had ever written make Kate the leading expert on Viv's communication style, or did sleeping with her for five years earn Jonah that title?

The thought of Jonah sleeping with Viv made Kate's stomach clench, but she made damn sure her face didn't show it.

"Did you know you can make wallets out of duct tape?" Jonah asked.

That earned him an eye roll from Amy and a slight waver in Viv's smile. With a sigh, he slid his hands down the thighs of his jeans. "Okay, fine," he said. "I admire Viv for her perseverance. She always talked about wanting to do a TV show someday, so I'm glad she made that happen."

Interesting, Kate thought, remembering her first conversation with Vivienne Brandt, when Viv had made it sound like she'd never considered the possibility of TV. Was that false modesty, or something else?

A flash of discomfort in Viv's eyes suggested she wasn't thrilled at being outed, and Kate wondered if Jonah had done it on purpose.

"My turn," Viv announced. "I admire that Jonah adopted a cat from the shelter." She smiled, and Kate thought she might stop there with a seemingly sincere compliment, but Viv kept talking. "Rescuing a homeless animal is such a noble thing. And having the self-awareness to choose a pet in sync with one's own personality is such a bonus. Cats are cool and aloof and detached and—"

"I admire Viv for finding a way to be catty while complimenting my cat," Jonah interrupted. "If that's not a made-for-TV moment, I don't know what is."

Viv's eyes flashed. "Well, I admire Jonah for finding a way to inject negativity into an exercise designed to reflect the *positive*. That takes some real creativity!"

"Okay!" Kate said, clapping her hands together and glancing down the hall. Where the hell were Sam and Elena? "Jonah? Did you want to go?"

"God, yes." He started to stand up, then stopped. "Wait, is that not what you meant?"

Amy snorted, while Vivienne gave an exasperated sigh. "Honestly, Joe—"

"I admire Vivienne for her outstanding memory," he interrupted. "I've only told her a handful of times that I fucking hate being called

Joe, but she committed that to memory so she could make an extra-stellar effort to use that name when she's trying to rile me up."

Viv folded her arms over her chest and looked at Kate. "Is this what you had in mind for the exercise?"

"Not really," she admitted.

"Um, good job, guys," Amy offered with a nervous glance at Kate. "Way to tap into that sense of conflict. That's really going to shine through once the cameras are rolling."

"I don't doubt it," Jonah muttered, throwing a look of resignation at the unmanned camera.

CHAPTER NINE

Filming with Viv and Jonah wrapped up early at three. Combined with the B-roll they'd shot over the course of the last week, they were off to a solid start. Their first sit-down with Viv and Jonah had just enough edge to give the production team some juicy sound bites for promotion.

Sam and Elena—the couple they'd chosen for the pilot episode— came off as sincere, sweet, troubled, and just a little bit weird, which was the perfect combination for television. Sam had complained about Elena spending thousands on shoes, and Elena had countered with a jab about Sam's taste for expensive cigars, but they'd held hands without prompting for most of the conversation. It was going well, all things considered.

Mostly.

She watched as Jonah hustled out the door, giving courtesy fare-wells to the crew while looking a bit like a man fleeing a house fire. Kate watched his car pull out of the driveway as she stood at the window coiling a cord for the cameraman.

"Don't you think so, Kate?"

She turned to see Viv in the doorway looking thoughtful and serene. "What's that?"

Viv's gaze flicked to the window where Jonah's taillights were just fading around the corner. She watched them for a moment before directing her attention back to Kate. "I was just saying I think the patients are going to do really well with a little Imago Therapy and maybe some work on Compassionate Communication techniques."

"I agree," she said. "I'm eager to see if they take the advice you gave them."

"Yes. Well, some people have a hard time taking criticism."

Viv turned and began rearranging a cluster of lilies in a red vase on the side table next to the door. Kate watched, wondering if Viv had something on her mind. Was she here seeking praise on her performance, or something else?

It's her house, for crying out loud. You're looking for issues where there aren't any.

Kate cleared her throat. "I think you and Jonah did well," she said. "We got some great footage of that fast-paced banter you had about whether Sam and Elena should try sleeping in separate bedrooms."

"Yes, that was a healthy little bit of conflict, wasn't it?"

Kate nodded, not sure if they were talking about Sam and Elena or Viv and Jonah. Something about Viv's posture told her it was the latter. "You play off each other nicely."

"We do, don't we?" Viv's looked up from the lilies and glanced out the window again, to the edge of the shrubs where Jonah's car had disappeared moments before. "We always did work well together."

Kate swallowed hard and set the cable down on top of a chest filled with audio equipment. She grabbed another cord and began wrapping it around her arm, elbow to thumb, elbow to thumb, keeping her mind distracted. It was easier than fixating on the tight knot that had lodged in the center of her chest in the middle of filming when she'd watched Viv reach over and touch Jonah's arm, lingering there with a tender familiarity. Or the moment near the end of the day when Jonah had caught Viv in his arms and held her there, smiling up at him, as they demonstrated the proper way to do trust falls.

Kate set the coiled cord aside and took a few calming breaths. She used the method Viv had suggested in *But Not Broken*, in the dog-eared chapter on self-care. *In for four seconds, hold for seven, out for eight.*

"There you are."

She looked up at the sound of Amy's voice to see her assistant producer in the doorway. Amy glanced at Viv, then stepped past her to continue into the parlor. She wasn't smiling, and she clutched her iPhone like the handle of a hatchet. Her eyes met Kate's, and she gave a familiar eyebrow lift that signaled the start of every conversation that began with the unspoken words, *You're not going to like this.*

"I just got off a conference call with the guys from the network." Amy stopped behind the black leather loveseat and rested her hands on the back of it like she was standing at a lectern. "They're really enthusiastic about some of the early footage we've shared. I sent them the clip from today with the scene in the kitchen, and they were super pumped."

"But?" Kate prompted. She knew there was a *but*. She could tell from the twin lines between Amy's brows and the way she kept glancing at Viv, like she wasn't sure whether to have this conversation here or in private.

Viv drifted into the center of the room, her flawless forehead creased with concern. "Is everything all right?"

"Everything's fine. Just a little unexpected twist." Amy gave Viv a placating smile before returning her gaze to Kate. "You know how we're set up to do this as a self-contained show?"

"What's a self-contained show?" Viv asked. She glanced from Amy to Kate. Seeming to sense this conversation could take a while, she folded herself into the same orange leather chair Jonah had picked the first time they'd all assembled here.

Kate rested her hand on the pile of coiled cables and stayed standing. "Every episode stands on its own," she explained. "They can be played in any order, and it's easy for viewers to jump in at any time."

"Shows like *Intervention* and *Deadliest Catch* and *Undercover Boss* and *House Hunters* are good examples," Amy added. "Those are all self-contained programs."

"Also referred to as closed-ended shows," Kate added. "Networks love them because they can get a lot of mileage out of reruns no matter what order they show the episodes."

"Right, right—of course." Viv tucked her legs beneath her, looking elegant and serene like an origami swan. "I'm familiar with the concept. I just wasn't familiar with the term."

Kate glanced at Amy, trying to get a read on her. She could guess where this conversation was headed, but part of her hoped she was wrong. "The opposite of a closed-ended show in unscripted television is an arced show," Kate continued for Viv's benefit. "That's where there's a story arc that continues through the whole season. You can't watch them out of order, or they won't make sense."

"Right." Amy met Kate's eyes and nodded once, almost imperceptibly. "Shows like *The Bachelor* or *Survivor* are examples of arced programming," she continued. "Viewers need to start at the beginning to really feel invested in the story."

"Okay." Vivienne glanced warily between them. "And we all agreed that our show would do best as a self-contained program." She looked at Amy again. "Right?"

"We did." Amy took a deep breath. "But Empire TV's executive director is asking for a small tweak."

"Chase Whitfield." Kate uttered the name like a curse, then glanced at Viv. "He's a brilliant director, but he can be—*challenging*, sometimes."

Viv gave a small smile. "I suppose that's true for most of us."

Kate looked back at Amy, wondering if Chase got a sadistic pleasure out of making them jump through hoops. Plenty of directors worked like that, not happy unless they made sweeping changes to someone else's concept.

"A small tweak," Kate repeated. "How small are we talking?"

Amy tucked a wayward curl behind one ear. "They still want each episode to be self-contained as far as the couples go. That's not changing. Each couple will still have their story conclude—for better or worse—at the end of each episode."

"Thank goodness," Viv said.

"But they want to see some sort of arc laced into the bigger picture," Amy continued.

"But how?" Viv ran her palms down the arms of the chair like she was soothing a cat. "Are we inviting couples back for continued counseling?"

"No," Amy said. "They'd like the series arc connected to the show's stars."

Kate watched Viv straighten a little at the word *stars*. It was a subtle shift, but Kate noticed and mentally applauded Amy's word choice.

"So they want an arc with Viv and Jonah," Kate said slowly. "Did they have something in mind?"

Amy held up her hands. "I know, I know. Don't worry. The first thing I told them is what Jonah said about not pretending they're still married. I made it clear that's non-negotiable, and they seemed fine with that."

Kate nodded once and curled her fingers into her palms, letting her nails bite into the soft flesh. "So what then?"

"They threw out a few ideas, but wanted us to brainstorm," Amy said. "They're thinking of something along the lines of Vivienne dealing with a crisis related to her new book and Jonah weighing whether to step in and help. Or exploring the mixed emotions between Viv and Jonah as one of them starts dating again. Those are just examples, though. They want us to come back to them with more ideas."

Viv went very still. Her hands stopped moving on the arms of the chair, and she looked from Kate to Amy and back again. "They didn't specify what the arc needs to be?"

"They left that up to us," Amy said. "They want it to be organic to the show and to the characters."

"Personal stories sell well," Kate said. "Since you and Jonah anchor the show, it makes sense to have this stem from what's happening in real life for one or both of you."

Kate focused on breathing, on trying not to react to the notion of tying the show more closely to the relationship between Viv and Jonah. This was just business. Just a matter of giving the network what they wanted.

"Real-life stories are best," Amy agreed. "And it will help if it's a little juicy. Something that will really draw viewers in."

Viv looked thoughtful, but not upset like Kate expected. That seemed . . . odd. Then again, Viv wasn't the one who'd be most annoyed by another form of personal intrusion. It was Jonah they needed to worry about.

"Did they say why they're asking for this?" Viv asked. "It seems a little strange to throw this in after we've already started filming."

"They think it'll give viewers a more intimate connection to the show," Amy said. "You know, provide a sort of voyeuristic thrill about peering into your lives."

Kate's stomach churned, and she hated where this was going. Not as much as Jonah was going to hate it, though. She glanced at Viv, who looked serene as always. "Viv? Do you have any ideas?"

Vivienne tilted her head to the side and gave a slow nod. "Perhaps. Let me give it some thought. How soon do they need to know?"

"Within a day or two," Amy said. "I told them we'd put our heads together and get back to them."

Kate picked up the coiled cables and moved across the room. Depositing them in a crate next to the door, she straightened and looked at Viv.

"Should we call Jonah in for a meeting?" Her voice sounded casual enough, but eagerness fluttered right under her breastbone. "We could get him on a conference call if we don't want to drag him back here."

Viv looked at her, seeming to consider it. "No. Let me do it in person. One on one."

Kate nodded in agreement. "Of course." That was best, obviously. The less time Kate spent with Jonah, the better. Let Viv handle this. "That sounds perfect. Maybe the two of you can go have coffee or something and hammer out your thoughts."

"That's a wonderful idea." Viv smiled and stood up. Her silk slacks were remarkably unwrinkled, and Kate wondered how she managed that. "If you two don't mind, I'm going to head into my study and do a little brainstorming for this. Will you excuse me?"

Kate nodded. "Absolutely."

Viv smiled, moving toward the doorway. As she approached, Kate stepped aside to let her pass. A tickle of Viv's perfume hovered in the air, something spicy and earthy and mysterious.

"Thanks for all your hard work today, Vivienne," Kate said. "You did a fantastic job."

"You, too, ladies." Vivienne looked back at Amy, then returned her gaze to Kate. She held it for a long time, and Kate ordered herself not to break eye contact. Not to flinch at all. Viv smiled. "I hope you know how much Jonah and I appreciate what you're doing."

Kate swallowed and nodded. "Thank you."

"Tell Jonah hello for us," Amy called. "Make sure you let him know we think he did great, too."

Vivienne smiled again, her eyes still locked with Kate's. "I certainly will."

◆　◆　◆

Jonah walked through the door of the animal shelter with a skinny Labrador on a leash, more eager than he'd been in weeks to put his damn shirt back on.

"Getting chilly out there?" Jossy asked as she grabbed the lab's leash and handed Jonah a wad of clothing he recognized as his own.

"Actually, it's a lot warmer than it looks." He fumbled with his sweatshirt, trying to untangle it from the T-shirt he'd left twisted inside. "And Bruno here does great on a leash."

"Good boy!" Jossy bent to scratch the dog's ears as Jonah dropped the sweatshirt on the counter and began wrangling his T-shirt right-side out.

"I could have done without the woman who stood there for a full minute watching Bruno lick his dick before turning to me and asking if that gave me any ideas."

"Eew!" Jossy pretended to gag. "Jesus. What the hell is wrong with people?"

Jonah yanked the hem of his T-shirt out of the armpit, cheered by his sister's indignation. "I told her Bruno seemed to be doing a fine job cleaning it himself, but that he'd let her know if he needed a hand."

"I feel like I need a shower."

"You and me both." Jonah located the neck hole of his shirt and had just started to yank it on when the door chimed. He looked up to see Vivienne standing in the doorway.

She'd changed into a flowy black top and soft-looking lavender leggings that reminded him of a pair she'd owned when they were married. Back then, she used to wear them around the house on nights they'd cook dinner together. He'd graze her ass with his palm, brushing past her en route from the granite island to the stove, and Viv would gasp and pretend to be shocked.

Jonah always knew better. She'd liked his occasional flares of cave-man behavior. At least she had when it served her purposes.

"Jonah." Viv's gaze drifted over his chest and lingered for a good three seconds before she lifted her eyes to his.

He hurried to pull the shirt over his head, struggling to stuff his hands through the arm holes. As he yanked down on the hem, he felt better about not being so exposed.

"You just put your shirt on backward," Viv pointed out.

"I like it that way." He yanked the hem down again as Viv continued to study him. "What brings you here? Christ, I've seen you more lately than I did when we were married."

The thought didn't cheer Jonah all that much, but Viv just smiled. He waited for her to answer, but her gaze swung to Jonah's left instead.

"Josslyn," she said. "It's so good to see you. Would you mind if I stole your brother for just a minute?"

"That's kinda up to my brother." Jossy looked at Jonah, her expression flat. "His shift as my shirtless dog walker is over, so his schedule is up to him."

Jonah heard the prickliness in his sister's voice and wondered if he should do something to soothe it. He also wished they had some sort of secret sibling signal to cue an impromptu game of make-believe. An ear tug to indicate Jossy should fake a fainting spell, or maybe a chin scratch to suggest she play along if he announced a need to reroof the building today.

The memory of his game of make-believe with Kate gave Jonah a sharp pang of longing. Hardly convenient with his ex-wife standing here, appearing unlikely to leave until he agreed to chat with her.

"Yeah, fine," Jonah said at last. "I'm free for a few minutes, I guess. I do have somewhere to be in an hour, though."

"A date?"

Jonah stared at her. Since when was Viv interested in his personal life? "Not a date," he said. "Something at the bookstore. Come on. You want to hit that coffee shop around the corner?"

"They have tea?"

"I'm sure they have tea," he said.

He marched toward the door and pulled it open, then turned back to see Jossy pantomiming a gag. He started to give her a dirty look, but caught Viv smiling up at him and decided to ignore his sister.

"Thank you," Viv said as he held the door open. "You know, we didn't get to finish our exercise before filming began. This is another thing I always appreciated about you—the way you hold the door open for others."

"Yeah, I'm a real fucking gentleman." He sounded like an asshole, and he tried to figure out why he was acting that way. Something about Viv being here in his space. Well, Jossy's space.

Stop being a dick, he ordered himself.

Shoving his hands in his pockets, he started toward the coffee shop. He glanced over to see her shiver a little in the autumn breeze, and he instantly felt sorry for her.

"I appreciated a lot of things about you, too, Viv," he offered.

"Like what?" She looked up expectantly as she fell into step beside him, and Jonah scrambled to come up with something meaningful.

"Your feet," he said. "You have nice feet."

Viv burst out laughing, then stopped walking and lifted one sandal-clad foot. "You're a real romantic, Jonah."

Funny, the way she said it with fondness now instead of shouting it at him the way she had a year before the divorce. Jonah walked faster, trying to escape the memory of those words.

"I'm just asking you to meet me where I am," she'd said in that way Viv had of yelling without raising her voice at all. "To offer some romantic gesture to show you even see me anymore—"

"Here we are!" Jonah announced unnecessarily as he jerked open the door of the little coffee shop. A bell tinkled, and he gestured for Viv to walk through first. She smiled and floated across the threshold in that stately way she always had of moving through the world.

He let her order first, then asked for a plain black coffee and a blueberry muffin. He couldn't remember the last time he'd eaten anything. The day's filming had left his stomach too knotted up to do much more than pick at the elaborate spread the TV people had laid out in Viv's kitchen.

Since Viv didn't whip out her wallet, Jonah paid. That earned him a show of gratitude that seemed much more effusive than a ten-dollar tab warranted.

"Really, Jonah," Viv gushed. "That's so thoughtful."

She clutched her mug of chamomile tea and drifted to a quiet table in the corner. Jonah followed, wondering what the hell she was up to. He'd find out soon enough.

"So," Viv said when they were finally seated. She wrapped her fingers around the mug of steaming tea, but didn't take a sip. "How did you think today went?"

"Fine. It went fine." He wanted to leave it at that, but her expectant look told him he was supposed to say more. That he needed to "unpack it," as she used to say.

Jonah sighed and stirred some sugar into his coffee. "Having cameras in my face like that was a little intense," he said. "But Sam and Elena seemed nice. Well, once they stopped hamming it up for dramatic effect."

"Do you think the marriage can be saved?"

He looked at her a moment, trying to read her expression. How often in their marriage had she ever asked his opinion? Ever really sounded like she wanted it?

"Yeah," he said slowly. "I think they can save it. If they're willing to do the work."

Viv's face broke into a grin. "I'm so glad to hear you say that."

Jonah grunted and picked up his coffee. He took a big gulp before remembering it was really fucking hot and also that he didn't even want coffee. It was just something to order, something to hold in his hands as a prop so he could look like a motherfucking adult having a motherfucking grown-up conversation.

What was it about being around Viv that made his subconscious swear so much?

He took another sip of coffee, waiting for her to say something. It was another elicitation technique, one of his favorites he'd honed on his last tour in Kabul. Just waiting for the other person to get uncomfortable and rush to fill the silence. They always did.

Especially Viv, who never could stand it when people weren't making a constant effort to communicate.

"So, Jonah," she said. "The network folks made another request today."

"They want me to do the show shirtless?" He grunted again and blew on the coffee. "Yeah, they already called and asked."

"What?" Viv blinked, then laughed. "Oh, you're kidding? Right, of course."

Actually, he wasn't kidding, but there was no point detailing his phone conversation with Chase Whitfield. Man, that guy was a piece of work.

But that didn't seem to be why Viv had tracked him down. He didn't really give a shit about shooting some B-roll of him working out in the little gym he'd built at the bookstore. Free publicity for Cornucopia Books was never a bad thing, plus the network had agreed to pay Beth to run the shop on days Jonah was filming. He felt like he owed them.

"Anyway," Viv said. "The network wants to do an arced story line."

"A what?"

"An arced story line," she repeated. "It's where there's a story that carries through the whole season of episodes. Some little thread that ties everything together."

"You mean besides the fact that both of us are *in* every episode?"

"That's the starting point, of course," she said. "But it would be something more than that. Something more—personal."

"More personal than having cameras stuck in our faces for ten hours a day?"

Viv took a sip of her tea and gave Jonah a look of practiced patience. "They want to focus on some element of *our* story," she said. "You and me."

"You and me." The words came out flat, and Jonah wasn't sure why he needed to repeat them. To hear them land in the middle of the table with a dull thud.

Viv pretended not to notice. "Exactly. For instance, say one of us were involved in a new romance. The producers might chronicle how that unfolded, maybe explore each spouse's emotional reactions to the new development."

Jonah felt a pang of alarm, but willed himself not to react. Had Viv picked up on something between him and Kate? Maybe caught a lingering glance between them, or noticed the way Kate smiled and rolled her eyes when the makeup girl swooped in for the third time to powder his face and rest one of her silicone-enhanced breasts on his shoulder.

Jonah gripped his mug a little tighter and tried not to picture Kate's face. Or her bare leg, disappearing into a delicious froth of bathtub suds. Or the kiss in Ashland, or the one at the bookstore, or the kiss at his place—

Christ. How many times had they kissed?

Too many for two people who'd pledged not to do it at all.

Not enough, considering how much he wanted to do it again.

Jonah looked at his ex-wife and focused very, very hard on not blinking.

"I'm not seeing anyone," he said slowly. "Are you?"

"No!" She brought her hand down on the table a little too quickly, sending a teaspoon clattering against her saucer. "I'm not. I'm not dating anyone at all."

"Okay, then," he said slowly. "You think one of us should start Internet dating or something?"

"There's an interesting idea." She picked up her tea and blew on it, then took a cautious sip. "I suppose I could float that out there with the producers. One of us joining a professional online dating network or something."

"How about if we make it you?" Jonah said, already regretting having broached the subject. "I don't think I'm really cut out for Internet dating. It all seems like too much exhibitionist bullshit for my taste."

Viv cocked her head to the side and studied him. "Says the man who walks dogs with his shirt off?"

"Not the same thing," Jonah said. "That's for a good cause. Gets people through the door and looking at adoptable pets."

"Of course, I understand." She looked at him over the rim of her mug. "Actually, that's not a bad idea. Maybe there could be some story line about your shirtless dog-walking duties and all the women you attract."

"Thanks, but no thanks."

"Really? I thought you'd want to bring the attention to the shelter. Maybe generate donations for Jossy's cause or more interest in adoptable animals."

Hell. He hadn't thought of it like that. "I guess. Maybe." He made a mental note to talk to Kate about it. Maybe that could be a way to help Jossy and the shelter without having to fight her to take money from him directly.

"This is wonderful!" Viv smiled. "Let's keep brainstorming. I like the way this is going."

Jonah didn't particularly, but he refrained from saying so. "You mentioned something about remodeling your upstairs bathroom. Maybe they could focus on that."

"Hmm. Yes. I think they're looking for something a little more *personal.*"

Of course they were. Jonah knew it already, but he'd hoped Viv might take the bait. Might be happy with the prospect of something that put more focus on her. It was her damn show, after all.

"What if we spent some time analyzing what went wrong in our own marriage?" Viv said. "Maybe some clips where we each reflect on the role we played in the breakdown of our relationship. I know I have plenty of regrets. Plenty of mistakes I could own."

Jonah looked at her, wondering if he was supposed to say the same thing. It was true, but was there any benefit to rehashing that now? "Sure," he said. "I know I fucked up plenty."

"So maybe that's a way we could lend some personal insights to the couples we're helping," she said. "A way of sharing from our own experiences."

Jonah frowned, but didn't reply right away. He didn't like the idea of tossing out all his dirty laundry for the camera. That's not what he signed on for, dammit.

Then again, she had a point. He'd learned a few things through the unraveling of his marriage and the whole messy process of divorce. If that could be useful to someone else, maybe he owed it to the world to keep some other poor schmuck from tanking his relationship.

"Maybe," he said slowly. "I guess I'd be willing to consider it."

"Wonderful!" Viv beamed at him, and Jonah felt like a student who'd just answered an algebra question correctly. "I'll add that to the list they're sending the network director."

"Sure," he muttered, ready for this conversation to be over. "Whatever you want."

Her brows lifted a fraction of an inch, and she tilted her head to the side. "So overall, you'd say you're fairly open?"

"I don't know." He looked at her, not sure why he felt leery all of a sudden. "I guess I'd want to know about it beforehand, whatever they decide."

"Of course."

"And if it's all the same to you, I'd rather the story be more focused on you than me."

Viv laced her fingers together on the table and nodded. "That's good feedback." She stared at him a moment longer, then unlaced her fingers to reach for her tea again.

Jonah glanced down at his own mug, surprised to see he'd already drained it. He hadn't touched the muffin, but his stomach wasn't feeling up to it anymore. Would there someday be a point where being around Viv wouldn't make him feel this way? Like someone grabbed hold of one of his testicles between a cold thumb and forefinger, not pinching, but not letting go either. Like he was waiting for the ache that may or may not happen.

He stood up too quickly, banging his knee on the table. "If we're just about done here, I should probably run," he said. "I've got some stuff to do at the store."

"I understand." Viv smiled, but didn't stand. Just sat there, looking up at him with fond familiarity, like she knew exactly what he was thinking. He used to love that look. Loved the idea of someone peering into his brain and liking what she saw.

Now it just unnerved him.

"Thanks for brainstorming things with me," Viv said. "I'm glad we're able to work together again like this."

"Yeah." Jonah cleared his throat. "Me, too. Good seeing you, Viv."

He turned away, not sure whose lies were the boldest. Hers or his. She had to hate this as much as he did, right?

He felt Viv watching as he carried his mug to the bus tub and set it inside. Pushing the door open, he refused to turn back and make eye contact. They'd said their goodbyes. There was no point dragging it out.

Jonah walked fast with the muffin in one hand, desperate to put some distance between himself and his ex-wife. It was already growing dark, but he didn't head back to the shelter. Not yet, anyway. He needed some fresh air and a chance to get a little space from the conversation.

He slowed down, glancing over his shoulder to make sure Viv hadn't followed. There was no sign of her, so Jonah pulled his phone out of his pocket. A twinge of guilt pinched his chest as he scrolled down to find the number for Kate. But there was no reason to feel guilty, dammit. He had plenty of professional reasons to call the producer of the show he worked on, didn't he?

Even so, Jonah found himself crossing to the other side of the street, turning a corner to take him the opposite direction of the animal shelter. He hit the button for Kate's number, annoyed at himself for the way his pulse kicked up.

"Hello?"

Her voice sent a rush of adrenaline through him, but he ignored it and put on his best professional-guy voice. "Hey, Kate. It's Jonah. I was hoping to talk to you about this whole arced story line thing."

"Oh. Right. Yes, of course."

She sounded distracted. Muffled. And was that trance music pounding in the background?

Jonah took a bite of his muffin and chewed, trying to make out the din of conversation in the background on Kate's end. "Did I catch you at a bad time? It sounds like you're in a bar or something."

"Uh, I am," she said. "I think. I guess it's sort of like a bar."

Her voice definitely sounded odd. And what the hell was "sort of like a bar," anyway? It was probably none of his business.

"Should I try you back another time?"

"No! I, uh—I want to talk to you."

A peal of laughter sounded in the background, then something that sounded like a muffled moan.

"Are you okay, Kate?" he asked. "You sound a little weird."

"Maybe. I'm, uh—at a swingers club."

Jonah inhaled a muffin crumb. He stopped walking and coughed, trying to get his breath back.

"A swingers club?" he wheezed.

"It's where couples go when they want to swap partners for sexual—"

"I know what a swingers club is," he said. "I'm just wondering why you're in one."

"Location scouting," she said. "For the couple we're considering for episode eight. They've been talking about trying an open marriage, so Amy and I wanted to check this place out."

"You're there with Amy?"

"I was." The music kicked up a notch louder, and Jonah heard somebody cheering. "Amy got an emergency call and had to leave, so I'm here—"

"Wait, you're alone? In a swingers club?"

"Yes. Yeah. Um, yes."

Jonah wasn't sure whether to laugh or cry. "Do you want company?"

"Oh dear God, yes."

The eagerness in her voice sent a thrill through him. He took a deep breath, pretty sure what he was about to say was not his smartest course of action.

"I'll be right there."

CHAPTER TEN

Kate took a sip of her vodka soda and tried not to make eye contact with anyone. Not the woman strutting past in a purple corset and fishnet leggings. Not the guy in latex pants and a red denim vest dotted with metal studs. Not the leather-clad octogenarians Kate felt fairly certain used to play in her grandmother's bridge club.

"Ma'am? Are you looking for someone?"

Kate's pulse kicked up, and she turned to watch Jonah slide onto the barstool beside her. She'd never been so glad to see anyone in her entire life.

"Jonah! Thank God you're here. I was hoping they wouldn't give you any trouble at the door."

"That was a first for me." He grinned. "Having my name on a guest list at a members-only sex club."

Something about that grin dissolved the tension in her shoulders, and Kate began to relax. "Thanks so much for coming. I didn't want to leave without getting a feel for the place, but—"

"You didn't want anyone getting to feel *you*?"

"Exactly."

"Quite the crowd they have here."

She watched as Jonah studied the scene, hands clasped on the bar in front of him. Kate followed his gaze, watching as it skimmed over the dance floor, then up to the second level, where a row of people leaned over the balcony with drinks in hand. She wondered what he thought of all this.

Lights throbbed in time to the music, bathing the room in a glow of pink light and perfume. A disco ball swirled overhead, casting glittery rainbow spots on a dance floor packed with writhing bodies. Some were dancing and some were . . . um, that definitely wasn't dancing.

"I had no idea this was even legal," Kate admitted.

Jonah glanced at her, then followed the direction of her gaze to a couple undressing each other in the corner.

"Huh," Jonah said. "They're really going for it, aren't they?"

She nodded. "I guess I thought the sex part would be more discreet. When the owner gave me a tour, she showed me all the playrooms. Some have doors that lock and curtains you can close."

"Or leave open, I assume?" Jonah shrugged. "I'm guessing a place like this is the perfect spot for exhibitionists and voyeurs to get together and turn each other on."

"I hadn't thought of it like that."

Jonah laughed. "I'm guessing neither of us had given much thought to sex clubs before this." He raised one eyebrow as a woman at the other end of the bar began playfully spanking a woman wearing nothing but a red bra-and-panty set. "Can't say I even knew this place existed."

"I find that tremendously comforting," Kate said. "That you're not a regular part of the swinger scene."

"My most memorable swinging experience was on a porch in Ashland with you." He grinned and leaned closer, making Kate's heart skitter in her chest. "That's probably not scandalous enough to be part of an arced story line, huh?"

"I take it you've talked with Viv." Kate felt her smile start to wobble, but she held it steady.

"Yep."

He said nothing else as he made an unsuccessful attempt to signal the bartender. The guy was focused on lining up a large tray of beers for a man wearing leather chaps and a dog collar. "Viv seemed pretty focused on wanting one of us to get back out on the dating scene," he said.

"This probably wasn't what Viv had in mind for the dating scene."

"Probably not."

Kate's gaze landed on two topless women groping each other in the corner while their male partners watched. Startled, she looked back at Jonah.

"Maybe we should keep our eyes on each other for now," she said. "Some of this can't be unseen."

He laughed. "Good idea."

"Let me buy you a drink. It's the least I can do since you came down here to rescue me."

"I'd definitely feel better if I had something to do with my hands." He winced. "Besides the obvious."

Kate gave a nervous laugh and caught the bartender's eye. He gave her a just-a-minute signal, so she turned back to Jonah. "What can I get you?"

She watched as he leaned across the bar, squinting in the dim light of the club. "Looks like they've got Boneyard on draft."

"Is that the name of a cocktail, or was that slang for a sex act?"

"It's a beer. Made by Boneyard Brewery. They make the best IPA known to man." The bartender approached, and Jonah looked up at him. "Pint of RPM, please."

"Can you put it on my tab?" Kate added.

"Sure thing."

Kate watched the guy pour the beer and wondered if she should spend some time Googling the brewing industry. She had no idea what

RPM or IPA stood for, but she was curious. The beer she'd sampled at Jonah's had been a pleasant surprise, and she wanted to try more.

She spun her glass of vodka soda on the counter and looked around again. Two women and a man linked hands and disappeared through a doorway Kate knew led to one of the playrooms. Her mind filled with images of what might happen next. Touching and kissing and undressing. Writhing bodies, skin slick with sweat as breath came faster. The sound of gasps and moans and—

"How would you even film in a place like this?"

She looked back at Jonah to see he had his beer already. He was watching her over the rim as he took a long sip.

She swallowed and hoped like hell he couldn't read minds. "We'd have to do some tricky things with lights, but—"

"No, I meant legally. Surely they're not going to let you run around with a camera crew in a swingers lounge."

"Oh, that. I've already talked with the owner. If we go ahead with it, she'd open the club during off-hours and invite members to show up if they want to be on camera. They'd all sign waivers, of course."

"You think enough people would do it?"

"It's like you said about the voyeur thing," Kate said. "If enough people like being watched, we'd have no trouble."

"Anything for five minutes of fame."

Jonah took another sip of his beer, then set it down on the bar. "Damn, that's good. Seriously the best IPA on the planet."

She bit her lip. "May I try a sip?"

"Be my guest."

He nudged the glass in front of her, and Kate picked it up. She sniffed it first, trying to remember what Jonah had told her about olfactory senses and beer tasting. "It smells like pine-tree sap," she said. "And citrus. Lemons, maybe. Or tangerines."

"I know they use Citra hops in there, so that makes sense."

She took a cautious sip. "Wow." She tried a bigger swallow. "That's really good. It's—I can't think of the right word."

"Hoppy," he said. "IPAs are known for having a high hop content, and this is one of the hoppiest. I'm actually a little surprised you like it. IPA isn't usually a good starter beer for people who aren't used to it."

"I love it. Actually, I might like to have my own." She caught the server's eye and signaled her for another, nudging her vodka soda aside.

She took the frosty pint from the bartender and folded her hands around it. "Thank you," she said. "This is good enough to actually drink."

"As opposed to what?"

"Holding it like a prop, which is mostly what I was doing before," she said. "I might have to grab some food from the buffet so this doesn't go straight to my head."

"There's a buffet?"

Kate nodded toward the hallway that led toward an area the owner had described as the Group Playroom. "It's down there," she said. "Apparently the buffet is the only place in the club where you're not allowed to have sex."

"There go my plans for the night."

Kate grinned, though something about the gravel in his voice made her skin tingle pleasantly. She couldn't keep her brain from picturing what Jonah might look like pushing aside the fruit platter, then reaching for his belt buckle and—

"I hear the food's pretty good!" she said with a little too much enthusiasm. "They switch to breakfast at midnight."

Jonah looked at her oddly and took a sip of his beer. "I guess people work up an appetite fucking each other senseless."

"I guess so." Kate took a deep breath and tried to focus on the job she was here to do. "The film editors will have their work cut out for them if we end up shooting here."

"How do you mean?"

"All this nudity means a lot of editing. A lot of black boxes to add."

"You really think they'd want to shoot here?"

"It's perfect for the sort of salacious footage viewers love. Something a little taboo, a little forbidden—"

She stopped talking and took a sip of beer, hoping Jonah didn't read too much into her words. Surely that's what was happening here, right? She wanted him so badly because he was off-limits. It was as simple as that.

Glancing over, she saw his mossy amber eyes fixed on two couples headed up the spiral staircase in the corner. They reached the first landing and kept going, headed for the third level.

"The orgy bed is on the third floor," Kate said. "In case you were wondering."

"I wasn't, but thanks." Jonah sipped his beer and shook his head. "Holy shit. I feel like I'm getting an education here."

"You and me both."

He grinned and set his glass down, studying her with an intensity that made her skin hum again. "You know the Five Things exercise you had me do with Viv on set?"

Kate swallowed hard, wishing it didn't bother her that he'd brought up his ex. "It's a great exercise."

"Right. Well, this is one of the five things I really admire about *you*," he said.

Kate laughed, surprised by the turn in conversation. "That I drag you out to swingers clubs to spend time creepily staring at strangers?"

Jonah smiled and spun his glass on the bar. "I meant that you're so open-minded. That you go out of your way to experience new things."

"If you're talking about orgies, I don't think that's on my bucket list."

"I meant the beer, but good to know."

"Right." Kate grinned and sipped her beer. "Trying new things usually pays off for me. At least half the time, I end up discovering something I love."

A heavyset man with tattooed arms the size of tree trunks skidded to a halt in front of them and looked at Kate. "If you want to try new things, there's a frog chair up on the second floor. I could grab my wife and my girlfriend and the five of us could—"

"Actually, we're just here observing for now," Kate interrupted.

"For now," Jonah agreed. "But the second you see my wife heading for the sex swing over there, that's your signal to join us."

The man grinned and gave them both a conspiratorial wink. "Got it. We'll see you around."

As the guy walked away, Kate leaned closer to Jonah. "You're a whack job, you know that?"

"Hey, you're the one who wanted to observe a swingers club," he pointed out. "What better way to observe than to play along?"

"In case you hadn't noticed, I'm not exactly dressed like I belong here."

Jonah's eyes skimmed over her body, and Kate reminded herself she'd just invited him to do it. It's not like he was checking her out. He was just critiquing her choice of the fitted boat-neck dress with a zipper that ran all the way from knee to neck.

"I've never seen you wear white," he said. "It looks good on you."

"Thanks. It's Amy's dress, actually. She said it would glow under the black lights."

"Amy has good taste. You should probably unzip it a little if you want to fit in."

Kate started to laugh. He was kidding, after all. But something about his words made her feel bold. Like she wanted to surprise him.

She lifted her hand and caught the zipper pull between her thumb and forefinger. Jonah's eyes widened as she tugged it, exposing a few inches of skin between her breasts. "Thanks for the tip."

Jonah's throat moved as he swallowed. "Thank *you*."

Their gazes stayed locked for a moment, and Kate focused on breathing in and out. Jonah broke eye contact first, but he didn't look away from her. He let his gaze travel down her body, slow like a caress. Kate shivered, watching as his eyes lifted to her cleavage and stayed there for a few beats.

Then he picked up his beer and took a sip, muttering something that sounded like *"Christ on a motherfucking cracker."*

She wasn't sure why, but it sounded like a compliment. Kate picked up her own beer and sipped it. "So what were the other four things?"

He looked back at her, startled, and Kate hurried to explain.

"You said there were five things you admired about me. I was curious about the other four."

She held her breath, hoping that didn't sound desperate. Hoping she sounded like a bold, confident woman instead of one who'd spent way too much time reading self-help books and practicing ways to infuse her voice with the perfect pitch of casual nonchalance.

"Let's see," Jonah said. "You're smart. Not just book smart or look-at-me-and-my-vast-collection-of-abstract-expressionist-art smart. You're intellectual, but you're also clever. Good at thinking on your feet. I kept noticing that today during filming. Everyone kept hitting you up with technical problems or gripes about the timing, and you always seemed to find a solution to everything."

Kate felt her chest swell, which was dangerous, considering the position of the zipper. She took a swallow of beer to keep from grinning like a big, dumb idiot.

"Thank you," she said. "I love my job."

"It shows." Jonah spun his beer on the counter and studied her again. He wasn't looking at her cleavage this time. He seemed to be taking in the whole package, a thought that thrilled Kate.

"Item number three: you're tenacious," he said. "You don't take no for an answer, whether it's from me or Viv or the TV people. Someone puts up a wall, you find a way over it, under it, or around it."

Kate had a hard time breathing. How did he know what to say? That he was homing in on the things that made her proudest. The things she liked most about herself instead of the things she wanted desperately to change.

She swallowed hard, not sure if she wanted to hug him or kiss him. Neither seemed like a good idea in a swingers club, so she was grateful when he kept talking.

"Number four: you're kind," he said. "I watched you make up a plate of food for that camera guy who hadn't gotten a break all day. I watched how you interacted with Sam and Elena. How that guy from the network kept trying to get her to cry, but you called for a break in filming. I get it, you guys need the tears for the show—but you know these are human beings you're working with. You're not willing to crush someone's spirit for the sake of ratings."

Kate swallowed hard, feeling a pinprick of tears behind her eyes. No one had ever talked to her like this. Not even Anton, when they'd done the Five Things exercise themselves. He'd fired off single-word descriptors like he was choosing them at random from a thesaurus, while Kate had stood there with her own two-page list gripped in a trembling fist.

"Jonah—" she said, wanting to thank him. Wanting to stop him. Wanting something else she knew she shouldn't want but still desperately, urgently did.

He grinned. "Okay, it's your turn." He picked up his beer and took a gulp before setting it back on the bar. "And yes, I know that was only four. You have to do me before I tell you the fifth."

Kate's brain short-circuited a little on *do me*, but she took a deep breath and picked up her beer. She took a cold swallow, trying to smooth down the lump that had formed in the back of her throat. She looked around the room, trying to get her bearings. Trying not to notice the couple in the corner, the woman whose naked back arched with desire as the man slid his palms up her thighs and beneath her leather skirt.

Kate shifted on her seat, undone by a heady mixture of desire and affection and the sense that this was probably not the setting Jonah and Viv envisioned when they'd written the Five Things exercise.

She licked her lips and set down the beer. "It feels like I'm just repeating what you said, but I really do admire your intelligence," she said. "Not just your geeky trivia about theater plays and books and owls, but the more understated stuff. The way you don't just guzzle beer, you study it. The way you learn the subtle nuances and what makes it all come together. I admire that."

Jonah smiled and spun his beer around on the counter. A pair of lacy black panties hurtled through the air and landed on the bar next to him, but he never broke eye contact. "Thank you."

"You're selfless," Kate continued. "I know you don't parade around shirtless because you want to show off your hot bod, though you obviously have one." Kate hesitated there, watching his eyes flicker. Watching his response. She held her breath, hoping she hadn't crossed some line. "You know it'll help find homes for the animals at your sister's shelter. Hell, you created a cat sanctuary in your bookstore, even though you flat-out admitted you're not a cat person."

"I might be becoming one," he admitted. "Marilyn's been persuading me."

"And that's another thing I admire," she said. "You're not afraid to change your mind. You don't dig in your heels and insist the thing you've always believed is the only way it can be. You let your heart be open to a cat when the right one came along. You listened to me tell you all the reasons you should do the show, even though you'd already decided not to do it. You allow yourself to be persuaded."

Jonah took a swallow of beer, then set down the glass. He held her gaze for several long seconds, not saying a word. Kate held her breath.

"Maybe I just wanted to sleep with you," he said slowly. "Did you consider that?"

Kate felt dizzy. She was still holding her breath, and her pulse throbbed in her head. The air was electric. Music throbbed and laughter trickled and sighs of pleasure drifted from somewhere far away, but all of it was background noise behind the echo of Jonah's words in her head. She took a slow breath, wanting to savor these last few seconds before she said something with the power to change everything.

"Do you?" she murmured.

"Want to sleep with you?" Jonah nodded once. "Most urgently."

Kate licked her lips. "But we—can't."

He said nothing. Just held her eyes with his, not blinking at all. In the dim lights of the bar, his amber-green eyes looked molten. Kate watched him, marveling at the stillness.

Nothing in her was still at all. Every nerve was firing at once. Her skin prickled with energy, and the damp heat behind her knee made her crossed legs slip apart.

The ball was in her court. She knew that. And she knew she wanted to grab it with both hands and run as fast as her shaky legs would carry her.

"Let's go," she whispered, then slipped off her barstool and headed for the door.

◆　◆　◆

Jonah drove faster than he'd ever driven in his life, worried Kate might change her mind. Worried he might.

But as she pulled him out of the elevator and practically dragged him down the hall to her hotel room, it occurred to him she might want this as desperately as he did.

"For the love of all that's holy, not now! Motherfucker!" Kate was jamming her card key into the lock with such force that Jonah considered the safety of his own appendages.

But a little risk seemed worthwhile at this point.

"Let me," he said, and gently pried the card from her hand. He had the door open in two seconds, and then she was clawing at his shirt. Clothes went flying—shoes, belts, a bra Jonah hardly had time to appreciate before it was sailing across the room to land on the television.

But the view of Kate standing naked in front of him was worthy of much more appreciation.

"You're so beautiful," he said as he reached for her.

She gave a nervous little laugh and slid her fingertips over his pecs. "So are you. It's no wonder women line up to watch you walk dogs down the street."

"You're the only woman I want watching me right now."

God, that sounded cheesy. But she smiled anyway, and the heat in her eyes was enough to make him forget he was hopelessly out of practice at this. At taking his clothes off in the presence of another person and giving everything he had to mutual pleasure instead of standing like some motionless statue to be admired.

Somehow they made it to the bed, kicking aside covers and pillows as they fell into each other. He couldn't get enough of her, touching arms and hips and belly and breasts and a few body parts whose names he couldn't recall in his lust-addled state.

"Condom," Kate panted as she let go of him and fumbled open a red plastic trunk the size of a small cooler. It was filled to the brim with foil packets, and Jonah felt alarmed again.

"How long are we planning to be here?"

Kate laughed and tore open a wrapper. "They're for the show. It's in the rider for all relationship-driven reality shows to have condoms on set at all times. I doubt they'll miss one or two."

"So it's product-testing, then." Jonah groaned as she slid the condom on, then rolled Kate onto her back. "Research."

"Unexpected job perks." Kate gasped as he slid inside her, and Jonah watched her fingers twist into the sheet. Then she let go and ran her hands up his back, holding on tight as he moved in and out of her.

The pressure built faster than he wanted, and he fought to keep his head in the game.

"Sex is the most natural expression of our humanness," Viv coached in his brain. *"When two people join together as—"*

"Shut up," Jonah growled.

"Sorry."

"No! Not you. I swear, I just—"

"I know," she murmured, smiling up at him.

And he thought maybe she did.

He moved again, and Kate arched tight against him, gasping with pleasure. He wondered if she really did know, if the voices in his head and the voices in hers were sometimes whispering the same words, hinting at the same old ghosts.

"Jonah, I'm—oh, God—"

He felt her break open beneath him, clenching and clawing and making the sweetest, most joyful cries he'd ever heard in his life. That's all it took to undo him. He let go with a soft groan of his own, driving into her again and again until they both lay breathless in a shocked and sweaty pile of wonder.

When he finally rolled away, he pulled her with him. They lay facing each other for a few moments, breathing fast, with Kate's eyes closed and her lashes fanned out on her cheeks.

"That was unbelievable," he said.

Her eyes fluttered open, and she laughed softly as she reached up to brush hair from his eyes.

"I can't say this is how I expected to end my day."

"Me neither. But I'm glad it happened."

"So am I."

Neither of them said anything for a long while. They lay there wrapped in each other's arms, legs twisted together and the sheets kicked somewhere near the foot of the bed. She shivered once, and Jonah reached down to pull the covers up. He arranged them over the top of their bodies, then pulled her close, nestling her snug against his chest. They were still facing each other, but so close you could barely slide a bookmark between their bodies.

"Kate." He planted a kiss along her hairline, then another on her earlobe. "No matter what happens, this was never a mistake. Things like this don't happen by accident."

She opened her eyes and looked up at him. There was something wary in them, something startled. She started to pull back, but he held her against him.

"I didn't mean that to sound ominous," he continued. "I just meant—shit, that came out wrong."

"No, I get it," she whispered. "I think I know what you mean."

Jonah tucked a strand of hair behind her ear and breathed in the grassy scent of her shampoo. "This might make things complicated," he said. "Or maybe not. But no matter what, I don't regret it. We were pulled into each other's orbit for a reason."

She stared at him for a few moments, then nodded. "I agree."

Jonah stroked her hair again, needing to touch her. He lowered his mouth to hers, kissing her more gently than he had before. The urgency had ebbed, leaving them here in this big white bed wrapped in a feather duvet. They were just two people craving each other's touch, exploring each other's bodies, warming each other's souls.

As Kate slid her palm over his shoulder blade, Jonah could almost pretend it was as simple as that.

◆　◆　◆

Kate slipped into the bathroom sometime around five the next morning. She'd always been an early riser, and having Jonah spend the night in her bed had left her too flustered to sleep well. She kept opening her eyes to look at him, hardly believing this was real.

"No matter what, I don't regret it. We were pulled into each other's orbit for a reason."

Okay, so he'd quoted his ex-wife in bed. Not a verbatim quote, exactly, but the part about being pulled into each other's orbit was something Viv had used in *But Not Broken.*

It was possible he didn't even know. It's not like Viv had trademarked the expression, and it wasn't such a unique turn of phrase that no one else could have said it. Kate probably wouldn't have picked up on it at all if she hadn't read Viv's books a million times.

She stepped under the shower spray, trying to rinse the anxious thoughts from her head. They had a busy day of filming ahead of them, and so much to do.

Get footage of Sam and Elena walking in the park together.

Film Sam at his office for clips to demonstrate job stress.

Grab B-roll around downtown Seattle to lay groundwork for the second couple.

Try not to look like you just slept with Jonah Porter.

Kate was smiling before she knew it. She ordered herself to knock it off. This was serious business, after all. She could be jeopardizing her working relationship with Viv, her future on the show. Her whole career, dammit.

But still, she was glad it had happened. Grateful she'd had a chance to be with Jonah like that, no matter what came next.

She finished rinsing the conditioner from her hair and stepped out of the shower. Grabbing the lone towel off the rack, she dried herself off and wrapped up in one of the plush hotel robes. The towel rack was empty, so she padded back into the room and phoned the front desk with a whispered request for more towels.

"Hey there."

His gravelly greeting made her turn, then smile at the sight of his tousled hair and his bare chest peeking over the edge of the sheet. "Hi."

He smiled back and watched her with sleepy eyes at half-mast. "You're up early."

Kate padded back to the bed and sat down on the edge of it. Leaning down, she nuzzled the side of his neck, planting a soft patch of kisses just behind his ear.

"Mmm, that's nice," he murmured.

She sat up again, making her robe gape open in front. She started to reach for it, but Jonah caught her hand. "You're so beautiful. I love looking at you."

She smiled. "I should get dressed."

Part of her didn't want to, but she knew she couldn't linger here all day. Jonah sat up and scrubbed his hands over his eyes. "I take it you're an early riser?"

Kate nodded and stood up, cinching the belt on the robe. "It's my secret to getting so much done in a day."

Jonah groaned and flopped back on the bed. "I'm the opposite of an early riser," he said. "A lazy ass?"

"You're not lazy," she said with a little more vehemence than she'd aimed for. But she remembered their conversation about dyslexics feeling lazy or stupid, and it seemed important that he know she didn't believe that. "You're one of the hardest-working guys I know. Your body clock is just different from mine."

He reached up and brushed hair off her forehead. "I never told you the fifth thing, did I?"

She smiled and shook her head. "Nope."

"It was a toss-up, actually."

"Between?"

"Your willingness to look for the best in all people, or your stellar ass."

Kate laughed and began shuffling through the closet. She stopped at a navy pencil skirt she'd always thought flattered the latter feature. "Which were you leaning toward?"

"Ass," he admitted. "Might as well stick with Average Joe mode. But I appreciate the other stuff, too."

Kate selected a V-neck top that dipped just a tiny bit lower than she normally chose for work. She felt sexy this morning, her skin humming with delicious energy.

She set the clothes on the dresser, pulled out a bra and panties, and began to get dressed. "You know, I only gave you three," she said. "Last night at the club? I only told you three of the five things I appreciate most about you."

"Intelligence, selflessness, and an openness to changing my mind," Jonah recited. "Were there really two more, or did you just sleep with me so you wouldn't have to come up with the rest?"

She laughed and fastened an earring on her left lobe. "Guilty as charged." Slipping the other earring into place, she sat down on the edge of the bed again. "Actually, that's not true at all. You want the other two?"

"Absolutely."

"Loyalty," she said. "And your sense of humor."

"Why those?"

Kate pulled off her towel turban and began to rub her hair dry. "Well, sense of humor because it's hands down the sexiest trait a guy can have," she said. "And because you've been making me laugh from the first day we met. Since before we met, actually. Your parts in *On the Other Hand* were hilarious. There were so many things in that book that made me want to cry the first time I read it, but then I'd flip to one of your sidebars, and suddenly I'd be smiling again."

Jonah reached up to catch her hand in his. He planted a kiss over the top of her knuckles before releasing it. "Why loyalty?"

"Because you're always looking out for other people," she said. "You came to my aid last night at the swingers club. You made sure Viv was really okay with you being part of the show before you agreed to do it. And you look out for others—the animals at your sister's shelter, your sister herself."

Something flashed in his eyes. A darkness Kate couldn't quite place. Then it was gone, and she wondered if she'd imagined it.

"I think you'd like my sister," he said.

The words startled her a little, the implication that she might actually meet his family. She knew that would never be possible, but—

"Speaking of my sister, Viv brought up a pretty decent idea yesterday."

Kate went back to toweling her hair, ignoring the twinge in her gut. So what if he brought up his ex-wife while they both sat on the same bed they'd made love in the night before? Modern relationships were complicated, and this wasn't even a relationship. It was only sex, wasn't it?

Jonah must have seen something in her expression, because he reached up and touched the side of her face. "Hey. I know this is weird. Dating's hard for anyone post-divorce, but when you throw in the high-profile nature of my previous marriage—"

"And the fact that your ex-wife is my longtime idol?"

"Yeah." He smiled. "It makes things a little more raw."

"It's fine," she said. "Like you said, nothing's ever a mistake. Sometimes it just feels weird, that's all." Kate tucked a damp strand of hair behind her ear. "What were you saying about your sister?"

"Oh, right. You know how the network folks have been after me to shoot a bunch of footage with my shirt off?"

Kate grimaced. "For the record, that wasn't my idea."

"No, it's fine. I'm actually okay with it, and I thought maybe we could tie it to Clearwater Animal Shelter. You know, explain why I do the whole shirtless dog-walking thing, maybe shoot a little promotional footage that draws attention to the shelter."

"That's kinda brilliant." Kate beamed. "We can build a whole promotional campaign around it, really get people excited for the show before the pilot even airs."

"I'm glad you like the idea." He sat up and stretched, then glanced at the alarm clock on the nightstand. "I should probably get going. I fed Marilyn in the evening, but she probably wants breakfast."

"Not to mention we're all shooting today."

"Right." Jonah gave her a lopsided smile. "Hopefully it won't be too weird."

"Oh, it will be." Kate smiled and stood up again. "But I'm a professional. I deal with weird all the time."

"Perhaps not this precise brand of it."

"True. I don't usually sleep with the stars of the shows I work on." She turned to face the mirror, resting one hand on the headboard as she smoothed down the front of her skirt. "Just the camera crew. And the lighting guy. And the makeup artists. And the—"

She shrieked as Jonah grabbed her around the waist and pulled her back down on the bed. He tickled her until she was breathless from giggling and her cheeks were pink with laughter. Her blouse came untucked and her skirt hiked up and she gave serious thought to just crawling back in bed with him and calling in sick for the day.

Then he stopped tickling and planted a soft kiss on the tip of her nose, followed by one more on the lips. "Enough," he said, taking his hands off her. "I suppose we both have to go to work."

"Right." Kate sat up reluctantly and heaved herself off the bed. She groaned as she glanced at the bedside clock. "Damn. I was hoping to be on set in fifteen minutes."

"You'd better get ready, then."

She pushed herself off the bed, then leaned down for one more kiss. Then she scuttled away, hustling toward the bathroom as Jonah eased off the bed behind her. "Let me just grab all my stuff out of here so you can shower and get ready," she called.

"No rush," he answered from the other room. "I'm going to see if I can get this complicated-looking contraption to make us some coffee."

"And I'm going to see if I can use this complicated-looking contraption to dry my hair." She pulled the blow dryer off the holder on the wall and started to switch it on when she heard the knock at the door.

She set the dryer down and poked her head out of the bathroom. "That's housekeeping. I asked them to bring a couple more towels so you'd have one."

Jonah looked up from where he was standing next to the door, fiddling with the coffeemaker. He wore nothing but a pair of blue-striped boxers, and Kate's stomach did a somersault at the sight of all that flesh on display. How was it possible she wanted him again?

"I'll get it," he said. "You finish getting ready."

"Thanks." She picked up her hairbrush again and watched for a second as he moved toward the door. A faint track of parallel lines ran across one shoulder blade, and she remembered putting them there, raking her nails down his back as she arched under him.

Quit staring, she commanded herself as she slid back into the bathroom and faced the mirror.

Her finger was on the switch of the blow dryer when she heard the thunk of the door handle, followed by Jonah's voice: "Thanks so much for—oh."

Silence, followed by a familiar female voice.

"Well, well, well. What do we have here?"

CHAPTER ELEVEN

All the blood drained from Jonah's head as he stood in the open doorway and stared at the unexpected visitor.

Footsteps thudded behind him, and he turned to see Kate running into the room with her shirt untucked and her feet still bare. "Amy! What a nice surprise! I thought we were meeting on-set this morning."

Jonah—who'd been doing his best to keep his lower half hidden behind the door—took a step back as Amy pushed her way into the room. She surveyed him from head to toe and gave a cluck of approval.

"Oh, very nice." She grinned. "No wonder everyone wants to get your shirt off."

Jonah did an inward grimace but ordered himself not to look down at his boxers. If his dick was hanging out the fly, there was no point drawing attention to it. "Amy," he said. "Nice to see you again."

Kate had somehow managed to tuck in her shirt while Amy ogled him. She stepped forward now, doing her best to divert the assistant producer's attention. "What brings you by so early, Aim?"

Amy grinned and folded her arms over her chest. "My morning conference was canceled, and you're always up by five," she said. "So I figured I'd grab my dress back and borrow your navy one for tonight's meeting." She shifted her gaze back to Jonah and gave a nod of appraisal. "Obviously, I didn't anticipate you'd have company at this hour."

Jonah sighed, wishing he'd at least thought to pull on his jeans. Maybe he could pretend they were reviewing promotional ideas or story arcs or—

"So you're sleeping together," Amy said. She didn't sound perturbed by it, but Jonah did a mental groan anyway.

"Just this once," Kate said, and Jonah turned to look at her.

"Okay, twice," she admitted. "Unless you count that last time, when we just—"

"Whoa, whoa, whoa!" Amy waved her hands in the air like an air traffic controller. "Please stop! I don't need details." Her gaze flicked back to Jonah's chest, and she gave a salacious grin. "Well, maybe a few details."

"I think I'll get dressed now." Jonah spotted his jeans on the floor behind Kate, so he bent to retrieve them. "Stop looking at my ass," he muttered.

"Sorry."

The word was a chorus of two female voices, which almost made him smile. But he'd prefer to just hit rewind on the whole morning. Well, maybe not the whole morning. Not the moment where Kate leaned down and kissed his neck, baring her breast through the opening in her robe. He'd kind of enjoyed that part.

Jonah finished buttoning his jeans and turned back to where Kate and Amy stood watching him. Spotting her dress on the back of a chair, Amy reached out and snagged it. "Thanks for this," she said to Kate. "Looks like it saw more action than I've managed to give it."

"I'll, um—have it dry cleaned for you," Kate said. "As for what's happening here—"

"You don't have to explain," Amy said. "The less I know, the better."

Jonah found his shirt on the floor and tugged it on. "Is there any chance this all could stay right here in this room?"

Amy leaned against the edge of the bathroom door. "That sounds like a proposition for a threesome," she said. "Not interested, but I do know this little swingers club—"

"I know," Jonah said. "And the fact that you left Kate there alone is kinda how I ended up here."

"Ah, so it's my fault you two bumped uglies?" She turned to Kate and grinned. "You're welcome."

Kate sighed. "Technically, doesn't Chase Whitfield get credit? He's the one who called you away."

"I really think it's best if we never mention your sex life and Chase Whitfield in the same breath," Amy said.

"Agreed."

Jonah cleared his throat. "So about keeping this quiet—"

"It's okay," Kate said. "She knows how to keep a secret."

Amy laughed and tossed her blond hair. "You don't last long in show biz if you can't. Besides, it was pretty obvious this was going to happen."

"Obvious to whom?" Jonah asked.

"Obvious to *me*," Amy said. "Not to your ex-wife, if that's what you're worried about."

It annoyed Jonah that anyone would think he cared about his ex-wife's opinion on who he slept with.

It annoyed him a lot more that he *did* care.

Not about Viv, exactly. He cared about the working conditions on the show, and whether this might jeopardize his chances to earn the kind of money that would make a difference in Jossy's life.

Christ. Maybe this was a mistake.

He looked at Kate again and his stomach flipped over. Nope. Definitely not a mistake.

"We'll be careful," Kate said. "And it won't happen again. Right, Jonah?"

She gave him a hopeful look, and Jonah's heart skipped. He knew what the answer should be. He knew there was no future here, but still.

"Yeah," he said, raking his fingers through his hair. "It was just a onetime thing."

Was it his imagination, or did Kate's smile falter just a little? She looked away and met Amy's gaze again. "So we're all good?"

"Never better," Amy said. "And you two can act natural around each other on set?"

"I can," Kate said. "Jonah?"

"Sure." He nodded, doing his best to underscore his own belief in himself. "No problem."

Kate smiled, and Jonah did his best to pretend he was glad, too. To pretend this whole thing didn't feel like an icicle through the center of his chest.

◆ ◆ ◆

"Sam, why don't you tell Elena how you feel?"

Kate watched as Vivienne clasped her hands together atop her thighs and looked back and forth between the husband and wife who'd agreed to broadcast their marital woes on national television.

The husband cleared his throat and looked down at his feet. "When you nag me like that, you make me feel—"

"Sam, remember what we talked about," Viv interrupted gently. "No one *makes* you feel something. Using judgment words is only going to start the spiral of defensiveness."

"Trust me on this, man," Jonah added, crossing his arms over a green flannel shirt that brought out the color in his eyes. Not that Kate noticed.

"That shit goes on for a long damn time," Jonah continued. "And you've got better things to do. Like watching reruns of *The Man Show* on YouTube."

Vivienne nodded sagely. "What Jonah is saying is that you need to let her know how you *feel*, but do that independent of any judgment of her actions."

"What Jonah is *saying*," Jonah interjected with a look of irritation at his ex-wife, "is that criticizing, blaming, or processing someone else's actions through your own fucked-up filter is a surefire ticket to heartache. Is that what you want?"

Sam frowned. "But she's wrong about—"

"Buddy." Jonah shook his head, and the compassion in his eyes made Kate's chest ache. "You can be right or you can be married. What's it gonna be?"

Next to Sam, Elena sat with tears shimmering in her eyes. From across the room, Kate thought she saw a glint of emotion in Viv's eyes, too. Kate signaled Pete to zoom in, wanting that shot. This was so important. For viewers to see how much the doctor really cared, to know these couples weren't just names on a chart to her.

"I know you're hurting." Viv reached out and took one of Sam's hands in her own. "And you have a right to your feelings. You and Elena have both done things to wound each other, whether you did it on purpose or not. But wouldn't it feel good right now to stop fighting? To put down your sword and build a bridge instead?"

Perfect, Kate thought. *Insert a dramatic pause, maybe a close-up of Elena's face, then of Sam's, then cut to a commercial before we—*

A movement in the corner of her eye caught Kate's attention, and she glanced at the doorway to see Amy waving to her. She cast a quick look at the center of the room, where Viv was putting an arm around Elena and offering her a tissue. Jonah had his head bent low, talking close with Sam in a low tone she knew would be picked up by the gazillion mikes they'd placed all over the room.

They had things covered. She'd see later how this ended.

Kate tiptoed out of the room and met Amy in the hallway. She pulled the door closed behind her.

"Is everything okay?" she whispered.

"Yeah," Amy said. "I just talked with Chase. He reviewed our mock-ups of the promotional videos and went nuts. I wanted to give you some notes about a couple tweaks at the midpoint, but that's not the most important thing."

"What's the most important thing?"

"He said this is almost certainly in the bag for us. Like unless one of the cast members dies or something, we've got it nailed."

"That's amazing!" Kate's heart was pounding, and this time it had nothing to do with Jonah.

Reading her thoughts, Amy glanced back toward the door. "You doing okay in there?"

"I'm fine. Everything's fine. The couple is endearing, Vivienne is intelligent and compassionate, and Jonah is—"

She stopped, fumbling for an adjective that sounded professional and indifferent instead of like the words of a woman who'd spent the whole day remembering how his mouth moved over her breasts.

"You think *you've* got it bad for Jonah," Amy muttered. "I swear Chase has a big, fat man crush on him."

"How do you mean?"

"Chase won't stop congratulating himself over coming up with the idea to pull Jonah into the show. He's seriously going to dislocate his shoulder with all the time he spends patting himself on the back."

"I'm glad he's pleased with the decision."

Amy looked at her for a few beats, then leaned closer. "I wasn't asking you about Jonah as he relates to the show," Amy added. "I just wondered how you're doing. If you're feeling weird about things."

"I'm a professional," Kate said. "I'm here to do a job, and it doesn't matter if—"

"You're also a human." Amy put a hand on Kate's arm. "And my friend. And I'm asking how you're feeling."

The kindness in Amy's eyes made Kate take a deep breath before responding. "Yeah. I'm fine. I mean—you tell me. Do you think I'm acting unusual?"

"You've avoided eye contact with Jonah, but you've been doing that from the start," Amy said. "I doubt Viv has noticed."

"I'm glad. And I'm glad tomorrow's filming schedule has them in different places. I just—" She stopped herself, not entirely sure what she'd been ready to say. How much she wanted to admit. "I don't want to mess things up."

"And you haven't. Everything's fine. If you want to know the truth, I'm glad you did it."

Kate frowned. "Why? So we can drag my skeletons out of the closet if there's a ratings slump?"

"No, hon. Because you needed to get laid."

She sighed and glanced at the closed door. Shaking her head, she looked back at Amy. "Could I have possibly chosen a worse person to scratch that particular itch?"

"You tell me," Amy said. "From the look on your face this morning, I'm guessing he wasn't that bad."

Heat crept into Kate's cheeks, but she couldn't resist smiling a little. "That isn't what I meant."

"I know." Amy grinned. "Look, it's not like they have any claim on each other. Even if she found out—"

"She can *never* find out! Can you imagine how unprofessional that would look?"

"Relax, Kate. I'm just saying, they're divorced. They've been divorced for a year. That means neither of them has any say in who the other sleeps with."

"I know that. In theory." She sighed, trying to think of how to explain this. "It's just—she's been this constant presence in my life, getting me through all the toughest stuff. And now I'm repaying her by sleeping with her ex-husband?"

"She's a professional colleague, Kate. Not your girlfriend. Not even your shrink."

"Well, you're my professional colleague, too."

Amy laughed. "A professional colleague who loaned you a dress to get laid in. And if I had an ex-husband, you could borrow him, too."

"You're a good friend, Amy."

Amy grinned and gave her another squeeze. Then she glanced down at the buzzing two-way radio on her hip. "Looks like they're about to break for the day."

As if on cue, the door pushed open, and Kate and Amy sprung apart like two teenagers caught kissing. Viv floated into the hallway with her shimmery orange silk top billowing behind her. She wore black velvet pants that fit like a second skin, and dainty red boots that laced up the back. The second she spotted Kate and Amy, she beamed.

"We did it!" She clasped each of them by a shoulder, practically radiating joy. "We had a major breakthrough in there just now."

"That's wonderful!" Kate kicked herself for missing it, but at least it was on tape. She'd see it later. "So they decided to save the marriage?"

"It was beautiful," Viv gushed. "Sam confessed to Elena that his greatest fear is losing her, so he's been pushing her away to test her. And Elena explained how that was bringing up all these memories of her father leaving when she was six, and the way her mother used to—well, you'll see it all when you watch the tape."

"Congratulations," Amy said. "Sounds like a job well done."

"Thanks." Viv closed her eyes and tilted her face toward the ceiling. The gesture would have seemed weird from anyone else, but from Viv, it looked like a prayer. "It feels so incredible to be part of something like that. To know I played a role in someone deciding to fight for a marriage instead of throwing in the towel."

There was a wistfulness in Viv's voice, and Kate wondered how many clients she'd had just throw in the towel. It had to feel good to get the hard-earned happily-ever-after. Kate studied Viv, hoping the cameras had done their job capturing this exact look from the doctor. If they had, the viewers were going to eat it up.

Viv opened her eyes again and sighed. "Do you think you got the footage we needed?"

"We had four cameras in there," Kate said. "I was looking over Pete's shoulder and saw some of the shots he was getting. It's safe to say you nailed it."

"The network guys are happy so far," Amy said. "They love the rough clips we sent yesterday."

"Good," Viv said. "I'm so glad. It's wonderful when all the pieces fall together like this. It's like it was meant to be."

The parlor door pushed open again, and Jonah stepped into the hall. He blinked, looking startled to see them, and Kate's heart lodged in her throat. The two exes locked eyes for an instant, and Kate wondered what separated a couple who threw in the towel from one who decided to stay and fight.

"Hey, Jonah," Amy said. "Nice work in there."

"Thanks." He cleared his throat. "You were great, too, Viv."

He said nothing to Kate, but he gave her a friendly nod of acknowledgment. There, they could do this. They could play it cool, pretend nothing had happened.

"How was last night, Jonah?" Viv asked.

He frowned. "What?"

"You said you had plans at the bookstore," she said. "I assumed you had an event or something."

"Oh." He cleared his throat again. "Right. It was great. Everything was great."

"Wonderful! I haven't been in there for so long. I'd love to come by sometime and see what you've done with the place. Is your manager running things while you're on set?"

"Yeah. Beth's in charge," he said. "Everything's running fine."

Kate looked away, worried her gaze was making him nervous. She focused on Amy instead, whose eyes held a hint of sympathy.

"We're actually going to do some filming at the bookstore next week," Amy said. "Some B-roll backstory stuff with Jonah working out, shelving books, filling cat bowls—that sort of thing."

"Sure," Jonah said, and Kate turned to see him nodding along with Amy. "Did you have a chance to talk with the execs about doing some stuff at my sister's animal shelter?"

"I ran it by Chase on the phone," Amy said. "He gave it the green light. Kate can give you a call tonight to work out the schedule for those segments."

Kate nodded and tried not to look alarmed. This is how they'd normally split up the work. There was nothing suspicious about her being the one to work directly with Jonah. So why was she having trouble looking at Viv?

"I can also shoot you an e-mail with some times," Kate offered. "If you're too busy to chat."

"Let's play it by ear," Jonah said.

"Let's."

Silence stretched out for a few beats, and Kate glanced at Viv. Was she noticing anything? Or was the awkwardness all in Kate's head?

Viv was smiling up at Jonah, still riding the wave of pride in their on-screen victory with Sam and Elena. "Thanks again for being here, Jonah," she said. "I'm excited about what we're doing here. What we're accomplishing together. This is important work."

He nodded once. "Sure thing. Beats baling hay or cleaning sewers for a paycheck."

Viv laughed and touched his arm. It was probably meant to be a playful swat, but coming from Viv's delicate hand, it looked like a caress. Kate breathed deeply, trying to ignore the sensation of someone grabbing her by the throat.

She turned back to Amy, needing to get her eyes off the friendly exes. "You want to go grab some coffee? We can go over the figures for—"

"Actually, ladies, I was hoping to talk with you quickly before you leave."

Kate swung her gaze back to Viv, who had blessedly removed her hand from Jonah's arm. "Any chance you have a few moments?"

Kate's pulse thrummed in her ears, but she found herself nodding. "Of course."

"Excellent." Viv reached up and tucked a strand of hair behind her ear. "There's something—*private*—I'd like to discuss. I'd really rather do this in my office if you don't mind."

The words hung there in the air for a moment, and Kate froze. Did Viv know something? Had she read it in Kate's face, or had Jonah given it away somehow?

She avoided looking at him, but heard him mumble a farewell. Conscious of his footsteps retreating down the hall, she managed a faint wave, then turned to follow Viv the opposite direction. Amy fell into step beside Kate and gave her a discreet elbow nudge.

"What the hell?" she asked with her eyes.

Kate pressed her lips together, not daring to shrug as she watched Viv's back moving down the hall ahead of them. Did Viv know something? Kate's mind raced with excuses, with justifications for what happened between her and Jonah.

It was just one time.

There's nothing serious going on.

I would never do anything to compromise the show.

Viv used a key to open a door at the end of the hallway. Pushing the door open, she waved them inside. Kate looked around, feeling like a terrified fangirl in Viv's office. The desk was huge and uncluttered, and the bookshelves held an eclectic assortment of art and reference books.

An unlit candle on the corner of an end table filled the room with the scent of sage and cedar. A cozy-looking red loveseat occupied one wall, but Kate sensed that wasn't where she should sit.

She turned and chose one of the padded leather chairs in front of the desk. Amy did likewise, folding her hands in her lap as they both watched Viv lock the door. Then she moved behind her desk in solemn silence. She seated herself in a tall leather chair, her posture unusually straight. Kate watched, on alert as Viv took a deep breath and laced her fingers together on the polished mahogany surface.

"Thank you for meeting with me." She looked at Kate, then Amy, then back to Kate. Her gaze held there for a few beats, and Kate could scarcely breathe.

"I'm sorry to be dramatic, but it's important to me that this conversation be discreet," she said. "The walls and doors are soundproofed in here. I want us all to feel confident and secure that the conversation we're about to have will stay within the confines of this safe space."

Kate swallowed hard, ordering herself to nod and look calm. "Of course. You have our word."

Amy nodded beside her. "Absolutely. The contracts we've all signed have nondisclosure clauses that extend to private conversations like this."

"That's comforting." Viv cleared her throat. "I spoke with Chase Whitfield this morning."

The hairs on Kate's arms prickled. "With Chase Whitfield," she repeated, trying to sound cool. Trying to pretend it was no big deal that the on-camera talent was making covert calls to Empire TV's executive director. "That's—unexpected."

"I know," Viv said, nodding once. "I realize that probably feels like I'm going over your head. But I had a good reason."

Kate found her tongue suddenly didn't work, so she was grateful to Amy for speaking up. "What's the reason?"

Viv looked up at the ceiling a moment, almost as though she was gathering her thoughts. Kate shoved her hands between her knees and prayed no one would notice they were shaking.

"It has to do with Jonah," she said. "Well, more specifically, with the idea of my ex-husband dating again. Dating and having sex and falling in love and all that might entail."

Kate's mouth went dry. She opened it, ready to stammer an explanation, but Amy put a hand on her knee. "You mean what we talked about yesterday?" she said. "About the possibility of using that story line for the arc?"

"Right," Viv said. "When I sat down yesterday with Jonah and started talking about the idea of one of us dating again, I was hit with this overwhelming sense of clarity. Clarity like I haven't experienced in years."

Kate swallowed hard. "What sort of clarity?"

"Clarity about Jonah. And the reason I don't want him dating anyone else."

Oh, Christ.

"What is the reason?" Amy asked.

"Because I love him. Again. Still, I mean—I don't think I ever stopped. And it's become crystal clear to me that I have a lot of work to do to win him back."

Kate's stomach lurched. Her palms were sweating, and she wondered if Viv had any idea. "I—um—wow. I didn't see this coming."

"How does Jonah feel about this?" Amy asked.

Kate glanced at her, grateful to her for asking the right questions. The questions she herself couldn't ask without her voice trembling, her hands shaking. Amy sat stone-faced, looking composed enough for the both of them.

"That's the thing," Viv said. "I know I preach open and honest communication, but I'm still processing my own thoughts. Considering the best way to approach things."

Amy tilted her head to the side. "You mean dating your ex-husband again?"

Viv sighed. "The divorce was my idea. I'm the one who initiated it. I take full responsibility for that mistake."

"Mistake," Kate repeated, trying to follow Viv's train of thought. "I'm not sure I understand. What does Chase Whitfield have to do with this?"

"I had an idea," Viv began, "A thought about sharing my feelings in a rather—unconventional way. And I wanted to get his take on it. To see how he thought a bombshell like that might impact the show."

The words took a moment to sink in. They were still sinking in before Kate could find her voice.

"Wait," Amy said, catching up more quickly than Kate. "You're thinking of making this part of the show? The story arc they're asking for?"

"I wanted to get Chase's read on it, yes." Vivienne took a shaky breath and looked at each of them in turn. "You think it's a bad idea?"

"You're talking about dating Jonah again," Kate said slowly. "On television."

"I thought it might be something people could learn from," she said. "Seeing me put it all out there. Watching me be humbled, watching me lay my heart on the line. Letting viewers see the authenticity of our interactions with one another in a personal way."

Kate stared at her. "You're wanting to win back your husband."

"Ex-husband," Amy pointed out, and Kate wanted to kiss her. "What did Mr. Whitfield say about your idea?"

"Chase thought it was a compelling story line," she said. "That regardless of how it turns out, we could piece it all together after the fact in editing."

"I'm sure he did," Amy said. Her voice was completely professional, but there was an edge to it. An edge only Kate would catch.

The blond producer smiled and reached across the desk to touch Viv's hand. "Dr. Brandt—"

"Please, it's Viv. There's no need to be formal here. I'm honestly asking for your input."

"Our input." Kate hated that she kept parroting Viv's words, but she honestly couldn't find her own. "Our input on the idea of introducing this into the show?"

"Yes," Viv said. "That, and—well, you've gotten to know Jonah." She paused, and Kate held her breath. "I'm wondering what your impression is."

"Of Jonah?"

"Of whether there's any possibility we might rekindle things between us."

"I—I—" Kate's mouth was dry. "I honestly couldn't say."

Amy leaned forward. "Have you broached the subject at all with Jonah? Gotten some sense of how he might be feeling about rekindling things?"

Viv cleared her throat again and glanced away. "Chase Whitfield was of the opinion that we ought to keep it from him. Not to let Jonah know my intent up front. To let things play out on the air however they will."

"What?" Kate stared at her. She gripped the armrests of the chair as the bottom fell out of her stomach.

"That's insane," Amy said.

Viv frowned and met Amy's eyes again. "Actually, I think he has a point. How better to capture the honesty of the interaction?"

"By being dishonest with a member of the team?" Kate asked. Her words sounded more impassioned than she meant them to, and she ordered herself to calm down.

"It's not dishonest," Viv said. "While expressing feelings is important, so is holding them in check until the right time. What sort of world would this be if people went around sharing every feeling they're having with no checks and balances?" She gave an awkward little laugh and glanced from Amy to Kate and back again. "Just because you have sexual fantasies about the checker at the grocery store doesn't mean you should blurt it out the first time you feel a pang of longing as he bags your carrots. You need to ease into it. Let things play out slowly and naturally."

Kate's brain swam with words that weren't arranging themselves into any rational response.

Why would you—?

What happens if—?

How is Jonah going to—?

"Yes, there's an uncertainty about it," Viv said, reading Kate's thoughts, though hopefully not all of them. "That's part of what will make viewers connect with it. The authenticity."

Amy rested her hands on the edge of the desk. "You mentioned speaking privately with Jonah yesterday. Did you manage to get a sense of how he might respond to something like this?"

"Is he interested in—" Kate's voice caught a little, but she held it together. "In getting back together?"

"I didn't ask outright, of course," Viv said. "I'm only just realizing these feelings myself."

"Of course," Amy said evenly. "But we have to ask, before we start down this path. Before we spend a lot of man hours getting footage for something that might not pan out the way you're hoping."

Kate held her breath, dizzy and nauseated and desperate to flee the room. But she wanted to hear Viv's answer. Needed to hear it.

"I understand," Viv said softly. "And yes. I have a sense that Jonah feels the same way I do."

Kate's chest felt like someone was standing on it. She breathed in for four seconds, held it for seven, released it for eight. The exercise wasn't calming at all. Her lungs were on fire, along with the rest of her chest.

"I just want to go on record saying this seems like a risky idea," Amy said. "There are so many ways this could backfire."

Viv gave her serene smile. "Isn't love always worth a little risk?"

Kate stared at her, honestly not sure what the answer was supposed to be. She licked her lips and folded her hand on her lap. "Yes. Yes, I suppose it is."

"Wonderful." Viv smiled and stood up. "I'm so glad we had this talk."

"So you're going ahead with it?" Amy asked. "With trying to woo your ex-husband back on national television."

"Yes," Vivian said softly. She looked toward the window, her expression solemn. "I need to see this through."

"Okay." Kate gripped the armrests tightly for a few seconds, then let go. "So I guess we'll just—" *We'll just what, Kate?* her brain screamed at her, pointing out all the ways this could go horribly wrong for all of them. "We'll just wait and see how it plays out."

Viv stepped around her desk and leaned against the edge of it. Kate knew she should stand up, too, but she wasn't sure her legs would cooperate.

"Chase promised to send me a few notes," Viv said. "Some ideas about timing, and what might play best with a television audience."

"Good," Kate managed. "That's good."

"In the meantime," Viv continued, "I'm hoping to start laying the groundwork by spending more time with Jonah."

"Of course." Kate swallowed. Was it her imagination, or did Viv's gaze linger on her? Viv looked away, then smiled at Amy.

"Well." Viv pressed her hands together in prayer position. "I don't want to keep you two any longer. I know you had budget items to go over. Thank you for hearing me out."

"Our pleasure." Amy stood up, then reached down and pulled Kate to her feet like it was the most normal thing in the world to help an able-bodied woman perform a simple task. Kate said a silent prayer of thanks that her legs managed to hold her up.

"Kate and I will do a little brainstorming about what you've proposed," Amy said. "Maybe a SWOT analysis to look at all the possible angles."

"Lovely." Viv smiled. "Thank you, both of you. It's so wonderful knowing this program is in such good hands."

"We aim to please," Kate said a little weakly. She gave Viv the most normal smile she could muster, though her lips felt stuck to her teeth. "See you tomorrow, Viv."

"Have a lovely night," Viv called back as Amy towed her out the door and down the hall. Even when they were out of earshot, neither of them said a word.

They'd just reached the front door when Kate froze. "Wait," she said. "We need to clean up the—"

"Leave it," Amy said. "I'll text Pete to make sure everything's put away. We're filming here early tomorrow anyway."

She ushered Kate to the rental car, stopping to grab Kate's purse so she could extract the keys. Amy unlocked the doors with a beep, then nudged Kate into the passenger seat and ran around to the driver's side.

"What the actual fuck?" Amy said the second she pulled the door closed.

Kate stared at her, still too stunned to process. "So she's going to woo Jonah back."

"She's going to *try* to woo Jonah back," Amy pointed out. "There's no way to know how that will go."

Kate glanced back at the house, half expecting Viv to be watching them. There was no one at any of the windows. She turned back to Amy.

"I feel like we should tell him."

Amy shook her head. "Kate." There was so much emotion crammed into that single syllable. "You know we can't," Amy continued. "You heard what I said when we sat down. That was a private conversation. We're contractually bound to keep her confidence."

Kate knew that, of course. That didn't make it any easier to wrap her head around. "But there has to be a clause in there somewhere—"

"Unless one cast member is planning to kill another, we have to let it play out," she said. "You know as well as I do that blindsides and secret plots are the name of the game in reality TV."

"I know that," Kate said. "Maybe he wants this."

"Wants to get back with his ex-wife?" Amy snorted. "You don't really believe that."

"I don't know what to believe." Kate glanced back at the house and wondered if Viv had noticed their car hadn't left the drive. "What if I did know for sure that Jonah's not interested? Do I owe it to Viv to tell her?"

"Tell her what? 'Hey, I shagged your ex-husband six ways to Sunday and ruined him for other women, so I don't think he'll take you back.'"

Okay, it sounded silly when Amy put it that way. "No," Kate said slowly. "I don't think that's true. I think—hell, I don't know what to think."

"She does have a point," Amy said. "Stupid though it may be, it would make for great television no matter how it turns out."

"Fucking Chase Whitfield," Kate said, even though she knew it wasn't his fault.

"Come on," Amy said. "Let's skip the coffee and go straight for martinis. My treat."

She started the engine and Kate felt a fresh wave of gratitude that Amy was in her court. Amy looked over then and gave her a sympathetic smile. "You okay?"

"Yes."

"Will *you* be able to keep the secret?"

Kate nodded, pretty sure she was on the brink of setting a record for the most secrets kept in a single week. "Yeah," she said. "Mum's the word."

CHAPTER TWELVE

The next few days of filming passed in a blur for Jonah. Kate behaved like the consummate professional, orchestrating detailed filming schedules and pulling cast members aside for on-the-fly interviews (which Jonah had learned to call "OTFs" so the crew members didn't look at him like a dumbass).

He tried not to take it personally that Kate never handled his OTFs, always deferring them to Amy or one of the other folks on set. This is what they'd agreed, after all. They both had to pretend nothing had happened between them.

He couldn't help wishing Kate weren't so good at it.

A couple of times he tried texting her after hours. Once about a beer he thought she'd like, and another time with some silly message about bubble bath. He also messaged her about the filming schedule at Jossy's shelter.

That was the only text she answered right away.

He knew that was for the best. She was just sticking with what they'd agreed, and he was the idiot who thought maybe they could still make something happen. That there was some way sleeping together wouldn't affect the show or their friendship or anything else.

He knew better, dammit.

Even so, he couldn't stop his stupid heart from lurching at the sight of her coming up the walkway toward Jossy's shelter. She was still wearing the skirt and heels she'd worn all day on set, and he wondered if her feet hurt like hell. He thought about asking, but decided against it.

Her feet were none of his business. Neither was the rest of her body.

"Hey," he called as he pushed open the door.

"Jonah. Good to see you again." Kate gave a polite nod and slipped through the door with the camera crew marching along behind her. Jonah scanned the group, relieved to see no sign of Viv. His ex had been like cling wrap lately, always hanging around wanting to go over notes or have tea together.

It was nice to have some space for once.

"Jossy's in the back room wrangling puppies," he said. "She thought that might be a good place to start."

"Puppies are perfect," Kate said, smiling as she swung a big microphone over one shoulder. "Everyone loves puppies."

"Come on. I'll take you back there."

He led the way down the hall with the crew following behind. A tech guy named Dan was walking around with a gadget Jonah had come to recognize as a light meter. Pete kept holding his camera at odd angles and swooping in for different approaches to the same shot.

"Nice place you've got here," he mumbled as he moved past Jonah. "Your sister's doing great work."

"Thank you," Jonah said, remembering the text message he'd gotten from Jossy early that morning.

Did you say Pete Waller was the camera guy on your show?

Yeah, why? Jonah had texted back.

He just made a $300 online donation to the shelter.

Jonah had smiled and texted a quick reply. That sounds like Pete. Helluva cameraman, even better human.

Jonah watched him work now, wondering how he'd ended up on a show like this. With a demeanor that reminded Jonah of a kindhearted Sasquatch, Pete seemed infinitely more decent than most of the network folks. He brought doughnuts for the crew every morning and made it a point to know everyone's name—even the caterers and the lowliest intern. What drew someone like that to a career in reality TV?

As Kate fell into step beside him, Jonah wondered the same thing about her.

"Thanks again for fitting this in," she said. "I'm glad we could make it work."

"So am I," he said. "I'm glad you're here."

"Me, too," she said. "For your sister, I mean. I think it's great we can help the shelter."

He smiled down at her. "Just for my sister?"

She smiled back, and there was a wistfulness to it. She leaned closer, lowering her voice. "It's good to see you, too."

Jonah pushed open the door to the puppy room. The second he did it, eight pairs of eyes looked up at him. Seven pairs belonged to floppy little fur-covered bodies that came rushing toward the doorway.

The other pair was Jossy's. She grinned up at them from her spot on the floor. "Hey, there!"

She started to stand, and Jonah recognized she was having difficulty. The prosthetic leg must be giving her trouble again. He hurried over, but Jossy waved him away. "I'm fine, I'm fine. Just a little stiff today, that's all."

She got to her feet and stuck her hand out to Kate. "I'm Jossy, and I swear that's not pee on my hand," she said. "Puppy slobber, maybe."

"Puppy slobber I can handle," Kate said as she shook Jossy's hand. "I'm Kate Geary. Thanks so much for inviting us here."

"My pleasure. I was super pumped when Jonah told me about the idea to film here."

"We'll definitely do what we can to bring attention to the organization," Kate said. "Animal advocacy is always popular with viewers."

"So are shirtless men, apparently." Jossy flashed him a knowing grin, and Jonah rolled his eyes at her.

"This is the rest of the crew," Jonah said. "Pete Waller, Dan Kinny— is Amy not with you?"

Kate shook her head and glanced away. "She had some things to work on with Viv. Some details in the production schedule."

Jonah nodded and tried not to look too relieved. The fewer people, the better, as far as he was concerned. If he had his way, they'd just have him and Kate here with no one else.

"I'm glad to finally meet you," Kate said to Jossy. Jonah watched, wondering if she'd noticed the prosthetic leg. It wasn't obvious when Jossy wore pants, but today she'd chosen ankle-baring capris. Some people might not pick up on it, but Kate wasn't some people. Jonah already knew from working with her how observant she was.

He glanced over at Pete to see the cameraman zooming in, and he felt a pang of anger. Goddammit. It would be just like them to exploit his sister's disability. Jonah glanced at Kate and saw her look at the cameraman, then shake her head once with a frown.

Pete nodded and redirected the camera at the mob of puppies frolicking at their feet.

"They're so cute!" Kate declared. She knelt down among them, rewarded by a chorus of playful growls and tiny, nipping teeth. "You're so fuzzy," she cooed. "So fuzzy and so very, very *sharp*."

Jossy laughed. "They're teething right now. Watch your necklace. They'll grab hold and never let go."

"They're also potty training, apparently." Kate winced and glanced at her shoe. "I think little fuzznuts here just filled my favorite shoe with a little liquid love."

"Oh!" Jossy gasped and rushed toward her. "I'm so sorry. Let me grab some paper towels."

"It's fine, totally my fault," Kate said. "I know better than to wear good shoes to a shoot like this. I normally have an extra pair in the car, but I forgot today."

She rested one hand on the wall and pried the one off her right foot, then frowned. Glancing around, she spotted the area marked *Wee Wee Station* and hobbled over. "There," she said as she dumped out what looked like a zillion gallons of puppy pee. "That's better." She grimaced, then leaned down to put it back on her foot.

"Wait!" Jossy said. "What size are you? I think I have some ballet flats in my bag."

"Eleven," Kate said, glancing at Jossy's feet. Both the real one and the prosthetic foot were encased in Converse sneakers. "You look like about a six?"

"Six and a half," Jossy said. "Sorry, that won't work."

"I have some running shoes," Jonah offered. "They're a men's ten and a half, so probably a couple sizes too big, but maybe better than four sizes too small?"

Kate seemed to hesitate. "Are you sure? That seems a little . . . intimate."

It was on the tip of his tongue to remind her that he'd been inside her, so sharing shoes seemed beside the point. But obviously he couldn't say that. "It's fine by me, but your call," he said. "I promise I don't have cooties, but it might wreck the look of your outfit."

"Ha!" Kate blew a loose strand of hair off her forehead. "Frankly, I'd love to get out of these heels. I accept."

Jonah smiled. "I'll go grab them."

He hustled out of the room and located the running shoes he'd stashed behind the counter. They were new enough not to be smelly, though the bright-orange hue would clash like crazy with Kate's green blouse.

But she just thanked him as he handed them over along with a pair of freshly laundered socks in a gaudy neon yellow. She hopped over to a spigot and rinsed off her foot, then dried it with a nappy gray towel that Jossy handed her.

"Thanks, guys." She pulled on his shoes and socks, but kept her focus on Jossy. "You're right, this is a great spot for shooting. The puppies are perfect."

"That's what I was thinking," his sister said. "Even though puppies never have much trouble getting adopted, they're a good tool to draw people in."

Kate grinned. "Sort of like shirtless dog walkers?"

"Exactly like shirtless dog walkers." Jossy winked at Jonah. "Only much cuter." She looked down at Kate's feet and laughed. "Now *that* is a cute look."

Kate glanced at her own feet, and Jonah half expected her to recoil in embarrassment. Instead, she laughed, turning her foot from side to side. The shoes were a couple of sizes too big, and with the yellow, orange, and green, she looked like a well-dressed circus clown.

She looked adorable. Jonah felt a warmth in the center of his chest that had nothing to do with puppies.

"Okay," Kate said, clapping her hands together and turning her attention to the camera crew. "What do you think? Will this space work?"

Pete nodded. "Yeah. I'm going to set up in the corner over there."

"Cool." Kate turned away and got busy unpacking gear. "What do you think about saving the OTFs until the end?"

"Good call," Pete said, scratching his beard. "You want to give me a quick opinion about the lighting?"

As Kate slipped away, Jossy sidled up to Jonah and whispered in his ear. "What's an OTF?"

"On-the-fly interview," he replied. "I thought you were the world's biggest reality-TV fan."

"I watch it, I don't film it." Jossy's eyes followed Kate across the room as she helped Pete string cable from one side to the other. "I like her. Very unpretentious."

"Very smart," Jonah agreed. "Very good at her job."

"Yeah, but not in a Viv sort of way. She doesn't seem like someone who needs to overshadow everyone else so her light looks brighter."

Jonah nodded, but said nothing as Kate shuffled back toward them in her clown shoes. "Tell me a little more about the whole shirtless dog-walking thing," she said. "How has it worked out for you from a marketing standpoint?"

"Great!" Jossy said. "We've seen a thirty percent uptick in adoptions since my gross brother started stripping for charity. I'm thinking of trolling for other men to take a shirtless shift."

"Impressive," Kate said, and Jonah couldn't help noticing her gaze flick over his chest. But she quickly brought her focus back to Jossy. "Are the pets he takes for walks always the ones who get adopted?"

"No, that's the great thing. Once he gets people through the door, the animals sort of sell themselves. We've found homes for a lot of pets that might have been overlooked otherwise."

"That's terrific."

"Yeah," Jossy agreed. "Turns out my big brother can be kinda useful."

"He does have a certain charm." Kate looked at him and gave a quiet smile that gave Jonah a pleasant ache in the middle of his chest. He longed to wrap his arms around her and press his mouth against the warm skin behind her ear, but Kate turned back to the camera and lighting guys. "You guys about ready to roll?"

"Five minutes," Pete reported.

Kate nodded and bent down to pet a persistent puppy who'd started tugging at her shoelace. Jonah's shoelace.

"You can pick him up if you want," Jossy said. "It's good to handle them as much as possible."

"You just made my whole week." Kate bent down and scooped up the fluffy mop, pressing her face into his fur. She murmured something against the little dog's ear, then began strolling the perimeter of the room. Jossy fell into step beside her. Jonah stood watching, feeling like an outsider in his own life.

"Are you comfortable giving us an on-camera interview?" Kate asked. "It's okay if you say no. We'll keep the focus on Jonah."

Jossy glanced at him, looking for a cue. He nodded, trying to convey he was game for anything. "Sure," Jossy said, looking back at Kate. "I mean, whatever you think will help shed some light on what we do here. Puppies, shirtless ex-Marines, a crippled girl with a prosthetic leg."

Kate froze. She turned and looked at Jossy with an intensity in her gaze that made Jonah's breath catch in his throat.

"You have my word that we won't do anything to exploit you like that," she said softly. "That's not why we're here. Not at all."

Jossy smiled and reached over to stroke the ears of the puppy in Kate's arms. "It's okay. I was joking, mostly, but I don't mind if you do want to show it. You know, zoom in on the fake leg or whatever."

Kate shook her head. "If we do choose to show that—and I promise you'll get to consent if that's the case—I promise we won't do anything to make you look weak or helpless. If anything, there's a benefit to showing the normalcy of someone with a disability doing something amazing."

Jossy beamed. His sister had just made a new best friend.

"Come on," Jossy said. "Let me give you a tour of the rest of the place."

◆　◆　◆

By the time they finished filming for the day, the sun had long since gone down. Jonah glanced at his watch and tried to remember the last time he'd eaten.

He looked up to see Jossy yawning. "Come on." He slung an arm around his sister's shoulders and resisted the impulse to give her a noogie. "Let me take you to dinner. How about Cactus?"

"Tempting, but I'll pass," she said. "I'm pooped. Besides, I need to get home and feed all the assholes before they tear my kitchen apart."

Kate smiled as she packed pieces of lighting gear into a fancy-looking crate. "You have a house full of assholes?"

"I am the consummate crazy cat lady," Jossy said. "I have a soft spot for the ones no one else adopts. The ones with attitude problems or missing limbs or some weird fungus that makes their hair fall out in clumps."

"I love it," Kate said. She was still wearing Jonah's running shoes, and something about that made him feel happy. "I wish I could have a pet. Someday, maybe."

"Hey, you can come over anytime and pet mine," Jossy said. "Not tonight, though. Tonight I just want to put my PJs on and eat ice cream straight from the carton."

"That sounds like the perfect plan."

"It was so great meeting you, Kate." Jossy stepped up and pulled Kate into a hug, flashing Jonah a thumbs-up behind her back. *"Love her!"* Jossy mouthed, grinning at him.

Jonah nodded, trying to keep a straight face. Trying not to let on that he had anything other than a professional relationship with Kate.

"It was great meeting you, too," Kate said as she broke the hug. "I'm so impressed by what you're doing here."

"Thanks!" Jossy tucked a fire-red curl behind one ear. "Call me if you have more questions. Or if you just want to grab a drink sometime. Something besides the nasty beer my brother's always drinking."

"I've developed a fondness for the nasty beer," Kate said, flashing him a smile. "But I'd love to grab a drink sometime. I could use a little girl time."

"Sounds good." Jossy moved toward the door, then turned back to Jonah. "You okay locking up by yourself?"

"I've got it covered."

"You *promise* you won't forget to set the alarm this time?"

"It was just the one time," he muttered, prodding her toward the door with a boom mike pole that Pete had left propped next to the door. Jossy giggled and scuttled away.

"'Night, Joss."

"Good night, Shirtless Wonder." She squeezed him hard, standing on tiptoe to whisper in his ear. "Much better pick this time," she whispered.

Then she pulled away, scurrying out the door before he had a chance to ask what the hell had given her the idea that he had any interest in Kate.

Kate, who was now alone in a room with him for the first time since they'd slept together. Jonah looked at her and gave a small shrug.

"So here we are," he said at last.

"Here we are." Kate smiled, but there was something in her eyes he couldn't read. Something bothering her.

"You okay, Kate?"

She nodded. "Just tired. And hungry. And tired. Did I mention tired?"

"You might have."

"Thanks for the shoes." She tipped her foot to the side and smiled down at them. "Do you mind if I wear them home and give them back tomorrow?"

"No problem. Keep them as long as you like. The clown look is a good one for you."

Kate laughed, and Jonah took a step closer. He didn't touch her, of course, but something in him ached to have her nearer. "Thanks for everything you did tonight," he said.

"What do you mean?" she asked. "I did my job."

"No, you didn't," he said. "You went above and beyond your job. You promised Jossy you wouldn't play up her disability without her blessing, even though we both know damn well audiences eat that shit up. Even though she probably signed the same crazy-ass contract the rest of us did that says you're free to run with whatever story line you choose."

Kate bit her lip. "We aren't heartless, Jonah. The show is about playing on human emotion, sure. But not at the expense of the humans involved."

"That's good to know." Jonah stretched, feeling tired all of a sudden. And hungry. Still really, really hungry.

"Could I interest you in dinner?" he asked.

She seemed to hesitate. "You mean that restaurant you mentioned? Cactus?"

"Sure, or wherever you want to go."

Kate glanced down at her shoes. His shoes. "Under the circumstances, I should probably—"

"How about my place?"

Shit. He hadn't meant to blurt that out. But Kate looked up at him with something that seemed like relief. "You *are* less than a mile away."

Jonah's heart did a funny little hiccup in the center of his chest. "True."

"Okay, I can grab takeout," she said. "I saw a drive-through Thai place down the street."

Jonah grinned. "Why don't you just be honest here, Kate."

Her eyes widened like he'd just stepped on her foot. "What?"

"You just want to see my cat." He smiled and watched her face, wondering what the hell had prompted such a strong reaction. "It's understandable."

Kate gave an uneasy laugh and clamped the lid down on the crate. "You caught me," she said. "So do you want to meet at your place in fifteen minutes?"

"Sounds good. You pick up the Thai food, and I'll move all the socks and underwear out of the living room."

"Your house is neat as a pin," she said. "I stopped by unannounced before, remember."

"Oh, I remember." He remembered a lot more than that. "I'll see you in fifteen minutes."

CHAPTER THIRTEEN

Kate rang Jonah's doorbell with her elbow. She had a bag of takeout Thai in one hand, a six-pack of IPA in the other, and her heart in her throat.

"Hey there!" Jonah threw open the door and grinned at her, then stepped aside to usher her in. "Looks like you found a way to change clothes."

"Yeah. There was a Victoria's Secret right by the Thai place, so I ran in and grabbed sweatpants and flip-flops."

"I like it," he said, and Kate's cheeks grew warm. Maybe she shouldn't have mentioned Victoria's Secret. And maybe she shouldn't have bought the cute bra-and-panty set she'd grabbed on impulse, reassuring herself it was only because her black undies might show beneath the new white sweatpants. None of it had anything to do with Jonah.

"Denial is a form of self-abuse," Viv chanted in her head. *"You're lying to yourself instead of someone else."*

Kate gritted her teeth and gripped her purchases a little tighter.

"Let me take that." Jonah grabbed the six-pack from her hand and started toward the living room.

"I notice you grabbed the beer first," Kate said as she followed behind him.

"That looked the heaviest," he said. "Besides, I wanted to see what you got."

Kate watched him head toward the couch and felt relieved. Something about that seemed more casual than sitting at the dining room table with placemats and straight-backed chairs. It had nothing to do with wanting to cuddle up close to him on a soft surface.

She almost believed that as she began unpacking the food on Jonah's coffee table, piling compostable containers of coconut rice and lemony tom kha gai soup in neat little rows beside his remote control.

"Nice choice on the IPA," Jonah said. "Crux makes some of the best beer in Oregon. Where did you find Gimme Mo?"

"There was a little grocery mart next to the Thai place," she said. "At first I wasn't sure about buying beer in cans instead of bottles."

"No, this is great." Jonah held up one of the purple cans and studied the label. "Canned beer has been making a comeback. Aluminum preserves the freshness of the beer better than glass does. Something about light and the way the cans are sealed."

"Plus I can crush it on my forehead when I'm done."

Jonah laughed. "I would pay a lot of money to see that."

Kate took the pile of paper plates and napkins he handed her and set them up on the coffee table while Jonah arranged plastic forks and a can of beer for each of them.

"Want a glass?" he asked.

"Nah, I'm good." She popped the top on hers, and something about the click and hiss gave her comfort. It made this whole thing seem more like a platonic meeting between two colleagues than a clandestine rendezvous between two people who'd slept together and might wish urgently to do it again.

Maybe that was just her.

Kate glanced to her right and spotted Marilyn looking at her with intense skepticism.

Kate could see her point.

She tore her eyes off the cat and took a sip of beer. "It's really good," she said. "Different from the Boneyard one the other night."

The second the words left her lips, she wished she could take them back. The last thing she should do was remind Jonah of their visit to the swingers club. Of what happened after that.

But Jonah didn't seem to notice. "You have a sharp palate," he said. "The Crux beer has more of a mosaic hop flavor to it. At least I assume that's where the name comes from."

He held up the can to study it again, which gave Kate the chance to study him. He was still wearing the green shirt from earlier, though he'd undone several buttons in front. He wore a white undershirt beneath it, but she could make out the light dusting of chest hair at the neck of it. She remembered what that felt like pressed against her bare breasts, soft and springy and—

"Okay, Kate." Jonah set his beer down on the coffee table. "What did you want to talk about?"

Kate licked her lips and rested her beer can on one knee. "What makes you think I wanted to talk about something?"

Jonah studied her for a moment, and Kate tried not to squirm. There were definite downsides to spending time with a guy trained by the military to ferret out spy secrets. It felt like he could read her mind.

He said nothing, which Kate knew damn well was meant to get her talking. To prompt her to volunteer more information.

She shrugged and took another sip of beer. "I was hungry for dinner, and your place was close," she said. "And being here instead of a restaurant keeps us from being spotted by crew members or Amy or—"

"We're coworkers, Kate. Is it really that suspicious we'd have dinner together?"

"I don't know." She fiddled with the tab on top of her beer can. "I'm leery about what people read into things. What shows on my face. I may have studied acting, but I'm actually not a very good liar."

"That's a plus." He grabbed two coasters and set one on the table in front of each of them, giving Kate the chance to take the beer can off her knee. "I'm glad you suggested this," he added. "It's nice to be able to let my guard down a little. Not to have to keep up some sort of front for Amy or the crew or—anyone else."

There was something in that pause, a name they were both avoiding. Kate could see it hanging in the space between them, Viv's name in big block letters. It was as noticeable as Viv's voice echoing in her head all the time.

"I love him. Again. Still, I mean—I don't think I ever stopped."

She shook her head to clear the voice and reached for one of the containers of food. Viv was in a meeting tonight, so at least there was no chance of her dropping by with the hope of wooing Jonah. Not that she'd do that here. Knowing Viv, she'd want to save all the best footage for when the cameras were on them.

Kate kept her eyes down, intent on the task of opening boxes and reading lids and trying to recall what she'd chosen. Beside her, Jonah began opening lids to reveal a fragrant array of food.

As the silence stretched out, they took turns doling out spicy curry and coconut rice. Kate wondered what he was thinking. If this felt as awkward to him as it did to her. If he was as aware as she was of the warm body just a few inches away.

Once she'd filled her plate, Kate leaned back against the sofa and tucked one leg under herself. As she forked up her first bite of food, she thumbed through the index cards in her brain, trying to find a topic of conversation. Something casual. Something friendly. Nothing that involved Viv or sex or marriage or—

"How did Jossy lose her leg?" Kate bit her lip, pretty sure that wasn't the fun quip she'd been aiming for.

The startled look on Jonah's face underscored her suspicion.

"Sorry," she said, eager to backpedal. "You don't have to answer that if you don't want. That's a personal question and Jossy's story to tell. That was really rude of me."

"No, it's fine. Jossy would be okay with you knowing." He forked up a bite of curry and took a long time chewing it. Kate waited, unsure how to conduct herself. She stabbed at a piece of eggplant but couldn't seem to get it onto her fork. At least the task gave her something to look at besides Jonah's face.

"You just surprised me; that's all," Jonah said. "I was going to let the silence draw out a bit so you'd tell me whatever was on your mind. I thought I'd have to wait longer than that."

Kate gave a small smile and took an equally small bite of pad thai. "My finesse might leave something to be desired, but I'm usually pretty direct."

"That's a good skill to have."

He still hadn't answered the question, so she waited. She was thinking of reiterating her insistence that he didn't need to tell her anything when he finally spoke.

"When I was eighteen, Jossy was fifteen," he said slowly. "I had my license before she did, so obviously I ended up driving her around. It was one of the conditions our mom set before she helped me buy a car."

Kate nodded and picked up her beer. She took a small sip but kept her eyes on Jonah. He wasn't looking at her. He was staring down at his plate, a rare moment of eschewing eye contact. Even Marilyn and her eyebrows seemed aware of a shift in the mood. She lay quietly on the back of the sofa, paws stretched in front of her like a sphinx. Her eyes were closed, and her face seemed unusually devoid of judgment.

"One night, Jossy called me from a party and said she needed a ride," Jonah continued. "I was in the middle of a date with a girl whose name I don't even remember. Krista or Kristy or something like that. Anyway, I gave Jossy a hard time. Asked if there was someone else who could come pick her up."

Kate watched the side of Jonah's face, noticing the furrow between his brows. The way he stared at his own hands, the plate of food forgotten in front of him.

"Did you end up giving her a ride?" Kate's voice was quiet, and she somehow knew what the answer would be before Jonah spoke again.

"No," he said. "I was a selfish teenage asshole who thought he had a shot at getting a blow job that night. Jossy—" He stopped there and took a shaky breath. "Jossy got in a car with a bunch of older kids. Juniors. Most of them had been drinking."

"The one behind the wheel?"

He nodded, gaze still fixed on his plate.

"Yeah. Yes." He looked up at her then, and the sadness in his eyes hit her like a punch in the stomach. "It was my fault. My selfishness cost my sister her leg. Left her with a lifetime of shitty pain and doctor visits."

"Jonah, no. You were just a kid."

He shook his head like he hadn't even heard her. "You want to know the worst of it?"

Kate nodded, though she wasn't sure she did. How could it be worse?

"Jossy was a competitive cyclist," he said. "She was really good, too. Fifteen years old, and the USA Cycling team was already starting to let her train with them. She had a future." He shook his head and set his beer down hard on the coaster. "A future I fucking ruined."

It was on the tip of Kate's tongue to insist that he couldn't blame himself, but she stopped herself. Was there really a point to that? If he'd spent eighteen years telling himself it was his fault, no flippant remark from her would change that.

"Can she still ride a bike?" Kate asked in a soft tone. "I don't know how prosthetic legs work, exactly."

"It's tougher when the amputation is above the knee like Jossy's was," he said. "There are computer-controlled knees that have settings for things like biking and skiing, but they're insanely expensive. Hundreds of thousands of dollars once you factor in fittings and maintenance and things like that."

"And insurance doesn't cover it?"

"Most don't," he said.

A light flickered in the back of Kate's brain, and she finally understood. "So that's why you're doing the TV show," she said. "That's why you changed your mind after I showed you the budget."

Jonah nodded once and spun his beer on the table. "Jossy knows computer-controlled prosthetics exist, obviously. But it's never been an option before. She's never wanted to talk about it."

"Does she know that's why you're doing the show?"

He shook his head. "But I figure if I find myself sitting on a huge pile of cash, she'll have a hard time saying no."

"Jonah." This time she did reach out and touch him. A hand on his knee, which seemed like a pitiful gesture once she saw her own five fingers sitting there useless and small. He looked at it for a long time, almost like he was wondering how it got there.

"That really fucking sucks," Kate said. "For you, for Jossy—hell, for the other kids in that car, whether they died or got injured or have to live with what they did forever. It fucking sucks for everyone."

Jonah burst out laughing. He laughed so hard that for a moment, Kate worried he'd slipped into hysterics. Even Marilyn seemed alarmed, her eyebrows lifting as she repositioned herself a few inches away.

"Oh, Kate," he said, shaking his head with laughter in his voice. "You say the best things sometimes."

Kate grimaced, wondering if she should back up and try again. "I'm sorry for your—for her—loss."

He shook his head, still laughing a little. "You know what Viv said to me the first time I told her that story?"

Kate felt a pang at hearing Viv's name, but forced herself to stay focused on the conversation. "No. What?"

"She said, 'Guilt is an emotional warning sign that there's something here for you to learn. Self-examination can be healthy, and this is a beautiful opportunity to grow and mourn and flounder and breathe.'"

"That's beautiful," Kate said. "Much more put together than what I said."

"Sure, it's great. Textbook example of what to say to someone who's grieving and blaming himself. Literally—it's from a book. A book she wrote."

"There's nothing wrong with that," Kate said, not certain why she felt like defending Viv. "She has wise insights to share. She's articulate and—"

"Kate, I know. You don't need to sing my ex-wife's praises. I know she has fans, and I know you're one of the biggest. It's just—sometimes people don't want the platitudes. They just want connection. Something real. Something genuine. Something heartfelt, even if it's, 'that really fucking sucks.'"

Kate twirled her fork around in the pad thai. "There was still a more poetic way to say that."

"Probably. But I didn't invite you to dinner for the poetry."

"Didn't I invite myself to dinner?"

"All the more reason I'm glad you're here."

Jonah picked up his plate and took a bite of curry. The frown lines relaxed in his forehead, and though he wasn't exactly smiling, he didn't look as melancholy as he had a few minutes ago.

"I'm sorry about what happened," Kate said.

Jonah looked up. "Are you talking about the car accident, or what happened between us the other night?"

"The car accident." Kate bit her lip. "I'm not sorry about what happened between us. It can't happen again, of course—"

"Of course."

"But like you said the next morning: It wasn't a mistake. We were pulled into each other's orbit for a reason."

Jonah grimaced and looked down at his plate. When he looked up, his expression had turned sheepish. "You knew that was a Viv quote, didn't you?"

"Yes." Kate shifted a little on the couch, conscious of his closeness, of the riskiness of this conversation.

"I didn't realize it until hours later, when we were on set and it hit me like a ton of bricks. Forgive me?"

"For what?"

"For quoting my ex-wife in bed with you."

"There's nothing to forgive." Still, the apology meant a lot to her. That he'd even thought to offer it. "It's natural she'd still be in your brain all the time. Natural, even, for you to still have feelings for her."

There. She'd put it out there. She was treading on dangerous turf, but she had to test the water, didn't she? To find out how Jonah might react to Viv's pursuit. It was her job as a producer, for the future of the show.

"Denial is the worst form of—"

"Feelings?" Jonah bit into a spring roll and gave her a dubious look. "I hope you don't mean that the way people usually mean it when they talk about having *feelings* for someone."

"Would that be so far off the mark? You two were married, after all. You pledged to spend your lives together. You were so deliriously in love that you got matching infinity symbol tattoos."

"God, I wish we hadn't put that in the damn book," he muttered. "Or gotten the damn tattoos in the first place. Actually, I take that back. The tattoo is pretty cool."

"I know. I was admiring it the other night."

Jonah sighed. "Kate. All those things you just said—the life plans, the marriage, the tattoos—the operative word in all of that is *were*. Past tense."

His words flooded her with equal parts relief and guilt. What the hell was she doing here? Was this a fact-finding mission for Viv, or for herself?

"I'm just saying, don't ever say *never*," she said carefully. "Things change. People change."

"Jesus, Kate." Jonah frowned and stabbed a big hunk of chicken. "You're starting to sound like Viv."

Kate would have found that flattering under normal circumstances, but she could tell he didn't mean it as a compliment. She started to pick at a spring roll, but stopped when Jonah spoke again. "Look, I appreciate what you're trying to do."

Kate's throat tightened. "What am I trying to do?"

"Reassure yourself that you didn't betray your idol by sleeping with me," he said. "But I can promise you there's nothing between Viv and me anymore. Nothing but a reasonably cordial working relationship and a few good memories mixed with some not-so-good ones."

"You're positive?"

His eyes locked with hers, and Kate felt certain she'd never seen him look so earnest. "I am absolutely, positively, one million–percent sure that I will never reconcile with Vivienne Brandt," he said. "It's a certainty that eclipses any amount of certainty I felt when I said, 'I do.'"

"Okay." Kate swallowed and picked up her fork again. Guilt and relief swished around in her belly like oil and vinegar. Guilt from knowing Jonah's certainty meant Vivienne's heartache.

But relief because he'd misjudged why she'd been asking. He hadn't guessed at her motive. More importantly, because it meant the man she was falling for wasn't in love with someone else.

That counted for something, right?

Even if she couldn't have him, even if they had no business sleeping together, at least she knew Jonah's heart didn't belong to someone else. *"Someone else" is Viv,* she reminded herself. There went the guilt again.

She looked up again to see Jonah watching her. "I love spending time with you like this," he said softly. "You know that? There's no one else I'd rather share Thai food with."

"Thank you," she murmured, giving him a careful smile. "Are you going to eat that last spring roll?"

He laughed and picked up his beer. "Help yourself."

She plucked it off his plate like they were old friends. Good friends. The kind of friends who shared spring rolls and old stories. Not the kind who shared anything else.

But as she bit into the spring roll and felt his eyes on her, felt her own body respond to his proximity, she knew that was a lie.

They could never be just friends.

◆　◆　◆

It was almost eleven by the time Kate made it back to the hotel. As she slid her key card into the slot, she heard a door open across the hall.

"Kate."

She turned to see Amy poking her head out of her room. Her face was bare, and she wore a serious expression, along with fuzzy pink pajama bottoms and an oversized black sweater.

"Hey, Amy," Kate said carefully. "You're up late."

"So are you." Amy slipped out the door and leaned against the wall, hands tucked up inside the sleeves of her sweater. "Pete texted as you guys were finishing up at the shelter a couple hours ago. Said filming went really well."

"It did. Everything was great." She waited for Amy to ask where she'd been in the hours since filming wrapped, but it was probably obvious. And it was obvious from the look on Amy's face that she'd already guessed.

"I didn't sleep with him again," Kate blurted.

Amy smiled, but didn't laugh. "I didn't ask," she said. "And I wouldn't judge if you had. But I do need to talk to you about something."

Kate glanced at her watch. If she went to sleep now, she'd still get six hours. That sounded heavenly. "Can it wait until morning?"

Amy shook her head. "No. It can't, actually."

Something in Amy's tone, in the tenseness of her expression, made the skin prickle on Kate's arms. This was more than a conversation about Chase Whitfield's latest request. More than a briefing about drama between the test couples or a suggestion from Viv about the direction of the show.

Kate slipped the key card into the front pouch on her purse and turned to face Amy. Hopefully they could keep their voices down and get this over with quickly. "Okay, but let's make it fast," she said. "What's up?"

Amy shook her head. "Not out here. This isn't a conversation for the hallway. Let me grab my laptop, and I'll meet you in your room in two minutes."

Kate sighed and tried not to be irritated. Building drama was part of Amy's job. She couldn't blame her for not flipping the switch after hours.

But she also knew whatever this was could wait. "Amy, I'm tired and I have to pee. Can you just spit it out now so we can—"

"He's married," Amy said. "Jonah's married."

Kate's blood went cold. She'd heard that expression before, but this time she was sure she felt flecks of ice pricking her veins from inside. She grabbed hold of the door handle, unsure whether it was for balance or an urge to get away. To duck into her room, burrow under her covers, and pretend she hadn't heard those words.

He's married.

Jonah's married.

Amy watched, her expression wary. "Kate?"

She nodded, even though there'd been no question asked. But she knew Amy was right about one thing. This wasn't a conversation for the hallway.

"Come on," she said, fumbling for her key card again. "Come inside and tell me everything."

CHAPTER FOURTEEN

Kate stared at the paperwork spread out across her hotel bed, too dumbfounded to comprehend the words dotting the pages like blood spatter.

She looked up to see Amy watching her with a nervous expression. "Say something," Amy urged. "What are you thinking?"

Kate swallowed, trying to get her bearings. "So the divorce papers were never officially filed," she said. "Which means the divorce never happened."

"Right." Amy nodded like a teacher responding to a pupil prone to hysteric outbursts. "As soon as I uncovered all this, I called Viv."

"What?" Kate knotted her fingers in the bedspread and ordered herself to keep breathing. "You called Viv about this?"

Amy reached across the bed and laid a hand on Kate's arm. "No, not like that," she said. "I didn't tell her what I found. I just asked a few questions about the divorce paperwork. She knows I've been working on all the due diligence. The background checks and legal stuff."

"Right. I'm sorry, of course."

"I wanted to see if I could figure out what happened. Get a handle on things so we know how to proceed." Amy gave Kate's arm a squeeze, but didn't draw her hand back. "I gave Viv this totally convincing story about some other show we worked on where an actor's divorce was filed in the wrong state and his ex-wife came after his checks and—well, it doesn't matter. She bought it. She didn't seem suspicious about me trying to track down copies of their divorce certificate."

Kate looked down at the paperwork again, willing there to be a divorce certificate somewhere in the jumble. She saw photocopies of driver's licenses and birth certificates and something that looked like a Costco card.

But no divorce certificate.

"There isn't one," Amy said, reading Kate's thoughts. "According to Viv, they handled the divorce themselves to make sure it stayed out of the media. It was an uncontested divorce, so all they had to do was file a Petition for Dissolution of Marriage and then have a lawyer prepare a QDRO."

"A cuatro?"

"No, a *QDRO*—it's legal shorthand for a Qualified Domestic Relations Order." Amy picked up a sheaf of papers from the pile and waved it at her. "It's a legal document for splitting up things like retirement accounts and pension plans."

"Okay," Kate said, not sure she was following. "So what happened? Or what *didn't* happen?"

"According to Viv, they divvied up the tasks. They did all the paperwork together—"

"How chummy," Kate muttered, hating the bitterness in her own voice.

Amy, bless her heart, ignored Kate's snark and continued. "Apparently they worked out a big list of who'd get what. She was very proud of that—that they didn't use a mediator or lawyers or anything. Just made this great big document splitting up all their assets and accounts and possessions."

"Okay," Kate said, pretty sure she was following.

"They decided Jonah would file the paperwork for the petition, and Viv would file the QDRO."

"You can do them separately?"

"Apparently so." Amy bit her lip and looked down at the papers. "And as far as I can find, Jonah never did his part."

"But—but—that doesn't make sense," Kate said. "Wouldn't there have been some sort of red flag when they did taxes or something?"

Amy shook her head. "It's only been a year. They had to file taxes together last time, since they were still married the preceding tax year," Amy said. "The red flag wouldn't have been raised until the next round."

Kate swallowed, unsurprised Amy had done her homework. It was the only thing here that wasn't a complete and total shock. "I still don't get it," Kate said. "How could you not realize your divorce wasn't final?"

"Viv did the QDRO," Amy said. "There would have been a lot of legal-sounding paperwork flying back and forth. It's possible they both just assumed it was a done deal. Viv does, anyway."

Kate opened her mouth to insist how improbable that sounded, but closed it again. Hadn't Jonah himself acknowledged his own forgetfulness? His failure to keep track of documents and remember important dates?

"Even Viv didn't catch it," Amy said, reading Kate's thoughts. "When I first started asking for paperwork, she gave me all these official-sounding documents, but nothing with an actual county seal on it. That's what raised my antennae. That's why I contacted the courthouse."

"But wouldn't Viv or Jonah or someone have realized at some point that they never saw an official divorce certificate?"

"That's what I asked the county clerk," Amy said. "She said it's not unusual. They don't automatically send you copies. You have to pay for them. And with all the QDRO paperwork flying around—"

"Jonah probably figured Viv had taken care of it," she said. "He told me once before how she was always giving him honey-do lists and then doing the tasks herself if he didn't jump on it fast enough."

"Sure, that's possible," Amy said. "All this time, Viv seemed so proud of how they managed to keep their divorce out of the media."

"And all this time, they weren't actually divorced." Kate had hoped saying the words aloud might make them easier to digest, but that wasn't the case at all. They still sounded sharp and cold, like little obsidian arrow tips.

Amy dropped the stack of papers on the comforter and nodded. "That appears to be the case."

They both looked down at the paperwork then, like the answer might be somewhere in that pile. Kate took a few deep breaths, trying to imagine how it might have all happened. Jonah with a big stack of paperwork, never quite getting around to filing his portion. Getting a stack of documents months later about the divvying up of assets and assuming it was a done deal. That it had all been handled.

Kate looked up again. "Who else knows about this?"

"Just the two of us, for now."

Kate nodded, letting the wheels turn in her brain. For once, she had no answer. No certainty about the right next move. Was this a deal breaker? A show killer or a show maker?

Beyond that, what did it mean for Jonah? For Viv? For all of them? Amy sat watching her, waiting for a response.

"We have to tell them," Kate said.

"Tell who?"

Kate hesitated. "Viv. Jonah. The network execs." She thought about the order of those names, about which needed to happen first. About their need to be discreet. "The show's lawyers."

"You're sure?"

Kate nodded, her brain working quickly, even though she wasn't sure. "We start with the lawyers. They'll know what to do."

"I thought about that," Amy said. "Surely the legal team has seen something like this before. Like maybe there's a simple solution. Some way they can just file the paperwork and get it over with and never need to alert Viv and Jonah at all."

"Right," Kate agreed. "Maybe it really is that simple."

They looked at each other for a long time. Neither of them spoke, but Kate knew they both realized there was no way it could be that simple. Not legally, anyway.

She looked down at the copy of the QDRO. Both bore signatures from Viv and Jonah. It would be so easy to trace those words, to imitate Viv's loopy cursive or Jonah's blocky lettering.

"No." Kate's voice was sharp as she glanced back at Amy. "We're not forging anyone's signatures."

Amy looked startled. "I didn't suggest it."

"I know." Kate took a shaky breath. "I'm telling myself. That's a line we can't cross."

"Understood." Amy was silent a moment, studying Kate with such intensity that she wanted to look away. "Kate?"

"Yeah?"

Amy seemed to hesitate. "I'll only ask you this once, and you don't have to answer if you don't want."

"Okay."

"Do you think Jonah knows? That there's some reason he did it on purpose or—"

"Stayed married to Viv?" She shook her head, waiting to feel any pinpricks of suspicion, any niggling tingles of doubt. There was nothing.

In a way, it was a relief to feel certain about one thing.

"No," Kate said. "I don't think he knows. It wasn't intentional."

"Okay," she said. "That's what I was hoping you'd say."

Amy gave Kate's arm one last squeeze before letting go. Then she picked up a stack of paperwork and began organizing it. Kate watched all the pages shuffling past, all those certificates and licenses and legal documents. Pieces of two intertwined lives.

Amy gathered them all into a thick stack and shoved them into a big envelope the color of baby food. When she closed it and looked at Kate again, she looked determined. "If I do my job right, maybe Jonah never needs to know," Amy said. "Same with Viv."

Kate nodded, wishing it could really be that easy.

In the back of her mind, she heard Viv's words again. A quote from *But Not Broken*, or maybe it was *On the Other Hand*. Kate wasn't sure anymore.

"If something seems too easy, get ready for certain heartbreak."

Kate touched a hand to her chest and tried to ignore the sharp ache.

◆　◆　◆

Jonah held a twenty-pound Main coon named Lucifer between his thighs and tried to remember why he'd agreed to do this.

"I love you, Jonah." Jossy smiled at him, then grabbed hold of Lucifer's rear paws before he could rabbit-kick Jonah in the nuts again. Jonah shifted in his chair, fumbling for a better grip on the cat.

"I'm having second thoughts about whether the feeling's mutual," Jonah muttered, though he knew damn well that's the why he was here at the Cat Café long after business hours, subjecting Lucifer to the world's ugliest manicure. Jonah held out his hand to accept a pink glittery nail tip from his sister. "Remind me again why we're putting Lee Press-On Nails on a cat?"

"Because Lucifer has a bit of a scratching issue," Jossy said. "That's why he's been rehomed six times."

Lucifer wriggled one paw free and took a swipe at Jonah's cheek. Jonah ducked back, glad the military had left him with sharp reflexes. He'd never expected to use them for cat wrangling, but it was a small price to pay for helping his sister. And this asshole cat.

"You remembered to put glue in it this time?" Jonah pressed Lucifer's squishy pink paw pad to reveal the claws on his right hand. Lucifer responded with a hiss that sounded like a malfunctioning espresso machine.

"Yes, I remembered." Jossy held the cat still while Jonah wrestled the nail tip onto the cat's first claw.

He drew back, admiring his handiwork. "Why the pink glitter?"

"Because the vet clinic was out of more manly colors." Jossy stepped back to fill another claw tip with glue. "Sorry, Lucifer."

The cat growled as Jonah slid the next claw tip into place. "You're seriously compromising his manhood here." He positioned another glittery pink object over the next claw. "And mine," he added as Lucifer delivered another rabbit-kick to his nuts.

"Sorry, Sorry." Jossy handed him another claw tip and grabbed the cat's rear wheels again. "Seriously, Jonah—I owe you for this. Declawing is such an inhumane thing to do to a cat, so this is truly a kindness you're doing for him."

Lucifer growled again, unimpressed by Jonah's kindness. Jonah grabbed another claw tip from Jossy and slipped it into place, getting more comfortable with the task even if Lucifer wasn't.

Maybe this would be a good time to broach the subject of the computer-controlled knee. They'd discussed it before, but not recently. And never when it was a real possibility. Never when Jonah was in a position to make this kind of difference in Jossy's life.

He was thinking about how to bring it up when Jossy interrupted his thoughts. "Have you seen the footage yet?" she asked. "The stuff they shot at the animal shelter the other day?"

"Not yet. Kate mentioned something during filming yesterday. Said post-production was putting together a promotional thing on YouTube."

"Will you get to see it before it goes out?"

"She offered, if we wanted to see it. Apparently they can't e-mail it out, but she's willing to pull it up on her laptop and show us when she gets the files tomorrow night. We could both meet up with her if you'd like."

"No." Jossy bit her lip and handed him another claw tip. "I think I'd be too nervous. Maybe you could watch it first and tell me what you think?"

"You're so weird." Jonah wiggled the glittery pink claw tip into place and held out his hand for another.

They lapsed into silence for a moment, each of them focused on the task of helping the uncooperative cat. When Jossy spoke, her voice was barely audible.

"Jonah?"

"Yeah?"

"I had a dream last night that I was riding a bike."

He looked up sharply, and Lucifer saw his shot at escape. Jonah gripped the cat tighter, subduing him without taking his gaze off his sister.

"Wow, that's—does that happen often?"

She shook her head, eyes glittering a little. "No, that's why I told you. It kind of shook me up. I mean—I've barely even thought about bike racing for eighteen years."

"Really?"

She shrugged and handed him another nail tip. "I mean, sure, I've thought of it. In that way you think something absurd like, 'I wonder what it would be like to buy a two-thousand-dollar pair of stilettos and sashay through downtown Seattle.'"

Jonah frowned and slid the next claw tip into place. "You lost me there."

"I just mean, it's impossible," she said.

"It's not impossible, Joss." Jonah kept his voice soft, both for Lucifer's benefit and his sister's. He couldn't believe his luck at having her broach the subject. This had to mean something. "We've talked before about the computer-controlled knees."

"Please." Jossy rolled her eyes. "You think two-thousand-dollar shoes are insane. A prosthetic like that? You could buy fifty pairs of those shoes for the cost of one of those."

"Call me crazy, but only one of those options sounds practical."

"That's not even remotely practical," she said. "Even if money were no object, it's a silly thing to spend it on."

He started to tell her money *was* no object. Thanks to the show, that was almost the case. But should he really count chickens that hadn't hatched? The show hadn't formally been picked up yet. Anything could happen.

Jossy shook her head and handed him another nail tip. "I wasn't telling you about the dream to complain. I just thought it was interesting."

Jonah nodded, not ready to let the subject go just yet. He thought about Kate's words the other night.

"That really fucking sucks."

It did suck on so many levels. He'd spent eighteen years trying to make it up to Jossy. Trying give back some of what he'd stolen from her. Trying to live up to his father's last request.

But shirtless dog walks and cat manicures could only go so far.

"What if a computer-controlled prosthetic just landed in your lap?" he asked.

Jossy snorted. "Ouch."

"I don't mean literally. Like what if insurance suddenly paid for it or something."

He kept his gaze on the cat, not wanting her to read too much into the "or something."

"I don't know," she said slowly. "There's no point in even talking like that. It's never going to happen, Jonah."

He took another nail tip from her and slid it onto Lucifer's claw. For the first time, he saw a faint shimmer of hope. Things would never be the same for Jossy, but if he could just make this happen for her—

"We're almost done," Jossy said. "Hang in there, sweetie pie."

"That's right, buddy." Jonah glanced at his sister and smiled. "The end is in sight."

CHAPTER FIFTEEN

"That's a wrap!" Kate called with a glance at her watch.

It was only four, which was a bit early to stop shooting, but they were starting to lose their light. Besides, the temperature had been dropping all afternoon, reminding Kate of the challenges involved with outdoor shoots.

"Think we got what we need?" Amy trotted up beside her, blowing on her gloved hands.

"I'm pretty confident," Kate said. "That last sequence with Elena running into Sam's arms on the sidewalk looked perfect."

"She totally nailed that." Amy grinned and glanced back toward the waterfront walkway, where the happy couple were still twined in each other's arms. "I love the way he picked her up and spun her around. He did that without prompting."

"Quintessential wrap shot," Kate agreed, already picturing it in her mind. They could dub in some voiceovers with the couple talking about their life together after the show. The camera would zoom in on the autumn leaves swirling around their ankles and Elena's blue-and-gold scarf fluttering in the breeze.

"I talked to the guys in post-production about the musical score," Amy added. "That will add a lot."

"Thanks for handling that." Kate shoved her hands into her coat pockets and wished she'd thought to bring along some hand warmers or maybe a thicker jacket.

"Fuck me raw with a blue potato." Amy blew on her hands again. "When did it get so cold?"

"At least it's not raining," Kate replied. "I expected it to do that all the time if we filmed in Seattle."

"Wait until next week. It's supposed to rain every day but Wednesday. Don't worry, I adjusted the schedule and e-mailed the updates to everyone. We can knock out most of the indoor footage with those next two couples."

"You're the best." Kate looked back at Sam and Elena. They were still holding hands, and Elena beamed up at her husband like he'd invented dark chocolate and multiple orgasms. The cameras had stopped rolling, which made it that much sweeter. This was the real deal.

"Great choice on her outfit," Kate said. "She looks adorable."

Amy looked back at the couple and nodded. "Yeah, Ginger found that white sweater coat at a boutique downtown. And those jeans—would you believe she found those at a thrift store?"

"Nice." Kate watched as Sam swept a stray lock of hair off Elena's forehead, then bent to kiss her again.

All those counseling sessions, all the awkward conversations. In the end, it had all been worth it.

"This is going to be a kick-ass pilot episode," she said.

"Yeah. I talked to Viv this morning," Amy said. "She had some really good ideas for the next two couples we're flying out here. And she also had a few thoughts about weaving in the story arc with Jonah."

Kate tried not to wince, but Amy caught it anyway. "Hey," she murmured. "There's nothing we can do about it. You heard what Chase said on the conference call this morning."

"Right," Kate muttered, hating the echo of his voice in her ears.

"I don't care if you're a zillion percent positive Average Joe doesn't want to bone his ex-wife," Chase had boomed over the speakerphone. "It'll make for fucking great television either way."

"God, what a dick," Kate muttered.

"But he's got a point."

"Doesn't mean it's a good one," she said. "Or that we have to like it."

"No, but our hands are tied." Amy sighed. "I talked with Rick Black in legal this morning." Amy glanced around, but there were no crew members nearby.

Even so, Kate edged a little closer and lowered her voice. "What did he say?"

"He asked a lot of questions about dates and legal proceedings. Had me send over copies of everything related to the divorce."

"Did he seem—hopeful?"

"He sounded like a lawyer," Amy muttered. "Guarded. But I explained the importance of discretion here. That we're doing our best to keep this whole thing quiet while we try to find a solution."

"So what's the plan?"

"He's going to do some research into Oregon divorce law," Amy said. "That's where they were married, you know."

"I know," Kate murmured, remembering the details from the book. Viv's glowing descriptions of the ceremony and vows and—

"Oregon divorce law isn't a specialty for an entertainment lawyer, obviously, though he has a couple guys on staff who know more than he does."

"So until then, mum's the word?"

"Yeah." Amy nodded. "At least until we know more from the legal end of things."

The buzzing of Amy's phone put a halt to their conversation, and Kate felt a flicker of hope it was the attorneys. Maybe they had an answer to the problem. Maybe Jonah and Viv would never need to know their marriage was still technically—

"Speak of the devil," Amy muttered as she stared at her phone screen.

"Chase or Rick?"

"I meant the other devil. The one who wants to woo her ex on national television."

Before Kate could reply, Amy tapped the screen to answer the call. "Hey, Viv. What's up?"

Kate strained to make out the reply, but Viv's breathy response was too soft to hear.

"We're actually just finishing things here," Amy continued. "Did you need us?"

More soft murmurs, and Kate watched Amy's brow furrow. "Let me check with Kate really quick."

Amy hit the button to mute the call. "Are you free to run by Viv's place right now?"

"I think so. Did she mention why?"

"She wants to go over concepts for wrap footage. She had some ideas for an on-camera interview segment where she starts laying the groundwork for getting Jonah back."

Kate swallowed hard and tried not to let her face show any reaction. "Does she want to test shoot it? I can grab Pete."

"Nah, let's use the handheld. It'll make it more authentic. It's just for practice anyway."

"I'll get us packed up."

Amy went back to the call while Kate hustled to help put away gear and fill the crew in on the next day's schedule. By the time they got in the car, it was after five. Traffic was lousy, but Kate didn't mind. It gave her time to collect her thoughts while Amy jotted notes about the upcoming shot lists. As Amy muttered to herself and shuffled through files, Kate watched orange-gold leaves hurl themselves like angry confetti against the concrete dividers.

It was nearly six by the time they reached Viv's place. A black sedan sat out front, parked haphazardly next to the azaleas. The plates were from Washington, but something about it made Kate think it was a rental car. She got out with an uneasy churning in the pit of her stomach.

"Looks like she has company," Amy said.

"Probably her gardener or masseuse or feng shui consultant or something." It sounded convincing, though Kate wasn't sure she believed it.

Amy got out first and waited for Kate to catch up before marching up the walkway. As they approached the front door, Kate spotted a note tacked just above the peephole.

Come on back, ladies! read Viv's artsy, flourished handwriting. *We're waiting in my office.*

Amy looked at Kate. "We?"

Kate shrugged. "Maybe she wants us to film the feng shui guy?"

"God, like I don't have enough release paperwork to deal with."

Kate slid the note into her purse and glanced back at the black car. It wasn't Jonah's, which filled her with unexpected relief. She'd been glad today's shooting schedule hadn't required him at all, or Viv for that matter. Frankly, she'd needed some time to process her thoughts. To remind herself that she needed to keep a business relationship with all of them.

Amy pushed open the door, then hesitated in the entryway. "Sooo . . . I guess we just show ourselves back there?"

"That's what the note seemed to indicate." Still, Kate hesitated, too, listening in the foyer for the sound of voices.

There was nothing.

"Soundproof office," Amy said, reading Kate's mind again. "I'm sure it's nothing."

"Right."

They moved down the hallway together, neither of them speaking. They'd left their gear in the car, not sure yet whether they'd need it or if this was just a brainstorming session.

As they rounded the corner, Kate noticed the office door was closed. She lifted her hand and gave three light taps.

Nothing.

She'd just raised her hand to knock again when the door flew open. A radiant-looking Viv greeted them. She wore white from head to toe, and Kate had a flash of memory. Viv and Jonah's wedding photo from *On the Other Hand*, a rustic black and white with Viv resplendent and beaming in a snowy dress with a handkerchief hem. Jonah had his back to the camera, but his shoulders looked broad and strong as he swooped his new bride in his arms. Viv's hair trailed almost to the ground as she laughed up at him.

Kate's breath caught in her throat, but she forced herself to smile back as Viv threw the door wide open and waved them inside.

"Kate! Amy! It's so wonderful to see you!"

There were at least three exclamation points in the sentence, and Kate found herself offering a tentative smile, caught by the contagious-ness of her enthusiasm. "Hello, Viv."

"It's good to see you," Amy said as she stepped forward into the office.

Kate started to follow, then halted as Amy froze like a statue. "Oh!"

Amy's gasp made Kate's heart jump, and she edged sideways to see what elicited such surprise. She let her eyes scan the room, taking in the familiar artwork, the spotless desk, the blood-colored sofa with a tall, beefy figure planted squarely in the center.

Chase Whitfield looked up from his phone and regarded them with a calculated nod. "Ladies." He smiled, showing way too many teeth and making Kate think of sharks. "This is some solid-gold shit right here."

Kate blinked. "Pardon me?"

Someone touched her arm, and Kate looked up to see Viv sweeping past her, an ethereal look on her face. "You must not have heard the good news yet."

"Good news?" Relief sluiced through her, but Kate remained on edge. "What's the good news?"

Viv looked at Chase, her smile widening as she tossed her hair over one shoulder and turned back to Kate and Amy.

"We're still married," she trilled. "Jonah and I are still married."

CHAPTER SIXTEEN

"Fucking lawyers," Kate muttered as she pulled the rental car into her parking space at the hotel. She switched off the engine, but made no move to get out yet.

"I'm really sorry," Amy said. "I don't know how that happened."

Kate turned to see Amy frowning in the passenger seat. Her blond curls looked like she'd pulled Viv's Zen garden rake through them, and the twin creases between her brows seemed deeper than normal.

"It's not your fault," Kate said. "We both agreed that involving legal was the right way to go. There's no way you could have predicted Rick would go straight to Chase."

Amy shook her head and looked down at her lap. "I thought with client privilege—"

"We're not the client," she said. "Chase is. Well, Chase and the network. Not us."

Amy sighed and looked up again. "I don't know why, but I guess I expected a little bit of decency."

"I don't know why either. You've been in this business long enough to know better."

Amy snorted. "Reality TV isn't the place to go looking for decency."

"That's 'unscripted television' to you, missy."

Amy gave an undignified growl and reached for the door handle. "At least Pete wasn't there to film it. Chase breaking it to Viv, I mean. Just an intern with a handheld. Maybe it'll turn out lousy. Maybe we won't have to see it."

"I doubt that'll happen," Kate murmured, knowing she'd have to watch the rough footage over and over during edits, not to mention on the inside of her eyelids when she couldn't sleep. God, Viv had seemed so happy. It almost made Kate wish the feelings were reciprocated. That Jonah really did still love his ex-wife.

No, you don't, her subconscious reminded her. *You don't wish that at all.*

Kate swallowed, trying to dislodge the guilty lump in her throat.

"Maybe Chase will change his mind," Amy said as she pushed open the car door.

Kate shook her head and stooped down to grab her things out of the backseat.

Amy kept going, afloat on her own stream of wishful thinking. "Maybe Chase will realize it's a terrible idea."

"For Viv to declare her love on national television?" Kate slung her bag over her shoulder and followed Amy through the front doors of the hotel.

"That, too," Amy said. "But also to blindside him with the news that they're still married. Chase has to know that's an awful plan."

"It's an awful plan for Viv, and an awful plan for Jonah," Kate pointed out. "It's not an awful plan for ratings. That's all Chase cares about."

Amy pushed the button for the elevator, then turned to Kate with eyes so wide they reminded Kate of Amy's first day on the job. She'd spoken up during a meeting when the production team was plotting out how to edit the season to make one participant look like a villain.

"But isn't that a little dishonest?" Amy had piped up.

Everyone else at the table had laughed, but not Kate. It was the moment she knew she and Amy would be friends beyond the parameters of the workplace.

But the way Amy was looking at her now gave her a fresh ache in the center of her chest. She looked like a kid whose sister had just spilled the beans about Santa and had turned to Mom for reassurance.

"If anything, I should have known better," Kate said. "Maybe if we'd gone straight to Viv ourselves. If we'd told her about the divorce not being official. Or maybe if I'd told Jonah first—"

"But now you *can't* tell him," Amy said. "You heard what Chase said. We're sworn to secrecy. Contractually bound to it."

"Right," Kate said glumly as the elevator dinged in front of them.

"So what do we *do*?" Amy's voice hitched up on the last syllable, making two women look over from the opposite side of the lobby.

The doors swished open, and Kate ushered Amy inside. She didn't speak again until the doors slammed shut, and the elevator began to rise.

"There's nothing we *can* do," Kate said, struggling to keep her voice even. "Not without risking our jobs. Hell, risking the whole *show*. You know what our contracts say. We practically signed them in blood."

"I know, but—"

"Amy." Kate swallowed, hating this as much as Amy did, but knowing there was no way around it. "Do you remember the clause about fines? The dollar amount we agreed to pay if we ever got caught releasing protected information?"

Amy bit her lip. "It was something like a million dollars," she said. "But I can't believe they'd actually—"

"Believe it. They'd hit you with a suit before you got six words out, and then where would we both be?"

Amy didn't say anything after that. Kate's stomach twisted into a knot of sour energy. It was possible that hunger was to blame for some of it. She'd grabbed half a turkey wrap at noon, but nothing else for more than eight hours. The thought of ordering room service again made her stomach stir with disappointment, and she longed for a home-cooked meal. That was ridiculous. She didn't cook, and the last home-cooked meal she'd had had been at Amy's house months ago.

"Something smells amazing," Amy said as they stepped out of the elevator.

That's when Kate realized her fantasy dinner wasn't only in her head. Someone in one of the rooms along their hallway must have ordered something delicious. It smelled like spiced meat and a hint of honeyed cornbread like her grandmother used to make.

"I wonder where they ordered that." Kate sniffed the air, feeling like a grizzly bear. "I'll check the menu folder in the room. Want to join me?"

"Don't tempt me. I promised myself I'd hit the gym for at least an hour."

"Suit yourself," Kate said as she turned the corner and drew out her key card.

That's when she spotted him. Jonah was sitting in the hallway beside her room with his back against the wall. His legs were stretched out in front of him and crossed at the ankles. Beside him on the floor was a canvas bag bulging with Tupperware containers.

He looked up as they approached and gave them each a slow smile. "Ladies." He got to his feet and hefted the bag in front of him. "I brought dinner. Jossy's famous white chicken chili. She's dying to know how the footage turned out but was too nervous to see it in person. I've been sent with a bribe and a plea to get the first look."

"Jonah." Kate flashed back to her conversation with Amy in the elevator and said a prayer of thanks that she and Amy had stopped talking before they'd stepped out onto the ninth floor. Even if they'd revealed something by accident, they could still be held liable.

"You did say the clips were being sent at eight, right?" He glanced at his watch, then back at her. "I thought about calling first, but I was afraid you'd say no, and Jossy's really dying to hear details." He gave the bag a little shake and grinned. "There's enough here for all of us. Did I mention Jossy makes the best chili on the planet?"

Beside her, Amy gazed at the bag with intense longing. She gave a heavy sigh and shook her head. "Thanks, but I have to take a rain check. I've blown off the gym all week. If I don't go now, I'll never make it."

"We'll save some for you." Jonah's gaze swung to Kate. "How about you? I have it on good authority that cornbread and homemade chili go great with this sour brown ale from New Belgium Brewing."

Kate's stomach growled loudly enough to serve as a reply, which saved her the trouble of finding her words right that moment. Jonah laughed and held out the bag of food. "Here. You're welcome to just stick your face in the bowl."

"Jonah." She stopped there, torn between telling him how glad she was to see him, how grateful for the meal, how desperate to tell him all the things she couldn't possibly say.

Oh my God, I slept with a married man.

The thought hit her like a kick between the shoulder blades. For some reason it hadn't registered until right that moment. Not in those words, anyway. She'd been wrapped up in the details of the show and Viv's announcement.

You slept with a married man who doesn't know he's married, she reassured herself. *And who has no idea his ex-wife wants him back.*

She swallowed hard, wishing she could say something, knowing she couldn't, hating the way this was all going to play out.

But deep down, she knew she couldn't say no to a few precious hours alone with him before this whole thing blew up.

"Come on," she said, stepping forward to slide her key card into the slot. "For the record, I can always be bribed with food."

◆　◆　◆

Kate sat across from him at her little hotel table, each of them shoveling up spoonful after spoonful of fragrant chili. She reached out, and for a second Jonah thought she was trying to hold his hand. But no, she was just grabbing another piece of cornbread.

It was the first time in Jonah's life he'd felt jealous of food.

"So what did you think?" Kate asked, nodding at the laptop. "It's still a little choppy around the forty-second mark, and obviously we'll have to cut a lot in the shorter clips for TV. But that should play great with the YouTube crowd."

Jonah set down his beer, wrapping both hands around the bottle as he looked at Kate. "That was terrific. You're really talented."

"Please. I hardly did anything. It was all Pete and the guys in post-production. And you and Jossy, of course."

"You, too. It's your vision, Kate. Don't sell that short."

"It's a team effort," she conceded.

He watched as she broke off another big hunk of cornbread and swirled it around in her big bowl of chili. She put the whole thing in her mouth and chewed, closing her eyes in bliss.

"This is *so* good."

"Jossy does that," he said, and watched as she opened her eyes again. "She can't eat any kind of soup without dipping something in it."

Kate grinned and broke off another piece. "I think your sister and I are kindred spirits."

"Actually, I think you're onto something." He took another sip of beer, enjoying the cool tart of the ale and the warm sweetness of Kate's company and the pleasant way those two things mingled. "She hasn't stopped talking about you."

"Your sister?"

"Yeah. She asked if it was too late to trade me in and have you as a sibling instead."

Kate laughed. "That's sweet."

"That's Jossy. She either loves you or hates you. There's not much in between."

He watched as Kate seemed to hesitate. She sat poised with her cornbread above the bowl, but didn't take a bite. "Did she and Viv get along well?"

"They didn't fight, if that's what you mean."

"It wasn't exactly what I meant. I guess I was just curious if they were close."

"Not close," he said. "I know you're the president of the Dr. Vivienne Brandt fan club, but my sister—"

"Not so much?" Kate took a bite of cornbread.

"She used to call her Snobby McBitcherson."

Kate laughed, then started choking on cornbread crumbs. Jonah stood up and whacked her on the back a few times, grateful for any excuse to touch her.

"You okay?"

"I'm fine, I'm fine. God, I'm such a jerk. I shouldn't laugh at other people's expense. That's karma right there."

"Cornbread karma?"

"Exactly." She set the cornbread down and picked up her bottle of beer.

Jonah watched her drink, relishing the pleasure on her face. He flashed on a memory of that same look in a different setting. Kate naked and arching beneath him, crying out as he drove into her.

God, he wanted her again. Maybe when this stupid show was all over—

"We haven't really talked beyond the first season," he said, picking up his beer again. "You said before that the first season would be fourteen episodes, but what happens after that?"

"If the show is a success?" Kate shrugged and dunked another piece of cornbread in her bowl. "We hope for as many seasons as we can get."

"What's normal?"

"It's anyone's guess, really. But you look at shows like *Survivor* or *The Bachelor* that have been going for twenty or thirty seasons—that's what everyone hopes for."

Jonah felt a sick twist in his stomach. Is that really what everyone hoped for?

Then he thought about the money. About what cash like that could buy for Jossy. Even if he only did the first season or two, maybe that would be enough.

He took another sip of beer, considering the options. "Do characters sometimes leave after a couple of seasons?"

Kate lifted one brow and chewed. "You're thinking of quitting before we get started?"

"Just wondering how things usually work. If characters shift around much on a reality-TV show like this."

She studied him a moment, then nodded. "Sometimes," she said carefully. "Are you not happy with the way things are going?"

"It's fine," he said, not sure how much more he should say. "You guys are great. The whole crew has been terrific to work with. It's just—I guess I never really imagined myself on TV."

"Is it the television aspect you don't like, or the part about working with your ex?"

He shrugged. "Working with Viv hasn't been that bad," he said. "I have to admit, I've remembered some of the things I liked about her."

Was it his imagination, or did something change in her expression? She covered it quickly, taking a slow sip of beer. Maybe he'd imagined it. Or maybe she was just happy to have him not bitching about Viv. He should probably do more to be a team player. To assure Kate he didn't see his ex-wife as the antichrist.

"What sort of things?" Kate asked with such practiced casualness, he suspected it was forced.

"We had a good chemistry," he said. "We made each other laugh. I remember this one time we went camping in Utah."

247

"Utah?"

"Mesa Verde," he said. "Viv wanted to see the Anasazi ruins, so we spent a week backpacking around the area."

"Right, I remember. She wrote about that in *On the Other Hand*. The reverence she felt crawling around the prehistoric cliff dwellings. It sounded like a great trip."

Jonah felt a flare of frustration he couldn't explain. It wasn't like he hadn't consented to have his vacations, his conversations, his *life* turned into a self-help book.

But he'd always wanted to hold a few things back.

"It was a great trip," he agreed. "I think my favorite part was this day it rained for like six hours. We couldn't leave the tent at all."

"I'm not sure I want to hear this," Kate murmured as she took a sip of beer.

"It's not what you're thinking," he said. "Not exactly, anyway. We just stayed in the tent all day and made up silly games."

"Like what?"

"Like we tried to come up with a body part for every letter of the alphabet," he said. "Whoever came up with an answer had to kiss that part on the other person's body. It's not as sexy as it sounds—*A* for ankle, *B* for brain, *C* for collarbone—that sort of thing."

Kate laughed, though Jonah could have sworn he saw a flash of sadness in her eyes. "Some of those must have been tough," she said. "What did you do for *X* and *U*?"

"Viv got xiphoid process," he said. "She took a lot of anatomy classes in college."

"What's that?"

"Breastbone," he said, tapping his knuckles against his own sternum. "I tried to convince her to kiss my uvula."

"I'm afraid to ask," Kate said. "My anatomy knowledge is a little rusty."

"The little dangly part at the back of the throat."

"Ick."

Jonah laughed and scooped up a spoonful of chili. "We settled for a peck on the ulna," he said. "That's the bone in the forearm."

"Sounds like you had fun together," Kate said. There was a wistfulness in her tone. "Why didn't you include that in the book?"

"I didn't want to," he said. "I liked the idea of holding a few things back. Keeping some things private, just the two of us."

"That sounds like real intimacy."

"I suppose so," he said.

"Do you miss it?"

He noticed she said *it*, not *her*, and he sensed it was a deliberate choice. That it was the latter she really wanted to ask about. "I miss intimacy sometimes," he said. "Having someone to curl up with in bed at night, talking until we both fall asleep."

She looked at him oddly. "So what if you could have that again? If you could have it all back?"

"I will. Someday, I mean."

Kate swirled a hunk of bread in her bowl and didn't meet his eyes. "With Viv?"

"Christ, no!" That came out a little harsher than he meant it to, and Kate gave him a startled look. Reminding himself to tread carefully, Jonah dialed it back a notch. "She's a terrific person, don't get me wrong. I'm sure she'll find someone else someday. Someone who's *not* me."

"Oh." Kate took a sip of beer, making it tough for him to read her expression. "I guess that's—good. For both of you. Right?"

He picked up a piece of cornbread and studied her face. "Why do you keep asking about that?"

"About what?"

"About Viv and me? About whether there's any chance we'd ever rekindle things?"

"No reason." She held his gaze, but something in it seemed off. He wasn't sure what, but he had a sense she was hiding something.

"As a TV producer, I'm supposed to ferret out the stories," she added.

"There's no story there."

"Still. I'm supposed to ask tough questions."

"That's not a very tough one. Try again."

"What?"

"I mean, asking whether I'd ever get back with Viv is like asking whether I think I'll ever give up the bookstore and join the circus. Did I mention I hate clowns?"

She smiled a little at that and took a sip of beer. "So what's an actual tough question?"

"Something important. Something thought-provoking."

Kate dabbed a cornbread crumb off the edge of her plate and licked it off her finger. "Example?"

He thought about it. "Like if I had to drink eight ounces of someone else's saliva, whose saliva would I choose?"

Kate laughed, and Jonah admired the faintest hint of a dimple on her left cheek. God, she was beautiful.

"That's your idea of a tough question?" Kate asked.

"You've gotta admit, it's a difficult one. Do you go with a family member or a lover? Considering how much tonsil hockey a couple might play over a lifetime, you probably do consume about a cup of saliva, if you really think about it."

She gave him a pained look, but she was still smiling. "I'd rather not think about it."

"Okay, here's another tough question," he said. "If you could give one person in the world the biggest, most uncomfortable wedgie imaginable, who would you pick and why?"

"This is a real question?" She seemed to consider it, though, twirling her beer bottle on the table as she watched it with a thoughtful look. "John Peckenham."

"Who's John Peckenham?"

"My boyfriend when I was twelve years old. He broke up with me at recess and then told everyone I kissed like a goldfish. For months afterward, everyone went around making fish faces at me."

"If it's any comfort, you don't kiss like a goldfish."

"Thank you." She grinned. "I've had time to practice."

Jonah desperately wanted to ask for a demonstration but knew they shouldn't start down that path again. Even if they wanted to. Even if he desperately, urgently wanted to touch her just one more time—

"Okay, here's another tough question," he said. "What's the weirdest thing you've ever done in front of a mirror?"

She laughed and grabbed another piece of cornbread. "I've read *Our Bodies, Ourselves*. I'm not ashamed to admit I straddled that mirror like a pro and figured out what was what. I think I was in college."

Jonah laughed, not wanting to admit how sexy he found that image. "How very enlightened of you."

"I try." Kate nibbled and looked thoughtful. "My turn to ask one."

"Fire away."

She scrunched up her face the way she always did when she was pondering something. Jonah wanted to reach out and trace a finger over the lines in her forehead.

"Tell me the most embarrassing thing your parents have caught you doing," she said at last.

"Trying to stick my dick in the vacuum cleaner," he answered without hesitation. Kate's look of surprise made him think he should have hesitated just a little. "I was eleven or twelve years old and had just learned what a blow job was. Suffice it to say, it didn't work out well for me."

"Oh my God! Did you get hurt?"

"No. But I did require a little outside assistance to extricate myself."

Kate burst out laughing, shaking her head as she smeared her bread through the last of her chili. "You're nuts." She snorted and popped the bite into her mouth. "No pun intended."

"I haven't done it recently," he pointed out. "I am capable of learning from my mistakes."

"I'm sure you are. I didn't mean to sound judgmental."

"Now you have to volunteer your own sexual mishap," he said. "While we're on the subject."

He expected her to balk or change the subject. But she surprised him. "Anton—that was my last boyfriend—"

"I know," Jonah said, biting back a flare of jealousy he knew he wasn't entitled to. "You've mentioned that a few times."

"Right, of course. Sometimes he'd text me in the middle of the day and ask me to send him a sexy pic."

"Typical guy."

"You've done it?"

"Probably."

Kate laughed, not looking too perturbed. "I could have refused, but it seemed like a pretty harmless way to spice things up," she said. "Then again, it's tough to feel sexy when you're sitting on the toilet in the ladies room, yanking your boobs out of your bra between meetings."

"Is this supposed to be turning me on?"

She grinned, but ignored him. "Anyway, this one time I was in a hurry, so I snapped this really quick up-skirt photo while I was sitting at my desk eating lunch."

"Hot," he said, not caring that he sounded like Average Joe.

"Not quite. I went to text it to Anton, but instead of hitting the message icon, I hit the icon right above it. The one that says, 'Tap to Share with AirDrop.'"

"Oh no."

"Oh yes. And since I was at work, the AirDrop user closest to me was the person in the next office."

"God." Jonah shook his head. "Was it your boss?"

"Thankfully, no. It was Amy. She still teases me about it sometimes."

Jonah laughed and picked up his beer. God, he loved this. Not the dirty story swap, though that was fun, too. He loved sitting here with her like this, laughing together at themselves and each other. Not caring about showing each other their very best sides, but letting their silliness show, too.

This is real intimacy.

He almost said it out loud, but stopped himself. It didn't seem like the right thing to say. Not now, not with what they'd agreed.

Still, he felt closer to her. Did she feel it, too? He looked in her eyes and knew the answer. There was an intensity there that made his chest ache. A longing he knew matched his own.

"Kate—"

"I should let you get home." She stood up fast, nearly sending her chair toppling. She righted it and began stacking paper plates and bowls into a pile, arranging the plastic utensils in the top bowl. She wasn't meeting his eyes, so he stepped forward and touched the side of her face.

"Kate," he said again, softer this time. She lifted her chin, meeting his eyes at last, and the urgency in her gaze made his chest feel tight.

Then his lips were on hers, gentle at first, waiting to see if she'd respond. She did respond, kissing him back with a hunger that sent his pulse racing. She tasted like hops and honey and something unbearably sweet.

He tunneled his fingers into her hair, while his other hand still cupped the side of her face. Deepening the kiss, he knew this went beyond lust. Beyond desire. In thirty-six years, he'd never had such a deep-seated longing to connect with another human.

He broke the kiss but didn't let go of her. Looking deep into her eyes, he knew she felt this, too. "Please," he whispered. "Let me make love to you again. Just once more."

Something flickered in her eyes. Desire, yes, but something else. If she said no, he'd accept it. He'd walk away and never ask again. But holy mother of hell, it was going to hurt.

The silence stretched out so long he began to count his own heartbeat. Or was that hers? They were pressed against each other, chest to chest, heart to heart.

"We shouldn't," she whispered.

"I know." He tried to step back, but something held him there. Maybe it was Kate's palms pressing against his shoulder blades, but it felt more than physical. "It's okay." He meant it as a reassurance that he was fine walking away. That he could step back and exit the room with his pants zipped, his job safe, his heart intact.

But the longing in Kate's eyes was unmistakable. She didn't let go. She took a shaky breath that made everything ache in the center of Jonah's chest.

"No, I need this," she whispered, and kissed him again.

CHAPTER SEVENTEEN

"This feels weird on so many levels," Kate muttered to Amy in the elevator the next morning.

Amy gave her a sympathetic smile. "You mean attending a TV network meeting in the same building where you shagged the show's star the night before?"

Kate grimaced as she watched the buttons on the elevator counting down to the awkward meeting. *Five, four, three . . .*

"God, I shouldn't have slept with him again," Kate whispered.

"Will you stop it? You're both consenting adults. And don't give me that bullshit again about how he's technically still married. As far as he knows, he's been divorced for a year."

"Yes, but as far as *I* know—"

"Don't." The elevator doors swished open, but Amy put a hand on Kate's shoulder to hold her back. With her free hand, she hit two more buttons and sent the doors sliding shut again. The buttons began to light up once more, this time in ascending order.

Kate looked at Amy. "We're going back up? What did you forget?"

"Nothing, but this seems like one of the few places for a private conversation."

Kate glanced around, half expecting to see hidden microphones in the walls. How did that little emergency-call button work, anyway?

"Look, Kate," Amy continued. "Don't turn this into a moral issue. You know as well as I do that the marriage only exists on paper. This is a technicality. One we can fix easily enough with a good lawyer and some hastily filed paperwork from the couple."

"But that's not what everyone wants," she said. "Not Viv, anyway."

"So? You can't force someone to stay married to you. This is reality television, not Vatican City. Jonah wants to be divorced, right?"

Kate hesitated. "Right," she said, hoping it was true. God, it felt true last night when he held her in his arms, murmuring about how he wished he could stay there in bed with her forever.

"Besides," Amy continued. "If you hadn't slept with him last night—"

"I shouldn't have told you that," Kate interrupted, prompting an eye roll from Amy. "I *shouldn't*. I know better than to kiss and tell."

"Please," Amy said. "The man showed up with dinner and didn't leave until two in the morning, which I know because I was up all night working on scheduling and heard him leave. You think I'm dumb enough to believe you ate cornbread for six hours?" She shook her head, not giving Kate a chance to retort. "Like I was saying, he would have just gotten suspicious if you'd eaten his dinner and sent him on his way home with a pat on the head."

The elevator doors swished open again, this time on the eleventh floor. A man in black holding a room-service tray looked startled to see them. "Are you going down?"

Amy hovered a hand over the elevator buttons. "Which way are you going?"

"Down."

"Sorry, we're going up."

She hit the close button and sent the elevator surging upward again. Kate looked at her. "I'm not sure whether to be more concerned that you just implied it would be suspicious for me not to sleep with a guy who brought me food, or more concerned that you're treating the elevators as our private mobile confession booth."

"There are plenty of things to be concerned about in this situation," Amy said. "Those aren't the most important ones."

"What are the most important ones?"

"Keeping the show running smoothly," Amy said. "And keeping Chase Whitfield from doing anything stupid."

And keeping Jonah on the show so he can help Jossy, Kate amended in her mind. She hadn't told Amy about the accident or Jonah's role in it. Unless Amy remembered that brief line in *On the Other Hand,* she probably had no idea Jonah's dad was dead, or how that had sparked Jonah's urge to protect his sister.

That was Kate's secret to hold. There were so few opportunities in this job for her to protect other people's private stories. To protect their hearts. Something about that detail made Kate want to hold it tightly to her chest.

"I swear, Chase is like a bloodhound when he gets the scent of some juicy, heartbreaking story line," Kate muttered.

"It makes me hate him as a person," Amy agreed. "But as a network exec, it's what's made him successful."

The doors swished open again, revealing a tall, beefy figure standing in front of them on the fifteenth floor.

Speak of the devil, Kate thought as she pasted on her most professional smile.

"Chase," she said. "It's great to see you. I didn't realize you were staying here as well."

"I normally wouldn't, but they were all booked at the Four Seasons," he said. "That's why we're in the conference room here this morning."

"I wondered about that," Amy said, shuffling through a stack of papers in her arms. "Here's that post-production report you asked for. It's coming along nicely."

"Excellent work." Chase took the folder as the doors opened into the lobby. He stepped out ahead of them and took off at a speedy clip, leaving Kate and Amy to exchange a covert glance.

The three of them trooped into the conference room with Chase barking orders at the concierge about coffee service and scones. Amy walked around the table, laying a briefing at each spot, and Kate checked her phone for any messages.

There was one from Jonah, sent just a few minutes before.

I miss you already. Last night was amazing. I wish we could—

"Kate!"

She looked up sharply to see Chase looming in front of her. She clicked off her phone and said a silent prayer he hadn't seen anything.

"Yes, sir?"

"I've been thinking about how to do the big reveal."

Kate set her phone facedown on the conference table. "The one where Viv tells Jonah—Joe—that she's still in love with him?"

"That, but also when he discovers they're still married. What do you think about sending him on some made-up errand to the courthouse, where he'll realize he fucked up and never filed the papers?"

Kate swallowed hard and concentrated on keeping a steady expression. "I think we'd run the risk of making him feel stupid," she said. "And that's something we promised not to do."

"Promises broken." Chase snapped his fingers. "That's brilliant! That's a great title for the first episode, don't you think?"

"Um—"

"Okay, how about this," Chase continued, oblivious to Kate's objections. "We get the two of them in the hot tub together—"

"The two of who?"

"Viv and Joe, of course." Chase waved a hand as though to indicate the details were irrelevant. "We make up something about needing them to model some form of hydro therapy for couples or some shit like that. Anyway, they're sitting there in the hot tub when the lawyer walks out—"

"Is the lawyer in a Speedo?" Amy pulled out her notepad, and Kate watched her starting to scribble words on the page.

"No, the lawyer isn't in a Speedo." Chase scoffed like it was the dumbest idea he'd ever heard. Dumber than getting two ex-spouses into a hot tub together or having one of them reveal her love for the other in front of millions of viewers. "Anyway, the lawyer comes in looking all official and says he has something important to tell them."

"Cut to commercial break," Kate said, hating that she could picture this so clearly in her mind. That she knew it would make great television.

"Exactly," Chase said. "And then when we come back, he delivers the news about the divorce papers not being filed. Boom!"

"Boom," Amy repeated with a lot less enthusiasm. "So are we setting this up for the season finale, or one of the earlier episodes?"

"That's the beauty of this, isn't it?" Chase said. "Post-production can edit to make it look like it happened at any point. We can splice it together so it seems like the big news came after months of filming, or we can do it early in the schedule so the whole season arc is about what happens next."

It was on the tip of Kate's tongue to echo Amy's words from so long ago. *Isn't that a little dishonest?*

But she knew better. And she could see Chase's mind was already made up. "I say we do it fast."

"What?" Kate took a steadying breath at his words. "But why? What's the rush?"

"News spreads fast in this business," he said. "I don't want any leaks. I'd rather spring it on Jonah fast so we don't risk someone else spilling the beans."

Kate swallowed hard and nodded. "Right. There are bloggers who get off on spoiling shows months before they release."

"I've already heard about Reality Steve sniffing around the camera crew," Amy added, prompting a sour look from Chase. "Don't worry—Pete wouldn't do that. He's one of the most honest guys I know."

Chase nodded, though it occurred to Kate that wasn't necessarily a plus in the boss's book.

"So what are you thinking?" Kate asked Chase. "How soon?"

"Now. In the next couple days." Chase folded his arms over his chest and leaned back against the table. "It seems smart, don't you think? If he learns the divorce isn't final after Viv's been throwing herself at him for weeks, he's going to react with suspicion, right?"

"Right," Kate said slowly, knowing that was probably true.

"But if we do it now, when it's truly coming from out of nowhere, we catch him on tape with shock that's authentic. He'd be truly stunned."

Kate nodded, knowing that was true as well, and also that she hated it.

"But is that really worth it?" Amy asked. "Like you said, we can edit in a shocked reaction from some other scene."

She sent Kate a frantic look, and Kate recognized she was grasping at straws. Amy knew better than anyone the importance of continuity. The fact that she was even trying to convince Chase otherwise made Kate want to hug her.

"Nah, we need things to be authentic," Chase argued. "We need footage to show Joe in the same outfit, sitting in the same setting, wearing the most genuine look of shock we're ever going to get from the guy." He snorted and leveled Amy with a look. "Come on, he's no actor. Besides, how's he going to react if he finds out at the end of the season that we knew all along about the divorce?"

"Pissed," Amy said, and Kate felt grateful that she wasn't the only one weighing in on Jonah's emotional responses. That they weren't counting on her to be the authority on Jonah Porter.

Still, it was Kate that Chase turned to when he spoke his next words. "We want him a little pissed," Chase said. "That's part of his persona. It makes for good ratings."

"You're messing with a man's life here," Kate pointed out. "With Viv's life, too, but at least she's in on the plan."

Not all the details, of course. She didn't know about Kate and Jonah sleeping together, or that Viv's quest to win back Jonah was unlikely to succeed.

"We've got him on contract for fourteen episodes," Chase said. "He's not going anywhere."

Amy shifted a little and lowered her notepad. "I agree that Joe might not react well if he thinks we've been hiding things from him."

"Exactly," Kate said, telegraphing silent thanks to Amy. "There's a difference between having him a little angry in general and having him pissed off at the whole show. At everyone involved with it."

Chase looked at her again, and something in his expression made her wonder how much he knew. Made her question whether the elevator or her hotel room or her breakfast tray had been bugged after all. She knew that wasn't possible, but she got a slithering feeling down her spine from the way he stared at her.

"Then you need to do whatever it takes to keep him around." He held Kate's gaze for a few beats longer, and she fought the urge to look away. "It's your job to keep him happy, isn't it?"

Kate swallowed. She opened her mouth to respond, but another voice echoed in the room.

"It's no one's job to keep someone else happy."

Kate turned to see Viv floating into the room. She was beaming from ear to ear and wearing an ivory tank top printed with a mandala, and olive-green yoga pants that made her look like a cross between a ballet dancer and a pixie.

Viv swept through the entrance and put a hand on Chase's arm. "Sorry to interrupt," she said. "I just overheard the last of what you said and wanted to point out that people are responsible for their own happiness and no one else's." Her smile faltered a little then as she glanced from one face to the other. "I'm sorry, did I come in at a bad time?"

"No, it's fine." Kate offered her best imitation of a smile and hoped like hell Viv hadn't heard anything too damning.

"Vivienne," Chase said, putting an arm around her and steering her toward the head of the conference table. "It's lovely to see you again. You're a little early, aren't you?"

"I know, I'm sorry. I had a yoga class just down the street and decided to pop by." She glanced back at Kate and Amy. "Were you talking about the show?"

"Employee relations," Kate said before anyone else could speak up. "Just making sure everyone who's part the show is taken care of financially, spiritually, emotionally—"

"Physically," Chase added, his eyes still locked on Kate. "I know we can all trust Kate to handle everything, though."

"She's very good at it," Viv chimed in, offering Kate such a genuine smile that it nearly broke her heart. "The best at making sure everything and everyone is handled with care."

"The very best," Chase agreed, sending a shiver down Kate's spine.

◆ ◆ ◆

Jonah had distinct memories of basic training as a young Marine. Of twelve-mile night marches and 3:00 a.m. stick battles designed to test a recruit's stamina and hand-to-hand combat skills.

But the filming schedule they followed over the next few days was making that look like a cakewalk.

On top of that, Viv was acting weird. At first he chalked it up to her mugging for the camera. She'd share some poignant memory from their past, always as a means of illustrating a point she was making for a couple they counseled. He'd catch her smiling at him a little long, or reaching across her desk to touch his hand.

He tried not to react, even though instinct made him want to yank his arm back and tell her to knock it the hell off. That wasn't exactly the best way to model positive dialogue for the couples they worked with.

As the days wore on, Jonah was starting to wonder if all this time on camera was making everyone a little loopy.

"Here's the Speedo they want you to wear."

Jonah turned to see Amy looking sheepish and offering him a garment the size of an eye patch.

He frowned. "I thought they were kidding about the hot tub scene."

Amy shook her head, still holding the Speedo like a steak entrée she'd been asked to serve a vegetarian. "Sorry. I didn't make the shot list. But we already know the shirtless stuff has been playing well with focus groups."

Which Jonah could grudgingly admit was a good thing. They'd had something like a gazillion hits on the teaser video they'd floated on YouTube. The result had been a slew of donations to Clearwater Animal Shelter, and a growing buzz about the show. Jonah didn't understand how it all worked, but everyone kept using the word *viral*. The video had laced footage from Jossy's shelter with clips from Viv's appearance on *Oprah* several years ago, hyping the whole thing up as America's hottest new reality show.

The wording had bugged the hell out of Viv, which Jonah could understand. Hell, he could even understand her being irked by how much attention he'd been getting. This television shit was horribly sexist, so maybe he owed it to her to take one for the team.

He stared at the Speedo. "I'm not wearing that," he said. "I'll do the hot tub thing, but I'll wear my own shorts. I think I have a gym bag in my car."

Amy smiled and tucked the Speedo back in her bag. "Great! They'll see you out there in ten."

She walked away, leaving Jonah wondering if the whole thing had been a gimmick to get him to agree while letting him feel like he'd won some small battle. He sighed and glanced at his watch. God, this was shaping up to be their longest filming day yet. At least Beth was holding things together at the bookstore.

"Jonah?"

He looked up to see Kate hovering in the doorway of the makeshift greenroom. There was no one with her—no cameraman, no sound checker—and Jonah tried to remember the last time they'd been alone together.

In her hotel room, he remembered, and tried not to picture her naked.

She must have had the same thought, because her cheeks turned faintly pink. "I just heard you agreed to do the hot tub scene."

"News spreads fast in this business."

She looked at him a little oddly. "Right. Yes, it does." She glanced behind her, then took a few more steps into the room, bringing her close enough to touch. Not that there could be any touching between them. Not here, anyway. "You look exhausted," she said.

Jonah laughed. "Gee, thanks."

"No, I mean—if you want, I can talk to the production guys about putting this off," she said. "Maybe we can reschedule or something."

"You're sweet to be concerned," he said. "Actually, I'm looking forward to it."

"To getting in a hot tub with your ex-wife?"

He frowned. "Viv's going to be there?"

"Shit." Kate frowned. "Yeah. I take it they didn't mention that part?"

He shook his head, feeling irritated. "No, they didn't. Are they doing some bullshit thing where I walk out there and act all surprised to see her in the hot tub?"

"No, nothing like that. They won't make you fake anything."

The look on her face wasn't very reassuring. "So what's the setup?"

"You're just supposed to act like you're unwinding together after a long day of filming," she said. "Technically, that's true, right?"

He frowned. "Sure, if I were in the habit of stripping down and taking a bath with my ex-wife."

"Don't think they didn't kick the bathtub idea around," she muttered. "Be grateful they went for the hot tub. At least it's huge. Plenty of room for you to have your own space."

Jonah sighed, hoping this wasn't going to get played off as some romantic interlude between them. "They're not going to make us sip wine and laugh at each other's unfunny jokes, are they?"

"There's no requirement that you tell jokes," she assured him. "Funny or unfunny. And actually, hang on."

She hurried out of the room, then returned a few seconds later with a four-pack of beer in cans. "Look—no wine either."

"You got me 3-Way IPA?" He grinned as she handed it over.

"It's from Fort George Brewery," she said. "I know you like IPAs, so—"

"This is great." He tucked the cans under one arm. "Is this some sort of product placement deal or something?"

She shook her head, and there was something almost sad in her expression. "No. I just wanted you to have something you'd like. Something that's just for you."

"I appreciate that."

They looked at each other for a moment, neither of them saying anything. If there were no risk of anyone walking in, he probably would have kissed her by now. Hell, he might have asked her to skip this whole stupid hot tub thing and come home with him. He was still entertaining that fantasy when she spoke again.

"Look, Jonah." Her voice was soft, and she darted a glance at the door before speaking again. "Remember what you said to me that first morning after we—after the night we went to the club?"

"I said a lot of things that morning," he said, shifting the beer from one hand to the other. "You'll have to be more specific."

"You said, 'No matter what happens, this was never a mistake.' I just want you to know that meant a lot to me."

He studied her a moment, trying to get a handle on what she was saying. On why she was speaking in code. "Okay," he said slowly. "Kate?"

"Yeah?"

"Is there something you're trying to tell me?"

She shook her head, then opened her mouth to say something else.

"Come on, already! Take your clothes off!"

They both turned to see Amy in the doorway tapping her watch. "Sorry, guys, but we need to move this along. We're paying the whole crew overtime right now. Jonah—you think you could maybe hustle?"

"Sure. No problem."

He looked back at Kate. "Can we talk more later? Like maybe after this shoot? When this is all over?"

Kate nodded, and that darkness in her eyes flickered again. "Yes. When this is all over."

CHAPTER EIGHTEEN

"Places, everyone!"

Kate clapped her hands together and surveyed the film crew. That seemed easier somehow than focusing on the scene they were set up to capture.

Jonah and Viv sat a few feet apart in Viv's massive hot tub that had been designed to look like a rock grotto. Rounded boulders lined the edges of a bubbling pool shimmering with flecks of pink and silver, reflecting the setting sun. A breeze ruffled tiny field violets blooming among the rocks, and Kate breathed in the scent of damp fern and ozone.

The setting was perfect. The lighting was perfect.

Kate's stomach was *not* perfect. It felt like a cement mixer someone had filled with Jell-O and cold rocks before turning the crank with agonizing slowness.

"Can you move a little to the right, Joe?" One of the lighting guys waved Jonah closer to Viv, and Kate tried not to cringe.

Jonah's arms were stretched out over the rock-lined rim of the tub, his infinity tattoo prominent on one sculpted pectoral muscle. Over his heart. Kate wondered if that's what the film crew was trying to capture.

"Beautiful, Vivienne," someone called. "Turn a little this way. There you go."

Kate forced herself to watch. This show was her baby. Her monster. She had to own it.

Viv's hair was piled loosely on her head, and she wore a simple black maillot that showed off her yoga-sculpted shoulders and arched collarbones.

Collarbones, Kate thought, remembering the game Jonah had described. How they'd taken turns planting kisses on the spots they named as they worked their way through the alphabet. God, she wished she didn't know. About the game, about the secrets, about everything that was going to happen in the next twenty minutes.

"We're ready to roll," Pete called, snapping Kate back to the present. He looked at her and nodded once, and Kate wondered how much he suspected. How much anyone here suspected.

Amy stepped up beside him and glanced back at Kate. Her expression didn't change, but Kate could feel her telegraphing the words.

"Are you okay?"

Kate nodded and forced her attention to the hot tub. To the scene unfolding before them. Viv was laughing at something Jonah had said, inching a little closer to him at the urging of the sound man.

"And—action!" Amy stepped back and looked at Kate again, lifting her hands and offering an almost imperceptible flutter of her fingers.

It's out of our hands now.

Kate nodded and took a breath.

Then she flicked on the miniature handheld camera she gripped in the folds of her jacket.

"Okay, guys—just like we talked about," Kate said. "Casual banter about the day's shooting. No names, no specifics about the couple. Just general discussion about therapy methods and the sort of work you're doing."

"Got it." Viv smiled and turned to Jonah. "I think we're making some amazing progress," she said. "I feel really great about what we accomplished today."

Good, Kate thought. *Nice and vague. That'll make it easier to edit.*

"Yeah," Jonah said stiffly, then took a sip of beer. He glanced at the sound guy, who gave him a hand gesture urging him to elaborate. "They seem like a nice couple," he added, resting his beer can on the rock ledge.

Viv smiled and swished her fingers through the bubbling water, a perfect image of casual banter. "I agree," she said. "Of course, they could benefit from some improved communication. They need to learn to speak more constructively with one another."

"They need to stop acting like toddlers fighting over whose diaper stinks the worst," Jonah muttered as he spun the beer can between his fingers. "In the end, they're both full of shit."

Kate nodded, approving of the dialogue even if she hated everything else about this moment. About what she knew was coming. She ordered herself not to glance back toward the house, even as she kept the miniature camera aimed that direction.

"It seems like such a positive sign that they haven't given up yet," Viv said. "The fact that they're coming here to see us speaks volumes about their commitment to each other. About their willingness to work things out, even though they've had moments of doubt over the years. Who hasn't, right?"

"Sure." Jonah looked at Viv a little oddly, and Kate held her breath. Did he suspect something?

If he did, he seemed to shake it off. He took another sip of beer and kept talking. "Maybe we get them in a room and take turns duct taping each one's mouth shut so they're forced to listen instead of yammering at each other."

In her mind, Kate heard the doorbell. It was imaginary, of course, something they'd cut in during editing. But she knew that's how it would go. How the scene would unfold on viewers' television screens. The shot would jump to the lawyer in a three-piece suit standing on Viv's front porch with a briefcase in his left hand. His right hand would drop from the doorbell, and he'd stand there waiting with an expectant look on his face.

In reality, the lawyer was stationed in Viv's mudroom, waiting for his cue to enter. To walk out on set and deliver the big news. At least he really was a lawyer and not a hired actor. That had been Chase's idea, a way to throw a bone to some favored member of his legal team.

Kate held her breath, waiting.

Right on cue, the side door swung open. Kate glanced down at her hand, making sure the camera was aimed right at the pathway leading from the house to the hot tub. She took a step back, getting into position. They'd reshoot this part later, of course, but this was about capturing authentic reactions. The ominous march of the lawyer's wingtips across Viv's cobblestone patio. The steely look on his face. The way he adjusted his tie, preparing himself to deliver the unexpected news.

Kate watched it all unfolding, knowing without a glance down at the handheld that she'd gotten the shot she needed. Pivoting to the right, she angled the tiny camera toward the hot tub, keeping it tucked in her jacket. This was her chance to snag backup footage that Pete and his crew might not get.

Back in the hot tub, Jonah hadn't yet noticed the lawyer's entrance. He was still nursing his beer, still making guarded conversation with Viv. Kate wanted to stop time. She wanted to preserve everything about this moment. This perfect, oblivious instant before everything changed forever.

"Excuse me?"

Viv and Jonah looked up. The surprise on both their faces was real. Even Viv hadn't been clued in about how this would all go down. She knew about the divorce, of course, but her surprise in the moment was genuine. That had been Chase's idea, too, a chance for the big reveal. An opportunity to catch everyone off guard.

Just like they'd hoped, Viv looked startled. "Oh. Hello. I—I didn't realize we had company."

"The crew at the door let me in." The young lawyer stepped to the edge of the hot tub. "I'm sorry to intrude, but there's some urgent information I need to share."

Jonah frowned at the lawyer, who was pulling a chair to the water's edge. They'd practiced this last night, the way he'd rest his briefcase across his knees and give the couple a solemn, meaningful look. Kate held her breath, watching the lawyer, not daring to look at Jonah.

"I'm Ashton Solomon with the law firm Myndee, Solomon, and Pierce," he continued, his face fixed in a perfect expression of concern and professionalism. Kate had coached him on it in the studio earlier, making him say the words over and over until she'd heard them echoing in her brain all night when she couldn't sleep.

"I represent the Empire Television Network," he continued. "And I need to let you know there's been a new development in your divorce."

Kate looked at Jonah and caught the flash of a frown. She knew before he opened his mouth what his response would be. She'd crafted the lawyer's statement to prompt it, knowing Jonah well enough to anticipate how he'd reply. What he'd say.

"Our divorce?" Jonah scowled. "You mean the divorce that's been final for over a year?"

In the final cut, there'd be a dramatic pause. Maybe a musical crescendo to build the tension.

In reality, only a few seconds passed. "That's what I'm here to talk about," the attorney said. "There's an issue with your paperwork."

Something about the melodramatic tone must have tipped Jonah off. Or maybe it was the panning of the camera, the way the audio guy scuttled across the patio like a teenager hiding beer cans after a party. Whatever the reason, Jonah's shoulders stiffened.

Kate watched, motionless. She kept her eyes fixed on his face as the words set in, as he braced himself for the rest of the news.

"What sort of problem?" Viv's words were like a distant murmur.

Kate didn't breathe. She didn't move. She just watched Jonah and waited.

He looked up then, finding her face in the crowd. Kate inhaled sharply. She felt his gaze spear through her like a hot skewer, puncturing a rib and a lung on its way through her heart. She watched as his expression shifted from confusion, to suspicion, to the one thing Kate feared most.

Betrayal.

◆　◆　◆

"What the actual fuck?"

Jonah couldn't recall if he was allowed to say *fuck* on television, or if it was one of those things they'd have to bleep out later.

At the moment, he didn't give a shit.

At the moment, the only thing he did give a shit about was the big stack of paperwork the man with the stupid orange tie had just locked in his briefcase with a taunting thunk.

"I've e-mailed you both a copy of the report so you can review it at your leisure," the lawyer continued, though Jonah wasn't sure the guy really was a lawyer. Did lawyers really wear ties that ugly? Or pronounce *leisure* like it rhymed with *pleasure*, which seemed unbearably pretentious?

"This is mind-blowing," Viv said. She swung her gaze to Jonah and held it there. She didn't look like he felt. Like he'd just been socked in the chest by a hundred-pound punching bag.

She looked . . . serene. Calm. Composed.

She looked like normal Viv, but there was something else. A sick feeling settled in his gut.

"Did you know about this?" he demanded.

Her expression faltered a little, and Jonah suspected that wasn't his line. If this whole thing was as scripted as he'd begun to believe, that's not how they'd expected him to respond.

Fuck that.

"I filed everything we agreed I'd file," Viv said, reaching up to brush a damp strand of hair from her cheek. "The documents to divide our retirement assets, the paperwork with the bank—"

"That's not an answer to the question, Viv." His voice rattled with anger, and he saw one of the sound guys step back. "How long?"

"How long what?"

"How long have you known?"

"Jonah, I'm just as surprised as—"

"Don't play me!" he slammed his fist down in the water, splashing himself and his beer and getting nothing on Viv. Of course. That was probably planned, too. "How long have you known about this?"

Viv pressed her lips together. "I found out a few days ago."

A few. That could mean two or three, or it could mean several weeks. Viv had always been vague in her concept of time.

Did it matter at this point?

He tore his gaze off her and looked straight at the camera. It was something he'd been instructed not to do, at least not in this scene. Doing it now felt like a rebellion of sorts.

"This is fucking bullshit," he said, aware that he sounded like one of the couples they'd been counseling. Like an angry, impetuous, scorned lover.

But that's what this felt like. Like he'd been lied to by someone he'd cared about, slept with, laughed with, loved.

Only in this case, it wasn't his ex-wife.

As he turned and found Kate in the crowd, he focused on her again. She met his gaze, not blinking at all. Her face might seem expressionless to anyone who didn't know her well, but Jonah knew her a helluva lot better than *well.*

At least he thought he had.

Maybe he'd been kidding himself. Maybe the remorse in her eyes was all for show. For *the* show—this goddamn, stupid reality-TV show.

He watched as she twisted one hand in the ruffled hem of her coat. She was blinking hard, and he wondered if it was the lights or the chlorine or some real show of emotion.

It couldn't be real. None of this was real.

Her mouth moved then, but no sound came out. Even so, Jonah could make out the words.

"I'm sorry."

He shook his head, so tired all of a sudden that he couldn't bring himself to respond. To even look at Kate anymore. He closed his eyes, inhaling the scent of wet stones and crushed fern while anger pounded so hard in his brain that his teeth clacked together.

"Fuck you," he muttered.

In that moment, he didn't know who he hated more. Kate? Viv? Himself?

"Fuck you," he said again, tossing the dark net of sentiment over all three of them. "I'm done."

CHAPTER NINETEEN

"Jonah, wait!"

Kate scrambled down the hall after him, slipping in the wet puddles of his footsteps. She regained her footing and kept after him, watching as he stormed toward the powder room just off the foyer. She felt the floor shake as he pushed the door open.

"Leave me alone, Kate!"

"Jonah, please—"

He slammed the door in her face.

A noise behind her made Kate turn. At the end of the hall, Pete stood with his camera trained on her. On the whole scene that had just transpired.

Of course.

The dramatic, impassioned exit of a reality show superstar. It was the biggest ratings grabber on the planet.

"Pete," Kate said calmly. "I'm going to ask you nicely to shut the camera off and leave the room."

"Sorry, Kate." He sounded genuinely sorry, but that didn't stop him from zooming in for a close-up. "Boss's orders."

"Pete," she said again, her voice remarkably calm even though her hands were shaking. "I'm going to start counting now. If you're not gone by the time I get to ten, I'm going to shove that camera so far up your ass you'll have footage of your tonsils."

He blanched a little at that, then lowered the camera. "I don't like this any more than you do, but you know the drill," he said. "This is the job."

"Believe me, I know. And I sympathize." Her breath caught a little there, and she wondered if he had any idea just how much she sympathized. How deep she'd gotten into all this.

Amy knew, thank God. She'd been the one ordering everyone to stay put when Jonah had stormed off set, sloshing water onto the sound equipment as he marched across the cold cobblestone path.

"Hold your places, everyone," Amy had shouted as Kate tore across the patio on Jonah's heels. "Kate's the one on our legal rider who's licensed to deal with situations like this. Plus she has advanced training in meltdown management."

It was total bullshit, but what did it matter? Amy was keeping everyone at bay for the moment.

Well, everyone but Pete.

Kate glared at the cameraman. "Pete," she warned, glancing at the camera. It was still rolling, even if it wasn't perched on his shoulder. "One, two, three . . ."

Pete rested one grizzly-bear paw on the edge of a built-in shelf, looking conflicted. He glanced back at the door behind him as though expecting Chase Whitfield to come charging through at any moment and fire him.

Kate could feel his pain. But she could feel her own a lot more vividly at the moment.

". . . four, five, six . . ."

She gritted her teeth and stared at the camera, wondering if she'd really do it. If she had it in her to break an expensive piece of equipment or risk her job. At this point anything seemed possible. She wanted to break something or smash something or—

"Um, Kate?"

She glared at Pete. "What?"

"I think your man just got away."

She whirled around just in time to see headlights flick on, followed by the rev of an engine. As she started toward the door, she heard gravel churning and the squeal of tires.

"Goddammit!"

She started toward the door but knew it was too late. Yanking a bobby pin from her hair, she stuck it in the lock on the powder room door and jimmied it open. Pushing her way inside, she spotted a trail of water leading to the door that opened onto the carport. She'd forgotten about the damn door.

"Fuck!"

She stared at the wet footprints on Viv's otherwise spotless wood floors. Then she turned back to Pete. "Did he just take off barefoot in his wet shorts?"

"He was pretty mad."

Kate balled her hands into fists and closed her eyes, wishing she could hit rewind on the whole evening. On so many other things.

She opened her eyes and turned to face Pete again. "Why don't you get packed up," she said slowly. "We're done here for now."

"Will do." He seemed to hesitate. "Are you okay?"

Kate nodded, but didn't say anything. She was gritting her teeth too hard. Pete continued watching her, looking leery about leaving her alone.

"Good work today," she said at last, straightening up. A lock of hair fell across her forehead, and she thought about putting the bobby pin back in place. Did it even matter? "It was a long day. Why don't you go home and get some rest?"

Pete still didn't say anything, but he watched her face like he wasn't sure what to do next. She could hear the chatter of voices outside on the patio, probably crew members who'd noticed Jonah's escape.

But here in the entryway, it was just the two of them—her and Pete—with sympathy warming the cameraman's dark-brown eyes.

"It's not your fault, Kate," he said softly. "You did what you had to do."

She swallowed hard, wondering how much he actually understood. She dug her fingernails into her palms, willing herself to stay calm. To be professional.

"This is so much worse than you think."

Kate wasn't sure what made her whisper those words. Maybe something about the kindness in the cameraman's face.

"I understand." Pete set the camera on the shelf beside him and rubbed his knuckles through his beard. "I have eyes, Kate. I see more than you think I do."

She shook her head, certain that couldn't be true. "No."

"Why do you think I wouldn't film that first blindside in Viv's office? The one where they told her about the divorce." He cleared his throat. "Why do you think I talked Chase out of having my crew tail you last week?"

Kate squeezed her eyes shut, not sure she could handle any more revelations. Not sure she had the strength to go back out there and talk to the crew. When she opened her eyes, Pete was watching her with a tenderness that made her chest ache.

"We do what we can to cushion the blow," Pete said. "To bring some humanity to this business. But beyond that, we do what the job requires."

"I know," she replied. "But knowing doesn't make it suck less."

"Sucking is part of life."

She snorted. "That's for damn sure."

Pete gave her a small smile. "We sound like self-help gurus."

Kate choked on a mirthless little laugh as her heart twisted tight in her chest. "Yeah," she muttered. "We should have a TV show."

◆　◆　◆

Two hours later, Kate leaned back against the headboard of her hotel bed and picked up her phone.

"Stop doing that." Amy snatched the phone from her hand and set it on the nightstand. In its place, she stuck a cheap hotel wineglass between Kate's fingers. "Drink up."

"I want a beer."

"No, you don't," Amy said. "You want Jonah, so you're trying to find him in liquid form."

"That's deep."

"Yeah, that's what happens when I spend sixteen hours a day hanging around a bunch of shrinks and self-help fanatics."

Amy scooted herself across the bed and slid into place beside Kate. Lifting her own wineglass, she took a sip. Kate watched her, grateful for the friendship even if she wasn't in the mood for a drink.

She set her untouched wineglass on the nightstand, using the excuse to glance at her phone again. There was still no reply from Jonah. No indication he'd gotten any of her text messages or voicemails or—

"Stop staring at it," Amy said. "He's not going to message you when he's pissed. Don't you remember that? *Average Joe's temper can run hot, so we're careful not to start conversations when one of us might say something regrettable.*"

"God." Kate closed her eyes and inhaled through her nose. "Please say you didn't just quote Viv at me."

"The woman knows her shit. Especially when it comes to Jonah."

That wasn't much comfort to Kate, but it was probably true. She sighed and picked up her wine. It tasted a little like cat pee, but not in a bad way.

"Marlborough sauvignon blanc," Amy said. "It's my favorite."

"Thanks."

Kate took another sip, then set the glass down again. "I just keep thinking I could have done something differently. If I'd gotten them to hold off on springing things on Jonah, or maybe if I'd worked harder to convince Chase that—"

"Kate, no. You did your job."

"I did my job like an asshole."

Amy shook her head. "You're one of the few compassionate professionals I've met in this business. Don't beat yourself up. This field is filled with people whose idea of compassion is making sure the knife is extra-sharp before slipping it between your ribs."

She shook her head, not mollified by Amy's words. "I knew there was a line I shouldn't cross," she said. "And I hurled my whole body over it like the damn thing was on fire."

"You didn't exactly throw yourself at him," Amy said. "The two of you were equally gaga for each other. He's just as culpable as you were."

Kate clenched her hands in her lap. "Maybe if I hadn't slept with him. If I hadn't fallen in love with him."

The words caught them both by surprise. Even Amy looked startled. "Wow. I knew you really liked him, but—wow."

"Goddammit." Kate shut her eyes. Now that the truth was out there, it didn't hurt any less. It hurt more, if that was possible.

A buzzing on the nightstand sent a jolt of adrenaline through her. Kate opened her eyes and fumbled for the phone, hands shaking so hard she knocked it off the edge.

"I've got it." Amy scrambled off the bed and dropped to her hands and knees, wedging her arm into the space between the bed frame and the nightstand. "I can almost reach it—"

She sat up in triumph, handing the phone over to Kate without glancing at the screen.

Kate loved her friend more in that moment than she ever had.

"What does it say?" Amy asked.

Jonah.

Kate studied the words, lips moving as she read them silently to herself once, twice, then one more time to be sure. Her heart squeezed into a tight, painful knot as tears clogged her throat. She knew she'd never be able read the message aloud, so she handed the phone to Amy without comment.

"According to my contract," Amy read, "I'm entitled to five days of sick leave per season and ten days of vacation time. Effective immediately, I'm taking all fifteen consecutively. My attorney has reviewed the contract and assures me that's legal, and that he'll be working around the clock to figure out how to get me out of this ridiculous sham of a show. Have a nice life, Kate."

Amy handed the phone back, and Kate felt a tear slip down one cheek.

"He's angry," Amy said, sliding an arm around her. "Give him time to cool down."

Kate shook her head. "It's not that simple. Think about how many people's livelihoods are on the line. How many people are depending on the whole team to show up on set tomorrow."

"So what are you going to do?" Amy asked.

Kate took a steadying breath, trying to get her bearings. Trying to decide whether to throw in the towel or keep flinging herself at the wall.

She looked up at Amy and felt emboldened by the earnestness in her expression.

"Same thing I always do," Kate said. "I'm going to take Dr. Viv's advice."

CHAPTER TWENTY

Kate stood on Jonah's doorstep, breathing in and out, watching raindrops spatter on rhododendron leaves that looked silver under the streetlight. She clenched her fists at her sides, steeling herself to knock.

"There's nothing braver than facing your own fears. Having the difficult conversation instead of running away."

The words echoed in her head, and it annoyed Kate to be standing here in the rain with Viv's voice in her ears. She tried to recall which book they'd come from. *On the Other Hand? But Not Broken?*

Hell, maybe she'd made them up herself.

She was still trying to figure it out when the door flew open.

"Jonah."

She swallowed hard and looked at him, trying to remember the speech she'd been rehearsing in her head. Something about forgiveness and professional obligations and—

"I said I didn't want to talk, Kate," he said. "I know you don't have a helluva lot of respect for other people's wishes, but this is flat-out trespassing."

The anger in his words made her throat squeeze up, but she swallowed hard to make her voice work. "I'm not here to defend myself," she said, even though a tiny part of her wanted to do just that. "I just wanted to explain what happened. Why I had to follow orders when it came to—"

"Right, of course." He folded his arms over his chest and leaned against the door frame. "Because you're such a rule follower?"

She swallowed again, ignoring the raindrop that slithered down the side of her neck. "Acting in the best interest of the show is my job," she said.

"Even when it comes at the expense of the people involved with the show?"

She balled her hands in the pockets of her jacket and forced herself to hold eye contact. "Jonah, you have to believe my hands were tied." Her voice sounded tear choked, and she struggled to get it under control. "I did everything I could to convince them not to go through with it. To do the right thing. I tried to tell them it was a bad idea."

"To make me look like a dumbass on national television? To blindside me with the news that I fucked up my own divorce, and I'm still technically married to the esteemed Dr. Brandt?"

"No one meant for you to look like a dumbass," she said.

Jonah sighed. He looked more sad than angry, but the dark edge in his voice told her there was a mix of both. "Kate, what was the one thing I asked for when I agreed to do the show?"

"Besides money?"

It was a bit of a jab, but she had to put that out there. To remind him that his involvement in the program wasn't just some benevolent gesture on his part. That there was something else at stake here. A chance to help his sister, to make a difference in her life.

Jonah glared but didn't take the bait. "I wanted a chance to repair my image," he said. "To stop looking like the idiot buffoon and have a chance to contribute something meaningful."

"You did contribute something meaningful," she said. "Those couples—"

"Are having a good laugh at my expense," he said. "The dyslexic dumbshit who can't even file his own divorce papers right."

"Jonah, no. It could happen to anyone."

"But not on national television," he said. "You could have chosen to handle it privately."

"I didn't have a choice." Kate shook her head, hating the hurt in his eyes more than the anger in his voice. "I did my best to stop the train wreck. I even thought about forging signatures. Trying to push your divorce through so no one would ever have to know."

"Forgery?" Jonah shook his head and looked at her with disgust. "A felony is your idea of doing the right thing?"

Kate gritted her teeth. "I said I *considered* it," she said. "I didn't do it. But I did try to stop them from going this direction. I explained to them what you'd shared with me about wanting to move out of Viv's shadow."

"So that's what it was all about?" He snorted. "It all makes sense now. Sleep with me to get the dirt to make the show better."

Rain lashed the leaves behind her, sending a trickle of ice water down her neck. She wished he'd invite her inside, but knew that wasn't going to happen. "That's not why I slept with you," she said softly. "That's not what happened at all."

It was almost like he didn't hear her. "God, to think I actually believed that was real."

"It *was* real, Jonah. You have to know that."

He frowned as if a new thought had just occurred to him. "Wait. Was this planned out from the start? When we met in Ashland that first time—"

"Of course not!" Kate snapped, stung by the accusation. "I was as surprised as you were when you showed up at Viv's house that first day. I had no idea who you were, and I sure as hell didn't mean to fall for you."

"When did you know about the divorce?" he demanded.

Kate fumbled around in her brain. Not for the date, but for the wording in her contract. Was that a detail she couldn't reveal? She couldn't be sure.

"I can't say," she said softly.

"Can't, or won't?"

"Can't," she repeated. "Look, I couldn't say anything. I still can't say too much about—"

"You've said more than enough."

Kate stomped her foot, irritated with herself for such a cliché gesture and for the fact that it only served to splash muddy water up her calves. "Dammit, Jonah. The execs had the information. You can't blame them for wanting to catch an authentic reaction from you on camera."

"Oh, it was authentic, all right. Probably the only authentic thing in this whole made-for-TV mess."

"That's not true," she said. "The way I felt about you—the way I *still* feel about you—"

"Spare me, Kate. People who care about each other don't let the other person get blindsided on national television. They don't plot behind that person's back to make the other person look like an idiot. You just don't *do* that."

Kate swallowed hard, wishing she could make him understand. Wishing she could make herself understand. "You were a Marine," she tried. "You know what it's like to have to carry out orders you may not agree with."

"Yeah, and I also understand about integrity and honor. About not sacrificing people for your own self-interests."

She took a shaky breath, wishing she could say more. Wishing her goddamn contract hadn't left her hands tied up like a Thanksgiving turkey.

"I know it's hard to understand," she said slowly, "but this show is important. Not just to me and to my career, but to potential viewers," she said. "If it can help even a handful of people who are struggling, isn't it worth a little sacrifice to get them to tune in and watch?"

"Spoken like someone who wasn't the one making the sacrifice."

She blinked hard, but her eyelids had given up the fight. A tear slipped down one cheek, then another. Or maybe that was the rain, trailing through her hair and down the back of her neck. She shivered under the porch light, wishing her brain weren't picturing how this would all look on camera.

It would be a terrific shot.

"I love you, Jonah."

A flash of emotion played across his face. Surprise, hurt, confusion. He stared at her for a moment, then glanced at the bush over her shoulder. "Let me guess. Are the hidden cameras documenting this?"

"What? No, of course not!"

"Oh, right—because you're above using a hidden camera to get the shot you want?" He shook his head. "I saw the one in your hand at Viv's place."

Ice slashed through her. "I was just—"

"Carrying out orders?" Jonah shook his head. "That's more than just a passive role in the game. You were in charge, Kate. And I was the dupe who fell for it."

Kate's gut churned. "No one meant to make you look stupid, Jonah. That's not what it was about."

"No? You mean it was just a happy bonus?" He snorted. "From the start, that's what everyone wanted. The chest-thumping Neanderthal who'd curse and say stupid shit and take his shirt off on cue."

"That's not true."

"That's exactly how it'll play on TV," he said. "Tell me I'm wrong."

Kate swallowed hard. He wasn't wrong. That was the worst of it. "Jonah, I never meant for it to happen like this."

"Yes, you did." The venom was gone from his voice, replaced by a tiredness that made Kate ache more than his anger had. "You wanted drama. You wanted a spectacle, and you got it. Congratulations, Kate."

And with that, he shut the door in her face for the second time that day.

◆ ◆ ◆

Jonah turned and stalked through his entryway without a word. Thunder boomed behind him like some fucking special effect in a TV show. In *his* TV show.

"Fuck you," he muttered, then felt like a jackass for cursing at the weather.

From the back of the sofa, Marilyn regarded him with silent judgment.

The person stroking the cat's back wasn't as silent.

"Don't you think you were kind of harsh just now?" Jossy said.

"No."

"Way to keep an open mind."

He stepped around the sofa but didn't sit down. He was too keyed up. He raked his hands through his hair and paced in front of the fireplace. "She played me for a fucking chump," he said. "It's bad enough that I seem like an idiot for botching my own divorce, but she set me up."

Jossy frowned and tucked her good leg up under her on the sofa. "Why are you pissed at Kate? You should be mad at the executives or Viv or the cameraman."

"Or myself," he muttered. "I'm the one who fucked up the damn paperwork."

"I wasn't going to point that out."

"God, I'm such an idiot," he said. "I remember all that shit show-ing up in the mail and thinking Viv had just gone ahead and filed.

That she'd given me a task to do, and then done it herself like always. I assumed—" He shook his head. "Never mind. Isn't that what they say about why you never *ass*ume anything?"

"Because it makes an *ass* of *u* and *me*?"

"Exactly."

"Owl," said Marilyn.

"You keep out of this," Jonah muttered.

"You're arguing with a cat," Jossy pointed out. "Don't you think you're overreacting just a little?"

He shook his head, still trembling with anger. "God, I'm such a dumbass." He kept pacing, but he felt his sister's eyes on him. Back and forth. Back and forth. He was such a pathetic cliché.

"So you're mad at yourself," Jossy said.

"Yes."

"And Viv and the producers and all the TV people."

"Yes."

"But you're taking it out on Kate."

He stopped pacing and whirled to face her. Something about hearing her name was like a bucket of cold water tossed in his face. He thought about her standing out there on the porch in the rain and felt his heart split right down the middle.

"I didn't spill my guts to Chase," he said. "I didn't sleep with the cameraman."

"That would make for one helluva reality show."

He glared at his sister. "Not in the mood for jokes, Jossy."

"Owl."

He glared at Marilyn. "You have something to say?"

The cat lifted both eyebrows in scorn, but refrained from further comment. He looked back at his sister, who was glaring at him with more heat in her eyes than Jonah had seen in a long time.

She pointed at the sofa. "Sit down."

"What for?"

"Because I said so!"

Jonah sat, not sure why he was following orders given by someone whose diapers he'd helped change. Then again, he'd spent a lifetime doing whatever he thought would make Jossy happy. Now wasn't the time to stop.

He picked up a beer can off the coffee table, knowing it was empty and had been sitting there all week. He just needed something to hold. Or maybe he wanted to crush it, feeling the aluminum crumple in his fist as he—

"What's pissing you off more?" Jossy asked. "That you might look dumb on national television, or that Kate kept a secret from you?"

"Why the hell am I supposed to pick?" he demanded. "Both are pretty shitty."

Jossy rolled her eyes and stroked a hand down Marilyn's back. The cat gave a chirp that sounded like a snort of disgust.

"Have you ever seen reality TV?" Jossy demanded. "Because this is how it works. They're always trying to blindside someone to get the big reveal. To get the ratings."

"What, you're an expert in reality television now?"

Jossy grabbed a balled-up napkin off the couch and threw it at him. "I've watched every episode of *The Bachelor* and *The Bachelorette* for twenty-one seasons. I think I have an idea how these stupid shows are supposed to work."

"Is this where you rub it in?" he said. "Where you tell me I should have been watching with you all along so I wouldn't be such a clueless twit?"

"Yes, that's my point exactly." Jossy's voice oozed with sarcasm. "I'm here to tell you that you would have been a lot smarter if you'd spent the last fifteen years watching strangers get naked and use questionable grammar on national television."

Jonah grunted and set down the beer can. He grabbed a handful of pretzels from the bowl on the table before remembering they'd been there since Tuesday. He looked down at them, not surprised to see someone had licked the salt off all of them.

He looked up at Marilyn, who closed her eyes and telegraphed her disgust. *What are you going to do about it?*

Jossy sighed, seeming to develop a little sympathy at last. "Let me ask you something, Jonah. Why did you decide to do the show?"

He scowled at the pretzels and didn't look up. "For the money."

"Right, I gathered that. But you got decent money off your book deal with Viv. And I know the bookstore isn't killing it, but you do okay, right?"

"I do fine."

"So why did you need more money?"

He thought about not answering her. About coming up with some bullshit story about fleshing out his artistic horizons or redeeming himself in the wake of the book.

But after a month filled with dishonesty, he probably owed her more than that. He took a deep breath and met his sister's eyes.

"To help you out," he said. "To make repairs at the shelter and maybe even buy you a computer-controlled knee. I thought if you had that, you could take up cycling again. Maybe not competitively, but if you could just ride again—"

"You might not feel guilty anymore?" Jossy shook her head, then reached out and rested a hand on his knee. "I thought it was something like that."

He sighed. "Look, Joss. You loved cycling so much, and it was just taken from you." *I took it from you*, he thought but didn't say. "There's no way to ride with the prosthetic you have now, and insurance will never pay for a computer-controlled one. I thought I could—"

"You thought you could sneak around behind my back and pull puppet strings without telling me?"

Jonah swallowed. "You're pissed."

"I'm not pissed. I'm trying to make you see you're being kind of a hypocrite here."

"I don't see the connection."

Jossy sighed again, and Jonah could tell she was on the brink of throwing something besides a napkin.

"I'd call you a dumbass right now, but you're clearly sensitive about it. So I'm not going to."

"Your restraint is admirable."

Jossy shook her head and stared at him. "You think it's okay for you to sneak around behind my back because it's well intentioned. Maybe you've convinced yourself it's okay because it's for my own benefit, or maybe you even have the self-awareness to realize you're doing it to ease your own guilt. It doesn't matter, actually. It doesn't change the fact that you're making decisions that affect my life without telling me about it."

He dropped the pretzels back in the bowl and frowned down at them. "It's not the same thing at all."

"It *is* the same thing," she said. "You love me, and Kate loves that damn show. Not just as a television program, but as a way of helping people. As a way of spreading a message that's had meaning for her."

He looked up at his sister. "You're not really comparing my love for my sister to a producer's love for her television show?"

"For what that show *stands* for, at least in Kate's mind. The power of love. The power of positive thinking. The power of not giving up on relationships or people."

He shook his head. "You're giving her too much credit."

"And you're not giving her enough," Jossy snapped. "You want to know why you're really so pissed?"

"Not particularly."

"Because you love her."

"No." Jonah shook his head.

"Yes."

"No."

"Yes."

"No."

Jossy stood up and grabbed the bowl of pretzels. Before Jonah could say anything, she'd upended the entire thing on his head. He sat there, dumbstruck, as twisted bits of pretzel tumbled into his lap.

"You did not just do that," he said.

"Damn right I did." She shook her head. "Seriously, people pay for your relationship insights and communication skills? You're talking like a petulant toddler."

"Do as I say, not as I do," he muttered, knowing damn well it was a weak argument.

Jossy shook her head. "There's no way you'd be this upset if you hadn't fallen for her."

He started to argue, but stopped himself. Did she have a point? Pissed as he was, could he at least acknowledge that much?

"Maybe," he muttered.

"So you admit it," Jossy said. "You fell for her."

"So? It's a moot point now anyway."

"Because you're walking away from the show?"

"That's right." Jonah started to rake his hands through his hair again before remembering his head was covered in pretzel dust. He sighed and dropped his useless fists into his lap. "I don't know."

"What if I said I wanted you to stick it out?" Jossy said softly. "That I really want that prosthetic leg? That I want you to do whatever it takes to get it for me."

Jonah's heart quivered. He turned and looked at his sister. "Do you?"

She stared at him for such a long time that Jonah thought she might not answer again. "Maybe."

It was a start. "Then I'll do whatever it takes to get it for you."

"Anything?"

"Anything." He meant it, too. If she wanted him to lie down on hot coals or stick paper clips under his fingernails or—

"Go back to the show," she said. "Give Kate a chance."

He stared at her. "Give her a chance with the *show*," he said carefully.

"With the show," she agreed.

On the back of the couch, Marilyn stood up and stretched, lifting both eyebrows with intense skepticism.

"*Owl.*" Her expression was one of disdain, though Jonah could have sworn he heard approval in the lone syllable. "*Owl!*" she said again, more adamant this time.

He looked back at his sister. "Just the show," he said. "If I agree to finish it out, that's all I'm agreeing to."

Jossy gave him a small smile and leaned over to pluck a pretzel from his hair. "We'll see about that."

CHAPTER TWENTY-ONE

At nine the next morning, Kate tapped on Viv's front door. They weren't scheduled to shoot until the next day, or maybe ever, depending on how things shook out with Jonah.

The legal team was working on that.

But at the moment, Kate had something she needed to get off her chest.

The door swung open, and Viv looked at her blankly for a few beats. "Kate." She smiled, but it wasn't her usual soaring, serene smile. It was a tired smile. The smile of a woman who hadn't slept well and perhaps had eaten six doughnuts for breakfast.

Maybe Kate was projecting.

"Good morning, Viv." She held up a white paper cup with an earthy cardboard sleeve around it. "I brought you some of that tea you like. The cardamom-rose black from Metolius Artisan Tea?"

Viv seemed to force the corners of her mouth a bit higher as she held open the door and waved her inside. "You're an angel, Kate. Such a good soul."

The lump in Kate's throat grew thick and sour, and she followed Viv into the parlor with guilt draped like a wet shawl around her shoulders. Her fingers felt numb around her own cardboard cup of tea as she looked about, almost surprised to see the space not cluttered with television production gear.

"Pete came by and collected everything this morning," Viv said. "He said they needed the equipment on another shoot." She gave a sad little smile and looked down at her fingernails. "He gave me a hug and told me not to worry."

Kate smiled back, even though she didn't feel it. "Pete seems like a guy who'd give good hugs."

"That's true."

The small talk felt stilted, and it echoed in the hollow spaces of the room. Kate looked around, noticing the empty spots where cameras and lighting equipment had stood only days ago. "It must be hard," Kate said. "Having the filming in your space. No privacy or escape."

Viv turned and offered a small shrug. "Yes, but it's what I wanted. What I asked for." She gave a brittle little laugh. "Admittedly I haven't always been a great judge of what's best for me."

Kate forced a smile of her own and wondered how much to read into that. Was Viv making small talk or offering something deeper?

"Please, sit down." Viv gestured to the seating area, and Kate hesitated before choosing the squash-colored club chair where Jonah had seated himself at that first meeting.

God. How long ago was that? It seemed like years, though it was only a matter of weeks.

Kate found a coaster and set down her cup of tea on the coffee table. Viv arranged herself on the dove-gray leather loveseat and tucked her bare feet beneath the hem of her linen skirt. Then she folded her hands in her lap and looked at Kate expectantly.

Kate took a deep breath. On the drive here, she'd practiced what she wanted to say, but now she was questioning her approach. She was questioning a lot of things, actually.

She cleared her throat. "In chapter sixteen of *But Not Broken*, you talked about having the hard conversations," Kate began. "You described the moment you had to tell your best friend that your relationship was over and you'd decided to leave—"

"Kate?"

"Yes?"

"Just say it." There was the tired smile again. Viv lifted a hand and tucked a thick swath of dark hair behind her ear. "Sometimes it's okay to just jump right in and say what you need to say."

"Right." Kate cleared her throat. "Okay. First just let me say how much respect I have for you. I've made no secret of how much I admire you both professionally and as a person."

"Oh, for the love of Christ." Viv closed her eyes and pressed her palms together just below her chin. As Kate watched, heart pounding, Viv lowered her forehead to her fingertips. She breathed deeply, in and out, eyes shut tightly. "Just say it already," Viv said.

"Okay." Kate licked her lips. Hadn't Jonah praised her for her way with words? But somehow it seemed harder now. Was it because she was talking to Viv, or because she *wasn't* talking to Jonah?

"So, Viv—"

"They're canceling the show."

"What?"

Viv lifted her head, blinking. "That's what you're here to tell me, right?"

Kate shook her head, not sure if the news she'd come to deliver would be better or worse. "No. Um, not even close."

"But after yesterday—"

"No, Chase loved it. He saw parts of the footage last night, and Amy and I gave him a full report on the phone this morning." Kate stopped there, not wanting to share too much. Not wanting to feel her gut churn at the memory of Chase's delighted laughter.

"This is solid fucking gold right here," he'd said. "The ratings are gonna go through the fucking roof with this epic blindside."

Of course, that might all be in jeopardy if Jonah really did walk away. The lawyers had told her to stay out of it for now, insisting they had things under control. That they were making progress with Jonah and his attorney.

Kate had been more than happy to step away. To leave the tough stuff to someone else for a change.

Viv looked at her, uncertainty etched between her brows. "So what did you come here to tell me?"

Kate licked her lips and took a breath. "It's about Jonah," she said. "See, the thing is—" Kate cleared her throat, annoyed with herself for bumbling her words. "There's more to my relationship with him than you realize."

"Ah." Realization dawned, and Vivian gave a sage nod. "I understand."

"You do?" Her stomach rippled with unease, but maybe this would be easier than she'd thought.

"It's okay, Kate." Viv smiled. "Believe me, you're not the first."

"What?"

"If I had a nickel for every woman who's developed a little crush on my husband—"

"No, that's not it." Kate dug her nails into her palms, thinking Viv had a point about just spitting things out. "I—we—" She took another deep breath and looked Viv in the eye. "I slept with him."

Viv blinked. "I beg your pardon?"

Okay, so there was a more delicate way to say that.

But Kate pressed on. "It's true. I didn't mean for it to happen, and I never meant to hurt you, Vivienne."

Viv pressed her lips together a moment, digesting the information. "In Ashland, when you met before?"

Kate shook her head. "No. It was true what we told you at that first meeting. That whole thing was just a stupid coincidence. I mean, we kissed, but that was it."

"You kissed in Ashland," Viv said, her expression still uncertain. "But more happened after that?"

"Right," Kate confirmed, wishing there were a way to just fast-forward through this conversation. To not spell out every last humiliating detail. "But as we got to know each other, we started to grow closer."

"I see."

"But I swear to you, I had no idea that you still had feelings for him when he and I slept together." *The first time*, her conscience whispered.

"The first time," Kate said aloud, and forced herself not to look away.

Viv stared at her. She didn't speak for a very long time. Kate ordered herself to sit quietly, to give her a chance to process things.

"Holy fuck."

Kate swallowed. "Right."

Viv sat and breathed for several long moments. Then she looked up at the ceiling, her perfect, pointed chin tilted toward Kate like an offering.

I can see up her nostrils, she thought, and then felt guilty.

Another wash of guilt hit her when Viv met her eyes again. "You know, if there were a camera in the room and this were all part of an unscripted television program, this is where I'd smile sagely and assure you that I knew all along," Viv said. "That I always had a sense about this, and that the two of you belong together."

"I—"

"But that's bullshit."

Kate jumped a little, and Viv sighed. "I don't mean whether you belong together. I have no idea about that. Although now that I think about it, this makes sense. The way he'd always look at you when he didn't think you were watching. The way his face lit up when you walked into the room."

Kate shook her head as a pang of loss rippled through her. "Not anymore. He hates me."

Viv gave a small smile and shook her head. "Joe isn't like that. He has a hot temper sometimes, but he's not capable of hate. It only looks that way because he loves so deeply."

Kate looked down at her hands. "I'm sorry, Viv. I could give you some excuse about how I never meant for it to happen, but it's like you wrote in chapter seven of *On the Other Hand*—"

"Kate." Viv clapped her hands together, and Kate looked up sharply. "Please stop quoting me to *me*."

"Right." Kate nodded. She needed to just say it. To spell out the rest of the story and live with the consequences, no matter what those might be. To stop skirting the facts.

"I knew you loved him and I slept with him anyway and I'm sorry," she said. "That's what I came here to say."

Vivienne nodded. She picked up the cup of tea in front of her and started to take a sip, then seemed to change her mind.

She probably thinks it's poisoned, Kate thought, and felt worse than she already did. How was that possible?

"I appreciate you telling me," Viv said. "Coming clean. That takes courage."

Kate nodded and gripped the armrests of her chair. "For what it's worth, it's over between us," she said. "Jonah and me, I mean. Having me betray him like that—there's no recovering from that."

Viv lifted one delicate eyebrow. "You mean the part where you did your job and kept my secrets from him and his secrets from me?" Viv shook her head. "That's not betrayal."

"It is to Jonah," she said. "And sleeping with my idol's ex-husband when I know she's still in love with him—" She stopped, not sure she wanted to go any further. "That's betrayal, too. A different kind."

"You're the one putting labels on things, Kate. Not me."

Kate swallowed hard and picked up her tea. The paper cup was still warm, but the liquid inside had turned tepid. She took a sip anyway, trying to wash the taste of guilt from her mouth.

"You want some unsolicited advice from a professional?"

Kate looked up and her heart picked up speed. Clutching the cup a little tighter, she nodded. "Yes, please."

"Stop looking to me for advice," Viv said. "It's time to start trusting your own instincts."

Kate choked on a small, bitter laugh. "My own instincts just led me off the end of a pier with a pocket full of rocks."

Viv laughed, too, but hers was real. It was tired and a little sad, but it was a laugh just the same. That made Kate's heart ache even more.

"So here's your opportunity, Kate," she said. "Your chance to learn to swim."

◆　◆　◆

Three days later, Kate watched as Jonah tugged at his shirt collar and glanced over his shoulder at the towering studio light behind him.

Even Kate had to admit the glare seemed extra hot today, or maybe it wasn't the light at all. Maybe she was feeling the gaze of Chase Whitfield, who'd shown up on set to watch the glorious return to filming after their short hiatus.

"Nice work, Kate," Chase murmured as he leaned close enough for Kate to smell onions and expensive aftershave. "I knew I could count on you to do what it took to keep the cameras rolling."

Kate grimaced, not sure what he was implying. "Thanks, but it wasn't me," she said. "His sister told me—"

"Quiet on set!" Pete shot them a pointed look and gestured to the mike.

"*Sorry,*" Kate mouthed, and edged away from Chase. Across the parlor, Amy flashed her a sympathetic look. Kate sighed and directed her attention back to the center of the room.

Jonah was seated next to Viv, close enough that either of them could touch the other if the mood happened to strike. Kate hadn't spoken to Viv since that day in the parlor. She had no idea if Viv had told anyone about their conversation, but Chase had been in constant contact.

"I've been working my magic with Vivienne," he'd told her on the phone that morning. "I'm making sure she doesn't back out on the plan to seduce Joe."

The thought made Kate's stomach churn.

She'd tried texting Jonah once since the night he'd slammed the door in her face, but the message had gone unanswered.

"He's processing things," Jossy told her when Kate stopped by the animal shelter with a short promo clip to share. "Be patient. He'll talk to you again as soon as he comes around."

Kate wasn't convinced.

She shook her head and ordered herself to focus on the set. Viv was dressed in a fitted purple tunic and black leggings that somehow made her look both regal and comfortable. Kate envied her on both counts.

As Kate watched, Viv leaned forward and spoke in earnest tones to the new couple she and Average Joe were tasked with helping.

"Roger, I can see you're hurting very deeply," Viv said. "You, too, Abby. I want you to know I understand where you're both coming from. Mistakes have been made on both sides."

Roger started to open his mouth, but Jonah cut him off. "If you're about to offer a tally of who committed the most errors, so help me God, I'll take that list, tear it into a thousand pieces, light it on fire, and force you to stomp out the flames with your bare feet."

Roger blinked and shut his mouth.

"Metaphorically speaking," Jonah added. "Was there something else you had to say?"

Roger shook his head and looked down at his lap. Abby looked triumphant for a moment, but Viv shook her head. "None of this is about winning or losing," Viv said. "Being right doesn't make you happy. There's very rarely a correlation between winning an argument and finding joy."

"Let's just agree that you've both fucked up," Jonah said.

Viv nodded, not even wincing at Jonah's word choice. "The thing that's important to understand here is that everything happens for a reason."

"And sometimes," Jonah added, "the reason is that you're an idiot who makes poor decisions."

A few people on set chuckled, and Chase gave him a thumbs-up. But Jonah didn't look at him. He kept his focus on Roger and Abby, and Kate's chest ached from the compassion in his eyes.

"I'm including myself in that," Jonah added. "God knows I've made plenty of dumb choices over the years. But I've always tried to learn from them."

"And that's what's most important," Viv added. "Moving ahead instead of spinning your wheels."

Abby sniffed and glanced at her husband from behind a curtain of caramel-colored hair. "I just don't know if I can trust him again," she said. "I know things weren't always great in the bedroom, but I never expected him to—to—to go looking in someone else's bedroom."

Roger put his face in his hands and shook his head. "I told you, Ab—it was a mistake. And it wasn't actual sex. I swear to God, I never even took my pants off all the way."

Kate glanced at Chase, unsurprised to see he was eating this up. God, there were some great sound bites. At least Abby and Roger were getting help. In the end, that's what mattered.

"Intimacy is something you treasure," Viv was saying. "Something special that—"

"Cut!" Chase waved a hand in the air, though none of the cameras stopped rolling. The crew knew damn well that the exciting stuff usually happened when no one thought they were being filmed.

Chase moved forward, bumping a camera with his shoulder and earning a glare from Pete. "You all sound great, but I was wondering what this would feel like if we moved the scene someplace more intimate," Chase said.

"Intimate?" Viv looked confused.

"Right. Since Roger and Abby here have been having trouble in the bedroom, maybe you and Joe could take them back there and show them a few things."

Jonah frowned. "Seriously?"

"You don't have to take any clothes off or anything." Chase waved a hand like that was the furthest thing from his mind, though Kate didn't doubt the thought had occurred to him. The whole thing gave her a sour taste in her mouth.

Chase leaned close to Viv, easing into his role as her BFF. "Just being together on the bed, maybe offering a few tips about how you might go about—"

"Stop!"

Kate felt her throat vibrate and her mouth form the word, so she must have been the one to say it. Everyone turned to look at her, and she could hear blood pounding in her head.

She stepped forward, heavy with the sensation of making her way through a swimming pool while wearing snowshoes. "Enough," she said.

The second she said the word, she knew it was the right one. She kept going, directing her attention at Chase so she wouldn't have to look at Jonah.

"You can't keep doing this," she said.

Chase stared at her. "Doing what?"

There was a challenge in his voice, something daring her to take it a step further. Kate stared back, telegraphing her own message.

I know you're trying to get Jonah and Viv in bed together. I know what you're doing, and I won't let you.

303

Chase didn't blink.

Kate took another step forward. "People aren't playthings," she said. "You can't stand here pulling puppet strings while the two people who have the most to lose just flail their arms and legs around with every tug of the handle."

It wasn't the most artful metaphor, but it made Chase scowl. "Be careful, Kate." His voice was low, the threat implied.

A few feet away, Roger and Abby glanced at each other. Viv was frowning, and Kate wondered if she had any idea what this was about. If she still thought Chase had her best interest at heart. That he wanted to help her win back her ex-husband.

Kate didn't dare glance at Jonah, but she knew he was confused, too. God, he still had no idea. Not a clue that Viv wanted to win him back, or that Chase planned to make a spectacle of him all over again.

Taking a shaky breath, Kate took another step closer. "I can't let this happen, Chase."

Chase shook his head and folded his arms over his chest. "You're treading awfully close to the edges of your contract."

"Fuck the contract," Kate snapped. She turned to face Viv, steeling herself for what needed to be said. "Vivienne, he's not on your side. The things you've confessed—the feelings?" She shook her head, trying to convey her message without humiliating Viv. "It's not going to pan out. They're playing you, but this won't go down the way you want it to."

She stopped there, wondering if she was starting down the wrong path. Why would Viv believe her, anyway? The woman who'd confessed to sleeping with the object of Viv's affection. Viv probably saw her as a jealous rival.

But she had to try. She had to warn Viv, to warn Jonah—

"Jonah, I know you hate me right now." Kate swallowed hard and met his eyes. Those mossy amber orbs speared through her, taking her breath away. She knew he wouldn't argue about hating her, but she needed to keep going anyway. "I know how much you hate blindsides," she said softly. "And there's another one coming."

Behind her, Chase growled. "Stop this right now, Kate," he said. "Or there will be consequences."

She looked back at him and knew he damn well meant it. *A million dollars*, she thought, staring into those steely eyes. Kate stared back, unblinking.

My soul is worth more than that, asshole.

She turned back to Jonah and Viv.

"Go," she said. "Both of you need to leave the set right now and find a private place to talk." She shot a warning look at Pete, who nodded once.

"No cameras," she said to Viv and Jonah. "And no coming out until the two of you have had the conversation you need to have without anyone else standing to gain from it. Do you understand?"

Viv pressed her palms together and looked at her. A small, serene expression was painted on her face. Kate couldn't tell if it was a smile or a frown. The studio lights were so bright.

"Are you finished, Kate?" Viv asked.

"Oh, she's finished, all right," Chase barked, moving close enough for Kate to feel the waves of fury radiating from him. "You're done. Pack your things and get out of here. You'll hear from the legal team within the hour."

Kate started to move back, but Viv's voice stopped her. "I need everyone else to stop talking *now*."

Everyone froze. Even Jonah, who was probably the last person on earth to want to follow Viv's orders.

But he was watching his ex-wife with something that looked like pride. Viv looked back at him, then reached out and took Jonah's hand. As she squeezed it in hers, Kate's heart clenched, too.

Jonah met Kate's eyes again. "I already know."

Kate stared at him. "Know what?"

"Know Viv's plan to win me back," he said. "To rekindle our marriage."

Kate looked at him, uncomprehending. She turned to Viv. "I never said a word. I swear to you."

"I know you didn't," Viv said. "I did."

"What?"

"I told him everything," Viv said.

"I—so—wow." Kate swallowed. "So you're getting back together."

"Jesus, no." Jonah frowned, then looked at Viv. "No offense."

"None taken." Viv smiled, bigger this time, more certain. "I had a moment of clarity when I was telling Jonah about my feelings. I realized I only wanted to resume our relationship because I was scared of the alternative. Of spreading my wings and learning to swim on my own."

"That's a god-awful metaphor," Jonah said, but gave her a fond smile anyway. "But I'm proud of you. For figuring it out. For owning your shit."

"Beautifully put," Viv said. "I feel like I finally have closure."

"I don't fucking care!" Chase whirled around to face Kate. He pointed one meaty finger at her, sputtering with fury. "You're still fucking liable. I want you off this set right now before I call the police."

Kate nodded once and turned to go. She held her head high, buoyed by the look of encouragement Amy flashed her. By Pete's supportive nod.

"And I expect you to turn in all your equipment," Chase said. "Everything that doesn't belong to you—"

"My *pride* belongs to me," Kate snapped, whirling back to face him. "And I'm damn sure taking that with me."

Then she turned and marched out of the room, shooting a mental apology to Amy for having to deal with the aftermath.

Behind her, she heard the confused voices of Roger and Abby.

"Is this some kind of weird therapy?" Roger mumbled.

"I don't know," Abby answered. "Like maybe we're supposed to recognize how destructive it is to shout all the time?"

Kate pulled the door shut behind her, heels clicking on Viv's cobblestone walkway. She'd made it halfway to her car when she heard footsteps behind her.

"Kate, wait up."

She froze in her tracks at the sound of Jonah's voice. Still, she waited a moment before turning. She took a few deep breaths, wanting to be ready for whatever he had to say. Wanting to be the one to speak first.

She turned and met his eyes. "I'm sorry, Jonah."

It was his turn to freeze. "For what?"

She gave a hollow little laugh, not sure where to begin. "For betraying your confidence. For fucking up the show. For embarrassing you just now."

"It's not your fault, Kate." He took a few steps closer, and the warmth in those amber-green eyes was almost more than Kate could bear. "I saw what you were up against in there. And I saw what you tried to do anyway."

"For all the good it did." She shook her head and looked back at the rental car. Crap, she was going to have to turn that in. And check out of her hotel. And book a flight back, which she knew the network wouldn't pay for. Maybe she'd get lucky and be spared the fines and the legal fight, since Viv had revealed her own secret. Maybe Kate could find another job filming—

"Kate, I'm sorry, too."

"For what?"

He shook his head, remorse heavy in his expression. "For losing my temper. For not listening to you. For failing to give you the benefit of the doubt."

She nodded, grateful they'd cleared the slate. At least they'd have that. "I enjoyed working with you, Jonah," she said. "Everything else, too. Not just the work, but the friendship. And the rest. That was real, no matter what you believe."

"I know it was, Kate." He was standing close, so close she could feel the heat from his body. God, she'd give anything to touch him one more time.

"Good luck with the show," she said. "For what it's worth, I think you're doing meaningful work."

He shook his head. "It'll be more meaningful with you running it."

Kate gave a brittle little laugh. "No chance of that happening. Chase made sure of that."

"Wanna bet?"

Kate stopped laughing as Jonah nodded back toward the house. "Right now, Viv's in there laying it all out for him. She'll start by pointing out that they have no legal recourse against you since she's the one who spilled her own secret. That's why she did it, you know."

She frowned, not sure she was following. "For me?"

He nodded. "We went over it together this morning. Right after we finished the divorce paperwork. For real this time."

"But Viv should be furious with me."

"She should?" Jonah shook his head. "No one tells Viv how she should feel. And no one manipulates her feelings either. That's what she's angry about. At Chase, not you. He's the one who tried to screw her over."

Kate shook her head, struggling to process it all. "Okay, but even if he doesn't impose the fine, Chase will never keep me on the show."

"Sure he will," Jonah said. "Once he learns both Viv and I plan to walk if he doesn't agree." He smiled and reached up to tuck a strand of hair behind Kate's ear. "Turns out the one thing my ex-wife and I agree on is that this show isn't worth a damn if you're not in charge."

She stared at him. "You're not serious."

"I am, actually."

"Wow." She knew she should come up with something more intelligent than that, but her head was spinning too fast to generate more than one syllable.

"Kate, it's your passion that makes this show work," he said. "Viv knows that, and I know that. Deep down, Chase knows that."

She ached to believe it. Wanted desperately for it to be true. "I don't think so."

"Chase isn't stupid," Jonah said. "He knows it can't work without the three of us together. The network will never find another world-renowned self-help guru with a surly ex-husband and the award-winning producer he's in love with."

"But he can't—wait, what?" Kate blinked, pretty sure she'd heard him wrong. That she'd mixed up the pronouns or something.

Jonah moved closer and lifted a hand to cup her elbow. "I love you, Kate," he said. "I'm sorry I was too wrapped up in my own bullshit to say it before. I love you and I miss you and I can't imagine my life without you."

"Holy shit."

He laughed and held out his arms. "Please say you'll forgive me."

"I forgive you." She hesitated, wondering if this was all a dream. If it was some sort of TV stunt or a cruel prank.

"Hug me, Kate. I'm getting old here."

She smiled and stepped into his embrace. As she looked up at him, his lips found hers. She kissed him back, soft and deep and exactly the way she remembered.

When she broke the kiss, she looked up at him with tears in her eyes.

"I love you, too, Jonah. So much."

"Damn right you do."

Then he was kissing her again, and Kate slid her hands up his arms, gripping his shoulders and clutching him like her life depended on it.

When they finally came up for air, Kate saw a flicker of movement. She peered over Jonah's shoulder to see Pete at the edge of the house, his camera perched on one shoulder.

A bubble of anger swelled in her chest. "Pete," she warned. "I need you to stop filming right now—"

"It's okay," Jonah said. "I asked him to."

"But—why?"

He grinned and slid his arms around her, pressing the heels of his hands into the small of her back. His eyes locked with hers, and he leaned close so only she could hear the words.

"Because," he said. "When we're old and gray and sitting in our nursing home together, I want to watch this moment again. I want to tell everyone—the nurses, the orderlies, the guy who shows up to change my diaper—that this is where it all started."

EPILOGUE

"How soon do you think we'll see them?"

Jonah glanced over to see Kate squinting at the finish line. She wore a black cotton sundress that reminded him of the one she'd worn the first time they met, and he felt a surge of fondness as familiar as his own pulse.

"Relax," he said, sliding an arm around her. "We've got another ten minutes at least."

Kate tilted her sunglasses up on her head and smiled up at him, giving him a flash of those toffee-colored eyes that had been melting him for almost a year now. "Bike racing is kind of a tough sport to watch," she said.

"It's not a race, exactly," he pointed out. "Just a fun ride. We're easing in slowly, remember?"

We meaning Jossy and her new knee. He and Kate weren't taking things all that slowly anymore. They'd moved in together four weeks ago, with Kate still commuting to LA once or twice a month. For the most part, she spent her time in Seattle, where they'd just started filming the second season of *Relationship Reboot with Dr. Viv.*

Season one was currently the most-watched show in its time slot, with a prime-time Emmy nod for Outstanding Unstructured Reality

Program. Even Chase Whitfield had grudgingly admitted they'd made the right call keeping cast and crew intact.

Kate peered back at the bike course while Jonah admired the sun-slashed glints of mahogany in her hair. "Before I forget," she said, "I invited Pete and Viv over as soon as we finish unpacking all the boxes."

"Given how many boxes it took to hold all your stuff, that'll be somewhere around the time their baby enters kindergarten."

Kate gasped and looked up at him. "Are you serious? They're pregnant?"

He laughed and planted a kiss on her forehead. "Not yet, but isn't it just a matter of time?"

"I know they're trying," she said, making Jonah do a little shudder. "What?"

"*Trying*," he repeated, giving one more shudder for dramatic effect. "That phrase makes me think of them grunting and gyrating like farm animals."

"Thank you for ruining the beauty of procreation and childbirth for me," she said. "And the sweetness of that relationship."

"I don't think anything could ruin the sweetness of that relationship," Jonah pointed out. "The two of them together are like a teddy bear cuddling a jar of organic wildflower honey."

"I'm just glad they're happy."

So was Jonah, honestly. Part of him had expected Viv's second chance at love to come in the form of someone powerful or pretentious or sophisticated. In the end, it had happened with a guy who was a cross between a grizzly and a walking hug.

Jonah could appreciate that.

Kate turned back to face the race course, glancing once at her watch. "I hope she's okay," Kate said. "I know Jossy was worried about the last part of the course. Something about technical terrain or hills or something."

"Will you relax? She's fine." Jonah gave her another squeeze, aware that he was reassuring himself as much as he was her. Despite Jossy's new independence and new leg, he still hadn't stopped feeling protective. Would probably never stop.

A clang of cowbells drew their attention to a bend in the road where the first pack of cyclists came into view. Jonah scanned the crowd, looking for his sister. Good Lord, how many bike racers were there? Big, burly guys with thighs the size of hams, and women who were almost indistinguishable from the men, aside from the pink and purple racing jerseys.

Suddenly, he spotted her. Jossy wore a yellow top, black bike shorts, and a grin so wide he could see it from two hundred yards away. As she surged ahead and then whizzed past, Jonah saw the Clearwater Animal Shelter logo on the back of her jersey.

He stuck his fingers in his mouth and whistled. "Way to go, Joss!"

"Woohooo!" Kate called. "Nice work, Jossy!"

His sister sped through the finish line in a blur of color and big smiles, then stopped to accept slaps on the back from her teammates and the crowd. Jonah's chest felt too big for his shirt as he watched his baby sister beaming.

Beside him, Kate slid an arm around his waist and smiled. "She looks so happy."

"Yeah. She really does."

As the crowd began to thin, Jossy broke away and ambled toward them. Her limp was still there, but barely noticeable now. If Jonah squinted, he might not see the scars at all.

"Wasn't that awesome?" Jossy gushed. "Did you see how I passed that guy at the end?"

"I did," Jonah said, wrapping his arms around her and squeezing so hard he thought he might crush them both. "Nice work."

"That was incredible," Kate said. "I know it wasn't a race, but if it had been, you would have kicked some serious ass."

"Thanks!" Jossy stepped back and wiped her forehead on the shoulder of her jersey, then took a drink of water from a bright-red bottle. "It's too bad you'll miss the event in Eugene."

"You decided to sign up for that one after all?" Kate said.

"Yeah, but don't worry—I promise I'll still be an attentive pet sitter for Marilyn. Maybe I'll bring her with me when I check in on the kitties at the bookstore. It'll be like homecoming for her."

"Oh, she'll love that," Jonah said. "Car rides are her favorite. They rank right up there with bath time and getting feline press-on nails."

Jossy laughed and took another swig of water. "Okay, maybe she'll stay home."

Beside him, Kate tucked a strand of hair behind her ear. "Are you sure it's no trouble? We could find another pet sitter if you—"

"Please," Jossy said, waving her off. "Now that I have a little help at the shelter, I have extra time on my hands."

"Well, it is Marilyn," Kate pointed out. "She can be kind of demanding."

"I love that I have that in common with my cat-niece," she said. "Besides, we have fun together. We'll sit around talking about owls and thinking judgmental thoughts about Jonah."

Jonah grinned and reached over to thwack the side of her helmet. "Maybe you could teach her another word."

Jossy laughed and wiped her forehead again. "Did you guys decide yet where you're going?" she asked. "Where your big romantic vacation will be?"

Kate smiled at Jonah, and he smiled back, hoping his face wasn't giving anything away. He forced himself not to glance at Jossy, afraid she might spoil the surprise by accident. He'd already shown his sister the ring and gotten Jossy's input on how to propose.

"Don't say anything dumb," she'd coached. "And don't look at her boobs."

"Thanks, Joss," he'd muttered, ruffling her hair. "What would I do without you?"

Now he looked down at Kate and imagined the moment of surprise. Not a huge surprise, of course. They'd talked about marriage, and even discussed rings.

But this would be his chance to blindside her just a little, and in the best way possible.

Kate slid an arm around Jonah's waist and looked at Jossy. "We haven't picked a place yet," she said. "We talked a little bit about Utah. I've wanted to see the Anasazi ruins for a long time."

"They're definitely beautiful," Jonah agreed, remembering her words in Ashland. About the importance of reclaiming special places for yourself.

Kate looked up at him again, those copper eyes flashing in the sunlight. "But I've been thinking we should try something new," she said. "Someplace that can become special for the two of us."

"I hear Brasada Ranch resort is nice," he said. "The Oregon high desert?"

Kate grinned wider. "I've been there once for a friend's wedding," she said. "I never even got to stay the night."

"It sounds lovely," he said. "Wild rabbits hopping around at sunset."

"Coyotes yipping and the smell of sagebrush in the air."

Jonah grinned and slid his arm around her, his heart so full he thought it might explode.

"It sounds magical," he said. "Sign me up for all of it."

ACKNOWLEDGMENTS

Humongous thanks to my early readers and critique partners for giving me the tools I needed to bring out this story's very best self. I'm especially grateful to Linda Grimes and Kait Nolan for your awesome insights and suggestions.

As always, I feel absurdly lucky to have Michelle Wolfson of Wolfson Literary Agency in my corner. Thank you for putting up with my unfunny jokes, my neurotic need to plan, and my freak-outs about things that usually seem trivial the next morning.

Few things in life make me happier than an e-mail from editors Chris Werner and Krista Stroever saying I nailed it with a new manuscript, and this one made me extra happy. Thank you for loving this book enough to help shape it into an even better version of itself. I'm also grateful to Anh Schluep, Jessica Poore, Kimberly Cowser, Marlene Kelly, Hannah Buehler, Claire Caterer, PEPE nymi, and the rest of the Montlake team for everything you did to get this book polished, pretty, and into the hands of readers.

Just as Kate idolizes the fictional Dr. Vivienne Brandt, I have my own stable of self-help gurus and wise souls whose thoughtful words have gotten me through tough times, given me new perspectives, or inspired me to be a better person. Thank you to Elizabeth Gilbert,

Glennon Doyle Melton, Cheryl Strayed, Robert Fulghum, and Mary Roach. Thanks especially to Dr. John Gottman and Dr. Julie Schwartz Gottman for your incredible relationship workshops and insights on the art and science of love.

Big thanks to James Dustin Parsons for answering my questions about prosthetic limbs and helping me flesh out Jossy's story. Thanks also to author Robin Covington for both your legal insights and your super-awesome books. Hugs and kisses and huge thank-yous to Meah Cukrov for being an amazing personal assistant, pet sitter, and all-around human.

Shout-out to Purringtons Cat Lounge and Club Privata swingers club for offering me what was hands down the strangest and most enlightening weekend of book research in the history of my career.

Huge props to my favorite trashy-TV viewing companions, Larie Borden, Bayley Killpack, and Maegan MacKelvie, for the evenings of wine-fueled laughter. You're definitely here for the right reasons, and I'm glad we've shared so many "journeys." Who knew all these years of *The Bachelor* would come in handy?

Oodles of thanks to the Visit Bend team for making it possible for me to continue this crazy dual life of an author and a day jobber. This balancing act wouldn't be possible without you guys. I'm also hugely indebted to my incredible street team, Fenske's Frisky Posse, for all your hard work and dedication. Love you guys!

Thank you to my parents, David and Dixie Fenske, and to Aaron "Russ" Fenske and his lovely wife, Carlie Fenske. I love knowing you guys are rooting for me, and that you read my books even when you're not really required to.

Thank you to my awesome stepkids, Cedar and Violet, for making me smile and making me see the world differently since you came into my life.

And thanks always to my husband, Craig Zagurski, for ensuring I'll never run out of love stories to write. I love you, hot stuff.

DISCUSSION QUESTIONS

1. When Kate meets Jonah in Ashland, he bears little resemblance to the Average Joe she knows through Viv's books. When he's with Kate, how is Jonah different from how he is with Viv? With Jossy? Are there different traits you see in Kate when she's with Viv versus Amy versus Jonah?

2. Being around his ex-wife brings out a side of Jonah he's not always proud of, though he fights to rise above it. What is it about Viv that sparks that response in him? How does Kate's presence affect him differently? Who brings out *your* best self?

3. Kate has a long history of fandom with Dr. Viv's books. Is her reliance on the wisdom of self-help books a benefit or a hindrance in her life? Does that change over the course of the story?

4. Jonah tells Kate that the only thing opposites attract is heartache. Why do you think he says this? How do you feel about that theory?

5. At several points Kate wrestles between doing what she thinks is right versus doing what's required of her for her job. Are there moments where you felt frustrated with her choices? When did you applaud her choices? Can you think of a time when your own job required you to do something you disagreed with?

6. What did you think about Jonah's reaction to what he perceived as betrayal from Kate? Was he angrier about the lie itself, or about looking stupid?

7. There are a number of blindsides and secrets revealed throughout the story. Which one surprised you most? Has there been a time in your life when you've had to guard a secret you didn't want to keep?

8. What do you think attracted Viv and Jonah to each other? What do you see as the chief reasons for their divorce? What makes either of them better suited to the partner they end up with at the book's conclusion?

ABOUT THE AUTHOR

When Tawna Fenske finished her English lit degree at twenty-two, she celebrated by filling a giant trash bag full of romance novels and dragging it everywhere until she'd read them all. Now she's a *USA Today* bestselling author who writes humorous fiction, risqué romance, and heartwarming love stories with a quirky twist. *Publishers Weekly* has praised Tawna's offbeat romances with multiple starred reviews and noted, "There's something wonderfully relaxing about being immersed in a story filled with over-the-top characters in undeniably relatable situations. Heartache and humor go hand in hand."

Tawna lives in Bend, Oregon, with her husband, stepkids, and a menagerie of ill-behaved pets. She loves hiking, snowshoeing, stand-up paddleboarding, and inventing excuses to sip wine on her back porch. She can peel a banana with her toes and loses an average of twenty pairs of eyeglasses per year. To find out more about Tawna and her books, visit www.tawnafenske.com.